The Roman Empire
120 AD

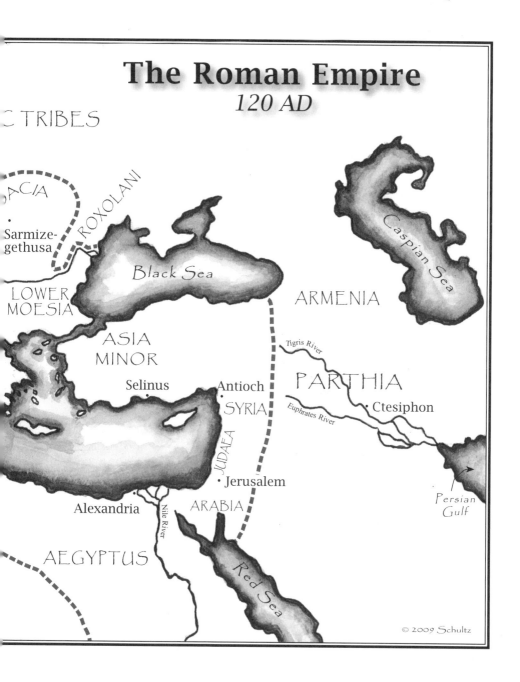

C TRIBES

ACIA

· Sarmize-
gethusa

ROXOLANI

Black Sea

LOWER
MOESIA

ARMENIA

Caspian Sea

ASIA
MINOR

Tigris River

PARTHIA

Selinus

· Antioch

SYRIA

· Ctesiphon

Euphrates River

JUDAEA

· Jerusalem

Alexandria

Nile River

ARABIA

Persian
Gulf

AEGYPTUS

Red Sea

© 2009 Schultz

C.R.H. WILDFEUER

TRAJAN
Lion of Rome

*THE UNTOLD STORY OF
ROME'S GREATEST EMPEROR*

Aquifer Publishing

An Aquifer Publishing book

Copyright © 2009 by C.R.H. Wildfeuer
Book design and maps by Jayne L. Schultz

Title page lion, book sections IV and Epilogue-
illustrations are works by William Martin Johnson
from the 1892 edition of *Ben Hur* by Lew Wallace.
Book sections I and II-illustrations © 2009 Jupiterimages.

Library of Congress Control Number: 2008934837

Wildfeuer, Christian R.H., 1961-
Trajan-Lion of Rome: The untold story of Rome's
greatest emperor / C.R.H. Wildfeuer

ISBN-13: 978-0-9818460-6-4
ISBN-10: 0-9818460-6-8

Printed in the United States of America.
Text set in Lucida Bright. Printed on acid-free paper.

AQUIFER
PUBLISHING

Order additional copies at www.aquiferpublishing.com

This book is dedicated to
the genius of the Roman People, now long vanished,
and to the long-lasting legacy it bequeathed.

It is also dedicated to the great men of the Roman Republic:
Camillus, Cincinnatus, Appius Claudius, Cato the Elder,
Scipio, the Gracchi brothers, Marius, Pompey, Cicero
and most of all Gaius Julius Caesar,
a man with no equal then and none today.
He set the imprint Trajan walked on.

My homage as a writer goes to:
Livy, Cicero, Caesar, Virgil, Horace, Ovid, Catull,
Sallust, Seneca, Pliny, Tacitus, Juvenal, Martial
and to the philosopher emperor Marcus Aurelius.

"HE DIDN'T ENVY NOR SLAY ANY ONE,
BUT HONORED AND EXALTED ALL GOOD MEN
WITHOUT EXCEPTION, AND HENCE HE NEITHER
FEARED NOR HATED ANY ONE OF THEM."

-Cassius Dio, Roman History, Epitome of Book LXVII

"MAY THE NEW EMPEROR BE
MORE FORTUNATE THAN AUGUSTUS
AND BETTER THAN TRAJAN."

*-Imperial inauguration prayer of the Senate in the fourth century AD,
according to Eutropius, Breviarium ab urbe condita, Liber VIII/5*

Dramatis personae

(Cast of characters)

Marcus Ulpius Traianus (*Trajan*)	The Emperor Trajan, Lion of Rome (ruled 98 – 117 AD)
Marcus Ulpius Traianus	Trajan's father, Roman general and governor
Pompeia Plotina	Trajan's wife and Empress of Rome
Publius Aelius Hadrianus (*Hadrian*)	Trajan's cousin and successor (ruled 117 – 138 AD)
Titus Flavius Vespasianus (*Vespasian*)	Commander-in-Chief of the Roman army in Palestine and Emperor of Rome 69-79 AD
Titus Flavius Vespasianus (*Titus*)	Emperor of Rome 79-81 AD, son of Vespasian, brother of Domitian
Titus Flavius Domitianus (*Domitian*)	Emperor of Rome 81-96 AD, son of Vespasian, brother of Titus
Domitia	Domitian's wife
Marcus Cocceius Nerva	Emperor of Rome 96-98
Casperius Aelianus	Praetorian Praefect under Domitian and Nerva
Lucius Licinius Sura	Roman nobleman, jurist and governor
Vibia Sabina	Trajan's grandniece and wife of Hadrian
Decebalus	King of Dacia
Lusius Quietus	Moorish general in the Roman cavalry
Pompeius Longinus	Roman general commanding on the Danube
Suburanus and Attianus	Praetorian Praefects under Trajan
Callistus	Trajan's secretary and friend
Harpenna	Slave in the Traiani household
Tiberius Claudius Maximus	Centurion in the Roman army
Titus Statilius Crito	Trajan's physician
Osroes	High King of Parthia
Exedares	Roman client king of Armenia
Parthamasiris	Parthian client king of Armenia

Contents

BOOK I

WAR IN THE EAST

Chapter 1

May 67 AD, Ptolemais, Syria Province

"What do you see out there, Roman?" Mago asked his host.

Marcus Ulpius Traianus broke a smile. The tall general was watching the bright orange ball of the setting sun on the horizon and the glistening reflection of its beams on the peaceful water of the Mediterranean. He stood with his back to the Phoenician councilman, at the latticed window of his second story quarters in the Roman fortress of Ptolemais. Down below, a multitude of war galleys and cargo ships was moored in the harbor. The sails' metal loops and rings were banging against the masts as wind and water had their way with them.

The sea reminded him of home, for the same water that gently rocked the ships here also touched the shores of his native Hispania. This could have been Gades were it not for the many galleys crowding the harbor and the unfamiliar harsh voices of Semitic merchants resonating from the paved streets. *Nothing beats a touch of home. This is Our Ocean, Mare Nostrum, as far as the eye can see... It connects the Roman world, physically and spiritually.*

The general turned around to his visitor. "I see Our Ocean out there. It gives me peace of mind and connects me to home - if you know what I mean, Councilman."

"I am not sure, Legate. Where is your home?"

"A valid question. My home is in Hispania because that's where I was born, but my loyalty is to Rome."

"Ah. Of course your loyalty is to Rome. I just wondered what you call home. Funny, isn't? Hispania is your homeland, yet you are Roman and not in the least torn by this duality. I wish it were like this here in Palestine."

A frown flitted across Traianus's face. "Palestine? Ptolemais is not part of Palestine. It's Punic like you, and part of Syria."

He looked closer at the councilman. The balding man, his sun-burnt face full of wrinkles, was dressed in a long checkered Phoenician tunic with half-long sleeves. Beaded necklaces adorned a thin neck, and deep creases flanked his black orbs on either side. Traianus avoided the sun. His shaven skin was pale like his white army tunic.

"On face value you are correct, but we are close to the troubles in Judaea and Galilaea," Mago countered. "What I wanted to say is this: While you Romans have managed to turn the people of your conquered lands into obedient subjects of the empire, I don't think you will ever succeed in Palestine. The Jews will never fit in. Never."

"I don't agree, Mago. You have."

"Yes, I have and my people have, but we matter not. We are a small community of merchants. Phoenicia is not even a country anymore. Our glory days are gone – ever since your people wiped out Carthage."

He peeked by the general and down at the hustle on the piers. "No doubt, the population of Ptolemais works well with you. They are Greek or Phoenician, businessmen who know how to turn a profit. They want to be on the winning side - your side. But go down to Joppa or Apollonia and it's a different story. The populations there are Jewish, and they hate you. Talk to Titus. His legion's infantry had to bypass many Jewish coastal towns on their way up from Egypt."

The squadrons of triremes and other galleys in the harbor were part of Titus's Fifteenth Legion *Apollinaris* and had turned the Phoenician port into a huge Roman base. Traianus's own Tenth Legion *Fretensis* and his colleague Cerialis's Fifth *Macedonica* had arrived a short while ago, joining Titus's troops. Throngs of auxiliaries had come with them, levied troops from Eastern client kings. Together, the assembled army in Ptolemais numbered over fifty thousand men now, commanded by the new governor of Syria Province, Titus Flavius Vespasian, who had summoned them to crush a Jewish revolt.

Palestine was of strategic importance. Rome couldn't let it slip away. As the land link between North Africa and Asia Minor Judaea was essential for control of the Eastern Mediterranean. In addition, it was the destination of caravans from Asia and India bringing silk and spices to the western world. A rebellion might even catch the attention of the Parthians and get Parthian Jews involved. Rome's great rival always had an interest in destabilizing the East. It would benefit, maybe even allow the Parthian king to conquer Syria and take its grand prize, the rich metropolis of Antioch.

"Dear Mago, gloom and doom, as always," Traianus said. "Do you not you grasp the importance of this moment? You may be right about the Jews now, but the army we pulled together changes everything. It is the biggest concentration of Roman power since Pompey's conquest of Syria. It will teach them. Do you perhaps believe the Iberian tribes of Hispania gave up their freedom without a fight? It took us a hundred years to conquer the Iberian Peninsula, and another hundred years to romanize it and integrate the natives into the Roman family of nations. They were tough fighters, but we were tougher. Yes, today Judaea is in open revolt and fighting for its independence, but tomorrow they will be a productive part of the Roman world. It may take time, maybe a long time. But it will happen. It always does. We aren't conquerors for the moment.

Think big, Mago. Like our bridges, roads and aqueducts, the Roman empire is built for eternity!"

The merchant stared at the legionary commander, shaking his head.

"I will never understand you. You Romans are scary."

Traianus shrugged. "Fine, back to business then. Did the Council agree to our request for camels? You keep tiptoeing around this, Phoenician."

"The Council doesn't like it, and I can relate. You are asking for a lot, General. You have no payment to give us other than loot from the pending war. And what if there will be no booty? What if you lose? What if the Jews kick you out of Palestine? The imperial Treasury is empty. Everybody knows that. Of course they are hesitant; they want hard cash."

"They will get cash. Just not now. Later. After the campaign."

"And how long do you think that will take?"

"I don't know. Three months maybe. Or three years. Hard to say. I believe it will be over before the end of the year, but I have always been an optimist. That's beside the point. Ptolemais will be paid. The Council needs not worry. Tell them that."

"What if they refuse?"

"All the same," Traianus replied without qualms. "We will appropriate the camels with or without your consent. And either way, the Treasury will pay you. We aren't thieves after all."

"I imagined you would say that." Mago sighed and shuffled to the open door of Traianus's office. "I hope you are right, Legate."

Traianus followed the man and grabbed his shoulders at the threshold, turning him around so that the trader had to look at him close up. The general tightened his grip and looked the merchant hard in the eyes. "I will be. You have my word," he said with resolve. Then Traianus dropped his arms and reached out for a handshake with his ally.

Taken aback, Mago furrowed his brows, but after a short tense moment he took the general's outstretched hand, shook it and left.

Traianus returned to the latticed window and again peered down at the cacophony of war galleys. The sun had set, but its orange shimmer was still lingering on the horizon.

The Jews... He didn't even know why they had risen up. Certainly, Governor Florus had maltreated them, hurting their religious feelings. Still, Judaea was not a poor province. The Jews would gain nothing from a war. There was more to this puzzle. Why were they so fanatic and why not only the people in Judaea, but also those in Samaria and Galilaea? Insurgents there had wiped out many Roman garrisons and allied themselves with the Sanhedrin in Jerusalem, the governing body of High Priests. Then there was the ferocious infighting among the different Jewish factions: Pharisees, Sadducees and many splinter groups. He had a lot to learn.

Chapter 2

On the following day Traianus called for an escort of four war-hardened legionaries and marched them to the local synagogue. He was hoping to talk to an octogenarian former Sanhedrin council member, a Sadducee, whom Vespasian had put under house arrest here.

Pages admitted the general and his men right away. The boys led the Romans straight to a seedy old man in the walled courtyard of the building. He was sitting on a stone bench and rose on his cane when he saw the visitors. His scruffy hair and long beard were white as snow. The beard seemed to never have seen trimming scissors. The man's head oscillated left and right like a cornered cat.

"Do not fear," the legate addressed him in Greek. "We mean you no harm. My name is Marcus Ulpius Traianus, a Roman commander in Ptolemais. I have some questions for you." Traianus paused and smiled at the elderly man. "I want to better understand the situation in your homeland. You may be able to help me - and help your people at the same time."

The man didn't answer, but he pointed his thumb over his shoulders and turned to the temple chambers. They followed him into an unadorned, but clean room lit with candles. With the help of a page the tattering Sadducee sank into one of several padded wicker chairs and invited Traianus to join him. The general bowed politely and waved his men out of the room. They hesitated, but Traianus's arching eyes and steadfast expression allowed no dissent, and they took up station outside.

The general was not afraid for his safety. He had noticed only maids and young boys on the synagogue grounds, going about their business as usual, and he knew Ptolemais's adult Jews had been mostly rounded up and were now populating the local prisons.

Traianus seated himself and came right to the point. "Why are the Jewish people rising up against Rome?"

"You are asking me that in earnest, Roman?" The old man slurred his Greek with a strong accent. Traianus barely understood him.

"Is it not obvious? You oppressed my people, raped the land, violated all that is sacred, terrorized everyone: citizens, priests, scholars and rabbis, men and women - and you are asking why there is a revolt? We are God's chosen people and we have suffered enough. It is time to reclaim our land and gain our freedom. Other conquerors have been here before. They left, and so will you!"

"Why do they feel that way? What you are saying is not new. Judaea has been under Roman rule for a long time. And before that, Herodes ruled the land as our client king. What has changed? What did we do to incite so much anger?"

The Sadducee's brows drew together in a menacing and hostile frown, his eyes glaring at Traianus. The general winced, but then the old man took a deep breath and said, "Well, Roman. Let me start with our faith. We are different from every other people because we believe in only one God - Yahweh. He forbids the worship of any other deity.

When the Governor Florus forced our priests to pay obeisance to the Emperor Nero we became upset. I do realize the Emperor Cult is not really meant in a religious way, but to us there is no such distinction. What Florus forced us to pledge was a sacrilege: 'Propitiate the Divine Augustus Nero'... Pah!"

The old man spit on the floor. Then he resumed venting his grievances. "The Emperor Cult is a desecration of our beliefs, and we have to reckon with Yahweh's fury. Needless to say, the events spiraled out of control when the governor took over four hundred thousand sesterces from the holy Temple Treasure in Jerusalem. I don't know why he did that, maybe to collect taxes. It doesn't matter. It was a provocation, and we reacted with public demonstrations, asking him to return the money. Florus reacted with brutal reprisals. Hundreds of our men were arrested, tortured and crucified, but it didn't help him: his garrison couldn't hold Jerusalem and had to flee. Ever since, the great city is ours again. Then the countryside erupted, and now you Romans are pinned down here in Ptolemais."

The Sadducee grinned, exposing his toothless mouth.

Religious fanatics - can that explain everything? Traianus felt anger for the greedy governor who had mismanaged a delicate situation. He had more questions for the old man, who babbled on about Yahweh's superiority, God's revenge, the Chosen People and their successful rebellion.

"It is true, old man," Traianus answered. "Your people control the cities and countryside of Judaea for now, but with the exception of one incompetent legion we have only responded with auxiliary troops. This is going to cha-"

A ragged young man suddenly burst into the room and threw himself on the general with a long sickle-shaped knife. Traianus moved aside lightning-quick. The knife missed the small gap on the side of his cuirass and bounced off the front plate with a clang. The man hung on to the blade and tried again, clutching it with both hands. Traianus drew his sword and feigned a step back. The stranger whipped forward - right into the general's double-edged *gladius.* The sharp blade cleaved into his unprotected chest to the hilt. He gurgled. Blood was oozing from his mouth. The man stumbled as Traianus pulled out his sword. Pain and horror warped the rebel's face into a ghastly grimace, and he crashed to the floor.

Traianus's escort scurried into the room. One of the soldiers wanted to dispatch the rebel right away, but Traianus held him back. The general crouched over the man's face, putting his ear close to his mouth to understand his last croaks. "Yahwe... is great... You will all die!"

"Listen to me. Who has sent you?" Traianus shouted as he was holding the man's head. Beads of cold sweat appeared on the rebel's forehead. He was shaking and said something else, but Traianus couldn't make out the mumbled words. He put down the man's skull, stood up and ordered the old man arrested. The Sadducee was leaning against a wall, wailing or praying in his native tongue. The general could not tell. Old or not, this octogenarian was an enemy of the State. He must have known about a young rebel fugitive inside the synagogue.

Traianus's glance returned to his attacker on the floor. The wretch was in Charon's clutches - he could not be saved. To end his suffering Traianus sliced his throat with a quick cut of his still blood-dripping sword. Then he wiped it clean with his scarf. He condoned harsh punishments but was no friend of unnecessary suffering.

The legate signaled his men. They put the stammering Sadducee in their midst and dragged him out of the room. Traianus followed them. The march back to the Roman fortress would be short.

Back in the citadel, Traianus encountered Vibius Volusenna, a knight who had been on Governor Florus's staff. "Vibius, I need to talk to you."

"What about? I am leaving for Rome. The Treasury wants to know how many taxes and tolls we collected last year, how much we should have collected and what tribute payments we should impose after this war. I am glad I am still alive, Legate, but I barely made it out of Jerusalem. I cannot wait to leave this pit called a Roman province."

He pulled away from Traianus and dashed off. Traianus asked him to stop, but Volusenna wouldn't. The general lurched after him, grabbed a fold of his toga from behind and jerked him around. "Not so fast. I have important questions for you, Vibius. You will answer them. How long did you serve in Judaea?"

Pinned against the wall, Volusenna cringed under Traianus's grip. "Three years."

"Then you must know about this place. Tell me about the economy."

Vibius sighed. "Fine. Judaea is a rich land with all its trade and agricultural irrigation. However, the leading class has long lost touch with the common people. And we lost touch with them because we only dealt with the priests, the merchants and the noblemen. We enforced harsh levies that looked good on paper but squeezed the common people hard. Prissy Florus didn't make things better by squeezing even more than his voracious prede-cessor." He paused.

"Go on."

Volusenna tried to shake himself free, but Traianus kept him pinched against the wall.

"All right, all right. Many peasants were forced into debt and had to sell out to wealthy city dwellers. Over the years, class hatred grew stronger and stronger, and so did the animosities toward the cities. People deem the rul-ing class in bed with Rome. They fall for leaders who promise them a better life. Some of these men are rich and don't want to share the spoils of the land with Rome or a client king. They use the traditional Jewish beliefs to manipu-late the pious masses. Fortunately, some of them hate each other even more than they hate us because they know they will compete for leadership once we are gone – or so they hope. This is why you see a lot of infighting. Not even the faction chiefs in Jerusalem see eye to eye."

Traianus was learning something after all. Volusenna shook himself free, cursed the general and scampered off. He was barely gone when the general heard army heralds calling for an assembly of officers. A passing tribune gave him details. "Placidus is back with his men. His mission failed. Vespa-sian wants all of us to hear his report."

The mission failed? How was that possible? Traianus couldn't wait to find out. He followed the tribune to Vespasian's quarters, already overflow-ing with Roman officers of all ranks: tribunes, centurions, *optiones*, *duplicarii* and *decuriones*. Placidus was answering agitated questions from all sides. The begrimed young officer was wearing battle armor, but he didn't seem to be injured.

Vespasian sat behind his huge cedar desk, chatting with his son Titus and General Cerialis. "Ah, Traianus is here now," Vespasian bellowed. "We can start. Silence, officers, silence! As all of you know, I sent the Tribune Placidus with a detachment of seven thousand men to break the siege of Sep-phoris, the only town in Palestine that is still loyal to our cause. Placidus was supposed to chase the rebels away and rally the town. He was also ordered to intimidate the villages of Lower Galilaea along the way. Placidus, your report."

The young officer stepped forward, putting on his most serious face. "I will make it short, *milites*: We failed. Sepphoris is still under siege. We were repulsed, and I decided to withdraw because we were seriously outnumbered. In my estimate, over thirty thousand rebels are besieging the city now. They are not well armed, but by Jupiter, they are determined."

Most of the assembled officers kept their composure, but Traianus could hear some murmurs in the back.

"I decided to launch a surprise attack on Jotapata on our way back," Placidus continued. "However, the enemy must have scouted us and the town was prepared. In fact, we ran into an ambush when we approached it. I have to admit - had it not been for our superior armor and the discipline of my men, the whole detachment would have been lost. But we retreated fast and orderly, losing only seven men, Governor. I couldn't count the Jewish losses, but they were minimal. Both sides had many wounded, however. In summary, I can say with certitude that Jotapata is well garrisoned and fortified. Retaking Galilaea will be no picnic, soldiers." He bowed to Vespasian. "*Legatus Augusti*, I have failed you and would like to return my commission."

"Request denied!"

Placidus stiffened.

"You will have plenty of opportunity to redeem yourself, young man," Vespasian assured him. Turning to the other men in the room he said, "It is time for us to make our move. The rebels are about to take Sepphoris, the only friendly place left. They are getting feisty because they haven't seen a Roman victory in a long time. My original plan was to bring succor to Sepphoris three days from now, but given the situation, we will leave tomorrow."

Hearing that the men's murmurs grew into a crescendo. Conversations erupted everywhere in the room. Even the generals exchanged ponderous looks.

"Quiet!" Vespasian shouted, raising his arm. "Quiet. The army will stay together to show our strength and terrify the villages. I will not disclose the destination of our march until the morning. The Jews have spies in town, and I want to keep our true destination from them as long as possible. Not even the legates know." He pointed at Cerialis, Traianus and Titus, and continued. "The allied ethnarchs and their officers don't know either. They will find out on the march. However, they know to expect an all summer campaign and have arranged for the appropriate logistics. We will also receive one thousand camels from Ptolemais's City Council. Use them to replace some of your mules. This will give us greater operational flexibility in the heat.

That is all. Pray to your *lares* tonight. The family gods are important. Make sure they are on your side. Titus and I will do so too. I will see you tomorrow. Dismissed."

Chapter 3

At the same time in Hispanic Italica, Traianus's eleven-year-old son Trajan was on his way to the toy shop in the portico of the town's theater. Yesterday he had tried to re-enact the sea battle at Actium between Mark Anthony and Octavian in the *impluvium*, the low water basin in the atrium of his parent's villa, and noticed that he didn't have enough skiffs to represent the Roman fleet. The boy was hopeful to dig up more toy ships at rock-bottom prices in old Bassus's store.

The plaza in front of the theater was crowded with people milling around and standing in line to buy tickets. Trajan traipsed around the growing lines and was entering the toy store when he heard an urchin scream nearby. The voice sounded familiar. It came from a small street connected to the northern end of the theater plaza. Curious, he spun around and scooted to the end of the massive portico.

He recoiled at what he saw: His friend Quintus was being thrashed by their common archenemies Lucius and Manlius, boys who were both older and stronger than Trajan and Quintus. Trajan hesitated.

"Trajan, help me," Quintus screamed at him when he saw him appear at the street corner.

Lucius and Manlius were distracted for a moment and turned their heads at Trajan for a short moment before hitting Quintus again. Lucius held Quintus from behind so he could not move or defend himself, while Manlius jabbed at him. Quintus shrieked as if he had been declared the main sacrifice at the Ludi Romani Festival.

Trajan had seen enough. Ignoring the odds, he ran forward and threw himself on Manlius. His fists flew through the air, hitting Manlius in the eye. The boy howled and tumbled back, covering one eye with his hands. Lucius tried to hit Trajan, but he moved too fast. Trajan grabbed Quintus's hand, and they both ran off as fast as they could, with Manlius and Lucius in hot pursuit. The older boys were catching up fast, but Trajan and Quintus reached the busy theater plaza in time.

Manlius and Lucius stopped behind them shouted, "We will get you, don't you worry! We will get you!"

Trajan turned around for a split second and flicked his tongue at them. Then he and Quintus disappeared in the crowd. Finally Trajan had a chance to ask his friend, "What in the world was going on back there?"

"Nothing. I was peacefully walking on the street when they came after me."

"And why did you not run away?"

"I didn't see them in time. They came so fast," he sobbed.

"Cheer up, Quintus. I don't fear them. We out ran them!"

"Yes, on short distance."

"Well, I knew how far it would be to the theater."

Quintus looked at him with big eyes. "You always amaze me."

Trajan shrugged. "Nah, it's not that hard. I wished I could run faster, like a legionary. What would I give to be in the Army..."

"It is not going to happen, Trajan. The closest legion is far away. All we have here are boring *lictors* assisting the magistrates."

"I know, but I tell you, Quintus, when I am old enough, I will join the legions - no matter where they are."

"Trajan, we have a much more urgent problem on our hands: Lucius and Manlius will want revenge."

"Most certainly." He didn't want to think about it. That was a problem for another day.

Chapter 4

An hour before sunrise dozens of tuba blowers woke the Roman troops. Thousands of soldiers scrambled from their cots, packed their battle gear, trenching tools and personal belongings, and marched to their stations outside of Ptolemais. Officers and enlisted men alike hustled in all directions – yet, there was logic to the madness. Every soldier knew exactly what to do and where to go. Within the hour, the units were assembled and ready to push off.

Vespasian smiled with pride when he mounted his gelding in the midst of all the gumption around him. He wore his legate's uniform with the trademark scarlet *paludamentum* cloak and an iron muscle cuirass, but no helmet. Fine woolen breeches covered his stocky legs, designed to supply perfect riding comfort on the Roman four-horned saddle. His shoes were enclosing and laced leather *perones*. A *parazonium* was dangling from his belt, the type of dagger only senior officers carried. Two adjutants in the rank of tribune flanked him. His generals, Titus, Traianus and Cerialis, were at the head of their respective legions by now, supervising the departure preparations of their units.

After a last craning peek at Ptolemais, Vespasian and his aides rode off, passing through the city gates and followed by a unit of horse troopers and a body of spearmen assigned to protect the baggage train. After arriving on the other side of the portal the governor upraised his right arm and then lowered it in one fell swoop. Responding to the signal, *cornicens* on the ramparts blew their horns to convey the final departure signal to all units.

Vespasian gently kicked his mount, and the column got under way. In marching formation the army was going to be eight miles long. It would take a full day for the last unit to set out and join their camped colleagues after nightfall.

The commander-in-chief and his entourage on horseback, however, were supposed to catch up with the infantry soon and merge with the main body of men. Vespasian had placed light-armed auxiliaries and bowmen at the head of the long column with orders to repel sudden attacks and search nearby woods that might provide the enemy with cover for an ambush. Next, he had drawn up a massive body of light and heavy infantry and cavalry, followed by a detachment of legionaries carrying instruments to survey and stake out the campsite for the night. The army would pitch a camp every day, protecting it with a ditch and mobile palisades rammed into the compacted wall of dirt piled up in front of the ditch.

Behind the surveyors rolled the senior officers' baggage train, guarded by a strong cavalry force and soon complemented by the spearmen of

Vespasian's personal guard. The legionary cavalry followed, one hundred and twenty horses per legion, then the mules, asses and camels that carried the small-range catapults. Oxen pulled the heavy artillery, such as long-range catapults, ballistas and scorpions, and also the huge battering rams. *Signifers* followed behind the animals, bearing the sacred standards and *vexilla of* every legionary unit, square pennants that were now fluttering in the wind. Only three of them carried a golden eagle to represent each legion as a whole - the ultimate symbol of Roman power and the soldiers' greatest pride. With them marched the horn and tuba touting *cornicens* and *tubicens,* wearing bearskins over their helmets and down their backs. The front leg skins and paws were crossed over their chain mail-clad chests. The main body of legionaries defiled behind the *signifers*, six soldiers per row, accompanied by centurions on either side to maintain formation. The legionaries marched in full battle kit, with *pilum*, sword and shield. They also carried their own cooking utensils, some digging gear and personal belongings on a pole attached to their back-mounted shields.

The whole trek of fifty thousand men seemed to have no end, reaching as far as Vespasian's eyes could see. Thousands of non-combatants concluded the column - squires, pages, servants and others, outside of the general's view. They were in charge of the heavy baggage like tents, palisades and the weightier digging utensils, hauled on wagons or carried by more camels and mules. Elite infantry units from the Tenth Legion formed the critical rearguard.

On the first day the army marched straight to the border of Galilaea. There, Vespasian ordered the first camp pitched and called for an immediate war council in his billet. Titus, Traianus and Cerialis as well as the tribunes and centurions of every legion were present.

"Before we sit down for dinner and you brief your staff, I would like to use this opportunity to recap our strategy and update you on my plans." Vespasian pointed at a map on his burl wood desk in front of him, outlining all of Palestine: Galilaea, Peraea, Dekapolis, Samaria, Judaea and Idumaea.

"All these lands are unfriendly to us," he explained. Then he pointed at a place in Galilaea. "The only exception is Sepphoris - here.

Our first task is to dispel the Jewish siege army. They are using Cestius's pilfered artillery for the investment. Needless to say, Sepphoris was hit hard. The city is in bad shape and desperately needs our help. Breaking up the siege will be the easy part. Regaining control of the countryside will be a lot more difficult. We will terrify the villagers, but in the long run we can only be successful if we conquer key hilltop cities like Gabara, Jotapata and Japha. This will require a lot of siege warfare. We are prepared, but it won't be a walk in the park. We may even have to build siege towers on site."

His officers nodded.

"The mountains in this country run north-south. Going east will be a challenge if we can't use the roads. Your pioneers will brief you on the terrain and can tell you what we can make accessible and where you will have to go around a hill or a canyon.

Now, the enemy is concentrated in Jotapata. Our spies are saying Jotapata is pivotal, but we don't know for sure how determined the Jews will resist our offensive. Let's expect the worst and be cautious and methodical.

The rebels have appointed one Josephus Ben Matthias as Governor of Galilaea. He operates out of Tiberias and will likely head the army that is going to oppose us on the way to Sepphoris. He is a Pharisee and was part of the Rome-friendly establishment, but now he is fighting against us. Josephus is said to be a political fox, but he has no military experience and no well-trained army at his disposition. He might surrender for terms if we make concessions. The rebel government in Jerusalem on the other hand – and this is somewhat based on intelligence acquired by Traianus - is a convoluted mess of moderates and radicals. Different ringleaders and high priests are vying for the leadership. There are many ways for us to take advantage of that later down the road. But first we have to pacify the North.

Soldiers, the Jews will not crack easily! They value the allegiance to their 'omnipotent god' higher than material considerations. Years of injustice, poverty and political ambitions have nurtured an inordinate amount of fanaticism among the poor. Unfortunately, this dissatisfaction is targeted at us. The simple folks are holding Rome responsible for their misery and hail revolutionary war as the solution." Vespasian paused and gazed at his men. He saw in their eyes the admiration for him, the glaze of unquestioned obedience.

Yes, they eat from my hands.

The governor liked his men, particularly Traianus and a promising young tribune named Casperius. Both were hardy and intelligent. Of course, he was most proud of his own son Titus.

He resumed his speech. "For the time being, I want the army to stay together," he said. "We will likely meet resistance at Garis, two and a half miles east of Sepphoris. It is the logical place for an attack. Note that we will bypass both Gabara and Jotapata. So expect assaults coming from that direction." The general pointed north on the map. "The Jews know that their hill-towns are key and will not risk sending out too many troops for fear of leaving their strongholds unprotected. Once Sepphoris is liberated, we will strike at Gabara and then simultaneously at Jotapata and Japha. From there, we will go to Tiberias. My goal is to take Galilaea within six weeks so that we have enough time to turn on Samaria. We must not make Cestius's mistake, who only cared about Jerusalem and was caught off guard in the hinterland. Once we own the countryside and the townships we can attack Jerusalem and only then. By Jupiter, the insurgency will end where it started!

One other thing: When it comes to taking prisoners, defer to me. I will decide what to do with them and how to treat the civilian population, using a carrot-and-stick approach. This will only work if we are smart and consistent about it. Don't forget, the line between active resistance and innocent population tangled up in this revolt is often hard to draw. I don't want to antagonize those who would like to stay out of this conflict, but we also need to hit the insurgents hard and kill them where we can. The latter is our priority, but I will decide that case by case. When I am not present and you are in doubt, send couriers and ask for guidance. Is that understood?"

"*Sic, Legatus!*"

Chapter 5

Josephus watched his men with anticipation. Most had never been at war. None had ever seen a Roman army and certainly not the approaching war machine of Roman legions in battle gear. They would have to prove themselves today.

Never in his life had he seen so many of his compatriots assembled in one place. They had come from all over Galilaea, but Josephus had left enough men in the townships to defend them against potential Roman surprise attacks. It had been hard because enemy vanguard units had intercepted Jewish messengers, disrupting the flow of communications to his captains.

The Jewish commander sighed. This would be a long and difficult struggle with terrible odds. Taking on the Romans, a people who dominated almost the whole known world was borderline to madness. Maybe it was complete madness. But if successful, it would be the greatest triumph since Alexander's conquest of Persia. Josephus couldn't fathom how they could ever make the Romans leave Palestine even if they were able to defeat them over and over again. But he also knew the Romans were vulnerable. Eleazar had shown that last year when he defeated Governor Cestius and killed thousands of Roman troops. It was this great victory that had inspired all Jews to rise up and try to break the yoke.

Josephus's men had taken up positions near Garis, a couple of miles outside the traitorous town of Sepphoris, but that awful town didn't concern him now. His mission was to slow the Roman approach, intercepting them here while his men were holding the hills. Galilaea was his responsibility; he would defend it to the last man.

"Josephus, Josephus!" an attendant shouted, pointing to the western plain in the distance. A huge dust cloud had formed and was spreading fast.

"What's that?" the attendant asked. "Is the weather changing? Are we getting a storm?"

"No," Josephus said. "That is no storm. It is the Roman army."

"Impossible!" The man shook his head.

"Not at all. It's a result of their numbers. What you see in the air is dust stirred up by over two hundred thousand feet of legionaries and auxiliaries. According to our scouts, Vespasian is fielding over one hundred thousand men. I think their estimate is too high, but it certainly is a big army."

Soon Josephus and his men could see the long and winding column of troops, crawling toward the Jewish lines like a gigantic worm covered with steel. Roman helmets and body armor glittered in the bright daylight, reflecting the sun. Thousands of *pila* javelins were sticking out over their heads like the thorny spine of a gargantuan hedgehog.

"Steady," Josephus admonished his aides. "Don't be afraid. You all know what to do. Don't act until I give the command, slingers first. Archers wait until they can target individual men. I will determine that moment and give the sign. Is that clear?" *The day has come. We must do well. Much depends on it.*

"Josephus, look!"

Josephus spun around, cringing: His men were leaving in droves, fleeing, panicking.

"Nooooooooo!" Josephus screamed and scrambled from his sheltered position to run after them, shouting, cajoling, cursing and threatening them, making promises and ordering them to come back. To no avail. His army was scattering in the wind. Meanwhile, the Romans were approaching, unleashing their cavalry.

"Quick, Governor, quick," his aides shrieked. "We have to go. We need to get away from here - fast!"

Josephus nodded like in trance. Numb and in shock, he followed them to the horses. They jumped on and wheeled east. Sepphoris was lost... "Back to Tiberias," he ordered. Their fast steeds allowed them to escape unscathed.

After the retreat of the Jewish field army Sepphoris's succor had been a breeze. Vespasian didn't lose any time and pressed on, targeting the rebel township Gabara.

Vespasian monitored the city from a neighboring hill for a short while. Then he ordered three attack columns to form and take up hillside positions around the town. He did not know the exact number of defenders in Gabara, but there had been no sallies, usually an indicator for limited resources inside the beleaguered city.

Vespasian shrugged and gave the signal to attack. They would find out soon. Roman horns trumpeted, and the columns pushed off. To his surprise, Gabara put up no resistance and the city was taken within hours. He decided it was time he would introduce himself to the rebels. "Have everybody killed, old and young," he ordered. "Spare only the small children. It's payback time! Also, burn down the smaller towns and villages in the surrounding countryside and carry off the population into slavery."

His officers acknowledged the orders. Only General Traianus protested. "You cannot do that. That's murder," he said defiantly.

Vespasian arched his eyebrows in surprise. "No, it's not, Marcus. It's war," he said without raising his voice.

"It's not right. Governor, it will not achieve what you want it to."

"And what do I want it to achieve?"

"Undermine their morale, intimidate them, make them lose their will. Think about it. It will only increase their determination because now they have nothing to lose."

"Not necessarily. Gabara didn't surrender at their own volition. It was ill-defended."

"But that's not the civilians' fault," Traianus argued. "They are at the receiving end of this. General, I beg you. By the gods of eternal Rome, have mercy."

"Silent," Vespasian barked at him. "I told you and the other officers that this would be my call to make - for a reason. It takes guts to keep an empire. I know what I am doing. The Jews need to know how we deal with insurrection, and that we mean business. This is the stick, later comes the carrot." He squinted at Traianus. "Marcus Ulpius, don't forget. The Gabarans were behind the rebellion every step of the way. They were siding with the insurgents in Jerusalem from the beginning and sent many of their men south to ambush Cestius."

He put his right arm on Traianus's shoulder. "I am sorry."

The general shook off his hand and scurried out of the command tent. Annoyed by Traianus's unexpected reaction Vespasian glared at the other two generals. He could see that Titus and Cerialis were also taken aback. "What are you gawking at?" he yelled at them. "Get out. You have your orders."

They saluted in haste and scuttled after Traianus.

Soon dead bodies were piling up everywhere on the streets of Gabara. It took days to remove and burn or bury the corpses. The stench was horrifying, but Gabara was no more.

In Tiberias, Josephus dictated a letter to the Sanhedrin leadership in Jerusalem. He included a report of his failure near Sepphoris and told them he had reorganized his troops now and fortified both Jotapata and Tiberias. He also let them know he could not hold Galilaea without bloodied troops and requested reinforcements with the men who had repulsed the former Roman governor. Furthermore, he wanted to know whether Jerusalem was willing to sue for terms. If not, he insisted on battle-tried troops to save the territory.

While dictating the letter a messenger demanded to see the governor. He waved him in. "What is it?"

The man would not talk. He looked at Josephus, then down on the floor, at Josephus again for a split second, and down on the floor again.

"What is it?" Josephus repeated impatiently.

"Gabara," the courier choked as the words came out of his mouth. "They... killed every one..."

Josephus froze. He turned chalk-white and stopped pacing. He wanted to say something, but his lips wouldn't obey. Aghast, he stared at the scribe at his side. The man looked back at him, dropping his reed pen. His arm went limp altogether and swiped the terracotta inkwell from his desk. It crashed on the floor and shattered into many pieces, splashing ink everywhere. Bewildered, Josephus glimpsed at the black dripping mess, reminiscent of blood, the blood of his countrymen in Gabara... All dead, slaughtered, massacred by a heartless enemy.

The governor swallowed. "You can go now," he told the messenger. "Go!"

He glanced at the embarrassed scribe. "Don't worry about the inkwell, Jacob. Are you all right? Can we finish this letter? It's more important than ever before. Our lives depend on Jerusalem. We can expect no mercy from the Romans."

"Yes, Master," the man said, still shaking. "I will fetch another well."

Upon his return Josephus dictated frantically. He ordered ten copies made and had them sealed with hot wax. After handpicking couriers he sent them all off to Jerusalem with instructions to ride day and night, hoping that at least some of them would make it through the Roman lines.

Chapter 6

Class was boring as always. Four boys and a girl named Cordula joined Trajan on the long bench of a rented forum shop. Outside, Trajan could hear obnoxious merchants stridently advertise their produce on the forum plaza.

He was not used to having a girl in class. Most families only sent boys to school. School was not deemed important for girls, but he knew the Cordii had a different view. Unlike most everyone else, they treated boys and girls alike. Cordula's presence bothered Trajan. He slid back and forth on his spot on the bench, avoiding eye contact with her at all times.

"Trajan," the *paedagogus* addressed him. "Did you study the text in front of you?"

"No, he did not," a perky boy named Sergius piped up. "He studied Cordula."

Trajan blushed while the other boys all laughed at him. "Not true," he protested. "Not true at all. This is just Sergius's dirty fantasy."

"Quiet!" the *paedagogus* ordered, lifting his hazelnut stick. Trajan fell silent. The teacher had used it in the past, and Trajan remembered all too well how badly it hurt.

"So, Trajan," the teacher addressed him again. "Why did Julius Caesar land troops in Britannia? He obviously had no intention to conquer it, did he?"

Trajan had no problem answering the question. Julius Caesar was his hero after all. The boy's thoughts turned to Caesar's account of the Gallic War. "Caesar wanted to send a message to the Britannian tribes because they kept sending troops and supplies to the Gauls to help them against us. He didn't want them to feel safe anywhere, not even on their own island. And Caesar wanted to learn about their fighting skills, manpower and resolve to repel a potential Britannian invasion later on."

"Very good, Trajan." The *paedagogus* was pleased. "Let's read the next chapter."

After class Trajan stormed out of the forum shop right away. He didn't want to talk to the other boys, certainly not to Sergius, but he also wanted to avoid Cordula. How awkward. Hopefully she didn't believe Sergius...

Trajan was still reeling from the embarrassment when he suddenly noticed he had strayed from his usual route home and accidentally entered the other side of town. Quintus called it the "danger zone," a part of town that was inhabited by the lower classes - a scary place for outsiders. Trajan turned around and hurried back, but it was too late. Four boys he had never seen before blocked his way.

"Hah, whom do we have here?" one of them shouted. He measured up to Trajan in size but was chubby. Like his three friends, he held a small club in his hand. Trajan looked for a way around them. This was not good, not good at all.

Another boy shouted, "Hey, I know who that is. Let me get Lucius."

Oh no! It dawned on him now. These were friends of Lucius and Manlius. He needed to get away from here fast. Trajan looked back over his shoulder. He knew he could not possibly fight them straight on. They were too many and they had weapons. He would need to outrun them. Trajan was about to spin round and take off when he heard Lucius's voice behind him. He winced. Sure enough - there were Lucius and Manlius, grinning at him. He was trapped.

The Roman army was moving on Jotapata next, the Jewish base of operations in West Galilaea. The Romans had learned from a deserter that the city was packed with refugees from the countryside and that Governor Josephus resided there himself, directing the defense efforts. Vespasian sent the Tribune Placidus ahead with cavalry and ordered him to cordon off the town. He didn't want to let Josephus get away. The deserter had stressed how important both the governor and the stronghold were for the defense of Galilaea. He argued, if they eliminated both the insurgency would collapse. Vespasian had his doubts about that, but it would be the beginning of the end and a major blow to the rebels' efforts.

The Roman main force arrived a day after Placidus's men and struck camp to the north. Immediately, Vespasian placed a ring of infantry around Jotapata to foil any Jewish reinforcements. The infantry was pointed against Jotapata while Placidus's cavalry formed another ring pointing to the outside and protecting the legionaries from relief attacks. With both rings in place, Vespasian ordered the Roman assault.

The Jewish defenders manned the ramparts and were also positioned outside of their walls. The Romans bombarded them with long-range catapults and short-to-medium-range bows and slings, unrelentingly firing battle darts, arrows and rocks of all sizes. Some of the 'rocks' were in fact pottery vessels containing loose debris. On impact, it flung out in all directions with devastating impact on bystanders. After a long barrage Vespasian sent his crack troops forward to take Jotapata's lower battlements.

To the general's amazement, Josephus himself spearheaded an aggressive sally against the charging troops. After heavy fighting the Jews were able to stop the Roman advance but could not break through the Roman lines either. Furious fighting continued all day, inflicting heavy losses on both sides. Vespasian was pleased with the discipline of his men, but the Jewish defenders seemed to make up with motivation and zeal what they lacked in skill.

Traianus may be right. They have nothing to lose.

The assault continued for days. Each time, Roman infantry got entangled with Jewish fighters under the walls. The geography did not help either. Jotapata was almost entirely built on a precipice, accessible only on the northern side where the city was built on the lowest slope of a hill. Of course, that very ridge was included in the fortifications. Vespasian's efforts could only be wielded against this ridge, making it impossible to deploy his army as a whole.

Frustrated, Vespasian called for a war council. After long discussions, the generals decided to build a massive platform against the approachable section of Jotapata's walls, using earthworks and timber and protecting the work crews with plywood screens.

The Jews attacked the Roman craftsmen with snipers and slingers right away. Vespasian responded with artillery, lining up more than one hundred and sixty engines in a half-circle and firing numerous payloads of bolts, firebrands, spears and rocks around the clock. The salvos drove the snipers off the walls, but the Jews reacted with swift counter-attacks in small groups. They were able to tear away the wooden screens, interrupting the work on the platform. By linking the screens together, the Romans were able to regain the upper hand and the defenders fell back.

Over the next couple of days, the platform grew higher and higher and almost reached up to the walls, prompting the Jews to make their next move. Hundreds of stonemasons appeared on the ramparts to increase the height of Jotapata's exposed bulwarks. To protect them from the Roman missile barrage, the defenders installed railings on the battlements and covered them with raw ox hides. They even wetted the hides so they wouldn't catch fire when hit with firebrands. That way the masons raised the walls by thirty feet.

Vespasian was stunned. Several weeks had passed and his operation had made no progress. He would have to starve them into submission though they seemed to have grain in abundance. What about water? There was no prospect of rain, and Jotapata wasn't known to have springs. Yet, here were the Jewish defenders, soaking even those ox hide rails with water. Vespasian rubbed his hand against his chin. He began to admire their commander. He had prepared them well. Still, the water needed to come from somewhere.

The general called for Traianus. "I have a difficult assignment for you, Marcus. Your legion has our best scouts. Use them to find the source of Jotapata's water. It cannot come from cisterns or springs inside the walls, but it must come from somewhere. Somehow the rebels manage to get it into the city. Make it your top priority."

Several days later and after having searched the scarp around the township multiple times, Traianus's men still had nothing to show for. Then Traianus ordered night searches.

If we can't find the water, maybe we can find the men getting it into the city, and if I were them I would do it at night.

Nothing came of it. Traianus's sentries didn't notice any suspicious activities. The general decided to throw more men at the problem by sending hundreds of grooms, squires and pages into the area.

After a week of searching and probing, his adjutant Calvinus woke him up in the middle of the night. "Legate, one of the squires is reporting what could be a lead."

Traianus rubbed his eyes and scrambled from his futon. "Yes... What did he find?"

"He says he saw dogs with light furs move around in a gorge west of Jotapata."

"And?"

"He says the 'dogs' aren't moving the way dogs would. It's subtle, he says, but his father is a breeder who taught him a lot about canines. The squire is certain these 'animals' aren't dogs at all, but he doesn't know what they are."

"My armor. This is likely going to be a fool's errand, but it could be a breakthrough."

"*Sic*, my Lord. Pages!"

Within minutes Traianus was ready. He picked a *turma* of men and they cantered to the questionable area. Sentries were pointing the way. At the edge of the ravine they left their horses behind and met with the waiting squire. Together, they stepped down the embankment. Halfway down, the squire signaled them to halt and crouch low behind the sagebrush. He pointed his index finger at the 'dog' that was moving along the bottom of the gully, about two hundred yards away from them. Traianus squinted, barely making 'it' out. *It is peculiar,* he thought. "You have good eyes, squire, but it could be a goat, no?"

"A goat bleats when it's lost, looking for its flock," the squire replied. "Whatever this is, it's not a goat, General. I don't know much about scouting, but this could be a human crawling on the ground under some sort of fleece."

Traianus nodded. "Let's find out. Calvinus, if this is a ruse there will be Jewish fighters in this gorge waiting to spring a trap on us. Bring in all your men and send a courier to call for a century of legionaries. Our pickets are nearby. The men should be here soon, but we won't wait for them. Have the troopers fan out and surround whatever we are seeing. When our ring is complete they are to move in and apprehend whatever/whomever they find."

As the soldiers homed in on the target 'it' suddenly accelerated. The Romans took after it, disappearing out of Traianus view. "By Jupiter," he shouted. "I think it's a man..."

Minutes later, the soldiers reappeared, manhandling a recalcitrant Jewish rebel. "We caught him on the bottom of the gully, General. There is a tiny crack in the bedrock through which he almost escaped. I guess this is how they enter the city. And we found this-" The trooper tossed a large leather skin at Traianus's feet.

The legate whistled. He picked up the skin and popped the cork. Then he took a sip. "In fact, it's water. Is this how you do it? Speak, prisoner!"

The man wouldn't talk. No matter, in the course of the night, Traianus's men ambushed a dozen more Jewish water carriers. At dawn, they investigated the crack to see whether they could use it for an ambuscade, but it was too small. Traianus sealed it with cement and reported back to a delighted Vespasian. Jotapata was finally cut off.

Weeks passed without further Roman activities until the Jews suddenly launched ferocious suicide attacks. Wave after wave hurled itself at the Roman lines, forfeiting their lives but inflicting heavy losses. Vespasian shuddered. He had seen mayhem in his life, but nothing on this scale. The din was deafening. To reduce Roman casualties Vespasian ordered the legionaries back. Instead, he sent Arabic bowmen and Syrian slingers forward to take the brunt of the desperate attacks.

Traianus pulled the governor aside. "My Lord, do you now see what I was worried about? The Jews fight to the death because you condemned them to. What else is left for a people with no hope?"

Deep inside Vespasian knew he had made a big mistake killing the Gabarans. Traianus had been right all along. The massacre of Gabara made it harder now to squash the revolt. "You may be right, Marcus Ulpius. You probably are, but there is another reason for their madness. They are fanatics."

"That is true for some but not all of them. Look, I am not saying this mess is all the result of Gabara. What I am saying is our mission would have been easier if we had not massacred the people there."

"It's too late now. We need solutions, not self-incrimination."

Despite the fighting the work on the platform had never stopped. Vespasian gauged its progress once more. Yes, the pad was ready to support the weight of the battering rams now, and the men needed a new initiative. He had tortoise-rams brought up, protected underneath wheeled wooden sheds and covered with bronze plates. The legionaries pushed them into place at the feet of Jotapata's walls. To cover their approach, catapults again fired hundreds of bolts, arrows and rocks at the defenders on the ramparts. The whirring tension skeins of so many torsion engines shooting all at once and non-stop interrupted the Roman communications, but the barrage wiped the Jewish soldiers off their parapets. Once they were gone the battering rams started hammering the walls without delay, but -alas- now the defenders lowered large sacks filled with chaff to where the rams hit the walls. The sacks softened and absorbed each blow.

Vespasian threw up his arms in despair, but Traianus had an idea. He told his cavalry to tie their lances together and create long poles at the ends to which they attached sharp sickles. Using this counter-weapon, the Romans were able to cut down the sacks as soon as the defenders lowered them in place. They cheered, but then the Jews rushed out in multiple columns carrying tinder wood and putting fire to the rams, their covers and the platform as a whole. They had mixed the wood with brimstone and drenched it in bitumen and pitch. The flames were flying at the Roman soldiers from everywhere, scattering them in all directions.

Vespasian gave his generals a sullen look. What they had worked on for so long was destroyed within the hour...

In the hustle, Jewish bowmen also resumed their volleys. One of the shafts hit Vespasian's foot while he was watching in the distance. The general screamed in pain and went down. Blood was dripping down his right *caliga,* but his adjutants quickly jumped to his aid, took off the blood-drenched military boot and carried him to safety.

Medics examined the wound in the infirmary. The arrow had come loose and fallen off. It turned out the injury was only superficial. "The shaft must have come from a very long distance, General. It did not have penetrating power. You will be fine."

Vespasian breathed a sigh of relief. The medics were still cleaning his wound when Titus came running into the tent. Vespasian gawked at him dumbfounded. "What are you doing here? You have an assault to command!"

"But Father, you were injured. I wasn't sure," Titus protested. "I heard-"

"I am fine. I am fine. It's nothing," the general shouted from the stretcher. "Look at this puny cut. It's nothing. Go away, Titus. Leave! Tell the troops to regroup and get back on the offensive. I don't hear enough Roman thunder out there. Our attack has lost momentum."

After one more glance at his father, the young general dashed off and rode back to the front lines.

Roman discipline returned to the rankers in no time. The attack was on a roll soon, blasting Jotapata's battlements with projectiles. Vespasian could hear their thudding impact and the roar of the bawling soldiers. The

Jews, however, he was told later filled every wall breach with debris, defunct weapons and even dead the bodies of fallen comrades. They did it so fast that the Roman infantry could never bring scaling-gangways in position to take advantage of the artillery onslaught.

Still, they were getting close. In the morning Vespasian limped outside, convinced it would be the last day of the siege. He ordered the whole army together for the final assault and gave his instructions: Coordinated waves of dismounted horsemen in full armor, equipped with Macedonian lances were to force themselves through wall breaches to establish small beachheads onto which legionaries from the Fifth and Tenth could place Roman ramps. That way the legionaries should be able to enter the city at last.

Placidus heard the *cornicens'* attack signal from his post near the front lines. The honking horns incited a thundering battle cry from the Roman throats. Immediately, heavy artillery and arrow volleys darkened the sky. Infantry ran forward, carrying hundreds of ladders that they leaned against the ramparts of Jotapata in a feint to draw defenders away from where lancers tried to push into breached wall sections. But it was hard for the Jews kept their focus on the more critical areas and blocked the onslaught of Roman lances trying to poke their way into the city.

The young tribune had been waiting for this opportunity to redeem himself. Impatiently, he egged on his lancers. "Come on, come on, you can do it!" Many times it was close, but as hard as they tried, they couldn't push through.

After a shift of position Placidus came to be stationed near his colleague Casperius Aelianus who was directing a cohort of infantry equipped with gangways. Placidus dropped his own effort and merged his men with Casperius's unit. "Aelianus, my men can't punch through. Perhaps we can do it together!"

Aelianus nodded grimly. "Watch, Placidus. This might just do it."

Casperius's men were able to lock several gangway hooks onto a section of crenellated ramparts. The Romans howled with joy and scampered up the ramps with no delay. Casperius took the lead himself with Placidus right behind him. They were close to reaching the battlements when suddenly the defenders poured boiling oil on them. Aelianus screamed in pain as the fenugreek ran under his armor and burning his skin. He whirled around, pushing aside the bamboozled Placidus, who almost lost his balance but was able to hang on to the rails. The other troops on the gangway now bolted to escape the hot oil, with Aelianus in their midst, still screaming in agony. Having reached the ground at the other end of the gangway he came to a screeching halt and lost no time tearing off his armor. Medics rushed at him with cold water and a stretcher and carried him off the battle site.

Placidus was watching in shock. Then he peered back at the walls of Jotapata. He was still on the gangway - the last man standing. The Roman attacks were losing momentum and coherence everywhere around him even as fresh waves of infantry were pushing forward. To his right, the Jews poured more fenugreek on another gangway's planks, picking off the legionaries on it. Some fell off the ramp altogether and plunged to their deaths. Others were trodden to death by their fleeing comrades in a terrible jumble of armor and men.

Seeing that, Placidus yelled at the incoming reinforcements, "Noo! Get back! Pull off the ramps. The Jews have fenugreek. You can't cross!"

The men hesitated, but Placidus kept waving his crossed arms overhead. "I say, back with you! Remove the cursed ramps. This is madness."

The grumbling men finally obeyed, peeking at the eagle standards behind them to see whether the attack was officially being called off just as the *cornicens* in fact blew retreat, and pages took down the attack pennants above Vespasian's command tent. Płacidus tossed his shield and sword on the ground in frustration and hunkered down on one knee in exhaustion, propping his begrimed forehead on his shaking hands. Jotapata could not be taken.

Chapter 7

Trajan was desperately looking for a way out of his conundrum when his nemesis Lucius yelled at the fat urchin, "Grab him!"

The fat boy made a tentative step forward. Trajan now remembered he did have a weapon of sorts in his school bag - his stylus, a sharp stick made of bronze designed to scratch the wax on his writing tablet. Trajan ripped it from his pouch and wielded it at the group like a knife. When the urchin made another step forward, he pointed the stylus straight at him.

"Don't come any closer if you want to keep your eye," he shrieked. "Just ask Manlius."

Manlius's eye was still black from his previous encounter with Trajan.

"Last time, I only punched him. But this time I will not hesitate to use this stylus. I'll puncture your eye. You will be blind and bleed to death!"

The boy froze. His three friends looked at each other startled, but Manlius didn't let up. "You cowards! Get him! We are six against one."

It was time for Trajan to act. He lunged forward and punched the stylus into the fat boy's chest with all the force he could muster. The boy screamed in pain and went down. In the confusion Trajan whirled round and ran off, with Manlius and Lucius hot on his tail.

Trajan made a hard right turn at the end of the block and another hard left turn at the next but couldn't shake them. Then he saw an open grocery stall coming up. No one was standing behind the counter. Trajan dashed in and grabbed a long knife hanging from a side wall. Out of the corner of his eye he saw a befuddled clerk turn at him from the back of the shop, but the man came too late. Trajan dashed back out, sprinting as fast as his legs could carry him.

The short delay had allowed Lucius and Manlius to catch up. They were now close behind Trajan, passing old warehouses and decrepit homes. Soon they were breathing down his neck. They would take him down any time now. He stopped abruptly, put out one foot and tripped up Lucius. The boy crashed down hard on the cobble stone pavement, 'braking' with his hands and knees. He came to standstill banged up, bleeding and moaning in pain.

Manlius had avoided Trajan and turned on him now, but Trajan directed his new-found weapon, the long knife from the grocery stall, at him. Manlius pulled back. They started circling each other like paired gladiators in the arena.

"It's your choice," Trajan said. "You want to fight? Then fight. If not, you better run."

Manlius stared at Trajan's glittering knife. "Bastard," he called him. "Freak."

Trajan did not answer. He eyed Lucius on the ground. Together, the two of them could still be dangerous, but at the moment Lucius was no threat. He was shocked, busy with his wounds and glared at the other two boys. "Let him go, Manlius," he urged. "Don't you see? He has a knife."

Manlius did not answer. He just stood there, hanging on to his bludgeon. Trajan cautiously stepped away, but kept a close eye on them. When he reached the end of the block, they still didn't make a move. Manlius was now helping Lucius with his injuries.

Trajan turned away and ran home. Maybe they would leave him alone from now on. In any case, he did not feel frightened any more. Upbeat, he wondered whether Julius Caesar would have acted like him. This reminded him, there was a war going on in the East, and his father was in the midst of it... He missed him.

Night had fallen over Jotapata. The Roman army was tending to its laid up men and cleaned up the battlefield. To add insult to injury the Galilean city of Japha, which had submitted to the Romans had a change of mind and revolted once again.

Vespasian called Traianus. "Marcus Ulpius, we have to split our forces. Take one thousand mounted auxiliaries and four cohorts from the Tenth and quell the insurrection at Japha. Let me know as soon as you are successful. Garrison the city and return with the majority of your troops."

"When do we leave?"

"As soon as your men have recovered from today's fighting, but no later than tomorrow noon."

Traianus saluted and left. Vespasian sat back down on his *sella curulis,* a beautifully carved official's chair with grill-shaped armrests and no back. A *Legatus Augusti* was not supposed to slouch. *Jotapata be cursed,* Vespasian thought. *I am falling behind schedule.*

Traianus departed at daybreak. He planned to make good progress before the heat of the day would take its toll on his men. At noon, they rested in the welcome shade of some scraggly trees and kept going until nightfall halted their advance.

They reached the city in the late morning hours of the next day. Seeing the ramparts, Traianus winced. Japha had dual ring walls of great strength, and he had only half a legion with him. To his surprise, the city's defenders were waiting outside the walls to take on the advancing Romans, itching for a fight and harassing his skirmishers and slingers.

Our saving grace. They outnumber us five to one, but it's only an unorganized throng of lightly armored men.

39

The general called back his light infantry and ordered the savviest cohort to form a *cuneus*, a wedge battle formation designed to break through enemy lines using the momentum of a deeply stacked slab of heavy infantry. Judging the situation on the field, Traianus decided to give it a ratio of eight men per row and a whopping sixty-two men deep, one whole cohort not lined up by century but as a homogenous block. He intended to smash their lines, cut them off from the city and destroy them in the open.

The legate placed the *cuneus* in the middle, flanked on either side by nine centuries from the other three cohorts. The outer centuries were placed ahead of the ones hugging the *cuneus* thus forming a crescent with the *cuneus* in the center. The fringe centuries would hit the straight enemy line shortly after the *cuneus* had rolled into it to prevent the defenders from helping the center to stand its ground. The squadrons of the auxiliary cavalry protected the centuries' flanks, fifteen *turmae* on both sides. They were to engage once the Jewish front line was broken and the rebels were trying to escape back to Japha's walls.

The *cuneus* hit the vast enemy host like a hammer. The collision ripped through the defenders' convoluted lines as if they didn't exist, breaking their ranks at once. The Roman wings made their move simultaneously while the cavalry was blocking any escape to the side. The rebels folded shrieking and scuttled back to seek protection behind the city's walls - the legionaries right behind them. Both sides burst into the gates of the outer ramparts at the same time. Traianus's plan to cut them off failed. The rebels managed to get behind the outer wall, but so did his men. Naturally, Japha's garrison closed the gates of the inner wall to prevent the Romans from entering the city together with their own. At least, the twelve thousand defenders were now caught between the two battlements.

Not by the book, but it will do.

Traianus ordered the portals of the outer wall closed and told his men to occupy its ramparts dashing up the staircases behind the protection of their shields. Then the Romans targeted the trapped Jewish fighters with volleys of *pila*. The rebels implored their countrymen behind the inner wall to let them in, but in vain - it would have doomed the city. So the Roman projectiles killed the fighters by the thousands. Many others were killed by Japha's garrison when they tried to force their way in. Some took their own lives.

Traianus closed his eyes. He felt no euphoria. War was evil, necessary at times but evil nonetheless. He turned to Calvinus. "Let me know me when this slaughter is over."

He spurred back to his command tent and sent a messenger to Vespasian, requesting the presence of his son so that the young commander could finish Japha himself. When Titus arrived with fifteen hundred more men,

Traianus took command of the left wing. Titus took the right. The legionaries kept battering and targeting the walls of Japha's inner ring from close proximity with portable ballistas and waves of *pila*. Ladders were brought up everywhere. The ensuing fight on the ramparts raged for hours until the outnumbered defenders were pushed from the battlements. Bitter fighting followed in Japha's narrow streets. Even the women pelted the Romans from their rooftops with anything they could find: kettles, ladles, rocks, tiles, even chairs.

The Romans rounded up the last defenders after long and arduous street battles. Titus and Traianus spared the women and children and sent them off under guard to the slave markets in Ptolemais.

Chapter 8

When they returned to Jotapata, a cheerful Vespasian welcomed them. Titus deferred his father's compliments to Traianus. "Marcus did the hard work. He attacked them so ferociously in the field that we got our foot in the door early."

Vespasian shook Traianus's hand. "Well done, General! I am proud of both of you, but the best thing is that Jotapata is going to fall soon. We have overtopped their walls in your absence with three fireproof towers that we built on site. Our scouts are saying their night sentries are tired and tend to doze off in the wee hours of the morning. That might give us a chance!"

Preparations were made for a stealth attack. Vespasian charged Titus with leading it. They started an hour before dawn. With a handful of his best men, Vespasian's son hurried up the stairs inside one of the siege towers. At the top, his soldiers flung slinged ropes over to Jotapata's ramparts. The slings caught on the battlements and allowed them to climb over hand over hand under the cover of darkness. To Titus's relief the Jewish sentries were in fact slow to react. Too slow. They died without noise.

When the area was clear, the young general sent for more troops. Meanwhile his men swiveled a gangway to the cleared section and occupied Jotapata's citadel from there. When the beachhead was fully established, Titus led the army into the city. The Romans swept down in full strength, surprising its defenders at dawn. Heavy-eyed, they tried to hustle and get to their posts, but confusion ruled. A thick mist made it hard for them to distinguish between friend and foe. Many of them ran into Roman troops and were killed on the spot.

Josephus was in a fitful slumber when his aides shook him awake. Rushing outside, he saw the enemy's soldiers roaming the streets of Jotapata. Josephus scurried back and slammed the door shut. He looked at his aides - it was over and they knew it too. Somehow, the Romans had found a way in. His men had one option left: the subterranean caverns. He told his aides to hide there and convey his instructions to everyone else. Maybe he could save some of the men for another fight or to help defend Jerusalem.

His supporters dashed out in pairs of two; then Josephus followed. What he saw was grizzly: The Roman soldiers were retaliating for the lengthy siege, hunting down civilians and fighters alike, killing indiscriminately. They only spared women, toddlers and babies.

Have they learned from Gabara?

Due to the fog visibility was poor. Josephus managed to run from house to house, taking cover behind a wall or a horse trough whenever he saw ravaging soldiers close-by. He was looking for a sewer trap door. Finally, he encountered one behind the markets. Josephus lifted it up, jumped through the opening and closed it behind him. The smell was atrocious. His open sandals landed in muck, but he had no choice. Rats were scampering by, splashing in the mucky water. The smell... It was so strong he nearly passed out. Determined, Josephus tore off a piece from his tunic and tied it around mouth and nose. He stepped off, wading in the waste. After following the pitch black canal for several hundred yards, he arrived at a junction. He made an educated guess and walked left. Soon, the sewer line widened, terminating in a large cavern. A dim light came through from the ceiling.

Another trap door.

Much of the cavern was dry and on higher ground than the canal he was wading in. He stepped onto the dry cavern floor while up above he could hear the commotion of looting and killing.

My poor people...

Josephus concentrated on the cave again. He tried to guess its dimensions - maybe thirty by twenty yards and ten yards high. He sat down, shaking.

I am safe for now.

The Jewish commander spent half the day in the cavern. Then, other men joined him, exhausted, hungry, horror-struck. In the evening another man came and told them of a bigger cave ahead where some forty well-supplied fighters were hiding. Gladly, Josephus and the others followed him through the sewer maze. They could still hear the trampling of Roman soldiers overhead. They overturned shelves and sofas to find trap doors into the sewer canals.

Let them. The Romans would get lost fast in here.

Suddenly, Josephus's eyes were blinded by lights ahead. The cavern! It was well-lit by a hodgepodge assortment of dilapidated oil lamps. Boxes were stacked against its walls. There were no other light sources, but ventilation shafts seemed to provide enough air. The survivors greeted Josephus enthusiastically. He hugged every one of them, cheering them up, commending them for their tenacity. Maybe they could outlast the Romans down here and return to the surface later. After a quick snack of water and bread, Josephus studied their escape routes and checked on the closest Roman sentries.

Another day passed. And another. They could still hear the Romans rummage through the doomed city above. After three days, Roman officers appeared out of nowhere at the cave's entrance and demanded Josephus's surrender. They had found him!

The Romans guaranteed his safety, if he surrendered. Depressed and disappointed, Josephus refused. Then an old acquaintance from his time spent at Jerusalem, the Greek Tribune Nicanor, who was evidently serving in

Vespasian's army now, shouted into the cavern from outside the barricaded entrance. Josephus's mind moved back in time - they had been friends long time ago when Nicanor had served with the Roman client King Agrippa II.

Nicanor assured Josephus that the Roman offer was honest, that Vespasian admired him and wanted to see him face to face. "Why would Vespasian send a friend like me and taint a successful conquest with perfidy? My honor would never allow me to participate in such a trick."

It sounded plausible and was certainly better than starving to death or getting killed when the Romans eventually stormed the cave. But his men snarled at him. To them, an honorable death was preferable to the ignominious life as a Roman lackey. As hard as Josephus tried, he could not change their minds. On the contrary, they soon accused him of cowardice and almost knifed him. He backed off.

The next day Josephus had an idea. "So you want to die? Do you?"

"No, but what else can we do?"

"Well, you don't want to surrender, but we don't have much food or water left. There is no hope for help. And you don't want to give the Romans the pleasure of enslaving or crucifying you."

"Never, never!"

"So be it. Here is my proposal. Let us die honorably before we are too weak. We will draw lots and kill each other. That way we don't have to commit suicide, a crime against God."

They stared at him aghast, but soon agreed to the terrible plan. Josephus then went to work, designing the details for his 'lottery'. It was simple. When the first man's number was drawn, the man with the next higher number would put him to the sword. Then that man would be killed. And so on.

The slaughter lasted an hour. Josephus had been smart enough to assign the highest number to himself. Therefore, only he and another man were left at the end. Trembling, the other rebel looked at Josephus and the dead bodies all over the cavern. The stench of blood added to the filthy air. "Now is my turn. I have to kill you."

"Try if you dare," Josephus shouted in defiance, jumped forward and held his knife under the man's throat. He froze. "Josephus," he hissed. "This is heresy. You can't do that. You are betraying our cause – and God!"

"Oh yes, I can." Josephus nabbed the man's sickle knife from his belt. Then he pushed him away. "You can do whatever you want, but I will surrender. My time is not up yet!"

He left the cave with raised arms and open hands, the other fighter trudging behind him, head down on his chest. The Roman guards lurched forward, searched them, shackled their hands and brought them to the generals.

"Josephus Ben Matthias," Vespasian muttered when the governor was brought to him. He held his head high, proudly staring at the Roman commander-in-chief.

"Well, you have shown wile and put up a valiant fight. If you weren't Jewish, I could mistake you for a Roman officer."

"Thank you for the compliment, Titus Flavius Vespasianus. I am honored. Your troops fought well too. But know this, crushing the rebellion will be no cakewalk. Jerusalem is not Galilaea. It is the heart of the rebellion, and the fight will be long."

"I know. But we have you now, your topographical knowledge and your inside information. And they lost you, their most competent man. You know as well as I do that the end of the insurrection is inevitable."

"I know that, but my compatriots do not. They will die fighting. They don't want to serve you any longer. They believe God is on their side. Do not underestimate their religious zeal. Myself, I will not betray my people. I will tell you nothing but this: You are fortunate by taking this city. That was hard. One day you will be emperor – and create a dynasty of your own. I can clearly see that."

The generals looked at each other, raising their eyebrows.

"You are crazy. How can you make such a bold prophecy? Are you a soothsayer?" Titus asked him.

Josephus didn't answer.

"I am talking to you," Titus barked.

His father raised his hand. "Don't, Titus. The governor interests me. Take him away, give him shelter and feed him well. He is to stay our prisoner until the war is over. And keep him separate from the other captives."

BOOK II

THE YOUNG SOLDIER

Chapter 9

Seven years later (75 AD), Antioch, Syria Province

The *decurio* and his soldiers were rolling dice in the portico of the Syrian governor's residence, the Praetorium, when the clatter of trotting horses caught their attention. The men were sweating in their woolen tunics even without wearing armor. Syria's merciless summer heat felt like a furnace. Not the slightest breeze provided Antioch with any relief.

The *decurio* casually raised his head. Who would be crazy enough to be out and about in the middle of the day? But against all reason, two young men dressed in dusty white tunics headed towards them. One rider was scrawny looking; the other, a well-built young man, exuded confidence. He reined in his horse and dismounted in a fluid motion by quickly sliding one leg over the horse's mane. The brawny traveler hit the ground with both feet, cushioning his landing with ease. Then, using his wrist, he wiped the sweat off his forehead and looked at the baffled soldiers.

Suddenly recognizing the wide purple stripe on his tunic, the men jumped to their feet and saluted the stranger, evidently a military tribune of senatorial rank. The *decurio* stretched out his arm and grabbed the horse's reigns.

"*Ave*, soldiers," the newcomer greeted them. "A bit hot today, isn't it? Is it like this every day?"

Where did this tribune come from and who was he?

The tall youngster possessed a well-proportioned body: wide shoulders, muscular arms and a pronounced torso buttressed by long athletic legs. His face was unremarkable: a straight nose and inconspicuous but firm lips. He wore most of his dark hair short, but thick ripples covered his forehead and eyebrows.

"Yes, it is, Tribunus," the *decurio* replied. "May I ask where you come from that you don't know that?"

"Excuse me, I forgot to introduce myself. My name is-"

At this moment, the doors behind them burst wide open and the governor's house slave Harpenna rushed out, throwing herself at the stranger. "Trajan, Trajan! I am so glad you are finally here. We were so worried about you."

The rider hugged her back, beaming. "Harpenna, so good to see you! It's been so long. Where is Father?"

"He is inside. Trajan, I prepared your quarters. Come in. Please, come in."

The *decurio* eyed Trajan with mixed feelings. *The governor's son...*

Another callow officer to deal with, but at least a friendly one.

"Who is your companion, Marcus?" Harpenna wanted to know.

The other rider had dismounted too and was tending to his horse.

"His name is Callistus. Officially, he is my attendant. Unofficially, he is my friend."

Callistus greeted Harpenna awkwardly.

"Let's go inside, Trajan. Where is your luggage?" Harpenna asked.

"I don't know. When we arrived at the port in Seleucia, they said they would take care of it. I guess we were faster than the baggage haulers. Not to worry, I am certain it will be here soon enough."

Inside the governor's residence Trajan said, "We are thirsty, Harpenna."

"Patience, patience, Trajan. Around this corner and - here is your room."

Harpenna opened the plain cedar door and pointed inside. Trajan entered, his gaze sweeping the *cubiculum* with great curiosity. He registered a well-appointed bed in one corner of the room that was covered by a neatly tucked-in blanket striped in red and white. Two rectangular crimson red army pillows adorned one end of the bed. Abutting it was a bronze nightstand with a terracotta oil lamp on it. "It is nice and cool in here," Trajan commented.

The room also contained a wax board cabinet, a scroll shelf and a desk. Someone had placed a water-filled decanter and several glasses on it.

"Perfect." Trajan filled one of the glasses and passed it on to Callistus. Then he poured another and emptied it himself in one swoop. He wiped off his mouth and belched. "That felt good!"

"Now, now! I guess you were thirsty," Harpenna admonished him and laughed. "It's been many years. You have become a man, Trajan, a very handsome man I might add."

Embarrassed, he lowered his head. "I guess so, but you are still the same, Harpenna. You haven't aged a bit!"

The slave blushed. "Thanks for the compliment, you charmer you. Serving in the House of Traianus will do that to you. Now, tell me about home. What's new? How is your Mother?"

"The house has not been the same since Father left and took you with him. Everybody misses you, Harpenna - your effervescence, your infectious laughter, your singing. Father should have never taken you away from us when he became Governor of Syria. I guess he wanted to enjoy your company too. Anyway, from what I can tell Mother is well. I haven't seen her in a year because I spent all of last year in Rome. Rome, Harpenna, Rome! An incredible city... You have not seen anything like it. It is simply breathtaking. The Forum is amazing, awe-inspiring. On the other hand, downtown is a big mess right now because they are building a new Amphitheater where the lake of Nero's Golden House used to be."

"I don't know, Trajan. There are too many amphitheaters in the world. All that effort to house spectacles of bloodshed..." Harpenna pouted.

"It's not a bad thing, Harpenna. The spectacles serve a higher purpose: They maintain the martial qualities of the Roman people. You can't have an empire and be squeamish. Anyway, the traffic from the quarries is a nightmare. Imagine the huge amount of material they need to bring in! The new stadium will be the largest ever built. I was told it will hold more than fifty thousand spectators, fifty thousand! But we may never see its completion in our lifetime."

Trajan fondly looked at the family's faithful servant he had grown up with in his native Hispania. "You know, Harpenna, I am a Tribune now. The government invited me to work as a *Triumvir Monetalis* at the mint in Rome until my transfer to the Sixth Legion *Ferrata* here in Antioch. That was something else. They involved me in coin design. I was allowed to suggest what kind of art to put on a coins, what kind of graphics or symbols - like a picture of a god or a goddess or a new building or landmark, and even what verbiage to stamp on it."

"Sounds exciting. Give me an example!"

"Oh, I proposed to use an imprint of the god of war Mars on the backside of all gold coins."

"Oh, Trajan. You are so predictable. Can't you think of nothing else but war?"

"Well... In any case, my proposal didn't make it. The Emperor Vespasian decided otherwise, but he likes me. And I am very lucky; Father helped him win the Jewish War. That counts for something. Now that Vespasian is Caesar it's downright brilliant."

"Brilliant indeed," Marcus Ulpius Traianus repeated as he appeared in the threshold of Trajan's room.

"Father!" Trajan jumped up from his chair and ran into Traianus's open arms.

"You are finally here. What took so long? We were concerned, Harpenna and I, weren't we?"

Harpenna nodded.

"But anyway, what matters is that you made it. What was the reason for your delay?"

Trajan shrugged. "Nothing special. Bad weather postponed our departure from Brundisium, and my position as *Triumvir Monetalis* held me up because we were in the middle of redesigning the empire's most valuable coin, the *aureus*. By Jupiter, so much politics, and then Vespasian's sons could not agree on anything. In the end Vespasian decided himself.

"I am so happy to be here, Father. Finally, I can join the Army. You know how long I have been waiting for this moment…"

"And how long I have been dreading it," Harpenna piped up. "It's not the fun you think it is, Trajan. It's dangerous. People get killed. I have seen injured legionaries."

Trajan put his hand on her shoulder. "I will be fine, Harpenna. Don't worry. Won't I, Father?"

Traianus smiled at them. "Of course, but don't take it lightly. You are only nineteen. You will have to learn and endure." He turned to Harpenna. "Girl, I am ready for a snack. Why don't you tell the kitchen slaves to prepare a little welcome meal? Trajan must be hungry. I can't wait to catch up with him."

"Yes, Master," Harpenna answered, bowed and left the room. Trajan hugged his father again, pressing him against his chest and enjoying the warm familiar embrace. Then they sat down on Trajan's cot.

"So, what's the latest in Rome, my son?"

"I don't know what you have heard last."

"It's been a month since the last dispatch, and it was about military matters only. By the way, do you have fresh instructions for me from the emperor? You would have been the natural choice for a new dispatch."

"I can help you with both," Trajan confirmed, searching in his pouch. "Here is the imperial dispatch."

He handed it to his father. Traianus glanced at Vespasian's seal and put the sealed and leather-wrapped scroll in his pocket. "Thank you, son. I will read it after we have talked. So, what can you tell me?"

"Hm, let's see here. I may be a Tribunus but at the College in Rome I was just a peon. I can tell you only what I have picked up from others. A colleague's uncle told him a story related to Vespasian's stinginess that he passed on to me. The Treasury is still empty after Nero's terrible spending spree, as you know. So Vespasian has introduced a sewer tax-"

"A sewer tax?" His father was half amused and half disturbed. "What for?"

"Anybody who uses public or private latrines in Rome has to pay a usage-based tax now."

"I'll be damned." Traianus shook his head. "Clever though. Typical Vespasian - pragmatic to the bone. But what's funny about it?"

"When his son Titus heard about the new tax, he went to his father and criticized the tax as disreputable and unworthy of the empire. Vespasian then picked up a coin and held it under Titus's nose.

'Does it stink?' he supposedly asked him.

A frown crossed his son's face. He sniffed at the coin and said, 'No, it does not.'

Vespasian's mouth broke into a triumphant smile. 'Exactly!'"

Traianus laughed. "Of course - Vespasian, vir vere Romanus - a true Roman of old."

"That's what they say."

Trajan scratched his head. "What else... ah, Berenice was visiting Rome when I left. It was THE topic on the streets."

"I can see why. She is a Jewish princess. And Jews are not exactly in favor after the rebellion. Titus should get rid of her. He is a son of the emperor, for crying out loud. Berenice is a liability."

"But she is his concubine, Father. Anyway, she is known for throwing glamorous parties on the Aventine Hill. Rome's finest ladies don't like her, compare her to Cleopatra. She must have certain talents if Titus is so fond of her, they say. Maybe they are jealous."

"I guess so. No obvious misstep from Titus's end?"

"No. He is very discreet, maintaining his dignity, at least publicly."

"Titus is too smart to expose himself. He will come to his senses and drop her one day. Mark my word. Anything else?"

"Well, huge construction projects are completely changing the area south of the Forum. And-"

Harpenna came back into the room. "My Lords, your meal is ready. Please follow me."

Chapter 10

The next day Traianus arrived at his father's office for his first military training. "We will get started without further ado, my son. My second-in-command, *Primipilus* Appius, is waiting for you on the drill field. A *primipilus* is the most senior centurion in a legion and also acts as camp commander. You will like Appius. He is tough and yet he has a heart for recruits. Bring a wide-brimmed felt hat so you don't get a heat stroke and a leather skin of water. After your first lessons, we need to take measurements and get your armor and uniform made. To that end, I will walk you to the armory in the evening, and we will pick your weapons and battle kit."

Trajan hugged his father and headed out. Traianus was not worried about him. He knew his son's modesty and can-do attitude. He would fit in with the other officers.

The governor sighed satisfied, sat down and opened Vespasian's letter. Traianus broke the seal and started reading.

From: T. Flavius Vespasianus, IMP CAESAR AUG
To: M. Ulpius Traianus, LEG AUG in Syria

Greetings, Marcus. I hope your son had a
pleasant trip. He is a wonderful young man, strong,
intelligent and hard working. I see greatness. One
day he will be a distinguished soldier like you.

The Parthian King Vologaeses has asked Rome for
help against invading Alans. I have denied his request,
as the Alans have not attacked Roman territory, and I
don't think they will. As you know, they have devastated
the Parthian client kingdoms of Armenia and Atropatene.
Vologaeses is about to face the Alans himself and is not
fond of us standing by idle. If successful, he might get
carried away and do something stupid – like come after
you and march into Syria. I would like to avoid that.
Therefore I want you to do the following: March
to Zeugma and take direct command of the Fourth
Legion Scythica. I am sending you Neratius Pansa
with the Twelfth from Melitene. He will be under your
command. Once you have arrived with the Twelfth,
get ready to march into Parthian territory. Take the

*two legions plus auxiliaries, cross the Euphrates and
march into Mesopotamia but limit your army to twenty
thousand men. Intimidate the Parthians but don't
attack them. The subtle message is hopefully enough.*

*We want to front up to Parthia and get entrenched
at the border but not invade. This way we can move
both defensively and offensively, depending on our
needs. Let's be measured and firm. My expansive focus
is on Britannia and Germania right now, not Syria.*

*Second, secure and shorten our communications within
Syria and make the provisioning of troops easier with a
massive road-building program. Focus on the routes from
Antioch to Zeugma and from Palmyra to Nicephorum.
We need the ability to quickly shift legions back and forth
between the Mediterranean coast and the Euphrates and
between Egypt/Judaea and Palmyra/Nicephorum.*

*Third, increase the number of forts along the Euphrates
border from Samosata to Dura-Europus, and upgrade the
existing forts and posts. I leave the details to you, but we
need enough fortifications so the troops can march from
one place to the next within a day in order to avoid night
raids on temporary camps. In the atrocious desert climate
the heat is a huge drain on the effectiveness of our troops
and will give Parthia a strategic and potentially decisive
advantage if we don't address this problem aggressively.*

*Marcus Ulpius, I have increased levies and taxes
thoughtfully throughout the empire to finance these
projects. Your quaestor will receive supplemental funds
shortly. You do not need to establish a special levy for Syria.*

*Life in Rome is good. Titus keeps everybody
entertained with his romance. Very amusing. The
new Amphitheater I am building is making progress.
I hope to see it completed before I die. When you come
back, you will not recognize the Eternal City!*

Vespasian

Traianus was both surprised and electrified. The emperor had an astute
strategic mind and his orders made perfect sense, but how could they possibly pay for all this? The spoils from the Jewish War must have refilled the

Treasury. The conquests in Britannia might help too - and the tax increases.

On the other hand, he was happy to get away from boring Antioch and go on campaign again - for the first time with his son. What an excellent opportunity for Trajan to learn the ways of the Army!

In the evening hours the fort erupted with activities. Legionaries cleaned and sharpened their weapons, tools and siege engines, examined the health of their horses, oxen and mules, received supplies from the city and stored them in the legion's warehouses. In the middle of this commotion, Trajan and his father strutted over to the armory building.

"How was your first day, son?"

"Incredible. Exactly what I was hoping for! Boy, I am trying to remember the vernacular the soldiers threw at me and the millions of acronyms everybody uses. Of course, I enjoyed the sword practice the most. By Jupiter, the sword gets heavy when you have to hold it for a long time."

"And don't forget, Trajan. We don't use the *gladius* for individual fighting much. It is a collective killing weapon for frontline formations, used by legionaries dressed up in line. We use it to stab and thrust while pushing our shields into enemy lines."

"Oh, I know. Still, the *gladius* is much heavier than the drill swords we had in Rome for our youth drills on the Mars Field. But I don't mind. I better get used to it. It's the weapon which conquered the world."

"True – and our discipline and perseverance. Those qualities are even more important."

Inside the armory, Traianus showed his son hundreds of swords and *pila*, javelins, bows, arrows, daggers, mail shirts, cuirasses, helmets, slings and even some artillery engines like ballistas and scorpions. Trajan's eyes opened wide. "I have never seen so many weapons in one place, Father."

"You see, Trajan, sometimes we lose weapons or they break. Replacements must be ready at all times. Sometimes we have to recruit auxiliaries in haste. They need armaments too, and when troops transfer, they often need replacements. In any case, every legionary base has an arsenal of this type. I even set up secret depots throughout my province. This will allow the troops to pick up weapons along the way - no matter their destination."

Trajan walked through the endless aisles of military hardware. He picked up a *gladius* or a *pilum* here and there, and put on helmets of different types. A centurion joined him and his father to suggest specific weapons for the young tribune. When Trajan returned to the entrance, his equipment was waiting for him. "This is all mine?"

Traianus and the centurion nodded.

"Yes, Trajan. Take the gear to your quarters. Tomorrow we will have it serviced by our blacksmiths."

His first set of weapons... A glorious day! But it wasn't over yet. In the evening Harpenna wanted to show Trajan and Callistus around in Antioch's downtown district.

They had a wonderful time in the gorgeous town forum. Nightfall cut their sightseeing short, however. Thirsty, they walked into a tavern and ordered wine and cheese and some tasty dates, a local specialty. Trajan wasn't wearing military garb or his laticlavian tunic. He wanted to stay incognito and enjoy the evening unencumbered. Harpenna and Callistus were careful to mix their wine with water, while he drank it undiluted. It was too good to resist.

While chatting with the others, Trajan noticed a beautiful lady sitting two tables away. The woman wore her black hair shoulder-long. She had beautiful almond-shaped brown eyes, a small adorable nose, cute little ears and a lovely smile. The only "imperfection" was her size. She was no taller than four-foot eight. The woman looked to be in her twenties, and he compared her beauty to Venus, the goddess of lover herself.

Surprisingly, the lady was by herself and therefore likely unmarried. Trajan could tell from her dazzling jewelry and the elaborate green silk dress that she was Roman or Italian nobility. When she talked to the waitress, he noticed her Latin had a slight Campanian accent. "Who is this woman?" he asked Harpenna.

"Oh, that's Claudia Aemilia. She is the divorced wife of our quaestor. I don't know why she is still here in Antioch. There is talk she is going back to her family in Capua. Trajan, you are not seriously interested, are you?"

He paid no attention. So beautiful...

"Trajan!" Harpenna shook his shoulder. "Claudia has an iffy reputation. The divorce was ugly. Yes, her husband cheated, but there is talk that she is a strange woman. Trajan, listen to me."

He still gawked at the noblewoman. Finally, he turned his head away from her. "I heard you, but she is drop dead gorgeous."

Callistus looked at the ceiling. Something imaginary required his full attention while Harpenna rolled her eyes. "Looks are deceiving, Master."

In the morning the legion's tribunes were waiting for Trajan in his father's office. "Son, have you met your colleagues yet?" Traianus walked around his desk and pointed at four men in uniform who politely lowered their heads at Trajan.

"Not yet, Father." Trajan turned to the officers. "*Avete, Tribuni.* It is nice to meet you." He felt awkward, trying to think of something funny and downplay the fact that he was their superior's son.

"I am convinced you will get along well with my son," Traianus said, raising his voice. "He will not enjoy special privileges. I will treat him like I treat you."

One of the officers smiled. "We have no doubts, Legate. Apples don't fall far from the tree. Trajan, my name is Lucius Licinius Sura. It's an honor to serve with you and your Father."

Sura seemed genuine. Trajan chatted with him and the other men for a while. They didn't impress him as jaded or jealous at all.

After dismissing them Traianus briefed Trajan on his duties for the next couple of weeks. He also gave him an overview of the diplomatic situation with Parthia and summarized Vespasian's instructions.

"As you can see, we have our work cut out for us. We will go to Zeugma with one cohort of infantry and two thousand auxiliaries. You will meet their commander tomorrow. But go see Quaestor Aemilius now. He is expecting you and wants to fill you in on the legionary treasury, pensions and payrolls. I will need your help with the road-building program."

Trajan sighed. The mission sounded exciting, but first he would have to weather the boring matters of army bookkeeping.

When he arrived at the quaestor's office, the door opened in front of him. Out walked - Claudia Aemilia!

Trajan gawked at her, his heart beating faster than the chariots in the Circus Maximus.

"Why are you looking at me like that, young man?"

"Hm, uh, greetings, my Lady."

Claudia fixed her eyes on him. "*Ave*, soldier. What is your name?"

"Trajan. My name is Trajan."

"You must be new. I have not seen you before. Wait a moment - you must be the new tribune, Traianus's son."

"That's right."

Trajan was amazed he could get words out at all.

"Greetings, young Tribune, greetings. When did you arrive?"

"Yesterday, my Lady."

"Very well. Welcome. Have a good time in Syria."

Then she walked off - the greatest beauty ever to walk the earth. Trajan rallied all the courage he could muster. "My Lady, what is your name?" He didn't want her to know that he knew.

She turned around. "Claudia. My name is Claudia Aemilia."

Encouraged, Trajan asked, "Will I see you again?"

Claudia laughed at him.

"You are bold, young man." She gave him a facetious smile while Trajan followed her out to the street. Claudia stopped abruptly and turned to him.

"Not only are you bold, you are stubborn too."

Trajan looked at the ground embarrassed. What was he doing? Nearly choking, he said, "I would like to see you again. Would you give me the pleasure and let me invite you for dinner at the governor's residence?"

She arched her eyes and said, "How can I deny the wish of such a brave young man?"

Trajan beamed. "Thank you, my Lady. Let's say tonight, around the eighth hour?"

"Very well. I will see you then."

Trajan watched her until she disappeared from his view. His heart was still pounding, his throat dry like the desert sand. He couldn't believe it. Upbeat, he turned back to the quaestor's office.

Aemilius was aloof and businesslike and taught him a lot about bookkeeping. Trajan was glad when it was over. What a dull and dreary man.

Back at the Praetorium, Harpenna served a light lunch for him and his father. Afterwards Trajan pulled her aside and whispered in her ear, "You won't believe what happened today."

"What?"

"I met that Lady Claudia-"

"Trajan!"

"She was in the quaestor's office and agreed to come over for dinner tonight."

Harpenna raised her eyebrows. "I don't like it. There is something about her."

"Well, if you are right, I will find out. If not, she may just be what I think she is - a dream come true!"

Harpenna shook her head. "Oh, Trajan. I wish you were right. Oh well. I will get dinner prepared. Just the two of you?"

"Yes. You can tell father about it, but it will be only the two of us. Book one of the guest *triclinia*."

Chapter 11

In the afternoon Trajan met with *Primipilus* Appius. Appius covered legionary infantry and cavalry tactics with him, deployment schemes and signals, scope and purpose of auxiliaries and pioneer units, defense infrastructure and the pitching of camps, field intelligence and scouting, command and control in and between tactical units, and more. Trajan soaked it up like a sponge. This is what he had come for.

At the end, he asked the *primipilus*, "Appius, when can I go out in the field myself?"

"Very soon, Trajan, very soon." Appius smiled. The officer seemed to like him. His father would be pleased to hear that.

"Great. I can't wait." Trajan saluted and went back outside. The wind had picked up, wafting an unwelcome scent from his arm pits to his nose. He had to take a bath before the upcoming date with Claudia and went straight to the bathhouse. After tipping the porter, he dropped his clothes in a niche of the *apodyterium*, the dressing chamber, picked up a large towel, slipped into a pair of clogs and entered the *tepidarium,* a rectangular ornamental antechamber heated by a hypocaust installation that circulated hot air underneath the floor and in tubes behind the walls. The *tepidarium* included a marble-faced pool filled with warm water. Trajan was surprised how small it was. The ones in Rome were definitely bigger.

Some officers were having a good time in the pool; others enjoyed massages on well-cushioned sofas. Trajan nodded at the men and joined them in the pool. They politely included him in their conversation, visibly considerate of the fact that he was the governor's son. He didn't have much time. As soon as he broke a good sweat he moved on to the hotroom, the *calidarium,* a large sauna that included on its short side a hot-water pool from wall to wall. A skylight was mounted in the middle of the ceiling and allowed the hot air to escape.

Trajan had seen many *calidaria* in Rome. The décor of the chamber didn't impress him much. There were the usual red walls, accentuated with yellow pilaster strips resting on a low plinth of marble slabs. The stucco strips were topped with traditional capitals, and a fluted vault crowned the whole room. He did notice that the white floor mosaics were exceptionally well-laid.

Thirsty, Trajan strode to the marble basin at the other end of the *calidarium* and imbibed cold water from the basin. Refreshed, he slid into the pool. *Ahh – hot… This will relax me.*

After a short while he returned to the *tepidarium* for cleaning and a quick massage. Then he finished the bathing cycle with a swim in the *frigidarium,* the cold-water room. In its center was an extra large circular pool, placed under a truncated cone-shaped roof with a glass skylight at the top. Deep blue frescoes on the ceiling showed a realistic imitation of the starry night sky and semi-circle *exedrae* showing off sumptuous garden scenes surrounded the pool on almost all sides.

Trajan jumped into the cold water with enthusiasm. He dived and swam, washing off the sweat and ointments the masseurs had applied on him before. Fresh and clean, he returned to the dressing chamber where army page-boys dried him with soft cotton towels.

By the time he had completed the whole bathing cycle, it was high time to be back in his father's residence. Harpenna had everything ready, and Claudia arrived on time.

She wore an elegant blue *stola*, a loose-fitting long tunic tied at the waist and below the breasts, made from the finest silk. An apple-sized golden brooch decorated her chest. Artfully wrapped around the *stola* was a stylish woolen shawl in green, a *palla*. Claudia's jewelry and makeup were spectacular: The necklace and earrings contained shiny gems that sparkled bright in the late evening sun. A multitude of silver bracelets covered her right arm.

Venus herself had come to Earth to visit him. The young tribune wore his best laticlavian tunic with the trademark purple stripe showing his patrician rank. They shared the medium couch.

"So," Claudia said, opening the conversation. "How come I am invited tonight inside these lofty walls?"

"Uh... well." The question hit him unprepared. His guest was so much more comfortable with courtship. But he was smitten enough to cut to the chase. "You are very beautiful. I have seen you in the city."

"My, my, I am honored. I assume you were pleased by what you saw."

"Of course. Do you like Antioch?"

"Of course not. It's too hot. I am looking forward to going home. There are still some financial matters that keep me here, however. I am waiting to get my dowry back from my husband."

"Why did you get divorced - if I may ask?"

"He cheated on me. Ran off with some local beauty. He hurt me very much." She glowered. "Did you come from Hispania?"

"No, I came from Rome. I have spent a year there as a member of the Board of the Twenty, assigned to the Mint. Ask me anything about coins and I can answer you."

"How exciting. Aren't you disappointed to be so far away from Rome, the center of the universe?"

"Not at all. I couldn't wait to come here. I want to become a soldier like my Father. The training in the Fourteenth Legion will be good for me."

Trajan started to relax and became more comfortable around Claudia.

They laughed and had a wonderful time. After dinner, he walked her to the door.

"Too bad you have to leave us soon," she said.

"It's most unfortunate. Maybe I can stay a bit longer."

"Yes, why don't you? I have finally met a nice man..."

Trajan didn't know what to say. He was torn, knowing that it was nearly impossible to stay behind while his unit was leaving. How should he explain this to his father or the *primipilus?* That he had found 'love'? They would laugh at him.

The long moment of silence was embarrassing. Thank Jupiter, Claudia seemed to understand.

"No, no, no. You can't stay without losing face, but be careful."

"I will."

"I want a letter from you every day, you understand?"

Though the request seemed over the top Trajan promised. Then he laid his arms around her shoulders – how tender they were! – and touched her warm cheek with his. When he pulled backed she beamed. Holding on to his hands she lunged forward and gave him a kiss. It was soft, yet firm. Trajan floated away. Her lips felt like the skin of ripe cherries. Heaven.

"It is too bad that I have to leave now, Claudia. But I will be back, you have my word. I·will be back!"

He hugged her one last time. Then he walked her to her litter, holding hands. She clambered on and waved at him with a big smile while the slaves carried her off.

They set out at dawn. Elite cavalry flanked Governor Traianus, his son and the other tribunes, followed by heavy infantry in battle gear. The baggage train rolled in the middle while Harpenna and Traianus's household slaves rode in the governor's personal carriage. She would keep an eagle's eye on the family's possessions.

The whole detachment was a spectacle and took Trajan's thoughts away from ever-present Claudia. He was amazed that only five hundred men, one tenth of a legion, were such an impressive sight. Later on, two whole legions would march into Parthian territory, twenty times their number. Inconceivable...

The march to the Euphrates River was uneventful and lasted a week. A messenger, sent by General Pansa, reached them two days before their arrival in Zeugma. He reported that Pansa's Twelfth was two weeks away. They would have to wait that long before the joint operation could be launched.

On arrival in Zeugma, the commanding general of the Fourth Legion *Scythica* had no news from Vologaeses's campaign against the Alans. The

Parthian king evidently had not engaged the invaders yet. On the contrary, thousands of refugees from Armenia and Atropatene were still pouring into his country. Some tried to find refuge in the Roman province of Commagene, which Pansa had granted.

After the long day's march, Trajan retired to his assigned quarters in Zeugma's Principia, the building hosting the senior officers. He was exhausted but still up when the door opened and Harpenna reported a visitor. "Who is it?"

"You won't believe it. Please see for yourself."

They walked to the entrance of the Praetorium together. At the doorstep, Harpenna slipped away. Trajan opened and there was – Claudia...

His jaws dropped. "What are you doing here, my Lady?"

"Shhhhh. My dear Trajan," Claudia said. "Not so loud. Can I come in?"

Still perplexed, Trajan shook his head.

"No? Well, then not." She turned around.

"No, no. That's not why I was shaking my head. I am just... stunned. Come in, dearest Claudia."

He pulled her inside and closed the door.

"You could have been attacked by brigands. The desert is dangerous."

"I wasn't afraid. Your trip sounded interesting so I decided to visit you here. We were riding fast to catch up with your detachment."

"And you did. Are you hungry?"

"No, I brought my slaves. They took care of everything. But nobody can take care of my love life as well as you can..."

He beamed and gave her a hug. Claudia didn't want to let him go, and they exchanged a long passionate kiss. Arm in arm they walked to his *cubiculum* where she threw herself on his bed.

"Undress me," she demanded.

Trajan was only too happy to oblige. Then they cuddled. She slung her legs around his thighs and torso while he wrapped his arms around her shoulders.

"I am so happy to see you, Trajan, my handsome man."

She kissed him again and again. The world was disappearing around him. Claudia clutched his groin through the fabric of his tunic, touching his male pride. Oh, the excitement...

"Nice cock you have," she said and pulled it out.

Trajan moaned softly. He glimpsed at her gorgeous breasts. They had the perfect size, not too big, not too small, round and firm. He touched them gently and rubbed her nipples. They were hard like the grommet of his uniform. Trajan gave them his full attention. Now it was Claudia's turn to moan with pleasure.

Their intimacy reminded him of his first sexual adventures with his childhood friend Quintus. But it didn't compare. Claudia slipped him in and started rocking up and down.

Trajan had never been in a woman. It felt strange but divine. With her on top, he didn't have to do anything. She moved her small body up and down, faster and faster, softly moaning. Trajan groaned in delight too, overwhelmed by pleasure. Claudia suddenly moaned louder and for what seemed a long time. She sighed, then rolled over.

"How about you, my friend?" she asked him. "Don't you want to come too?"

"Uh, sure."

Now he got on top and rocked back and forth, gentle and slow at first, then faster and faster. He improvised so as not to give away his virginal status. Everything was so strange - being at the fringes of the empire, making love. His first time. Trajan had to concentrate. At last, he was able to tune out the distractive thoughts and focus on his body and the pleasure he was feeling. He came with an explosion, feeling every tendon in his body. It seemed never-ending, unrelenting. He screamed so much that Claudia put her hand on his mouth. Then it was over. He fell aside, breathing hard, unable to move, unable to speak. They were both drenched in sweat.

"Uh," Trajan groaned. "Wow."

Claudia smiled at him. "This was your first time with a woman, wasn't it?"

He blushed.

"Did you enjoy it?"

"Immensely," he said. Then he looked her in the eyes. "I love you, Claudia."

"Not so fast. Love is a serious claim. You know, love develops in time. We just made love. That's a start but it's not love yet – if you know what I mean."

"But you came all the way from Antioch," Trajan protested. "It must be love."

"It may be, yes, yes. I certainly feel attached to you. But, Trajan, I have been hurt a lot in my life. I am careful. Be patient."

He had no idea what she was talking about. Later in the evening the young tribune walked her back to the inn where she stayed. They kissed passionately at the door. Elated, he returned to the fort.

Chapter 12

The next couple of days saw a lot of action as the troops prepared for the campaign. Traianus sent scout parties across the Euphrates and held a war council every other day where the tribunes and centurions gave their reports. Trajan was present every time, absorbing what he learned. In the evenings, he went to see Claudia, and they made love on end.

On the third day Trajan sent a messenger to Claudia once more to arrange an appointment but received no answer. Usually her answer came back within hours but this time – nothing. He sent another messenger half a day later. The courier confirmed that he had delivered the message to one of her slaves, but Claudia sent no answer.

What should he do? He waited in his room reading some of Catull's love poetry she had given him, but that made matters worse. What was wrong?

The next day she sent a short message.

> *Trajan,*
>
> *I am disappointed by your behavior.*
> *Please meet me at the inn after sunset.*
>
> *Claudia*

Trajan started to worry now. *Disappointed by his behavior?* When he arrived at the inn, a slave led him to her room. Claudia wore a beautiful dress. Lots of make-up adorned her face. She seemed ready to go out.

"So, young Tribune, how are you?"

"I am worried. What is going on? Why are you pouting?"

"Well, let's have dinner first."

"No, I want to know what is going on. What have I done that you are disappointed about?"

"I guess I should tell you right away. Well, it's one of those things that are difficult to address, and I don't want to hurt your feelings. Nor do I want you to start hating me because I am telling you."

Trajan gave her a quizzical look.

"I have been hurt a lot in my life, Marcus. More than you can imagine." She paused.

"And?"

"I am disappointed because last time we met you didn't walk me all the way back to the inn."

"I was tired," Trajan protested.

"Hear me out. It was your male duty to protect me. I felt abused. Since you are young, maybe you don't always know what is expected of you. I love you and therefore I am telling you even though it's awkward and I am risking to make you angry."

"I am not angry, not at all. On the contrary, I am glad you are telling me this. How else can I learn?"

"Good. Also, when you walked up to my litter the other day, you first welcomed the guests on the litter, not me. That's unacceptable."

"Excuse me, Claudia," Trajan protested weakly. "But when I approached that litter, you had just stepped off on the other side. I simply didn't see you."

Weird. Why was she being so difficult? He had never heard that a woman could be so easily insulted. It dawned on him that something was wrong with this woman, but he would deal with it.

She watched his face. "It's all right. I am hungry. Let's go."

Dinner was delightful, but they went back to her place early. She couldn't wait to have him that night.

Things were going great again, but a week later Claudia withdrew again and refused to see him for days. Then she told him, "I don't like Harpenna. She is sloppy, and gawks at me. I feel rejected. I am an *Aemilia*, Trajan, a Roman Patrician, and she is just a slave."

Trajan looked at her confused. "Why is she sloppy?"

"The bed sheets in your chamber. They smell."

"They smell? I didn't smell anything. Besides, that's the chambermaids' duty, not Harpenna's."

"But she is in charge of all the duties in the household for you and your Father, isn't she?"

"Yes, but-"

"Therefore it is her responsibility."

Trajan sighed. "Yes, I will tell her to fix it."

"Good. But there is more. One of the guards at the entrance didn't show me respect the other day. Have him reprimanded or transferred."

Trajan raised his eyebrows in disbelief but he said, "Fine. Anything else?"

"Yes. Two nights ago, when we were strolling along the riverbanks, I wanted to stop at one of the snack bars, but you ignored me and went straight back to the fort. I didn't like that."

"What? How can I read your mind? You need to tell me what you want. That's not asking for too much."

"I don't think so. YOU need to ask what I want."

"Fine," Trajan said exhausted. "I will."

Her second withdrawal was hard on him. He was afraid to lose the love of his life and nearly cried in relief after they talked again. Thankfully, she reiterated her affection. But from one moment to the next, she could become an entirely different person and switch from aggressive to soft, from suspicious to trusting. It could happen at any time and for any reason. *Mind-boggling.*

Trajan mentioned none of this to his father, Harpenna, or any of his friends. They believed he was madly in love and happy as can be. And he wanted them to think that way. His dignity demanded it.

They were still in Zeugma when he ran into Lucius Licinius Sura in the bathhouse. The officer was of ancient Roman nobility, a descendant of the famous Lucullus and Marcus Licinius Crassus. Despite the illustrious lineage, Sura was down to earth as can be and a pleasant colleague. Trajan liked him.

Over a massage, Trajan asked him, "Lucius, you aren't married, are you?"

Sura shook his head. "No, I am not. I should be at my age but I am in no hurry."

"But you have had lovers, right?"

"Of course."

"Have you ever been truly in love with any of them?"

"Not really. You know, most of them have been physical encounters with slaves of the household. I had a girlfriend for a while, but that did not go anywhere."

Trajan felt comfortable enough to tell him about his problems with Claudia. Sura looked at him flabbergasted.

"She is a lunatic, Trajan. Drop her. She is screwed up. Isn't she from Capua? Her name *Aemilia* is likely due to patronage only. I don't think she is a Patrician."

"I don't care about that, Lucius. But I want this to work, do you understand?"

"You are a pup. Don't worry. It will - one way or another. You always have me..."

What did that mean? Licinius Sura was certainly a good-looking man and a great friend...

Trajan shrugged it off, and they went on talking about the military situation.

"We are still waiting for Pansa's legion to join us," Trajan said. "I can't understand what's taking him so long. It's been three weeks now."

"There may be many reasons. For one, it's blazing hot. The troops can't march fast. Also, he needs to settle the refugee issue in Commagene. There are many more refugees than we expected. Maybe he does not trust them and wants enough troops on stand-by if things get out of hand. But he won't be able to delay his arrival forever. Vespasian's instructions are crystal clear."

"Father is getting impatient. Did you see how angry he was when a cavalry unit took too long to cross the river in yesterday's drill? He is afraid the soldiers are getting soft in Zeugma with its taverns, bars, brothels, baths and all the other amenities."

"I am not worried. They are fine fighters. Let them have some fun as long as it lasts."

The next day Traianus held a reception for Zeugma's councilmen, nobles, and representatives of the different ethnicities in this border town: Parthians, Jews, Medians, Arabs, Syrians - and Romans of course. Trajan was looking forward to bringing Claudia. Some of his friends had not met her yet because she wanted to keep their relationship private. But this time she had promised her attendance. At the last minute, however, Claudia sent a message that she wouldn't come. Trajan was beside himself, and when he did see her again she blew up once more. "I really don't like Harpenna. I want you to sell her, and get rid of Callistus."

"What? That's impossible, Claudia. She has served our family all her life."

"So? If you love me, you'll sell her."

Trajan was appalled. "Why if I may ask?"

"She reminds me of an aunt who didn't like me. She looks and acts just like her."

"That's insane. There is no connection."

"Well, I don't ever want to see her again."

Trajan shook his head. "I don't know how this can be arranged-"

"It can, it can," she assured him. They left it at that. Several days later, she visited again. Callistus led her to Trajan's office at nightfall where oil lamps provided some lighting.

The moment Claudia entered Trajan happened to close a scroll and open another.

"Aha!" she shouted. "Were you writing your other girlfriend?"

Trajan's jaws went slack. Puzzled, he raised his eyebrows. "No, why would I? I love you. These scrolls are army documents. See here."

But she spun about, scooted out of his office and dashed back to her litter with Trajan running after her, past some dazed soldiers and a frowning Harpenna. He caught up with Claudia in the portico. "You are completely wrong, Claudia. There is nobody but you!"

She pushed him aside. Her slave put down the stepping stairs, and she scampered on them. Up on the litter, she turned and looked back at him. "Cheater!" Then she closed the curtains. The litter slaves took off leaving a shaken young officer behind. *Paranoid. She must be paranoid. Paranoid of being ignored, paranoid of being cheated, paranoid of the people around her, paranoid of everything.*

Scowling, he walked back to his office, ignoring everyone around him. Humiliated, he locked himself in and wept. Many people had now seen how she treated him!

Nonetheless, Trajan tried to reconcile once more, and they met again, but the feelings were not the same anymore. He told her how much she hurt him, and she apologized. At the same time, she asked him why he bothered seeing her if he wasn't in good spirits. Trajan had enough. "You only want me to be a good-weather boyfriend? What kind of woman are you? Why are you so resentful? Why are you so paranoid? Why are you dating me at all? I can't take this any longer. Leave Zeugma. You make me lose my mind. I love you, but I am not sure you love me. I am not sure what love is anymore!"

Chapter 13

Finally, the Twelfth Legion arrived. It gave him something to do. Two days thereafter the Twelfth and the Fourteenth moved out as planned and crossed the Euphrates with ten thousand auxiliaries - a total force of almost twenty thousand men. Their invasion forced Vologaeses to cut his operations against the Alans short and secure Parthia's exposed Northwest.

Trajan would normally have been proud to see all this and be part of it, but he wasn't. He was still traumatized; the breakup with Claudia weighed him down. Nothing his father, Harpenna or Callistus said could cheer him up. Alas, the pain! He felt better only after spending much time with Appius and Sura. He soaked up Appius's know-how, and Sura became his best friend.

The army reached Carrhae where the road from Edessa crossed the Euphrates. They pitched camp at the crossing. Water and food were abundant, the legionaries upbeat despite the searing heat. In the evening the soldiers used their hand mills to grind wheat and bake bread for the next day. From his tent, Trajan could see thousands of smoldering campfires and the dull shine of brass kettles along the river. He felt better now. Army life - that was more like it. Better yet, Sura came for a visit, and they drank an amphora of wine together.

"I love this life," Trajan shouted. "Strong men all around us, powerful, stalwart, unwavering… the smell of steel and sweat in the air, muscles and mail in abundance, the flying sparks of our sharpening tools at work. This is glory, the only glory that there is!"

Sura pulled up his eyebrows. "You are really into it, aren't you?"

"Absolutely. Nothing gives me more satisfaction than being part of this - the greatest army the world has ever seen."

"Yes, we are powerful, but we will need to apply our strength with purpose and focus. There is always the temptation of arrogance."

"Not us," Trajan said with conviction, shaking his head. "Nothing has sapped our power yet. Nothing ever will."

They kept talking and chatting and joking for hours on end, thriving in each other's company.

"Trajan, I know it's a sore subject but I want to tell you one thing about Claudia," Sura piped up all of a sudden.

The governor's son frowned at him dumbfounded.

"How old do you think she is?" Sura asked him.

"Twenty-eight. Why?"

"She is not."

"But she told me herself. She is twenty-eight."

"And you believe that?"

"I do. Why wouldn't I?"

"Well, in fact she is forty-two."

"Impossible!"

"It's the truth. You were dating an old woman…" Sura giggled.

"Shut up. How do you know that?"

"I have my sources. Actually, it was easy. Her former husband Aemilius and I were talking a while ago. Somehow, the topic came up. He is about that age too, you know."

"What? Quaestor Aemilius is her divorced husband? Stupid me. I should have known. But even if I had I would have blamed their divorce on his dreary ways. He is a bean counter. Anyway, how do you know he didn't pull your legs?"

"Why would he? He has no reason to."

"To make me look like an idiot."

"Hogwash. He doesn't know you had a fling with her."

Cursed Claudia. What a liar. Forty-two! How could she have looked so good at forty-two? And how could he have been so blind? Must have been the makeup. He remembered that he had never seen her without makeup - not once.

"I don't want to hear about it. And don't tell anyone. I would be the laughing stock of the camp. My Father would think he must pick a good woman for me because I can't do it myself."

Sura chuckled but promised to keep it a secret. Then they talked some more about army matters and how strange the East was. Most people spoke Greek here although Latin was the official language and in exclusive use by the military and the courts. They also laughed at how effeminate the men were in these lands and speculated about the intrigues at the Royal Parthian Court in Ctesiphon. And they discussed the campaigns in the western half of the empire. How exciting it would be to join the action there.

Sura and plenty of wine helped Trajan get his mind off Claudia. *Much less trouble with men*, Trajan thought. *Jupiter curse the women!*

At the next war council, the military tribunes attended with the senior centurions, Appius, Pansa, and engineers from Antioch who had come to see the governor. When Trajan arrived, the engineers were leaving. He asked his father what was going on. Traianus smiled broadly. "It's going to be one hell of a road. They have developed awe-inspiring plans. We will also build a new waterway to shorten the distance from Antioch to Zeugma. I have just approved the plans. You will see the building site on the way back to Antioch."

"I can't wait, a canal…"

He had no idea how they could possibly dig a canal in the desert but he trusted his father's judgment.

Traianus opened the meeting. "Officers, thank you for coming. King Vologaeses is worried we might sail down the Euphrates and attack his Capital. He has moved his troops south to protect Ctesiphon. That means he can't strike to the west. Commagene and Syria are therefore safe. The Parthian king is marching back to his core territories. He has given up on regaining direct control over Armenia – for the time being. He may, however, try to recover Atropatene with auxiliaries, but anyway, the main body of his army is marching south along the Tigris. We have achieved our objective."

The officers were not pleased. Trajan could tell from their faces. "What? No fighting?" Sura asked.

"No. The Parthians worry about our presence here, but they don't want to fight unless we attack them in their heartland. And that's not Vespasian's plan. The empire is expanding in Britannia and Germania, not here."

The tribunes grumbled. Only Appius seemed to like it. "Young cubs, be glad. War is a bloody enterprise. This decision is a good thing, believe me."

"Easy for you to say," Sura protested. "But how can we distinguish ourselves if we never fight?"

"There will be plenty of opportunity," Appius assured him. "Get some experience first and if you want to fight, request a transfer to Britannia."

"Tell us more about your last war," Sura asked the veteran. "How was fighting against the Jews?"

"Bloody, very bloody. I participated in the siege of Jerusalem as did our commander here." Appius pointed at Traianus. "We lost many good men. The siege lasted half a year. And even after Jerusalem's destruction the rebellion continued elsewhere. At the end, we had pinned down the rebels in Masada. They were holding out in this promontory fortress for another two years until the glorious Tenth Legion under Silva built a huge ramp connecting up to the fortress... When we entered Masada, the Jews had all killed each other. Ugly, ugly, let me tell you. They were true freedom fighters. Not that I agree with them, but their courage was impressive.

I take that back. There were some women and children that we did find alive. They had gotten away and were hiding in an underground cistern."

Traianus nodded. "I didn't participate in the Masada campaign but I took part in the main conflict. It was tough, soldiers. And it's strange. We simply wanted to recover territory that we had taken many years ago, but it was harder than conquering a new country."

Then the governor issued orders to march the legions back to their bases in Melitene and Zeugma. Both Traiani and their Syrian staff would return to Antioch. A canal was waiting.

BOOK III

REBELLION

Chapter 14

*Fourteen years later (89 AD),
somewhere near Legio, Hispania Tarraconenis Province*

The two riders had been on the road for ten straight days, switching horses every three hours at the inns operated by the *Cursus Publicus*. They wore polished brass helmets and white tunics underneath red army cloaks. Their backs and buttocks were sore, the thighs agonizing. Every body part hurt from the hips down, and they were exhausted. But they had a mission to accomplish. The *Pax Romana* was at stake...

The riders squinted, hoping to soon see the walls of Legio. Nothing, nothing but rain-soaked grassland and lonely pine trees here and there – and a murder of crows sweeping through the air. They kicked their horses with their studded boots again to hurry them on. Go, go, go!

It had rained earlier on this desolate winter day in northern Hispania. The air was still fresh and clean from the spill but also bristling cold. The galloping Praetorians noticed the plumes of breath rising from their mouth. The road ahead of them was glistening wet from the downpour. If they maintained this speed, the horses might not survive the ordeal. It did not matter; they would get replacements. The only thing that mattered was their mission: carry a dispatch from the emperor to Legio. They were determined to arrive there today. Today! These were their orders. Everything was at stake, the empire's peace, the safety of the Roman People and Senate, even the emperor's life.

Picking up food and water at the imperial courier stations, they had never stopped, eating and drinking on horseback. To be light and fast the soldiers didn't wear any armor. Hispania Tarraconensis was a peaceful province and had been so for two hundred years. There was no need for protection, but just in case they carried two weapons: the *spatha*, a long cavalry sword, and the *pugio*, a belt-mounted dagger.

They had orders to personally hand the imperial dispatch to the commander of the Seventh Legion *Gemina* in Legio. How far did they still have to go? According to their calculations, the town should appear on the horizon soon. The riders kept worrying they might not make it on time. A bonus was at stake too. If they reached Legio today, both would receive an additional sixty dinars. This would go a long way to beef up their compensation.

A rebellion! Not since Nero's death had there been turmoil in the Army. Now this... How could Saturninus have done that, and why did he do it? No matter, he would be crushed – hopefully. What if other generals or governors joined him?

One soldier invoked a prayer for the well being of their Lord, the Emperor Domitian, son of Vespasian. The Flavian dynasty had been in power for over twenty years now. Vespasian, Titus and Domitian had been good to them, had always taken care of the needs of the Guard. They would not let the emperor down now. Where was Legio, by Jupiter!?

Gradually, crenellated towers became visible in the distance, partly shrouded by low hanging clouds. Yes, this must be the Asturian fortress of Legio, base of the only legion stationed in Hispania under the commanded of the Legate Trajan. He was the man they were ordered to hand the dispatch and only to him. As they came closer, more and more of the city walls came into view. Traffic on the road was increasing. They encountered farmers on their wagons or on foot, road maintenance crews, semi-stationary sutlers and their carriages and military patrols from Legio itself. The Praetorians ignored them all, even their fellow soldiers from the Seventh who greeted them with proper military salutes. Cloaks flying, the two Praetorians galloped past them. There was no time.

When they reached the *porta praetoria*, the main gate of the city, they finally reined in their mounts and identified themselves to the sentry posts. It only took a moment. Then the heavy arched gates swung ajar with a creak and the riders took off again. At the Praetorium they stopped for good and jumped off their sweaty horses, themselves grimy and beat; the long ride had taken its toll.

Their bodies didn't want to obey the mind. Ignoring the pain in their bottoms with iron will power, the couriers gimped to the Praetorium entrance. "We have an urgent message from the Emperor Domitian for your commander. Let us in, quick," they yelled at the guard.

"You can come in, but the legate is not here. He is in the countryside, supervising scorpion drills. He won't be back for hours."

"Hours? Do you have any idea how long we have been under way to deliver this dispatch? Send a messenger immediately and call him back. Now!"

The guard shrugged. "I'll see what I can do." He strolled inside but came back quickly. "The centurion on duty is sending a fast rider to the artillery range. Please, do come in and have some refreshments until the general arrives."

Satisfied, they entered the lobby. The legion's quartermaster ordered the kitchen to provide them with a warm meal.

General Trajan was back in no time, frowning at them. The legate was a tall man in his mid thirties with mighty shoulders and fierce eyes that stared at them hard. The Praetorians saluted. "Are you Marcus Ulpius Traianus, *Legatus Augusti Pro Praetore*, Commander of the Seventh Legion

Gemina?" they asked.

"Yes, I am. What is so urgent that you asked me to return to the city? It better be important!"

"It is, General. We have an urgent message from our Lord and Master, the Emperor Domitian. For your eyes only." The ranking Praetorian handed him a leather-wrapped imperial scroll. Domitian's seal was attached to the tie-down laces.

Still frowning, Trajan said, "Let's go to my office."

A servant was cleaning the room when they arrived at its doorstep. Trajan shooed him out. "Here we are," he said and waved them inside. He closed the heavy oak door behind him, sat down behind his desk and invited them to sit on the guest chairs. Then he removed the leather wrapper and broke the imperial wax seal. "So, what is so important?"

"Our orders are to hand over this dispatch and return with the acknowledgement that you have received it and that you will act on it without delay. Please dictate a letter we can take back to Rome. We do not know the exact content of Domitian's orders, but we do know that a rebellion broke out in Upper Germania. The People and the Senate and our Lord and God, Domitian Augustus Caesar, need your assistance."

"What are you saying? A rebellion? By whom?"

"The Governor of Upper Germania, Lucius Antoninus Saturninus, has declared against the emperor."

Trajan leaned back in his chair. "That's outrageous! No wonder you were in a hurry. Thank you, Guardsmen. That is all for now. My men will assign you quarters for the night. Feel at home and recover from the strenuous ride. How many days did it take you to get here?"

"Ten, General."

"Impressive. You will be well rewarded, I take it."

The men grinned at each other. "Yes, we will," one of them said with pride. "Sixty dinars each because we arrived on time." They stood up and left the room. A page showed them the way.

Trajan unfolded the imperial scroll and read it without a break.

> *From: T. Flavius Domitianus, IMP CAESAR AUG*
> *To: M. Ulpius Traianus, Legatus Augusti pro*
> *Praetore in Hispania Tarraconensis*
>
> *Dear Marcus,*
>
> *I hope this message will reach you before the end of*

*January. Saturninus, the Governor of Upper Germania,
has openly rebelled against Rome. He took control of the
savings funds of his two legions and thus forced them to
obey him. It is unclear at this point what Lappius Maximus,
his gubernatorial colleague in Lower Germania, will do. If
they unite, they would have four legions at their disposal.*

*I cannot allow this to happen. Therefore, I am on
my way to Moguntiacum to quash this rebellion. To help
this effort I need you to attack from the West. Take the
Seventh and march to Germania as fast as you can. Meet
me at Moguntiacum. Do not delay. Do not wait. Time is
of the essence. Your approach will force the rebel forces
to split up, making it easier for us to defeat them.*

*Dear Marcus, I am very sorry about this but
certain that you, like your father before you, will
serve the empire and the Flavian House well. Now is
the time to demonstrate your loyalty. Help me defeat
this revolt. A Civil War would tear Rome apart.*

*I will see you in Germania. May Rome's eternal
gods be with you.*

Domitian

Trajan put down the scroll in shock. He did not like Domitian but felt
great loyalty to the Flavian House. They had restored the peace after Nero's
dreadful years and ruled the empire well. Vespasian's younger son Domitian,
who had taken over after his brother Titus's short reign was the weakest of
the three, but he had been trying hard for years to pacify the volatile Danube
border.

Unrest in Germania would be a major setback to this effort. The earlier
they could stabilize Germania, the earlier the emperor could resume his efforts next summer on the Danube. And Domitian was an excellent administrator. He kept a close watch on his governors and magistrates to prevent
extortion and other excesses. Domitian also paid close attention to the needs
of the military, particularly the enlisted men. He had implemented a detailed
system that tracked the behavior of the centurions in the Army so they didn't
abuse their power over the rankers. Files were collected in all provinces and

sent to the Palatine every year as the foundation for the emperor's decisions whom to appoint, whom to promote, whom to punish.

But there was his other side, a cold and distant personality, jealousy, egomaniac tendencies and a religious fundamentalism. But Domitian was a Flavian. The Traiani had always served the Flavii. Trajan's family owed them its accession into the Patriciate. It owed them everything. Without Vespasian, his father would not have been consul and governor many times, and without his father, Trajan himself would not be a general today. It was obvious. He would do as his father had done. He would defend the House of Vespasian.

Trajan's fingers tapped on his blotter in rapid frequency while his mind wandered to Saturninus. This despicable pinnacle of depravity dared a revolt? He had become a senator under Vespasian and been appointed suffect consul a year after Domitian's accession to the throne. Why was he starting a revolt now? Maybe he was trying to preempt a move from Domitian. Saturninus's immoral lifestyle had drawn the wrath of the emperor, and Domitian could be harsh and unpredictable. He had once ordered three Vestal Virgins to be executed for breaching their sacred vows, and they had been buried alive... The people had detested this archaic punishment though it only followed the law on the books. Maybe Saturninus was afraid of being next on Domitian's moral crusade. Rumor had it the governor had cuckolded several of his own officers and smooched a tribune in public. Trajan had also heard of habitual orgiastic drink fests in Saturninus's residence.

Abruptly, he stood, opened the door and called for his officers.

Although disturbed, they cheered when they heard of Domitian's orders. He had hand-picked and trained his men well. The senior centurions had worked their way up the ranks, and even the tribunes were solid. Patronage, social class and family ties were all nice and good, but when it came to military appointments Trajan didn't compromise. He had commissioned them all based on talent and character.

Spurius Septimius, his *primipilus*, ran the day-to-day operations of the legion. Trajan had met him in Germania after his transfer to Colonia Claudia, capital of Lower Germania Province - an assignment he had preferred to returning to civilian life. Military action in the treacherous bogs of Germania had been more to his liking.

Trajan learned much from Septimius in those years and came to appreciate his expertise and loyalty. When Domitian gave Trajan command of the Seventh Gemina, Trajan had requested Septimius's transfer to help him whip the rusty Spanish legion into shape. It had not seen any fighting since the Civil War twenty years earlier. Septimius had accomplished much. The coordination between centuries was now outstanding, the equipment well-maintained, the precision of the catapult crews unmatched, morale high.

However, half the legion's men had yet to be bloodied.

Trajan deplored the rebellion, but he welcomed the opportunity. Careers were only made at war, and maybe he could find a way to yank Saturninus's control over the Rhine legions away through cunning. "Ready your units," he told his staff. "We will set out at the crack of dawn and leave only a small garrison behind. *Milites*, this will be no child's play. Forced marches all the way. I want to be in Moguntiacum within three weeks."

Chapter 15

It was raining again, really just a drizzle, but the boreal air made it chilling to the bone. Thick grey clouds were drifting east, filling the gloomy sky, dimming the daylight and adding to the misery of the cleaving drizzle.

Another bleak day in Germania, Governor Lappius Maximus mused as he peered down from the crenellated battlements of the *porta principalis.* His troops were about to leave Colonia Claudia. Vessels of the Rhine fleet were ready to take some units south; the others would march.

Lappius dreaded his own departure. The amenities of Colonia were hard to beat in this dreary land, particularly at this time of year. He cursed Saturninus for starting this messy revolt. The governor had no quarrels with Saturninus but decided not to join this knave's petty rebellion. Domitian was a harsh emperor, but Rome stood for unity, the Army for honor and discipline. Saturninus couldn't be allowed to get his way – even if it involved campaigning in terrible weather.

They were lucky it wasn't snowing. The Rhine had been frozen several times this year, thwarting troop movements up or down river, but at this point the gods were with Lappius. It was cold, but not cold enough for the river to freeze.

He had informed his men of the events in Moguntiacum and given them hope that their comrades of the Fourteenth *Gemina Martia Victrix* and the Twenty-first *Rapax* might not fight for the traitorous governor after all. Saturninus did have leverage over them through the appropriation of their payroll and savings cash accounts, but if they all turned against him, they could overpower the maniac and his cronies and recover the money. Everything was up in the air of course, and the news from Moguntiacum changed daily.

The emperor had sent word that he was on his way to reinforce Lappius's troops with the Praetorians. It should not be too hard to defeat Saturninus. His colleague had never been popular with the soldiers, but there was a wild card: the Germanic tribes. If he could bribe or find a willing Chieftain ally, the situation could spin out of control.

Lappius sighed and walked down the parapet. His adjutant was waiting below. He saluted the governor and said, "*Legatus,* your steed is ready." The tribune was a pup, barely seventeen. Lappius could see apprehension in his eyes - fear of combat. *Worse, the fear of fighting his own.* The young officer had not even been born when Nero had ruled the land.

"Very well, Tribune," Maximus said. "I will first send off the fleet. Keep the horse ready though. It should not be long, and make sure we have hot mead before we leave.

Don't worry, young man, this will not be as bad as you think. Rome always manages. We even survived Nero's follies. Saturninus is on his own. None of the other generals will rally to his cause. Norbanus, the governor of Raetia, has mobilized against him, and the emperor himself is coming up with the Praetorian Guard. Saturninus may not even have the two Rhine legions for long. Perhaps they have overpowered him and his knaves already. Relax, Tribune, everything will be all right."

The officer swallowed. "*Sic, Legatus.* Of course. It's just... I have a brother in the Twenty-first..."

"Ah. I see." Lappius grabbed the tribune's shoulders, squeezed them hard and looked him in the eyes. "Again, Tribunus, there may not be a fight. If your brother is smart, he will sneak out of Saturninus's camp and get away."

Lappius saluted the officer and stepped through the open gate, aiming for the docks outside the walls. *Primipilus* Papirius and linesmen of the fleet were waiting bundled up under thick *paludamenta* cloaks and doubled-up breeches beneath their *pterygae* flap armor stripes. Closed leather boots kept their feet dry.

Lappius and his second-in-command exchanged some final words. Then the legate gave the departure signal. Papirius jumped on board the lead vessel while the linesmen untied the heavy ropes and tossed them onto the boats. One by one, the vessels steered away from the moorings, stirring up some coots that were floating nearby, and the oarsmen put themselves to work.

Lappius watched the boats vanish in the mist. He invoked a quick prayer to the Rhine's patron god and turned back. Hopefully, the weather would not get any colder. They could not afford the river to freeze.

They had been on their way for a week now, forced marches throughout, with Trajan at the fore. Striding at the tip of the column made him feel like one of his men, and it made for good bonding. He wore the same clothes and the same armor, ate the same food, drank the same wine, cracked the same sordid jokes, indulged in the same ribaldry. The camaraderie delighted his soul. Still, he could not wait to arrive in Tarraco and see the ocean again. Many moons had gone by since he had seen the sea.

Spurius Septimius cantered up to Trajan from the rear of the marching legion.

"Everything in order at the heel, Spurius?" Trajan asked him.

"*Sic, Legatus.* The column is secure."

"Excellent. Spurius, what will you do first when we reach Tarraco?"

The *primipilus* didn't have to think long. "The Tarracian girls are beautiful and exotic, they say. It's a port town. They come from all over the world, even India. Need I say more?"

Trajan laughed. "No. Of course, I should have known better."

"And naturally, I can't wait to visit the baths. A massage, hot water and good wine will rejuvenate me for the next day's march."

Trajan nodded. Yes, he was looking forward to it too but also had to think of his wife Pompeia Plotina. He missed her, often sent letters. It gave him something to do and served as a diary on this trip.

They had met in Rome twelve summers ago. Pompeia had not at all been love on first sight. She was spindly and austere looking. The skin of her face was always pale, but her eyes were flashing brightly, indicating a secure grip on the world. Trajan had never gotten over his plight with Claudia though it had taught him that beauty wasn't everything. Pompeia wasn't very attractive but well-grounded, smart and full of surprises. He had grown very fond of her.

Pompeia was noble-born like Trajan. They had married *in confarreatio*, an aristocratic marriage contract that could not be dissolved. Trajan didn't mind. He adored her friendship and knew she loved him very much.

At this time she was supervising the education of his ward Publius Aelius Hadrianus, a boy of thirteen years whose parents had died a couple of years ago. Hadrian was the son of Trajan's cousin Hadrianus Afer. After Afer's death, Trajan had volunteered to become Hadrian's guardian. Due to his absence from Rome, it was Plotina's task now. She liked the boy. In her last letter, she had mentioned that the famous teacher and writer Scaurus would be Hadrian's Grammaticus - an excellent choice. Like Pompeia, Scaurus hailed from Nemausus in Gaul. She knew him well.

As much as Trajan was fond of Pompeia, he missed Sura even more. They had become intimate friends since their time in Syria and stayed in touch even after Trajan's transfer to Germania. When Trajan had commenced his civilian career in Rome, the *cursus honorum*, Sura lived in Rome also, taking up a lawyer's career. Like in the old days they spent much of their free time together. Trajan was attracted to Sura, admiring his athletic body. At the beginning he was appalled at himself, but in the end he had given in to his feelings. After a long night together in the taverns of Rome's Subura district they had lost their composure and confessed their mutual attraction.

Trajan didn't want to get married at all, but the social pressure being a Patrician had been unrelenting and ultimately carried the day. Thank Jupiter, Pompeia was a great choice. In fact, he felt so good around her he almost lost his homophile proclivity. The wedding night had been an epiphany, but soon lovemaking abated. He could never get as excited as with Sura. Pompeia cried her eyes out thinking - despite his assurances - that it was all her fault. She considered a difficult divorce but then dropped the idea to avoid a scandal, and they stayed together as friends. "I can't give you love," he had told her. "But I can offer you more than affability - I can give you affection."

To his amazement, their friendship and bonding had intensified over the years. They nurtured each other - in every regard but sexually. Pompeia had come to terms with the situation. Even when Sura stayed at their villa she wouldn't ask questions.

A vanguard unit reporting back from the Spanish seaboard interrupted Trajan's reflections. The *decurio* in-charge saluted the general. "*Legatus*, it will be two more hours to Tarraco. The first squadron has reached the city. They are setting up accommodations with the local garrison."

"Excellent. Ride down the column and spread the word. The men want to hear this."

Two more weeks to the confrontation with Saturninus...

Chapter 16

The imperial carriage was rumbling down the frostbitten Roman road when Domitian opened the shutters and stuck his head out. He was wrapped in mink furs although the coach's brazier mitigated the bitter cold. The emperor could not recognize much in the mist, but what he saw was anything but inviting. A thin snow cover lay on the ground like powdered sugar, all the way up to the distant hills that were shrouded in the fog. They were on the mountain pass between Augusta Praetoria and Octodurum, on their way through the Alpes Graiae. This was the shortest way to Germania, but in January the pass often closed. *Minerva be thanked, not this year.*

The winter had been mild, allowing the men of the *Cursus Publicus* to keep the road open. Domitian's carriage was well padded, and its walls were lined with the finest silk. Cushy tasseled pillows also helped absorb the shakes of the luxurious wagon on the bumpy alpine road.

Domitian scoured the landscape with furrowed eyebrows, but he took comfort in the Praetorian Century that surrounded his carriage. The whole Guard was on its way north, ten cohorts, a total of almost six thousand men. These Praetorians were front-line soldiers unlike the guard units of previous emperors and they had seen plenty of action in Flavian wars on Rhine and Danube.

When tiny snowflakes whirled in, Domitian closed the shutters annoyed and turned to his secretary. "How much longer to the Rhine? What's the word?"

"According to Casperius, another week, Dominus," Epaphroditus answered. "It will depend on the weather more than anything else."

"Really, Epaphroditus? Maybe it's more the speed of my Guard. Are they putting in enough effort?"

Epaphroditus shrugged.

"I am not a military man. I would not know how much faster several thousand men could march under these conditions. Even if they could, the horses and mules would start slipping-"

"You are useless," the emperor interrupted him. "Get out. Leave me alone and call the praefect. I need to talk to him."

Instead of an answer Epaphroditus grabbed his *palla* cloak, opened the back door and jumped off the rumbling carriage. The secretary closed the door behind him and Domitian could hear him jerk the bolt back into place - not to lock the door, but to make sure the rumble didn't yank it open accidentally.

Domitian scowled. He had his father's stocky body and sturdy limbs but was a bit taller than Vespasian. Domitian had lost his hair early too.

However, his face was well proportioned, the cheeks were smooth, his eyes always flitting. Like all Flavians, his lower jaw was pronounced, but the chin was slightly cleft and his nose classic Roman: prominent and crooked like an eagle's rostrum.

They are fools, all of them. Ruling is a hard and lonely business. And what dares Saturninus do, the wretched scum? Force me to go to frigid Germania to lop off his head instead of fighting the Dacians!

Domitian didn't know what to expect in the Germanic provinces. The intelligence was unclear. Evidently, Saturninus had two legions from Upper Germania under his control. The governors of Raetia and Lower Germania, Norbanus and Lappius, were marching against them, but no word had come from Trajan and none from the other two legions of Upper Germania. This was strange because the Praetorians were coming closer and closer to their bases in Vindonissa and Argentorate.

If the troops in the South were to revolt as well, he'd be in trouble. Vindonissa was only several days away. And who in the Senate was in cahoots with the renegade governor? He could not have possibly acted alone...

In the moonless night ten cloaked and hooded riders trotted into the village. The settlement seemed deserted, but Saturninus was confident it wasn't. There would have been signs of devastation or neglect. As it was, several thatch-roofed longhouses stood peacefully next to each other intact, each at least sixty feet long and twenty feet wide. There was no sound to be heard, not even the otherwise ubiquitous night creatures of the Germanic forest. All the Romans could hear was the snorting of their horses in the frosty night.

Saturninus reined-in his gelding, chopping his lips. The other Romans halted their mounts too. This was Chatti hamlet, about twenty-five miles north of Moguntiacum. Hostile warriors could surround them at any time now and finish them off. One of Saturninus's Germanic guides dismounted and strode to the entrance of the middle longhouse. Before he could reach it the wicker-and-hide cover was pushed aside and three chieftains stepped outside in full regalia, but without shields. They did have massive battle-axes attached to their stag leather belts. One of them greeted the apostate governor with a strong accent. "*Salve*, Saturninus, friend of Chatti. Welcome you."

"Welcome, Valdomarus. May you be blessed by Wotan and Fria, the gods of your people," Saturninus shouted. He dismounted and scurried forward to hug the Chieftain while his companions heaved a sigh of relief. The governor swung round after the ceremonial hug and ordered them to wait for him outside. Then he followed the Chatti chiefs into the longhouse.

The building was warm and cozy. A big smoldering fire in its center warmed tribal elders sitting cross-legged around it on ash tree logs. Brown bear and otter pelts covered floor and walls. A pungent smell from tanned hides wafted in the sticky air, complemented by dried herbs and hay. The three chiefs joined the elders and dropped down on the tree logs to sit close to the fireplace. Valdomarus waved Saturninus to follow him. The governor gladly took off his *paludamentum* and sat at Valdomarus's side. He had a hard time crossing his fat legs like the Chatti. *By Castor and Pollux, I hope this will soon be over.*

The newcomer's arrival did not seem to faze the chiefs. They kept on chuckling and gloating, passing around honey wine in flasks and horned cup holders. Saturninus could tell from the stained beards and wine spots on their checkered long-sleeved flax tunics that they had been drinking for a while; only Valdomarus was sober. He addressed his guest in barely intelligible Latin. "Roman Chieftain, you say you turn against thy Master. What has come?"

"Things are going well. The commanders of the Province are on my side. I have four legions now at my disposal and twenty thousand auxiliaries from Belgica, forty thousand men overall. If you join me, Valdomarus, we can liberate Germania and defeat the emperor. Just think of the plunder in Moguntiacum and Colonia Claudia and Colonia Treverorum! This is your opportunity to pay back the humiliation Domitian inflicted on you in his last war. In fact, I promise you his head if you join me!"

Saturninus was hoping Valdomarus would buy the story. There was the risk that he had somehow found out that the southern legions of Upper Germania remained loyal to the emperor. The auxiliaries from Belgica were an even more blatant lie, but in this case Saturninus was certain Valdomarus could not verify his claim. The Roman renegade was betting on the chieftain's thirst for revenge. Domitian's legions had inflicted heavy losses on the Chatti several years ago, and Valdomarus lusted for revenge and booty. He couldn't wait for the Roman cities along Rhine and Main to be sacked and destroyed.

"Good. My men primed. The River freeze soon and we cross within days and attack Lappius. My scouts see him not more than hundred thousand paces away."

Saturninus was aware of that. With the Chatti on his side, he wasn't worried though. Valdomarus could easily muster tens of thousands of men - many more than Lappius had. The governor needed these warriors. Fighting under duress, his own two legions would be pushovers. "Our plan will work out, Valdomarus. As soon as you strike, my legions will leave Moguntiacum and join forces with you. Lappius's troops will be outnumbered. After their defeat we turn south to defeat Domitian if he is still alive. The commanders of Argentorate and Vindonissa promised me to intercept him in the Alps." This was a lie too. His plan was to defeat Lappius with Chatti support but then to move south swiftly and destroy Domitian before the Eighth *Augusta* and the Eleventh *Claudia* could be mobilized. He was certain Domitian in his impatience would move north too fast and not wait for the legions of southern Upper Germania. Saturninus's agents in Argentorate and Vindonissa were spreading rumors and disinformation to hopefully paralyze the generals there.

"No, me want Domitian good so I can flay him living. No killing by Romans!" Valdomarus stamped his foot hard against the fire logs. Sparks were flying in all directions, but Saturninus kept his cool. "One more reason to get the business with Lappius over fast. Once we have our backs free, we can take on Domitian."

Valdomarus nodded grimly. "Me see. Tomorrow act. When River frozen, we cross and fight Lappius."

"Agreed." Saturninus had the Chieftain where he wanted him. Valdomarus rose. "No more talk. Leave, Roman traitor." The war council was over. Saturninus picked up his cloak, nodded at the chieftains and left the longhouse.

Chapter 17

The Seventh had left Tarraco a week ago. The men were making good progress in this race against time. Despite the grueling pace they were still far from their destination. Trajan, as always at the head of the column, let some units pass him by at times and encouraged the puffing men loaded to the gills with kit and weapons. "Keep it up, *milites*, you make me proud! It's only one more hour to the fording point. Keep up the pace, don't jostle. Be careful. Tripping will cost you extra energy."

He would often call his men by name, pick up from previous conversations he had had with them, yak about luck in the dice game or tainted love or the prospect of a nice state pension after twenty years of service or a man's desire for glory in battle. *They love me for it. We bond. It propels them forward.*

Despite the conviviality he was a tough commander when it came to matters of discipline. Only a few days ago, a centurion had caught a sentry post asleep. Trajan had him executed without thinking twice about it. These were the statutes – they all knew them. After all, a slumbering sentinel could spell the end for a whole legion. One for all, all for one.

They had reached the Rhone valley in southern Gaul. The sky was blue and bright as far as the eye could see. It should have been a wonderful day, but a nasty gale was blowing in their faces from the northwest, making breathing difficult. The men tied scarves around their mouths and noses to cope. On they marched, but the cursed squall slowed them down. Forty pounds of equipment on their backs plus the gale was too much to keep up the forced march. Trajan had to relent.

How often was the wind howling like this, he asked the native Gauls. They said it blew every once in a while but typically didn't last more than a couple of days. Trajan was comforted, but the men were getting impatient. His African rankers compared the howling squall to the desert winds blasting down from the Atlas Mountains. *The Rhone valley must channel the air at ferocious speed in African fashion.* Normally Trajan wouldn't mind, but now was just not a good time for them slow down their pace. The Seventh would not make it to Moguntiacum on time. At the current rate they wouldn't arrive there before mid February at the earliest - perhaps too late to have any impact on the conflict.

Trajan tapped his nose, shuddering. If Domitian lost, they might even be drawn into the abyss of an escalating Civil War... Since leaving Tarraco he had not received any new dispatch - neither from the Rhine nor from the emperor. Domitian must have crossed the Alps by now and would arrive first. What was the situation on the lower Rhine? Where was Norbanus? What was Lappius doing? Trajan couldn't wait to send out his own messengers and scouts.

In a way, the affair reminded him of his civil career in Rome. It had been slow sailing. Not long after marrying Plotina he had been quaestor, a boring office, but at least the government had not sent him to run the financial matters of a ghastly remote province. They assigned him to the Senate, a tedious but useful task. He had assisted Domitian in dealings with the august body, though often the young quaestor felt out of the loop and was overwhelmed by the political machinations. Afterward the *cursus honorum* had forced a customary five-year hiatus on him, allowing him to travel, spend time with his wife, parents and friends, and manage the vast family properties in Hispania. It was wonderful to be around Harpenna again - the two-legged sunshine in his parents' villa.

After that he had hungered to take responsibility again. He became praetor, presiding over the permanent courts in Rome. In this role he was able to make a difference, make sure justice prevailed. Then, two years ago, he had become eligible for a military command. And despite Callistus's protests, who worried for his safety he had jumped at the first opportunity. Domitian needed senior commanders on Rhine and Danube and less critical posts opened up elsewhere. Trajan snatched the command in Hispania. *What a coup it had been.*

Domitian did not like to commission patricians with the command of a legion. He more trusted knights or *homines novi*, men from outside the high nobility. Patricians constituted the old ruling class and were often jealous of the emperor's power. Trajan had been a recent addition to the senatorial order himself, but he didn't hail from the Famous Families in Rome. This had helped overcome Domitian's concerns.

Trajan's attention returned to the Rhone on his right. His troops were encamped on its western bank when suddenly a furious gust blew away numerous tents in the supply train. Canvas flew through the air, bouncing against mules, men and oxen and getting entangled with other tents, dragon standards and *vexilla* pennants. Trajan snapped at his adjutants and ordered the tarpaulins to be captured and folded up for transport. When would the cursed gale leave them alone?

North of Argentorate, Domitian's mood was improving. They had left the city with the Eighth *Augusta* and were marching north at the double. Enjoying the loyalty of Upper Germania's southern legions made him more confident. His strength had now doubled, but news of an alliance between Saturninus and the Chatti hung in the air.

The Chatti. We will see.

The numbers were unclear. True, with Lappius's two legions and count-ing the Praetorians he had five vs. Saturninus's two. Additionally, Norbanus would reinforce him with auxiliaries in the strength of half a legion, attack-ing Moguntiacum from the southeast. But how many Chatti warriors did Val-domarus have? How many chieftains had he rallied? And where were they?

Domitian and Praefect Casperius were mulling different scenarios: when and where Saturninus would attack, how he would deploy his men, and what they could do about it. A lot depended on the weather. If the Rhine froze, enabling the Germanics to cross the river in large numbers, Lappius could be in trouble even if they arrived in time to support him. It was critical to reach Moguntiacum soon. Norbanus's auxiliaries seemed to be three or four days away. He wanted to arrive within two.

The emperor was no longer riding in the carriage. He had mounted his warhorse, a black Arabic stallion of epic size, and was presently surrounded by elite horse troopers and bodyguards. Domitian had left the baggage train behind so the troops could march faster. The emperor cantered up and down the marching infantry yelling at the men to keep up the pace.

At noon the vanguard encountered messengers from Moguntiacum, sent by Lappius. Domitian's heart just about stopped. The emperor and Praefect Casperius spurred their horses to meet the couriers. He didn't care that the *turma* of cavalry right behind him would hear whatever news those messen-gers would bring – and spread them like wildfire.

"What is it? What news do you have?" Domitian shouted. He wheeled his stallion beside the arriving trooper's mount and stretched out his arm to grab the scroll from the man's hands.

The soldier was beaming at him. "Wonderful news, Majesty. We have won a great victory!"

Domitian broke Lappius's seal. He unfolded the scroll and raced through the dispatch:

> *I outflanked Saturninus and defeated him. He*
> *fell in battle. The Chatti could not cross the River*
> *and help him because the Rhine didn't freeze as they*
> *had hoped. His legions were feeble fighters. I tried*
> *to spare as many of the hapless men as possible.*
>
> *Now I am in Moguntiacum, mopping up*
> *and arresting his cronies. The Province is*
> *safe, Imperator. The revolt is over.*
>
> *Lappius*

Domitian handed the scroll to Casperius. Then he rose up on his four-pommeled saddle and turned to the troops. Cupping his hands around his mouth he shrieked, "We won. We won!"

He turned the skittering horse hard and galloped along the dazed Praetorian column. "The rebellion is over. Saturninus is dead. He is dead!" Up and down he rode, coaxing the agitated and snorting mustang back and forth. "We won. Lappius won a great victory. We won."

Casperius joined him now on the other side of the ranks, blurting the joyful news as he cantered down the column. The soldiers drew their swords and banged them against their iron shield bosses. "Victory, victory!" Bang, bang, bang!

Domitian ordered couriers to Rome right away to inform Senate and People.

At a more leisurely pace they continued the march north. How had it all transpired? What should he tell Trajan? The *Gemina*'s march was pointless now. And how would he explain Trajan's sudden arrival to Lappius? Anyway, the rebellion was over. The commanders would appreciate that.

Reining-in alongside the emperor, Lappius's messengers gave him more details. Their commander had made a pincer move against Saturninus's legions by sending troops up the River by boat and leading ground troops around Moguntiacum to attack from the south. The renegade governor had been caught by surprise, his two legions routed while the Chatti were forced to watch powerless on the other side of the River.

Chapter 18

Lappius pulled his beaver fur-lined *paludamentum* tighter. Cold wind was chilling his body as the governor was standing outside Moguntiacum's barracks, watching his troops escort prisoners from Saturninus's unfortunate legions into the city. The disarmed men were beat and hungry. Many officers would be charged with mutiny, flogged and executed. Should he decimate the rankers and have every tenth soldier be stoned to death by his comrades? Most of them had been dragged into a game not of their wanting. He did not want to punish them.

Lappius did want to find Saturninus's accomplices. His staff was setting up rooms filled with officers and petty officers from Moguntiacum's disgraced legions: *tribuni, centuriones, optiones, duplicarii, decuriones* and others.

Presently, a trooper galloped up to him and handed him a scroll with Domitian's seal on it. Maximus opened it on the spot.

> *Dear Lappius Maximus:*
>
> *Congratulations to your Great Victory. Messengers are on their way to Rome to tell Senate and People what you have done. We are in your debt.*
> *I am grateful for your loyalty and acumen.*
> *My troops are two days away, and I am looking forward to congratulating you in person.*
> *Do not release any prisoners. Punishment will be meted out according to the Law of the Ancients.*
>
> *Domitian*
> *IMP CAESAR AUG*

Curse you, tyrant. He knew Domitian all too well. The emperor would try to use Lappius's victory to exact revenge. Maximus was determined not to let that happen. To spoil Domitian's blood lust he intended to destroy as much incriminating evidence as he could and make it look like collateral damage.

Determined, he entered the Praetorium where Gnaeus Papirius and his men were waiting for the governor's orders. Maximus sent them out, with the exception of Papirius himself. "Gnaeus, there is some business we have to take care of. I mentioned it before. Many innocent lives are at stake because good men were taken for a ride against their will."

Papirius nodded.

"So, I want you to destroy all the scrolls and tablets you can find in here. Then burn down the whole *signifers'* wing with the payroll accounts, and while you're at it, burn the kitchen and the guards' billets too."

"Why that if I may ask?"

"Because it needs to look like fighting and the outbreak of fire. Rig it that way. We need to give Domitian a reason why the files were destroyed. If you can, have mute slaves do this work. Domitian must never know, do you understand?"

"Yes, General, but why the kitchen and the other rooms?"

"So it does not appear that the damage was limited to the payroll offices. And have some watchtowers and adjacent buildings singed as well."

"You have great courage, General. I will go about it at once!"

"Gnaeus," Lappius called him as his *primipilus* paced out the door. Papirius turned round. "Yes?"

"Domitian is two days away, but be ready tomorrow morning. The emperor might surprise us. He can be wily."

"*Sic, Legatus.* And what are we doing with Saturninus's cronies?"

Lappius shrugged. "That's not up to us. Domitian will execute them, as he should. I hate conspirators and would love to know myself who else was involved in this, both here and in Rome. I cannot imagine Saturninus acted alone. But then again, he may have. We may never find out."

Domitian's quarters in Moguntiacum were well-appointed and luxurious compared to the inns he had had to spend his nights on the trip north. The emperor had arrived late last night and immediately listened to Lappius's extensive report. Today he wanted to award the successful troops and commence his investigation.

The day was busy with individual citations and troop inspections. At the end, Domitian received Casperius, Lappius and Papirius in the dead governor's office. "I am very impressed, General," Domitian praised Maximus again. "You and your men did well and will be rewarded. Maybe I can even grant you a consulship down the road. But you can definitely pick your next command."

Maximus bowed to the emperor. "Thank you, *Imperator.* Your compliments are more than I deserve. I was only serving my country."

"No, no," Domitian insisted. "You went beyond your duty. You resolved a crisis before it spiraled out of control. I am realistic. Saturninus must have had supporters, perhaps even in the Senate. I hope to ascertain that, starting with the ringleaders still alive."

"The prisoners are at your disposition, Majesty. We know that ten officers have worked with Saturninus. The rankers are mostly innocent, but his cavalry chief was a conspirator and so were two of the tribunes. We know this from eyewitnesses, spies and the citizens of Moguntiacum. However, none of the prisoners has admitted any guilt. I suggest the establishment of a military court for the investigation and trial."

"Well said," Domitian replied without meaning it. "Lappius, you are so dutiful. Everything by the book, an example to us all."

His face broke into a forced smile, begetting their approval. "But I will exert my imperial prerogative, Lappius. Turn the men over to the Praetorians. We will investigate this."

"They are yours, Excellency."

Lappius pointed to Papirius. "Gnaeus, you heard the emperor, make it happen."

The chief centurion nodded at Casperius and rose from his chair. "This way, Praefect," he said, pointing to the door of Saturninus's office. He walked ahead, and both he and Casperius left the room.

"My dear Lappius," Domitian addressed the general with a generous smile. "I want you to go back to Colonia Claudia and resume your station there. The situation here is under control. I will also send the *Augusta* back to Argentorate. But I will not forget this. In the spring, you can pick any command you desire."

"Thank you, Caesar."

"Good. There is only one thing I don't like. It's a shame we don't have records. How did they get destroyed?"

"We don't know. There was heavy fighting when my men took the city. Collateral damage, I assume."

"Hmm."

It sounded plausible, and yet it was strange that so much evidence was missing. But Lappius had proven his loyalty. Domitian didn't doubt him. The fight in the Praetorium must have occurred while Lappius's troops had been outside the city. Every officer had corroborated Maximus's report. Domitian decided to leave it at that and focus on the prisoners. "There is something else I need to tell you, Maximus. The Legate Trajan will arrive here tomorrow with the Seventh Legion. I want you to swap quarters with him. Trajan will take over. His Seventh will garrison Moguntiacum together with the Praetorians."

Lappius raised his eyebrows. "Yes, Caesar, certainly," he said. "It will be a smooth transition."

Chapter 19

News of the battle had reached Trajan in Matisco, two weeks away from Moguntiacum. His immediate reaction had been a great void, followed by anxiety: What was next? He was glad to hear about Saturninus's death and relieved not having to fight against fellow Romans. But what was in store for him and his men now? They had covered hundreds of miles. Thankfully, Domitian had ordered Trajan to complete the journey and meet him in Moguntiacum.

Here they were, a mile from the city walls. The men of the defeated legions, the *Rapax* and the *Victrix,* teasingly hollow names now ('Predator' and 'Victorious'), were billeted in a vast tent city outside the city's battlements. Trajan's column was marching through clusters of frosty and shaggy tents, enviously watched by the crushed men.

Arriving at the walls, Trajan noticed some major battle damage. Strange. Had the conflict not been decided way north of here?

Domitian welcomed the young general in his quarters with a friendly hug. The emperor had visibly aged since Trajan had last seen him.

"Trajan, my friend, I cannot tell you how impressed I am that you came all the way from Hispania! Outstanding, truly outstanding."

"My pleasure, Caesar. We go where we are needed. How is the situation?"

Domitian gave him a quick report.

"So what about the Chatti? Are we letting them get away with this?"

"Of course not. They will be punished. I can't wait to strangle Valdomarus in person. But bringing Saturninus's accomplices to justice is more important."

"Very well. Majesty, if you don't need me for now, I would like to get settled and meet with the Commander of the Eighth. My orders are still to move my men into the Eighth Legion's barracks?"

"Yes, but that can wait, Marcus Ulpius. First, let's go see the prisoners."

The cells were not far away, guarded by Praetorians. Trajan shuddered when they entered the first stall. Three shivering prisoners were huddling together on the filthy floor of the frigid chamber, trying to retain as much body heat as possible under their dilapidated *paludamenta*.

Domitian barked at them. "Your names and rank!"

One was the quartermaster of the Twenty-first Legion *Rapax*; the other two were tribunes on Saturninus's staff. The emperor asked them about the events leading to the conspiracy. They said Saturninus had talked them into it. They regretted it all, they claimed, imploring the emperor to spare their lives.

Domitian wanted to know who else was involved, both here in Germania and in Rome. They assured him they knew of no one else and swore that Saturninus had acted alone, dreading the emperor's wrath to his licentious life style. Trajan could tell that Domitian didn't buy it. In a fit, he dashed out of the cell, leaving a puzzled Trajan behind. "Guards, send for Caro!"

Five disconcerting minutes later, a middle-aged centurion strode in.

"Minucius, I need these men to speak the truth."

Minucius Caro banged his fist against his mail shirt for acknowledgement. He came back with unmistakable tools and heated iron rods. Seeing that, the prisoners bawled in horror, begging for mercy. "Please, please, no torture. We are telling the truth and only the truth!"

"Take off your clothes," Caro ordered them. Then he had them lie down on their stomachs. Caro set one of the tribunes aside from the others and told him to spread his legs. Four Praetorians held onto his arms and legs. Without warning Caro took one of the heated rods and shoved it into the man's anus. The prisoner shrieked and squirmed and tried to get away, but the guards had a tight grip on him. Caro pushed the iron in deeper and deeper until only the wooden handle was sticking out. The man twitched in the Praetorians' hands, screaming off the top of his lungs. Trajan almost heaved, tried to leave the cell, but Domitian pushed him back.

"Watch this. You will see. The wretch will tell us all we need to know."

"No, he will tell you what you WANT to hear."

Trajan clenched his fists so hard it hurt. He told himself over and over again, Domitian was a Flavian, hailing from a glorious dynasty. He had done many good things for Army and empire. *My father served his father.* Still, these were the longest minutes of his life.

At long last, the man's ordeal was over. He had spilled all kinds of names that Caro had duly scratched on his wax board. Then his body went limp and he passed out. He would not survive this. Domitian grinned gleeful and pointed his sword at him. "Look at this animal. Evil life has but one purpose: to die!"

He sheathed his sword, spun about and left the grimy prison cell. His Praetorians hustled after him like specks of sand sucked through the hole of a sand clock.

Shaken and shaking, Trajan trudged back to his men. His duties kept him on the go all day long, but when he retired to his cot at night, he couldn't sleep despite his physical exhaustion. The image of the tortured soldier was etched into his brain. He couldn't find peace, dreading the next day. He knew he would have to deal with Flavian monster again. What should he do? How could he dodge this?

His mind was racing until the wee hours of dawn when his tormented soul finally found reprieve in the bliss of overpowering slumber.

"Caesar, I would like to find Valdomarus. My men are fully equipped and qualified to cross the Rhine," Trajan proposed to the emperor.

Domitian shook his head. "I don't know, Trajan. That's dangerous. Valdomarus has mobilized many warriors, tens of thousands. He knows his terrain, and it's winter - a mild one for now, but that can change at a moment's notice."

"I don't intend to conquer the whole land of the Chatti. What I want is Valdomarus's head. A surgical strike - that's what I have in mind, to surprise them. I have talked to Lappius's scouts and the sutlers in Moguntiacum. They believe, Valdomarus is expecting our attack in the spring and has started fortifying villages and moving people farther into the Hercynian Forest. Best of all, one of the scouts has family connections with another Chatti Chieftain. He has a good idea where to find Valdomarus himself."

"We don't have the resources to campaign on the other side of the Rhine, Trajan. On the contrary, I am going to send several legions to the Danube to prepare for the campaigning season there. Trouble is brewing with the Dacians, but also with the Quadi, Marcomanni and Roxolani. A week from now I will leave, taking the compromised legions with me. You will be alone with the Seventh. That's all you will have to protect the border. Under these circumstances, I am not convinced that a limited campaign is a good idea."

"Trust me, Caesar, I can do it. I will be back before your departure."

Domitian puckered his mouth, hesitating. "Fine, you can go after Valdomarus, but be careful – and return within a week's time."

Trajan was jubilant. "*Sic*, my Lord," he said and saluted.

They crossed the Rhine the same day, with three cohorts of infantry, about fifteen hundred men. The ground was too wet and slippery for cavalry. He also did not bring Callistus. His friend and secretary protested, but he could not change Trajan's mind. The general wanted him to be safe.

They marched at night only, covering everything metal with furs or strips of flax tunics to foil detection. After two days, the scouts pointed to a settlement in the distance, barely visible in the mist. "This is the place where you will find Valdomarus. Act now. He never stays long in any one place."

"It looks like the sentries have not noticed us. I will press this advantage and immediately surround the hamlet," Trajan said.

Half an hour later his men were in position. At his word, the troops showed themselves, walking out of the mist and banging their swords against their shields. Bang, bang, bang... Bang, bang, bang...

The fog muffled the din, but fur-clad Chatti dashed out of their long-houses at once, belts in their hands uncinched, swords clenched, looking for the reason of the hubbub. They scampered in all directions to find out what was going on. Soon the place resembled a beehive teeming with men, women and children, and stirred up goats and sheep and chickens.

Trajan cupped his hands and shouted into the village. "Valdomarus, you are surrounded by a Roman legion. Surrender or die!"

He could not determine who Valdomarus was but was certain the chieftain heard him. Trajan repeated his demand. Then Valdomarus answered, "I not surrend, Roman. Get me if can!"

The Chatti men chuckled, forming a wall of warriors around their chieftain. The scouts told Trajan Valdomarus was trying to send messengers out for help, but as far as they could tell the Germanics were being intercepted by the tight ring of Roman infantry quarantining the village.

"My men are telling me you are crying for help, but your messengers won't get through, Valdomarus!" Trajan shouted. "You don't stand a chance, Chieftain. You are trapped!"

Valdomarus sent men forward to break through the Roman line. Fifty Germanics hurled themselves against the legionaries, but Trajan's line was deeply stacked with heavy infantry. The Chatti tried several times, directing their efforts at different sections of the Roman cordon, but every time Trajan simply reinforced each point of impact. In addition, Roman *pila* killed or disabled many warriors while they were charging the Roman shield wall.

Trajan made an offer. "Valdomarus, I will let your women and children leave if you agree to a fight just you and me!"

After some time had passed Valdomarus answered, "Agree, but let all people leave before fight."

"No. I give you my word. They can go after the fight."

"No! How trust you?"

"You have no choice."

Trajan didn't want other Chatti to arrive before he and his troops had left the village. The men would have to stay.

After a while, the Chatti sent their wives and children forward - Valdomarus's way of agreeing to the ultimatum.

He thinks he can kill me one on one and then use the confusion to get away.

Trajan let the women and children pass the Roman lines unhindered by opening a small gap in the investment ring. It closed behind the last matron. Meanwhile, the Chatti warriors formed a small half-circle behind their Chieftain, keeping their distance to the Romans.

Everything was set: Trajan and Valdomarus stepped forward.

The Roman general wore plate armor, helmet and greaves, but he didn't bring a *pilum*. The main weapon in this fight would be his *spatha*. Longer than the *gladius*, it gave him equal range to Valdomarus's Germanic sword. A *pugio* was also cinched to his belt. Trajan's shield was a standard edition legionary infantry shield, rectangular and curved, four feet high and nearly two feet wide. It provided stupendous protection. Valdomarus used the Germanic flat oval shield. It was shorter but also lighter. If the fight took a long time, it would be an advantage. Trajan was determined not to let this happen.

Losing no time, he dashed forward and pushed his shield against the chieftain's. Valdomarus tried to poke around it with his sword. Trajan kept up with him, constantly changing positions to absorb the stings. At the same time, he waited for an opening to use the *spatha*. Not getting anywhere, Valdomarus became more aggressive and hit harder and harder, which required him to lift his sword higher and higher to dish out the blows. That's when Trajan changed pace, stepped aside lightning quick and slashed Valdomarus's chain mail with his sword. The blow was so hard that the Chatti Chieftain lost his balance and fell backward. Trajan was over him like the wind. He stepped on Valdomarus's shield to keep it out of the way and struck Valdomarus's sword so hard with his own that the chieftain lost grip. Without hesitation Trajan killed him with a blow to his neck. Blood gushed out like hot springs water, spraying the Roman general's *pteryges*.

The general stepped back disgusted, pointing at the dead body with his dripping sword. He lifted his eyes with calculated slowness. Then his sharp gaze swept the half circle of Chatti men opposite the Roman side. "The asp is punished. He tried using a Roman traitor to his advantage. Be warned, warriors. Rome will not tolerate such conduct. As long as Marcus Ulpius Traianus guards this border, peace alone will save you!"

The Romans left the village unencumbered and reached Moguntiacum unharmed. Not even five days had passed.

Domitian was satisfied with the situation in Upper Germania. Revenge had been taken, the Roman name rehabilitated. Trajan's legion was firmly established and the ringleaders of the rebellion had been killed. Unfortunately, the names yielded from torturing the prisoners had not implicated any senators or high-ranking magistrates in Rome. This was a reason for concern. Domitian was convinced that Saturninus had not been mad enough to declare against him without some support in the Senate. He wasn't happy about this but decided to leave Moguntiacum. The Danube border needed his immediate attention.

BOOK IV

A NEW BEGINNING

Chapter 20

Seven years later (96 AD), Rome

"**B**y Rome's eternal gods, where is Carnifex?" Pantherius barked. The clerks in the room winced at the Imperial Chamberlain's question, pulling their heads in between their shoulders.

"I need the program for the Games. Where in the world is he? Our greatest games, the Ludi Romani, will begin today, and I still don't know how many funds I need to release to pay the contractors!"

Pantherius had sent Carnifex to the praetor's office to fetch the final program for Opening Day. He was in a foul mood. Finding the money for the cursed Ludi had been hard enough. The Treasury was empty; too many wars, too much construction. The biggest expense had been the new Jupiter Temple on the Capitoline Hill. Its predecessor had burned down twenty years ago in the Civil War after Nero's suicide.

Pantherius sighed. Half a year ago, after repeated inspections of the treasury vaults in the temple of Saturn, he had thought he would not have enough assets to pay for the Great Games. Such a report would have been a career-limiting move. Domitian didn't like such news. He would not have appreciated being forced to skimp on the most important games in the city that ruled the world. So Pantherius had gotten creative, deciding to plunder temples all over the empire.

It would be all right, he assured himself as he operated his abacus, once more counting the Treasury's cash accounts. Contractors didn't like imperial warrants. They wanted hard cash from the Mint, preferably gold *aurei* or silver *denarii*. No help had come from the Senate. Rome's most venerable body of government was at odds with Domitian. The senators didn't like his autocratic style, his cruel character. Prominent members of the Senate had been executed on charges of High Treason. Last year, the emperor had even put his own cousin to death. The death verdict had included the man's sons, prospective heirs to the throne. The wife had been exiled. Domitian had accused the couple of rejecting the ancient gods. They had in fact sympathized with the new Christian religion, but nobody in the palace had seen it as a threat.

Pantherius didn't know what to think. He had served Domitian for years and been treated well. The Syrian freedman kept the palace organized and was a competent administrator. Pantherius felt safe from Domitian, but he knew the emperor was fickle. Missteps would have consequences. Moreover, Domitian always watched the delicate balance of power between himself and the Senate and the provincial governors. And yes, there were the People of

Rome too. That's what he was for – keep them happy with great entertainment. Like today.

Carnifex burst into Pantherius's office. "Here is the final program from Praetor Verulenus's desk, Lord Chamberlain," he gasped.

"Every time we have an event of this magnitude I get the program late," Pantherius grumbled as he picked up the casually wrapped papyrus scroll, but he knew it wasn't Carnifex's fault. Carnifex and the whole staff had worked all night with Verulenus's people to get it right.

"I don't know why I am looking at this at all. There isn't much I could change at this point anyway, could I?"

"Not a whole lot, Master, but we can make changes with the dancers and actors."

"Ah, yes, yes, you are right." He felt better now that the review was not just rubberstamping their proposal. "I will get back to you."

"Lord Chamberlain, we need the final list before the third hour," Carnifex pointed out uneasy. "The participants need to know their schedule, Master."

"I realize that. Out with you! I need to read this undisturbed."

So much to do and never enough time.

Over at the Circus Maximus, the 'Greatest Stadium' , the bleachers were filling up with spectators of all ages and classes. The grand procession honoring *Jupiter Optimus Maximus* would terminate there, followed by horse races, gymnastics competitions and theatrical events. Wager booths had opened, accepting bets on the chariot race teams.

At the imperial lodge, senators and knights entered at a steady pace. They were seated before the arrival of the emperor and his Praetorian detail. Only noblemen who had contributed funds to the Ludi Romani were admitted to the box.

Arrius Antoninus and Publicius Certus qualified for showing largesse. They arrived together.

"*Ave*, Publicius," Antoninus said. "What's happening? Tell me about your latest literary accomplishments."

"There is nothing, alas," Certus answered. "I wished there was, but I never have enough time. Betrothing my daughter is a full-time occupation." He chuckled. "And there was trouble at my Apulian latifundia. I spent a lot of time there."

Arrius Antoninus was too polite to ask what kind of trouble. He didn't know Publicius Certus all that well. The senator could be Domitian's man, an informer even. He had to be careful.

They exchanged some small talk until another senator arrived, Marcus Cocceius Nerva, a friend of Antoninus and the Elder Statesman in the Senate, a man of impeccable ancestry. An eagle's nose protruded from his long narrow head that was barely supported by a spindly neck. Arrius excused himself, joining Nerva. "We need to talk," he whispered.

"About what?"

"Everything."

"Ah, everything."

"Let's walk over there," Arrius suggested, pointing to the most distant corner of the imperial box.

They strolled to the corner spot and looked down to the arena and the hectic activities of public slaves preparing for the show.

"What is it, Arrius?"

"How long do you want to accept the status quo, Marcus?"

"The status quo?"

"The status quo - Domitian. His intolerable suppression of liberty, the Senate, everything Rome stands for."

Nerva pulled up his eyebrows, then turned his head to the arena, perfectly composed as if Antoninus had just asked him about the weather.

"You are itching, Arrius," he replied without looking at his friend.

Antoninus ignored the snipe. "Domitian is still young. If we don't act, there will be many more years of tyranny and many more dead senators."

"True, but what are you going to do about it?"

"There is an opportunity."

"Yes? Do say."

Arrius Antoninus moved closer. "Remember that Domitian dismissed Casperius a while ago, appointing new Praetorian Praefects?"

"Yes."

"Well, after the latest wave of executions I believe neither Petronius nor Norbanus feel safe themselves. There are rumors in the palace that Domitian has a list of men under his pillow that are next."

"Interesting. But how would the Praefects know they are on the list?"

"They don't. That's just it. They might be... What they do know is that complaints have been made to the emperor about them. Marcus, here is our chance! The Praefects are nervous. We should make them our allies and dispatch the monster - and make you emperor."

There was a long silence. Then Nerva shook his head. "The Senate has never appointed an emperor before. Why should the Guard listen to us?"

"Because there are no heirs," Antoninus said triumphantly, cupping one hand around his mouth. "The Flavian Dynasty is finished," Arrius whispered. "Domitian has killed all his male relatives. Despicable, but good for us."

"None of this is new to me," Nerva countered. "The only thing I didn't know is that the praefects are uneasy. That's good. But I do know that the rankers and centurions of the Guard adore the emperor. He has the Flavian touch. Don't forget, this Guard is not just a Palace Guard. It's an elite legion that has fought tough battles with Domitian in Moesia against invading tribes. They relate to Domitian; they have bonded with him, and he is shrewd enough to keep them happy with lavish pay and perks. A conspiracy would have to walk a fine line, involve only a small circle of the most trusted men - and would need help from inside the palace."

Nerva paused, waving at other senators that were taking their seats in their vicinity. He turned back to Arrius Antoninus and whiffed, "I cannot believe I just said that... I am getting carried away. Arrius, I am too old for this. Many emperors have come and gone. I have served the good ones and the bad ones - even Nero.

On the other hand, my age is also a responsibility, maybe a calling. My life is mostly over. Maybe... Maybe I can make a difference. Perhaps it is time to put everything on the line..."

Deafening blasts from hundreds of Praetorian *tubicens* and *cornicens* posted on top of the bleachers interrupted their conversation, signaling the emperor's arrival in the Circus. Arrius and Nerva gazed at the center of the Lodge, waving at Domitian along with everybody else.

"We should talk again, my friend," Nerva muttered against the backdrop of the blaring instruments. "But not here. Come to my house after the show."

They parted ways and returned to their assigned seats. The imperial lodge had filled up with dignitaries, but the Circus itself was not full yet. Many commoners were lingering in the Forum and watching the opening procession, which was about to step off from the Jupiter Temple.

Chapter 21

Keeping his gaze on Domitian and his entourage, Antoninus saw Praefect Petronius order his guardsmen to signal the consuls at the head of the
procession via a chain of flashing mirrors that they were allowed now to
set out. He couldn't see the parade until it entered the Circus through the
North Gates to the roaring cheers of two hundred and fifty thousand men
and women. Arrius covered his ears with his hands in pain. The racket defied
description.

The consuls, praetors, priests and the lower-ranking magistrates were
the first to enter the stadium. Behind them, young men on foot and on horseback paraded into the arena, some of them famous charioteers, piloting their
two- and four-horse rigs. Then, track-and-field athletes and tumblers wearing only loincloths burst into the Circus, catching the crowd's attention with
aerial stunts and other acrobatics. After them, flute and lyre players and war
dancers of all ages appeared, wearing shiny brass belts cinched around crimson red tunics, with swords, javelins and plumed helmets in all colors.

That's what we need. Someone who knows how to wield a sword.

The conversation with Nerva was still fresh on Arrius's mind. Meanwhile,
another group grabbed his attention: second-rate performers masquerading
as hairy satyrs in goatskins. They mocked and mimicked the war dancers
preceding them. The audience applauded the contrast on display.

Always fun to mix the somber with the bawdy.

Incense burners followed with urns, wafting the stadium with their
fumes. Next, the parade took on a more religious tone. Men carried litters
with the statues of reclining Roman gods, displaying the twelve Olympians
including Jupiter, Juno and Minerva, and also some Italian and imported
gods such as Saturn, Latona and the Fates and the Muses. Of all the statues,
Minerva's was the biggest and the only gilded one. She was Domitian's patron goddess whom he worshipped with ardor. Sacrificial animals headed by
beautiful white bulls concluded the procession. It covered one full lap inside
the Circus Maximus until it stopped in front of the imperial box. Domitian
rose and lifted his arms. The huge stadium fell silent, allowing the consuls
to hail the emperor.

In the background the sacrificial animals were being walked up to the
consuls so they could preside over their ritual killing. After obtaining the
emperor's permission, the priests went to work. They killed the mighty bulls
by placing long knives under their throats and then thumping them so hard
with oak clubs that the animals went down instantly, falling on the blades
and dying in a trice. The indirect slaying absolved the priests from bloodguilt
because - technically speaking - the animals killed themselves.

Attendants butchered the victims on site, seasoned each limb with *mola salsa* and carried them off in gold and silver vessels as the 'Gods' share', to be burnt in the temples of Rome and endowing the City with good fortune and the *Pax Deorum*, Peace with the Gods - considered as a guarantee for survival in all eternity. The remainder of the meat was cut up and would later be distributed amongst the families of magistrates and priests.

After his propitiation Domitian declared the *Ludi Romani* properly inaugurated. The audience thundered in excitement, and the competition could now begin, giving the people a day full of heart-thumping horse races, foot races, wrestling, jumping, throwing and acting, with interludes of musical performances.

Antoninus was impressed, but where did the exhausted Treasury dig up the means for sumptuous games like this?

The spectacles ended at dusk. In a lava-like crawl, thousands of spectators oozed from the Circus Maximus through a clever maze of hallways, arches and portals. Senators and knights headed back to their homes on litters, but only after Domitian and his detail had returned to the palace through a tunnel connecting the Circus with the Palatine.

Antoninus sauntered to Nerva's villa on the Esquiline Hill, making sure he wasn't being followed. The porter let him in right away. To his surprise, the villa's triclinium was brimming with eminent guests: the famous lawyer Tiberius Catius Fronto, the decorated General Verginius Rufus, who had been offered the Purple three times during the Civil War and had declined it each time, and the nobleman Aulus Larcius Priscus. Arrius smiled. Nerva, the old boy, wasn't losing any time.

On the other side of the Forum Romanum, Domitian was having dinner with his wife Domitia. The Praetor Gaius Verulenus and Lord Chamberlain Pantherius were their Guests of Honor in the new glamorous palace that now dominated the Palatine Hill. Managing the *Ludi Romani* made them Rome's most important officials for the next two weeks, and Domitian wanted to show them his gratitude. He was pleased with Opening Day and wanted to be apprised on the details of tomorrow's festivities.

"Gaius, did everything go to your liking?" the emperor asked in good spirits.

Verulenus bowed. "It did though it wasn't perfect. The two-horse chariot race could have been faster. But overall, I am satisfied and would like to thank my colleague Pantherius here for his financial genius." He pointed at the Lord Chamberlain. "He played the contractors expertly against each other, providing us with incredible savings. The great Crassus himself couldn't have done it better. We used the windfall to splurge more than we could have otherwise."

"No, no, my dear Gaius," Pantherius differed. "Though it is true that I like a good deal - the Games turned out well because you did an excellent job recruiting actors and dancers and signing up the most proficient riders and charioteers in the empire, and pairing them artfully. And, by Minerva, the choreography, the music - truly exceptional!"

Domitian chuckled. "Good to see you two are working well together."

His wife chimed in too. "I agree with my husband. Everything was brilliant, so colorful and engaging. I had a good time!"

After dinner, the Imperial couple withdrew to their suite. Slaves helped them undress and washed them in lavish marble bathtubs. While one of the chambermaids combed Domitia's hair she asked the emperor a question. "Titus, there weren't many senators in the box with us today. Why was that?"

Domitian grumbled. "I can't trust them."

"This is awful! You should be on better terms with them. How can you live like that?"

"I still have the knights on my side, most of them anyway."

"But you need the Senate. Not only is it the empire's most august institution; it is also the recruiting body for your governors and army commanders. You can't rule with freedmen secretaries and knights alone. That works in the palace, but out there-" She pointed at the elaborately framed windows. "Out there and in the provinces you need the nobility."

"Do I? Do I really? I am the Emperor, I am the Law!" Domitian snapped.

"Yes, you do. You can only propose or veto legislation, not make bills into Law on your own. And you know as well as I do that most bills are drafted by senators or people's tribunes."

"The Senate will pass any bill coming from me. You know that."

"Only because they are afraid of you. After those awful high treason trials I would pass any bill of yours too - not because I am for it, but because I am terrified." Domitia signaled the hairdresser to pause, touched her curls. She nodded satisfied and dismissed the maid.

Domitian glared at the empress. "What is the matter with you? This is none of your business."

Domitia stood, stepped to the window and turned back to her husband from there, hugging her elbows. "Doesn't it bother you that you have to live in constant fear yourself? Your attitude provokes plots. The way you behave tells me that you realize that and you are taking counter-measures, but what kind of life is that? Treat the noblemen better, and things will turn around. Domitian, I beg you, don't act like an eastern despot. One could mix you up with the High King of Parthia!

Why don't you work with them or at least give them the impression that you do. You need their loyalty in the Army; they are the commanders of your legions, Domitian, don't forget that."

"I know, sweetheart. That's why I keep rotating them so they are stationed far apart from each other. Domitia, the Senate is Rome's elite, but even they have to play by my book. I am the Emperor. I rule. My commands are the Law of the Land. If they turn into megalomaniacs, they die!"

Domitia lowered her head. "You don't understand. Rome is not Parthia. Its aristocracy does not put up with the rule of one man. They are proud and used to sharing the imperial power.

I am so tired of all this. You don't even trust the Guard anymore. How will this end?"

Then she remembered the execution of Domitian's cousin Clemens. "Clemens was no megalomaniac. He was no danger to you at all. Now we don't have an heir!" Her voice cracked, and tears filled her eyes.

"That's different," Domitian thundered. "He was impious, decadent and blasphemic. Wife, he had given up on the gods of Rome - the same eternal gods that have blessed this nation and our unprecedented conquest of the world.

If I had let him go on with his Jewish or Christian or whatever despicable ways – *nefas*! - the gods would have taken revenge and punished us for it – me and you and the State, the Senate, the People, the Army, EVERYONE. I am *Pontifex Maximus*. I have to preserve the Ancient Ways and the State Religion!"

He had talked himself into a frenzy and was screaming now. "Clemens was *nefas*! You hear that, *NEFAS*. I had no choice." His voice tapered off. He lowered his gaze, scowling.

"How can you say that about the Jews?" Domitia insisted. "Your own brother was in love with a Jewish princess. Don't you remember Berenice? Don't you remember anything? The fun we had as a family. How peaceful everything was when your Father was Emperor..." She heaved her shoulders, started sobbing.

Domitian walked up to her and caressed her curly hair. "I scared you. It's all my fault. I didn't mean to. Let's bed-wrestle!"

Domitia glimpsed at him aghast, pulled away and ran out of the chamber, banging the doors shut behind her.

"Then not. Chamberlain, Chamberlain!"

Carnifex scurried into the room. "My Lord?"

"Bring my favorite girl. Dress her up like the Goddess Minerva. You know what I mean? Beautiful and pompous, appropriate for an Emperor."

"Very well, my Lord."

Chapter 22

On the Esquiline, Nerva's dinner was well received. At its conclusion, he sent out the servants, had them close the triclinium doors and addressed his guests. "You all know why we are here tonight. There is a widespread belief that Domitian is no longer tolerable, is he?"

Antoninus, Rufus and Priscus nodded, but Tiberius Fronto injected, "Is it really inevitable? Why do we have to kill him? I feel like a wretched Caesar murderer!"

The other plotters arched their eyes.

"The common soldiers like him," he continued. "In Rome and in the provinces. The people like him. That was obvious again today. They cheered him and agreed with all his referee decisions. Listen, Domitian is a meticulous administrator and a hard worker. He is no Nero. In fact, we have never had such a well-managed administration. Of course, he wasn't always successful in the field but never lost a battle either; two of his generals did. In fact, Domitian employs intelligent border strategies that are keeping us safe. His image is a lot worse than the facts. Maybe we are only selfishly worrying about our own good fortunes."

Antoninus scoffed at Fronto. "I can't believe what I am hearing. Have you forgotten how many innocent men he has killed? Can't you see how the backbenchers in the Senate are trembling in the Curia every day? Every other session of the Senate is below quorum because people are too afraid to show up. Each of us could be accused of High Treason for some trumped up reason at any time. Do you want to live like this?

Yes, we worry. It's a matter of survival. You will find this out yourself one day at your own 'Violation-of-His-Majesty Tribunal' where sycophants will pile up far-fetched accusations against you, Tiberius!"

Nerva understood Fronto and deemed him on their side. The general just wanted to do the right thing: act in the interest of Rome and the empire and not just in the narrow interest of the nobility.

They discussed Domitian's pros and cons all evening long. At last Fronto nodded. "I guess you are right, my friends. It is self-defense AND it will benefit the empire."

"We are in agreement then," Nerva said relieved. "Domitian has to die. I am an old man and should not be in the forefront of this, but I see it as my patriotic duty to see to the healing of the State from this man's rapacious behavior. Some of you think, as *Princeps Senatus*, Leader of the Senate, I should be the emperor's natural successor. However, I am not falling head over heels for this. If somebody else volunteers, I will step aside."

Startled, the senators talked all at once. Aulus Priscus was able to make himself heard at last. "Marcus Cocceius, you are our man, and I am saying this though I have never been your political ally. I even remember you as a consummate politician serving many emperors and a man who somehow got along with all of them, even an abomination like Nero. But your diplomatic skills will keep the Senate together and prevent discord in our ranks.

You are the perfect candidate, experienced in all matters of State. You have the seniority, the authority and the competence to get it done. Your ancestry is immaculate. Your great-great-uncle mediated between Mark Anthony and Augustus. Your grandfather was a close friend of the Emperor Tiberius. He and your father were the leading jurists of their day. Your mother's brother was the husband of Julia, daughter of Drusus and Livilla and the granddaughter of Tiberius. The Senate respects you and will be glad to enunciate you Princeps."

Antoninus concurred. "Marcus, you are known for your practiced discretion. You have no baggage; you are not identified with any one political faction, and you are kind and friendly to everyone. I cannot think of any better man!"

Rufus laughed. "We sound like sycophants, but we are not. We mean it. You are the heart and soul of the Senate and you should be the First Man in the empire."

What all of you are not saying is, best of all you are old and have no military clout, allowing us to retain influence yourself... Nerva had no illusions about the motivations of his allies.

Fronto also weighed in. "Let's be realistic. Our friend Nerva here is acceptable to the army brass because he is not related to any of the consular legates and commanders. None of them will be favored over the other."

"How about the Praetorians?" Priscus asked.

"If we get the praefects on our side, everything will fall into place. This is in fact our opportunity: Petronius and Norbanus are nervous. They fear for their lives," Arrius Antoninus stressed.

"You want me to become emperor then?" Nerva asked.

"Yes, Marcus," they shouted. "We do. We offer you the Purple!"

"I must be crazy, but for the good of Rome in this difficult time I accept." He leaned back on his sofa and had a long sip from his chalice. Then Nerva clapped his hands. A servant led a newcomer into the *triclinium*, Vestricius Spurinna, deputy commander-in-chief of the Rhine legions. The senators rolled their eyes. Stern-faced, Spurinna bowed to them and joined Nerva on the host's sofa.

"I wanted to be assured of your allegiance before introducing our guest from the frontier," Nerva explained. "My dear Vestricius, we are glad you are joining us tonight."

"Glad to be here!"

"Spurinna, you know the Senate is upset with Domitian. You told me the Rhine Army is concerned as well because the emperor can't find a long-term solution to our escalating problems on the Danube.

Now, the younger Traianus defeated some Suebi tribes in a skirmish last month. That's excellent, but it will take more time and great military skill to pacify the Danube border as a whole. In other words, the Rhine Army thinks we need a new Princeps. Is that correct, Vestricius?"

"That is the majority opinion among the senior officers in Upper and Lower Germania, yes," Spurinna answered.

"And it is the opinion of the governors in Germania, is it not?" Nerva asked again.

"Yes."

"How about Trajan?"

"I don't know, but he is deemed staunchly pro-Flavian. Remember, he helped Domitian quell Saturninus's rebellion seven years ago. He might not come around, and I would ignore him. By the time he receives the news, it will be too late for him to do anything about it."

Antoninus disagreed. "Ignore him? I think not. What if he resents the plot? He is a distinguished commander. He might come after us, and if the Rhine legions or the Praetorians protect us, we might have a Civil War on our hands. That's an unacceptable risk!"

Nerva thought about it and said, "I concur with Arrius. We need Trajan on our side. At least, we need him to stay out of this. He is a well-liked general and enjoys fanatic loyalty in the Army."

Spurinna raised his eyebrows. "What if he doesn't play along?"

"That's our risk," Nerva replied. "Don't get me wrong. I wouldn't hold up our plans. If we get the opportunity, we will strike, but at least he was in the loop. Look, Trajan is astute. He and his father served the Flavian House for many years, but I don't think he appreciates Domitian's dark character anymore than we do. He will put the interests of the empire ahead of the interests of the Flavian dynasty."

"It is agreed then," Rufus said.

"Yes," Spurinna nodded without a smile. "Indeed."

Nerva closed the deal. "Vestricius, why don't you send a reliable soldier with a letter from the Senate to Trajan that says the following: 'The Senate and the People have lost trust in the Emperor.' He will know what it means."

Antoninus returned to the all-important subject of Petronius Secundus, the praefect. "I talked to Petronius the other day. He told me about accusations against him from disgruntled tribunes in the Guard who want his rank. Petronius is uneasy. I think we can inveigle him. It is a golden opportunity that may never come again."

"Agreed," Rufus shouted. "We need to tell him about the list under Domitian's pillow. That would get him started."

"But nobody knows whether he is in fact on the list," Priscus countered.

"It doesn't matter," Nerva said. "The list's very existence is enough."

"How can we find out who's really on it?" Fronto asked.

Antoninus pensive face broke into a smirk. "Have him ask the Empress. There is no love lost between Domitian and his wife. She might help us. I will talk to her beforehand and ask her to tell Petronius that he is on the list - even if he is not!"

Clever, Arrius, clever.

Fronto squinted. "What if he finds out she lied? What if she doesn't do it?"

"No matter. Once the deed is done, it's done. Besides, I will tell her to destroy the cursed list. Now, if she doesn't help us, there is nothing we can do other than try again."

They nodded. Antoninus would be talking to Domitia; Priscus would be talking to Petronius. Nerva pledged not to engage in any activities himself and as always participate in the emperor's council meetings.

Chapter 23

The *Ludi Romani* were in full swing when Domitia and Antoninus met. The empress and her guest could hear the bawling masses in the imperial suite on the Palatine. Antoninus didn't beat around the bush.

Domitia shuddered when he asked about the ominous list. *The risk he is taking.* She wasn't interested in mischief, but her husband had changed, eclipsed her affection. Domitia couldn't forgive him the seduction of his own niece Flavia Julia, the young daughter of his brother Titus. After Flavia had gotten pregnant, Domitian had ordered an abortion to keep a lid on the affair. The procedure had come too late, killing poor Flavia...

Taking a deep breath, Domitia promised to cooperate. When Arrius was gone she headed straight for the imperial *cubiculum*. It was a good time. Her husband was attending the Games, and only the chambermaids were around. She sent them out and locked herself in. Then she piled through the throng of pillows on the imperial divan. Sure enough, on Domitian's side she found a *parazonium* dagger hidden under the mountain of cushions and coverlets. Her husband evidently didn't feel safe even in his own bedroom. Attached to it was a scroll. She opened it with trembling hands.

It did contain names. Some were erased, some had been added on later. Right now, five names were left standing. Petronius was not one of them. Actually, he had been, but Domitian had scratched him out. The praefect worried for no reason, but his colleague Norbanus was on the list - and so was the Lord Chamberlain! Why him? Domitia put scroll and dagger back in their place and hurried out of the *cubiculum*. What to do?

Days later she arranged for an appointment with Petronius in his house on the Caelian Hill.

"*Salve, Augusta*," the praefect greeted her, kissing her hand. "I am honored."

"I heard you have great views from your house, Petronius."

"Absolutely, Domina, do you want to take a look?"

"I would love to."

They went up the stairs to the open-air second story of his villa. The large patio was covered with manicured box shrubs in huge t*erra sigillata,* fired-clay, planters. The plants were trimmed in the geometric shapes of triangles, circles, squares, stars and crescents. It was orderly and beautiful.

"You have good taste for a soldier."

"Thank you, my Lady. I am trying."

He pointed east. "*Augusta*, do you see the Servian Walls in the distance? And beyond them the plush meadows of our beloved Latium?"

The sun had just set, filling the azure sky with magenta colors. Back-lit stratus clouds hung over the horizon in pink streaks. Domitia enjoyed the peaceful scenery. They lingered for a moment until Petronius suggested walking back down for refreshments, but the empress held him back. "I have to talk to you, Praefect."

"Yes? What is it?"

"I heard you are feeling a bit uneasy..."

Petronius stiffened.

"Well, I have seen the list..."

"The list?"

Domitia nodded. "Yes, THE list."

The commander took a deep breath. "And? Who is on it? Am I on it? Tell me," he shook her arms, then backed off abruptly. "I didn't mean to scare you. Excuse me, Domina."

I can't blame you. So much is at stake. You are but a pawn in an ugly game.

"Petronius, you are on it," she lied.

The Praefect of the Guard winced. He closed his eyes, then opened them again and spoke to her softly. "It is true then. I am finished."

"Not necessarily. There is something you can do, but it takes courage. Oh, Norbanus is on it too - and Pantherius."

The following day she met with Antoninus in a remote corner of the Sallustian Gardens and told him the names on the list. "I made Petronius believe he is a target. That's all I can do for you, Arrius. If your plot succeeds, I will destroy the cursed roll. That's it. All depends on the praefects now. Petronius will impress the seriousness of their situation upon Norbanus and Pantherius, but will they have the guts? Norbanus - I believe so; Pantherius - hard to say. He is not a soldier."

She looked Antoninus hard in the eyes. "It's in the hands of the *fates*. May they have mercy with Rome's eternal soul."

Governor Trajan was in a good mood when Spurinna's dispatch arrived in Carnuntum, capital of Pannonia Province. The last several years had been good for him. He had accomplished what Domitian's other generals never had: victory over the Suebi tribes and a secure Danube border along the key stretch between Aquincum and Singidunum.

Spurinna's letter looked like any other dispatch. Trajan didn't pay any extra attention, added it to his pile. When Callistus reminded him to clear his inbox, he finally opened it.

From: Vestricius Spurinna, Legatus Augusti
pro Praetore in Germania Superior
To: M. Ulpius Traianus, Legatus Augusti
pro Consule in Pannonia

The Senate and the People have lost trust in the Emperor.

Spurinna

It hit him like a hammer. They planned to kill Domitian... Two parties seemed involved: the Senate, named explicitly, and the Rhine Army, involved implicitly through the addressor. But there were no details, nothing. They wanted him to know - and stand down.

Trajan's forehead broke into creases. Why let him know at all - to secure his compliance!

The message had come from the Rhine Army. It stood to reason that Spurinna and the other generals were backing the Senate and proffered protection should he, Trajan, come to Domitian's help. They were saying, 'Stay out of this. We know what we are doing. Don't launch a Civil War.'

Who were the ringleaders? There had been many conspiracies against Domitian over the years. This time, not just the nobility was involved. The plot had the backing of the Rhine Army. What about the Praetorians? They were not mentioned, but the plot could not succeed without them. The Rhine Army was too far away to protect the assassins in Rome. Maybe the conspirators didn't know yet whether they had the Guard's support. And who would commit the deed?

Trajan thought of Domitia Longina. She hated the emperor – for good reason. After the terrible execution of Clemens it had become clear that Domitian was losing his sanity, Flavian or not. Another Nero! By the gods, why did Titus have to die so early? Why did the Flavian House have to end like this?

And what should he do? What would Sura advise, Pompeia?

As awful as it was, he decided not to sit idle while others were deciding Rome's future. Perhaps the Senate and the Rhine Army were doing the right thing, but perhaps not. He wanted to know more about this. And whom had they picked as Domitian's successor?

Trajan tinkled the bell on his desk and called for his second-in-command. He ordered to send out riders and track down Spurinna. They were to ask for a meeting. He sent messengers to both Rome and Spurinna's Rhine headquarters in Moguntiacum. Other messengers were sent to find him on the main roads connecting Rome to the Germanic provinces - if he happened to be in transit.

Trajan's men found the general with a detachment of cavalry near Placentia, handed him Trajan's dispatch and returned to Pannonia with his reply. "The general pledged to change his itinerary and meet with you in Aquileia, Legate," they reported.

Trajan dropped everything and left for Aquileia. The two generals met at the house of one of the two *duumvirs*, the city's top magistrates. After exchanging niceties with him, the official retreated discreetly. A Nubian porter the size of a cupboard closed the massive oak doors of the villa's *triclinium* behind him.

Trajan looked at his colleague with pinched eyes. "Vestricius, what is going on?"

Glowering, Spurinna avoided Trajan's gaze. "Trouble is brewing in Rome. Domitian is unpopular. His latest actions are borderline to insanity. The senators fear for their lives. They want change. It is-"

"What do you mean by change?" Trajan interrupted him. He knew full well what Spurinna meant, but he wanted the other man to say the word.

"Hm, change... Well, I mean, change means that Domitian has to go."

"And how exactly do they want to accomplish that?" Trajan asked again, pushing the hot potato into Spurinna's face, but the other officer didn't go for it.

Trajan raised his voice. "How, Vestricius?"

"You know exactly how."

Getting impatient Trajan decided to force Spurinna's hand. "Fine. Here is what I assume is going on. The Senate has a conspiracy under way to assassinate the Emperor. I don't know how, of course, but you and the senators seem to be confident enough. Someone in the palace must be helping you, likely Domitia and some other officials, maybe even some Praetorians. Is that right, Spurinna?"

The general looked at the ceiling.

"I conclude from your silence that I am right."

"And if that were so?" Spurinna snapped.

"If that were so..." Trajan repeated Spurinna's words stretching them out. "It's treason."

Spurinna went on the offensive. "Are you telling me you condone Domitian's terror regime? Are you blind in your loyalty just because he is a Flavian emperor?"

"No, I am not. I am a man of honor and justice. You know that."

"Then you should be happy that someone is taking action, shouldn't you?"

Both men fell silent. A myriad of thoughts was racing through Trajan's mind. Much was at stake. He and Spurinna were representing two Roman armies. Trajan was senior in rank, but that wouldn't matter if they disagreed on this issue.

"What we meant to say in our message, Trajan, is that we, the senior officers of the Rhine Army, agree with the senators' decision and want you to be in the loop on this. Cut us some slack, would you? We took an immense risk after all!" Spurinna appealed to his colleague.

"Ah," Trajan shouted. "We... You are saying 'we'. Your staff is behind you?"

"Yes, they are, every one of them."

The men fell silent again.

"I am not surprised, and it sounds as if you are telling me to stay out of this. Is that so?"

"Yes. We don't want a fight with you or any other governor. All we are saying is that we approve of the plan and will protect the future emperor."

"That means you have picked someone already?" Trajan asked.

Spurinna nodded.

"Whom?"

Spurinna didn't answer.

"Is it a senator?"

"Before I answer your question – if I do answer it at all, I would like to know this: Did you call this meeting to tell me you want the Purple for yourself? I can't read you, Trajan. Who's side are you on?"

That's what they were afraid of. Not only that I would disagree, but that I might make a move of my own.

"I have no such intentions. My hands are busy on the border. The situation is in abeyance, but I enjoy commanding the Danube legions. That's where the action is. I am preparing an offensive and have no time for politics.

Vestricius, I have no sympathy for Domitian. You don't want to know what I have seen him do. But I am concerned for the sake of the empire and want to make sure you are doing the right thing."

Spurinna nodded. "Sounds reasonable. I am relieved to hear that. The change in Rome will not make your assignment any harder. On the contrary, we want you to succeed. We respect you. One of the reasons we don't like Domitian is that he wasn't successful on the Danube, and we worry he does not give you the resources to win out of jealousy. If you were successful where he was not, he would look bad."

"I see. You forged an alliance with the Senate out of convenience. They have their reasons; you have yours, but the bottom line is that Domitian has to go." Trajan paused. "Who is going to do the deed?"

"It's better if you don't know. It doesn't matter. The men are only pawns."

Trajan bobbed his head back and forth. "Fine. One last thing: Who was chosen to replace Domitian?"

Spurinna swallowed hard. "Nerva. We picked Nerva."

Trajan whistled. "A cunning choice. He is a resourceful and well-respected man. Thanks for trusting me, Spurinna. I do appreciate it."

He rose from his sofa and crossed to Spurinna's couch to shake his hand. "You have nothing to fear, Vestricius. Tell the commanders on the Rhine I will not interfere. Let's all hope the Senate gets it done and that it will be over soon. There is only one issue. Nerva is old and not a military man. The Praetorians will not respect him. He will be an interim emperor."

"True enough, but for now he is the best we've got. He will do fine. One thing after the other, Trajan."

Trajan returned to Carnuntum; Spurinna resumed his trip back to Germania. It was decided.

Chapter 24

Petronius didn't waste time. Soon after his conversation with the empress he met with Norbanus and Pantherius in the Praetorian Camp on Viminal Hill. Domitian was overseeing competitions he called the 'Olympic Games' which he had made part of the *Ludi Romani*. They were held in a separate stadium he had erected for this purpose on the Mars Field, dedicated to Olympic events like running, throwing, jumping, wrestling and others. Petronius was scheduled to join him, but he had sent a messenger to the palace telling the emperor he wasn't feeling well and assigned one of his senior tribunes to command Domitian's security detail.

When Norbanus arrived Pantherius was already in Petronius's office. "Hoh, hoh, hoh," Norbanus sneered. "Are we having a crisis today?"

"Yes, Petronius," Pantherius chimed in. "Why have you called us?"

Petronius Secundus scowled. "We are having a crisis indeed. There is something you need to know."

He asked them to sit down and rose to lock the door. Then he returned to his desk.

"You are scaring us, Petronius. What are you doing?" Pantherius frowned. "I don't like this. Why are you locking us in? What is going on?"

"Don't worry. It's for your own safety," Petronius calmed him down. "You both know about Domitian's alleged list, don't you?"

They nodded.

"Well, you are both on it!"

"Impossible!" Norbanus shrieked.

"Psssst," Petronius hushed.

Sullen, Pantherius leaned back in his chair staring out of the window.

Petronius continued. "I don't know how you've made the cut, be assured. I am on it too..."

"How do you know all this?" Norbanus asked.

"Domitia..."

"Domitia!" Pantherius bellowed. "The implications!

If she told you, she must disagree with her husband. That's good news, but the Praetorians will not hesitate to execute anybody on his orders, including their own commanders. There is only one way out."

"What do you propose?"

Norbanus heaved a big sigh. "We need to do something. Let's kill the monster before it kills us."

"Agreed," Petronius said. "And the key to success is you, Pantherius. You are the Lord Chamberlain. The only place where Domitian is not heavily guarded is the imperial suite, a place under your supervision."

Pantherius shifted.

"We need your help, Pantherius," Petronius urged him again. "You control access to the suite. We can't act in the open. Our soldiers would refuse. There are perhaps several close friends we could convince, but even this would give us only limited countenance. It needs to be over fast. Else there'd be fighting among the Guard, and I assure you, that would be a very bad thing. We'd lose."

Norbanus nodded in agreement.

"So, Pantherius, we need a plan and we need it soon."

"You are right, Praefects," he whimpered. "I hold the key. We need to recruit assassins and the empress's help. You two need to keep my back free. The shift on duty near the imperial suite needs to be on our side when we strike. See what I mean? I can hopefully take care of the rest."

"And do we have a plan for a successor? Don't we need to involve the Senate?" Pantherius asked.

"This has been taken care of," Petronius said. "Senator Priscus approached me the other day. They know about the accursed list. He pledged the Senate would welcome our move and has a successor ready."

The Ludi Romani were approaching their conclusion on the Ides of September. In a palace hallway, Pantherius stuck a note into Domitia's *palla* fold as they passed each other. They exchanged a quick glance, and Pantherius was gone. Heart racing, she strode back to her dressing room and read the message:

I will not die without a fight. See me in my office. P

The empress heaved a sigh of relief. The Lord Chamberlain was braver than expected. Life in Domitian's palace was tough enough, and many disgruntled officials failed trying to make a difference. Domitia was hopeful it would be different this time around. Never before had an alliance against the emperor included Praetorians, army officers, senators and palace staff.

Yesterday she had learned why Pantherius was on Domitian's list. Talking with him about this year's lavish Games Domitian had remarked, "Aren't they great? But Pantherius outsmarted himself. He plundered the temples in Italy including those of Minerva. Several priests complained to me – despite the Lord Chamberlain's bribes. I will never forgive him that. He dishonored the Roman contract with the gods!"

When she told the Lord Chamberlain in his office, he shrugged. "It was a calculated risk, and I should have known better. Too late. We need to look forward now and fight."

"Agreed. Domitian is still occupied with the Ludi Romani, but you and the praefects are in the greatest danger. My husband is seeking out successors as we speak."

Pantherius glowered. "I don't doubt it. And I am looking for assassins to kill him."

Could they beat him to it? To keep up the façade she even put up with Domitian's 'bed-wrestling'. Her mind somehow dissociated itself from the body and his insolent sex. *When will it be over? When?*

"Dearest Domitia, I have two people we can work with, both on my staff. You know them: Stephanus and Carnifex. They will help me in this desperate hour."

Domitia was startled. "What are you saying? No Praetorians? No soldiers? I would think you want someone who can wield a sword!"

"Too dangerous." Pantherius shook his head. "The praefects didn't agree. They barely have enough trusted men to take over the night shift when we strike. And neither wants to do the deed himself. It wasn't easy to convince them of the... ah, 'operation'."

It didn't sound right. Another bungle? "What is their motivation, Pantherius? Wait, Stephanus is Domitilla's freedman and holds a grudge against my husband for exiling her. I can see that. But Carnifex?"

"Carnifex is desperate because he is, correctly as I might add, accused of stealing in the palace. He is a moron, but I was able to direct his desire to escape punishment to our advantage. You know what I mean?"

She lowered and raised her head.

"There is something else," Pantherius continued. "We need your help preparing for this."

A chill went down her spine. "What for?"

"You are right, Majesty, not having soldiers for the deed is an issue. Therefore, we need you to remove Domitian's sword from its scabbard before the emperor goes to bed so he will be incapable of defending himself."

Oh no! Another risky intrusion in the bedroom while Domitian was gone.

But Pantherius was right. "I think I can manage that. What date have you picked? I will have to do it before we go to bed. Also, Domitian checks on his sword before falling asleep. The assassins need to follow us into the chamber. Do you understand that?"

"Absolutely."

"I have teased him about the sword and tried to make him feel ridiculous. Hopefully, it will help make him feel silly. He must not suspect anything."

"Excellent, we are all set then. I will give you the details very soon. We will strike right after the Ludi."

They ended up picking the last day of the Games, expected to be wild and crazy and terminating with a big public feast. The conspirators betted on

Domitian being inebriated and easy prey after the many hours of festivities, gluttony and crapulence.

Petronius broke the news to the empress during a joint stroll in the vast Horti Sallustiani. "Our men will take over tomorrow's night shift outside your suite. It is dicey because nobody else in the Guard knows anything, including the senior officers. By chance, some tribune might come and visit your husband. Domitian always has an ear for his men and would likely let him in, but we will have to take that chance, Domina. In any case, Norbanus and I will be close by and help the assassins finish the job before Domitian can get help from the Guard.

We have only one opportunity. If we fail, our fate is sealed, but we do have an escape plan. A skiff will be ready on the Tiber pier nearest the Velabrum to whisk us out of the city. But it's a long shot. Hope for the best, my Lady!"

Domitia thanked the praefect with tears in her eyes.

Chapter 25

Petronius spent the day with his master in the imperial lodge of the Circus, commanding the unwary daytime shift. Antoninus, Fronto, Priscus and Rufus were also in the Lodge. Old Nerva had excused himself with indigestion, nothing unusual for an elderly frail man. The plotters behaved as usual - polished and dignified.

Petronius's thoughts were with the chamberlain's assassins all day long. How were they doing? Did everything go as planned?

He scanned the ranks of the Circus, which was brimming with howling spectators of both genders and all ages. The people intently followed the furious conclusion of the Ludi Romani: the *quadriga*-chariot race.

Only two teams were left, the Greens and the Whites. Their two-wheeled vehicles, hurled forward by four Arabic-bred stallions each, thundered by the imperial box neck-and-neck, whirling up thick clouds of dust behind them as if Jupiter himself was thrusting them forward with lightning bolts. The charioteers whipped the sweat-drenched horses like furies, unrelenting and merciless, their faces begrimed with sweat and sand, eyes bulging out. One last bend - another half lap to go. They were still neck-and-neck...

Now the driver of the Whites started lashing his competitor with the horse whip. His competitor squirmed to escape the assault and desperately hung on to his bridles. Blood gushed out where the lashes hit his shoulder. But the aggressor couldn't crack the whip on his own horses while he was attacking the other driver. This lessened the urge on his steeds. It made the difference between victory and defeat. The Greens' chariot outran him by half a foot.

Petronius leapt from his feet, clapping for the winner. The winning charioteer gently brought his foaming and panting horses to a stop with a triumphant smile on his face. The loser tossed his lash and jumped off his chariot. Jostling his squires, he bunked out of the arena.

Domitian rose too, applauding the Green Team's victory to the frenetic hails of the masses. After awarding them the sacred palm trophy he left for the Jupiter Temple with Petronius and the Praetorian detail to attend the State Dinner on the Capitol.

Falernian red wine was being poured in abundance there. Domitian joined the feasting and carousing. "It was I after all who rebuilt this Temple," he boasted. "I was nearly killed inside the previous one when my uncle Sabinus defended us against Vitellius's men in the Civil War. He gave his life so we could live, but the Temple burnt down. Perhaps Jupiter wanted it that way because today his new house is even more beautiful, ornate and awe-inspiring." He raised his alabaster chalice and toasted with the dignitaries around him.

Once in a while Petronius and Domitia exchanged a quick apprehensive glance, but they were hiding their anxiety well. Disaster struck when Domitia couldn't leave the table. No matter the excuses she had, Domitian didn't let her go anywhere else than the latrines.

Petronius responded lightning fast, scribbling a sealed message for Pantherius:

> *Lord Chamberlain, be ready for the imperial*
> *couple. They will be back together.*
>
> *Petronius*

The courier wasn't supposed to read the note, but even if he did, it wouldn't tell him anything. Petronius hoped that Pantherius would read between the lines and realize that Domitia could not take care of the dagger because she was stuck at the banquet. He would have to do it himself.

Keeping his cool, the praefect didn't order the Praetorian messenger to rush his message to the palace. There was still time; a regular delivery should do. Now everything depended on Pantherius.

At the end of the feast, Domitian sent for his litter. Petronius and his men escorted the imperial couple back to the Palatine. Domitia was ardently hoping that Lord Chamberlain Pantherius had removed the dagger under Domitian's head pillow, but she had no way of knowing. Arriving at the palace, Petronius supervised the change of the Guard from day shift to night shift. His eight night guards took up their stations in the hallways and at the entrance doors to the imperial suite. Then Petronius retreated with one last subtle nod to the empress.

In the suite Domitian and Domitia took a quick bath. Afterwards slaves dried and dressed them in silky night robes, and they strode into their ornate *cubiculum*. The maids and chamberlains in the suite withdrew, including Carnifex. Domitia stared at him, but he didn't give her any acknowledgement one way or another as he left the room. The moment had arrived – they were alone...

The empress's hands trembled when she pulled back the bed linen. *Would the dagger be gone?*

Outside, the guards' rustling ceased. The friendly night shift should now be in place, but where were the assassins? Domitia's heart pounded faster and faster. Her husband stood on the other side of the bed and was about to take down his pile of fancy tasseled head pillows. *Where were the assassins?*

She decided to buy more time by flouting her husband. "Checking on your dagger again? What do you expect? That it might disappear into thin air? That I might attack you? Ha, ha, ha..."

Domitian slurred, "You never know. I don't have it because I fear you, Dearest, but because the world is a dangerous place and-"

Suddenly, the doors were thrust open. Pantherius, Carnifex and Stephanus scuttled into the room, closing the doors behind them. Domitian barked at them annoyed, "What are you doing here?"

The assassins pulled their knives and lunged forward. Domitia jumped off the bed while Domitian did the opposite, cursing. He tried to grab his dagger from the mound of pillows but only found an empty scabbard. He howled, picked it up anyway and slammed it at the closest attacker, Carnifex. Hit in the stomach, the man bent forward and went down with a gasp, losing his knife. But now Pantherius and Stephanus were on Domitian, stabbing him and dealing him blow after blow. They mostly missed, however, or got entangled in his voluminous night robe.

"This is for your paranoia," Pantherius shrieked, trying to run his dagger into Domitian's rib cage. At the same time, Stephanus cleaved the emperor's right arm. Blood was gushing out and Domitian screamed, "Guards! Guards! I am under attack! Guards!"

He twisted around, and Pantherius hit his shoulder instead of the chest. The Lord Chamberlain's face was turning red from the strain and stress of the fight. He was breathing hard.

Domitian howled again. More blood was gushing from his wounds now, but he managed to get all three of them entangled in his wide robe. Finally, Stephanus found an opening and rammed his weapon into Domitian's chest. The emperor gargled and gagged. Blood oozed from his mouth in spurts, and he fell to the cold marble floor.

Now the doors opened again, and other chamberlains rushed into the room trying to help their Overlord. One of the newcomers picked up Carnifex's dagger on the floor and ran it into the surprised Stephanus. At last, the guardsmen who had followed the servants into the chamber realized that the new arrivals were not in on the plot and instead were trying to save the emperor. They intervened and arrested the spoilers and dragged them out of the room after a quick worried look at the mumbling emperor's twitching body.

At this moment the praefects arrived and ordered the suite to be sealed. The guards took up their stations again and locked the imperial bedroom doors from the outside.

Petronius first checked on Domitia. She was shaken but unharmed. He gave her a warm hug. "It's over, Domina. The tyrant is dying."

Domitia pointed at the Lord Chamberlain. Drooping over Domitian's body, Pantherius was staring at Domitian's dead eyes.

Norbanus was checking on Stephanus. He shook his head - Stephanus was dead. Petronius withdrew from Domitia and hissed at the assassins. "Pantherius, Carnifex, get out! Stick to the plan. Meet with Nerva and let him know we succeeded. Then hide and don't come back until we tell you it's safe."

Outside, Domitia could hear a melee between the guards and Praetorian officers who demanded access to the suite. Armor was pushing against armor.

While the assassins sneaked out through the back door, the praefects examined the emperor's body to make sure he was dead. Despite the rustle, the yelling and the shoving in hallway the praefects kept hovering over Domitian's corpse - their last moment with the tyrant.

"What did he say all the time, Norbanus? 'Evil life has but one purpose - to die'?" Petronius muttered.

Norbanus covered the emperor's face with his blood soaked night robe. "So true, Domitian. Indeed..."

The commanders couldn't ignore the ruffle outside any longer. The argument had escalated to a brawl that stopped at once when they opened the doors.

"The Chamberlain Stephanus murdered the Emperor," Petronius told the stunned officers in a cheerless voice. "Domitian is dead. Our Caesar is dead."

Norbanus stood beside him, eyes downcast. Domitia's hands covered her face; she sobbed. The tribunes shot sharp glances at all three of them and scurried into the room.

In the Subura, Rome's crowded plebeian quarters, Pantherius and Carnifex arrived at their secret meeting place with Nerva.

"By the gods, this has been the longest day in my life. You are heroes!" Nerva shouted relieved when he heard the news. "Now, leave the city and go to your safe house." Then he sent messengers to the other conspirators and took his litter back to his villa to meet with them. The ecstatic plotters arrived in no time and rehearsed their plan of action for Nerva's acclamation in the Curia the following day.

Everything went smoothly. The Senate did proclaim Nerva Emperor; first inside the Senate building, then in public in front of the stunned Forum crowd. The senators condemned Domitian's memory, had his statues and images destroyed everywhere in the city, his name erased from public inscriptions, his laws nullified and all records of his reign revoked. Nerva announced the return of the Law and vowed that no tyrant would ever again put a senator to death.

Hearing about the dramatic events in Rome, Trajan felt rather indifferent. Nerva was a good choice, and Trajan liked the fact that the new ruler was on friendly terms with the empire's governors and generals. He was in fact the first emperor ever to be appointed by the Senate - a legal government certainly. Hopefully, he and Rome's august body would be up to the challenge. Everything spoke for him, but one thing he was not: a soldier.

Chapter 26

Petronius and an escort of newly appointed officers crossed the Forum on their way to confer with Nerva in the Domus Tiberiana. It was supposed to be his last meeting as praefect.

The veteran soldier was glad to see that life in Rome had returned to normality. The people in the Forum went about their business, not paying much attention to him and his men. The common folks had been apathetic to the news of Domitian's assassination anyway - as opposed to the jubilant senators.

Where he came from, however, in the Praetorian barracks on the other side of town, it was not so. Many soldiers were still upset, asking themselves how they had failed their emperor. Some of the officers accused both Petronius and Norbanus of complicity with the unidentified backers of the assassins. Others blamed Nerva because the Senate had appointed him so quickly, and all of them were furious at the guards of the night shift.

Petronius sighed. They wanted answers he could not possibly give them. He and Norbanus had been trying hard to quell the discontent. They had transferred the men of the night shift to the legions of Britannia and compensated them munificently for their sacrifice and support.

The praefects had also persuaded Nerva to grant each Praetorian soldier a sumptuous accession bonus. It had not been easy with the frugal Nerva, but realizing its importance the new emperor had agreed. Afterwards he had even gone beyond this measure and - to the praefects' horror - recalled the former Praefect Casperius Aelianus whom the Guard deemed as solidly pro-Domitian.

So this was it: one last visit with the Caesar, a discussion concerning the details of his retirement, civil duties maybe somewhere else in the palace. Then he would be dismissed and Casperius would take over. Petronius believed the appointment of Domitian's old praefect was a huge mistake, but Nerva had insisted that Casperius's appointment would get the fomenting Praetorians off his back. In a sordid way, Petronius was blithe about it; this wasn't his problem anymore.

After rearranging the military leadership in Rome, Nerva plunged himself into massive legislative efforts to win over the people and assure the senators that his new government was different – that it was humane, balanced, thoughtful and law-abiding.

Today was his big day. He had called the Senate into session to vote on his legislative package. All the leading men were present: Antoninus, Frontinus, Rufus, Tacitus and Priscus, and of course the presiding consuls.

The Senate building, the Curia, was packed with all six hundred members of the senatorial class. It was a rectangular building at the foothill of the Capitoline Hill with tall ceilings to keep the interior shielded from the summer heat. There were three floor levels on either side of the walls where the senators put down their stools to sit on. Backbenchers occupied the top level; senior senators sat up front. The presiding consuls and their staff occupied an elevated dais along the back wall of the lofty chamber, facing the mighty entrance doors on the other side of the building. They sat on their hallowed backless chairs, the *sellae curules*.

The senior consul opened the session with a short introduction and then allowed the *Princeps Senatus*, the Leader of the Senate, to speak first. That man was Nerva, now also emperor. When he rose to address the audience, the crowd fell so silent one could have heard a needle drop on the beautiful colored marble floor.

"*Patres Conscripti*," Nerva said, reverently bowing to the assembled noblemen on either side of the aisle. "Wise men of Rome and the empire, it is an honor for me to stand before you today as your *Princeps*."

He paused and raised his arms. Then he lowered them and touched his chest with both hands. "However, nothing inside me has changed. I still feel like a senator and I am still one of you!"

Excited, some senators stood up and hooted and clapped for Nerva. "Nerva *Imperator*! Nerva *Imperator*!"

The old man smiled wistfully. "We all have suffered terribly during Domitian's years of suppression, terror, cruelty and violence. This is now over. As long as I am emperor, no one and certainly no senator will ever be put to death without due process. This I swear, by *Jupiter Optimus Maximus* and the whole Capitoline Trinity!"

The crowd rose and cheered loudly.

"My reign will inaugurate a new era of moderation and fairness – and the return of the Law.

Patres, we are the people that rules the world. We need to show the world we are worth it. We want them to admire us. If they admire us, they will follow us. If they follow us, this empire will live in peace and be the pinnacle of human civilization forever more.

Look, I did not want to become *Princeps*. I am but a humble servant of my country. The *fates* put this weight on my shoulders, and I accept it solely because it is my duty to serve - to serve you and all the People of Rome.

The State needs healing. Our soldiers need renewed resolve to keep the peace on our borders. The people need freedom to pursue their lives unencumbered by tyranny.

I vow today that I will promote these needs, that I will heal the State, energize the military and increase the standard of living of every citizen in the empire!"

Nerva swept his gaze around the audience while they applauded him. There was Antoninus, flashing a smile of contentment. His glance moved on to Priscus and the others, and he remembered the many days and nights they had spent in fear, wondering whether they had a future. It had been worth it. Here and now, he could see that they were excited about a new beginning. Nerva was proud again to be a Roman.

He resumed his speech. "*Patres Conscripti*, let me now talk about the measures I propose today. They are carefully aimed at achieving what I just said and were drafted with your help. I hope they will find the whole body's approval, and I am looking forward to implementing them.

First, I am setting the customary imperial accession gift at seventy-five dinars per citizen. It will be commemorated on new coins. This measure will reassure the public that my new government has their interests and welfare foremost in mind.

Second, let us reduce the financial burden of the People of Rome and in Italia. I move to pass a new *lex agraria* that allows lots of land to be parceled out to poor citizens, administered by a senatorial commission that will buy the land and distribute. This is a powerful incentive for citizens to leave Rome and help alleviate the city's burdensome overpopulation. The allotted land will be used to found new municipalities all over Italia.

I also move to exempt our citizens from the expenses they incur when providing services for the *Cursus Publicus*, including the imperial staff and the military. They will instead pay a fair market price. Furthermore, I move to offer financial assistance to cities in need throughout the empire.

Third, let us reorganize our aqueducts and fix the related water supply issues. I suggest new granaries and a more efficient administration of the public grain supply. We need them. We shall have them. Every Roman citizen has an unalienable right to eat at affordable prices!

Let us also address the flood problems along the Tiber and repair the last inundation's damages. These floods are a disgrace.

You may ask, 'Marcus Cocceius, how can we afford all that?' Here is my answer:

First, I will sell significant amounts of my property, personal and imperial.

Second, I will donate the gold and silver content of Domitian's destroyed statues to the *fiscus*.

Third, I will set up a commission to systematically investigate ways to improve tax collection and eradicate wasteful public expenditure.

Patres, it can be done. It shall be done!

131

Finally, on the lighter side, I will re-allow pantomimes in Rome."

The senators chuckled at that. The insecure Domitian had banished the comedians because, in the best Roman tradition, they had made fun of him. Nerva beamed. Clearly, a more light-hearted government was replacing the old one. Then he rattled down more measures and ended by saying, "*Patres Conscripti*, I hope you like what you have heard today. Let us do our duties, let us revel in public service and restore the confidence in our government so that Rome once again becomes the shining beacon of the whole world."

The senators jumped from their stools and applauded him enthusiastically. The measures passed. Nerva's government had a mandate. Not all was golden though. Many noble families had suffered from Domitian's tyranny and lusted for revenge. Some did so by demanding compensation; others were not so moderate. A good number of Domitian's followers were found dead under mysterious circumstances.

Others yet tried to exact revenge by prosecuting Domitian's supporters in the Curia. The Senate was soon riveted by accusations and counter-accusations. But by vetoing individual prosecutions and forcing the Senate to take up recriminations as a whole, Nerva was able to tamp down on the revenge-seekers.

Chapter 27

At the Domus Traiana on the Aventine Hill Trajan's grandniece Sabina strode under the colonnaded peristyle of the house when through the open door of his bedroom she saw her great-grandfather's body lying on the floor. Terrified, she dropped the amphora she was carrying and screamed at the top of her lungs. Terracotta shards were flying in all directions.

Sabina's throat tightened - Trajan's father looked like he was dead. Shaking, she walked closer to his body. Before she could enter the room, Harpenna scurried around the corner with furrowed brows. She wanted to ask Sabina what was going on, but her eyes followed Sabina's petrified gaze to Traianus's lifeless body on the bedroom floor. The faithful slave arched her eyes and pressed her hands on her mouth. She squeezed past Matidia's daughter and hurried into the *cubiculum*. Harpenna kneeled at the *pater familias*'s body to check his pulse. Then she tried to turn him over because he was lying on his stomach, but didn't have the strength to do so. Sabina finally overcame her paralysis and helped her. Together, they carefully turned him on his back.

"He is still breathing," Harpenna cried.

The burden of gloom relented on Sabina's shoulders. "He must have fallen off his bed," she suggested.

"In the middle of the day?" Harpenna questioned. "I think he was out and about and collapsed. In any case, he needs immediate medical attention. Where is everybody?"

They didn't have to wait. The house steward and several slaves were rushing into the room. He grasped the situation right away and bellowed his orders, "Drusus, run to the doctor, quick! Everybody else, help me put our Master back on his bed."

While they picked up Traianus's body, old Marcia, Trajan's sister Marciana and Sabina's mother Matidia scuttled into the *cubiculum*, followed by Trajan's wife Pompeia. Grim-faced, the whole extended family in the Domus Traiana huddled around the bed. The ladies wailed; only Marcia kept her calm. Harpenna ran off and came back with a wet cloth to cool Traianus's pale face. A spot on his left forehead was swollen purple, presumably from falling down. She put pressure on it. Marcia held her husband's hand, settling nearest him on the bed sheet. The others stood around the bed, staring at the *pater familias*.

"He must have lost consciousness before hitting the floor," Pompeia said. "Just look at his swollen head. He will have a concussion."

Sabina nodded. *What would happen now? Would Grandfather wake up? Would the medicus be able to save him?*

On the same day, Antoninus hosted an opulent banquet at his villa. Many senators and knights were invited. So were officers of Guard and Army and their wives, including Pompeia. She hadn't wanted to go because of the uncertainty around her father-in-law's health, but the family had convinced her there was no point of staying home. She couldn't help anyway.

Hundreds of illustrious guests in togas and *pallas* were mingling in Antoninus's vast mansion. She ambled from table to table, picking bits and pieces of the scrumptious food. Her favorites were the boar with sautéed mushrooms in peach sauce, mullet served with a potpourri of dates, plums, beans and sprouts - and of course the prized oysters Antoninus farmed in the bay of Neapolis. They were so popular the house slaves couldn't remove the baskets with the piles of emptied shells fast enough. They toppled, fell on the floor and were crunched by the guests' sandals until the host sent more help from the kitchen.

Plotina found the mood cheerful overall, but something was not quite right. Maybe she was imagining it, but the guests still seemed anxious about the politics in Rome. The recent tumults in the Senate resurfaced every now and again in the revelers' many conversations.

"I am telling you, Rufus," Antoninus said to his fragile old friend who shared the host's sofa with him. "Nerva is too mild with the bunch. He should clamp down harder. It will come back to haunt him, I am telling you."

"I don't know, Arrius. I believe in restraint, I really do. We have seen enough terror," Rufus cautioned him.

"Right, Rufus, right. But can't you see? That's what did Julius Caesar in. His murderers were hardcore Republicans he had pardoned after the Civil War."

Pompeia sat down on an empty guest chair beside their sofa. "*Salvete*, illustrious senators. May I join you?"

"Good evening, Pompeia. Of course, please join us," Arrius welcomed her. "How wonderful you look tonight. Look at those locks, Rufus. A piece of art, drop-dead gorgeous."

Plotina was wearing her hair in Rome's latest fashion, a monumental construction of curls towering over her forehead, produced by metal tongs that were heated on a brazier before being applied on the wet hair. In the back, it was gathered into large swirling buns over her nape.

"Thank you, Senator." Plotina blushed at the compliment. She pointed at her curls as if they were some strange object. "If you knew how long my *ornatrix* had to work on this terrible array of pins, invisible nets and hairpieces to hold everything together, you wouldn't be so enthusiastic. Life is too short for such waste, but then again, what's the price of beauty?"

She giggled and self-consciously fondled the mother-of-pearl collets and emerald prisms of her necklace.

"Exactly," Antoninus concurred. "Your beauty is priceless for sure. How is the wife of Rome's most famous general doing?"

"I am quite well, but I am afraid my husband's father is not. We found him lying on the floor in his bedroom today. He looked dead, but thank Juno he was still breathing. We'll see what the doctors are going to say, but it's not good. Hopefully, it's not a coma..." Pompeia shuddered.

"I am sorry to hear that. Old Traianus is a good friend and a hero of the people. He managed his provinces well, not to speak of his military accomplishments as Commander of the Tenth in the Jewish War. I hope he will get better soon, Pompeia.

And how is your husband? Have you heard from him?"

"I miss him. He is so far away and always puts himself in danger."

"Yes, he does. But see, that's the secret of a successful general. I heard he even tramps in front of his column on foot like a ranker, foregoing horse or carriage. Remarkable."

"I guess it's a matter of perspective, but as his wife I don't have to like it."

"I understand," Antoninus acknowledged softly. "On a different note, what does Trajan think about our new government?"

"Trajan is glad things are changing in Rome," she answered. "He is happy that Domitian's terror has stopped. My husband, you know, appreciates civilized behavior above everything else."

The Senator Pliny joined them. "It is alarming, my friends, how much trouble we have had lately with revengists and would-be emperors. I am sickened. Everybody should be delighted that we are rid of tyranny. But no, instead there are these, hmm, shall I say, troublemakers! The Senate as a whole needs to stand together against its own black sheep and support Nerva."

"Absolutely, my dear Pliny," Antoninus agreed. "Don't you worry. At least I am on it, and I know you are." He chuckled. Then he scrambled from his sofa. "I shall mingle with my guests now. My Lady, Lords, I will see you later."

Arrius walked off nodding at them. Over in the villa's atrium, Plotina saw him jovially greet Casperius and other officers of the Praetorian Guard. They stood in a dark corner with sullen faces, sipping from their goblets.

Pompeia didn't like what she saw. The officers seemed unfriendly toward their host, oozing thinly veiled contempt. Arrius tried to cheer them up, but she could tell he did not succeed. After a short while he walked on. Before she had a chance to rejoin the conversation between Rufus and Pliny, a group of scantily clad dancing girls scampered into the peristyle, drawing everybody's attention. Their well-built bronze shimmering bodies moved ecstatically to the music of lyres, flutes and drums. A crowd formed around them instantly and clapped their hands to cheer them on. Some men shouted appreciating comments at host Antoninus.

Pompeia used the distraction to move on herself and ambled to the Senator Tacitus. "Publius Cornelius, do you like the show?"

"I do indeed," Tacitus replied without taking his eyes off the girls.

"Glad to hear. Your friend Pliny thinks we need to worry about Nerva's safety. Do you agree?"

Tacitus didn't answer. Then, with a darting glance at Plotina's curious face he said, "Maybe. Time will tell, Pompeia Plotina. I believe we do have a problem. Nerva is old and needs a successor. Nobody knows who this will be or how we will determine that. By senatorial election? I vote for that. Constitutionally, the Senate needs to approve the next emperor anyway. Or perhaps Nerva should adopt a capable man himself? There is no precedent because we don't have a dynastic system, and people are fed up with dynasties right now. Too many failures. And maybe, maybe we'll go back to the days of the Republic and abandon the Monarchy altogether, an intriguing thought... One thing is guaranteed, the uncertainty around Nerva's succession is a reason for the current unrest in the Senate."

Tacitus's eyes were still fixed on the dancers. Pompeia was impressed how well he was able to focus his thoughts on such a tricky matter in the midst of all the noise, music, hoopla and clapping around them. She wondered whether Tacitus was a hardcore Republican, possibly another 'troublemaker', as Pliny called them.

Finally, Tacitus pulled his head away from the spectacle and looked Pompeia in the eyes. She held his gaze and said, "Bold thinking, Publius. Does Nerva's Council discuss this matter?"

"Not at all. The Council is busy advising the emperor on governing matters. We are very busy and have not had an opportunity to talk about the succession issue, but we should. Everybody in the Council is working hard. Unfortunately, as the recent events have shown, there are others that are discontent, trying to outmaneuver us."

Tacitus paused and eased up to her, dropping his voice. "Pompeia, so far we have held up well, but Nerva's position is delicate. I am not even convinced the Praetorian Guard is behind him. Did you see Casperius today? He should be happy, but he is gruff and grumpy. And when I talk to officers of the Guard, they don't seem to care much about the new government. They are still coveting Domitian, asking themselves who was behind his assassination. I really wonder about their loyalty, Pompeia." He wasn't done yet. "The soldiers, who were involved in the plot are no longer in the Guard. Nerva had to dismiss or transfer them for their own sake. Ironically, we have a good emperor now, but he needs to fear for his life because the soldiers that are supposed to protect him adore his atrocious predecessor..."

Pompeia stiffened. *Tacitus fears the Guard.*

She was relieved to see her friend Attianus in the crowd. "Publius, Publius! Come over here. May I introduce you to the Senator Cornelius Tacitus? He is a book worm and one of Nerva's advisors. Maybe he will be appointed suffect consul this year."

The men shook hands and Attianus said, "Nice meeting you, Senator. How is Nerva doing? It has been a rough couple of weeks for him."

"Oh, he is doing well," Tacitus assured him. "After the dark years it's a pleasure for him to heed the call of liberty. You know, consensual government is always a messy business. If I may ask, how do you know each other?"

"Well," Pompeia replied. "Publius Acilius Attianus is a Roman knight and a native from Italica like my husband. He runs several shipping businesses. Attianus, weren't you just wheeling and dealing over there with some Spanish olive merchants?"

Attianus grinned. "Ever the attentive Pompeia! I wouldn't call it 'wheeling and dealing', but I certainly had productive talks with them. No wonder, with the who's who of the Roman elite assembled in this house tonight."

Tacitus excused himself and joined the crowd. After he was gone, Pompeia asked Attianus, "How is our ward Hadrian doing in the Army? Does he like his second tenure as tribune, now with the Fifth *Macedonica* in Lower Moesia? It's an eternity from here..."

"He is doing fine, Pompeia. Hadrian sends me letters all the time. He loves it there. Yes, it's far away, but he is learning a lot and has made many friends, not unlike your husband at this age. And he likes to see foreign lands.

By the way-" Attianus pulled Plotina closer and whispered in her ear, "Many soldiers of his legion do not approve of Domitian's assassination..."

Plotina pulled up her eye brows. "That's terrible, but I am not surprised. I don't think the Praetorians like it either. But tell me more about Hadrian. He writes me letters too, but you know, my letters are different. I am a woman, and he would never tell me if he were unhappy or dissatisfied with his assignment.

See, my husband loves the army life, but Hadrian is an intellectual, so I am worried a bit. Some even call him *Graeculus*, the little Greek guy. And you know how much my husband abhors hearing that. His ward – a *Graeculus*..."

Attianus laughed. "I know, but I don't think Hadrian is concerned. He is an independent thinker. Yes, he does love Greek culture. At the same time, he is a terrific soldier and passionate hunter. Trajan will recognize that. Hadrian has the mettle to be an excellent officer some day. Mark my word, Pompeia.

The only thing that worries me about him is his reckless spending. When Hadrian was stationed in Aquincum last year, under Trajan's command, remember, Trajan received many complaints about his reckless borrowing. Legates don't like that. It's a bad example for the staff."

"But Attianus," Pompeia countered. "He is young. Julius Caesar had lots of debt when he was a young, up and coming politician in the old Republic, and we all know what an incredible leader he was."

"Agreed, but as Hadrian's guardians we have to worry about that. In many ways, I feel like I am his father, more so than Trajan who never had the time to look after his ward. It is my responsibility, and you have an eye on him too. Anyway, we fret too much. The young man will do fine. Soon he will inherit his parents' estate and start his civilian career."

"If he doesn't get killed in some stupid war first! Oh, by the way," she added. "Did he tell you what he thinks of marrying Sabina? You know I am trying to get the two hitched. I have told you that, haven't I? Anyway, she likes him. They would be a great match. I really want to tie him closer to the family. Marrying Trajan's grandniece… All of Rome would gossip about that."

"We haven't talked about marriage. He certainly hasn't mentioned anything to me. I don't think it's on his mind right now. It's tough enough to be a soldier on the shores of the Black Sea. On the other hand, he undoubtedly misses Rome's finest women." He winked at Pompeia. "Let's talk about it when he comes home."

"Fine. I just thought I'd ask."

Chapter 28

Back at the Domus Traiana, Traianus had regained consciousness. Excited to hear that Pompeia scurried to his *cubiculum,* but the Greek doctor didn't let anybody into the room other than Marcia and Harpenna. So the rest of the family lingered in the *triclinium.* Disappointed, Plotina joined them for a glass of Amminean red. Remembering how Trajan always called them quacks, she didn't have much faith in the *medicus* or any other Greek doctor for that matter. Her husband only trusted his army surgeons. But then again, Trajan had never been seriously ill. The medics had been more than adequate to treat his wounds.

"Maybe we should call for a doctor from the Praetorians," Pompeia suggested. "Traianus served the Flavian House all his life. The Praetorians will appreciate that and send us someone. I am confident they would! At least we should get a second opinion. You all know what Trajan thinks of Greek doctors, including our family's *medicus.*"

Marciana was shaking her head. She had been widowed for twenty years now and never remarried. After the death of her husband Matidius, she had moved back to her parents' house to raise her daughter Matidia there. Unfortunately, when Matidia had come of age herself she married a young Roman nobleman, who died soon after the wedding. Several years later, she had married again and given birth to two girls, Sabina and another Matidia. Then bad luck had struck once more and her second husband died. Ever since, she and her children lived in the Domus Traiana.

"What good would that do?" Marciana asked.

"I don't know, but it's worth a try. Traianus has not enjoyed great health lately, but it looks dire now."

"Grandfather likes the *medicus.* Let's hear what he wants to do," Matidia countered.

The women nodded. Only young Sabina abruptly jumped on her feet and screamed, "I can't stand this uncertainty! Grandfather must not die. It's not fair. We should call ten doctors, maybe twenty, whatever it takes!" Tears rolled down her baby face. She burst into hiccupping sobs, heaving her shoulders. Her mother eased to her and wrapped her arms around her daughter in consolation.

What a sorry crowd we are, Pompeia thought. *If only Trajan were here.*

As the summer progressed, old Traianus's health improved, but he stayed homebound and needed constant attention. Harpenna was always there for him. She never accepted any help, only when he was too weak to leave his room by himself. Slaves would then carry him around the villa on a small litter. Traianus would humor himself and croak, "Too old to walk but too young to die, pups!"

'Pups' was his favorite term of endearment, referring to anybody younger than him, including his wife Marcia. It was a pet name everybody in the household loved to hear, even the slaves. It made them smile.

Traianus stayed upbeat and was determined to enjoy what life had still in store for him. He was a happy patient, never grumpy, never angry. His body was failing him, so he escaped into the world of Latin literature. He re-read his favorite books, Cicero's *De Re Publica* ('The Republic'), a philosophical treatise on government, and Livy's *Ab Urbe Condita* ('Since the Foundation of the City'), the National Chronicles of Rome.

Sometimes he asked Cornelius Tacitus to come over, and they would debate the different forms of government: democracy versus monarchy and the various hybrids in between. Both were relieved that liberty had returned under Nerva. Tacitus told Traianus that he planned to follow in Livy's footsteps and write a book called *Annales* ('The Annals of Roman'), covering the last one hundred years of Roman history.

"That's an excellent idea," Traianus encouraged him. "But hurry, I want to read it before I leave this world. I doubt the *Cursus Publicus* will deliver it into Hades, and *Charon* takes no bribes," he quipped.

The *medicus* was still concerned. He told the family patriarch that something was wrong with his blood. Traianus, however, didn't resignate. Every week he sent offerings to *Aesculapius*, the God of Healing, on the Tiber Island.

Plotina worried about her father-in-law too, but she was also apprehensive of Nerva's increasingly frail health. Tacitus kept the family abreast of the political developments in the Senate and the Guard. The new praefect had to deal with ever more recalcitrant officers in the Guard who resented the new government and demanded the punishment of Domitian's murderers. Word had leaked to them that Pantherius was involved, and the Guard took the dismissal of Petronius and Norbanus as an admission of their guilt. The latter had retired and moved back to his hometown, but the former still worked in the palace.

In the Senate, discussions kept lingering about Nerva's succession. Several players tried to position themselves, but there was no obvious candidate. Different factions supported different senators. The most influential faction around Antoninus was firmly behind Nerva and refused to discuss the matter. Others like Tacitus subtly promoted a return to republican government. He was encouraged because Nerva had allowed the ancient Centuriate Assemblies to vote on his agriculture bill.

In this tense situation, Pompeia sent a letter to Trajan at his headquarters in Pannonia.

Dear Husband:

I hope you are doing well. Rumor has it you are out in the field mopping up what is left of the Suebi. We have heard they are teaming up with Sarmatian tribes to make it harder on your troops. This sounds dangerous so I am asking you, please take care of yourself. Don't be reckless. Don't always be the first in line. Rome needs you. I need you - and I miss you.

Your father is not in good health. Since his collapse he has been fragile and weak. The doctor ordered him not to leave the house. As if he could do anything else! He mostly reads or sleeps. And we keep him good company. Even Tacitus comes over to chat with him. But the medicus is concerned and so are we, particularly your mother. Dearest Husband, please be prepared. Your father may not survive this year.

This reminds me. Verginius Rufus died last week. The old man never recovered from breaking his hip. The burial had a huge following, and Tacitus held a wonderful speech, praising his virtues. He is so happy about the return of liberty – I can tell from his enthusiasm. Tacitus made Rufus look like a great champion of freedom and fighter of oppression.

All of Rome seemed to have attended his pyre and watched Rufus's soul ascend to the heavens. The inscription on his tomb is moving too. It says:

'Here lies the man who claimed power not for himself but his country.'

The general was an amazing man. The Army had offered him the throne three times during the Civil War, and he refused each time.

Other than that, everything is quiet in Rome. As usual at this time of the year most senators are staying at their villas on the coast because it is unbearably muggy and hot in the city. Even Nerva can't be found on the Palatine these days - which brings me to his problems.

I am worried about the emperor, Trajan. The

Praetorians' loyalty is questionable. Nerva has no champion
for his cause in the Guard, not one. And he is in bad
health. People speculate who will succeed him. Some
senators are salivating to become emperor themselves.

How about the Army? What do you think? Your
cousin Hadrian tells us in his letters that many soldiers
in his unit detest Domitian's assassination. Some blame
Nerva. Do you hear that too? And how about the
governors at the frontier? Are they putting themselves
in position? Have you considered it yourself?

It would be a shame if Nerva died soon because he
has done great work, and many people feel free again.
On the other hand, his amiability and clemency leaves
the door open for trouble. Some misread it as weakness
and are waiting for the opportunity to strike him down.

Dearest husband, how much longer will you be
campaigning? I would love you to return to Rome.
Don't you miss me? Don't you miss Sura? You
would be warmer here than in the barbarian lands
- and I am not only talking about the weather.

One last thing, I think of Hadrian's future a lot. He is at
the age when it is time to get married. I am fond of Sabina,
your grandniece. Wouldn't they make a wonderful couple?

My dear Marcus, excuse my gloomy writing. I don't
want to distract you, but you need to know these things.

May Rome's eternal gods protect you.

Love,
Pompeia

Trajan dictated a prompt reply to Callistus but deemed it too risky to let
her know that the Rhine army backed Domitian's assassination. Uninvited
eyes might see the dispatch. He wrote:

Dear Pompeia:

Your worries are much appreciated, but cheer up:
I am in no danger. Every step we make is carefully
planned. Scouts scan the landscape before any unit is

*set in motion. I don't intend to die in some ambuscade
in the woods. Yes, I am campaigning in enemy lands,
but we never camp far from the Danube. I have not
been successful yet in eliminating the danger from
Suebi and Sarmatian incursions. There are so many
tribes north of the river, and it's difficult to stay on top
of their plans. We try our best to divide and play them
against each other. But when push comes to shove it is
the might of our legions that secures the long border.*

*My prayers are with my poor Father. I hope he will get
better and I desire much to be home and spend time with
him, but I can't. For Rome's sake. I have to do my duty;
too much depends on it. Many lives are at stake. Father
would not want me to leave my post only to see him.*

*And give Tacitus my greetings. I am thankful
that he is such a good friend. No doubt, the two
of them will solve the world's problems!*

*By the way, have you sent for doctors from the
Praetorian Guard? Please do. We must not leave any stone
unturned and give Father the best medical treatment
Rome can offer. I rely on you, my dearest Pompeia, and
Mother. Please, move heaven and earth to save his life!*

*I am sorry to hear that old Rufus died. He was a
good Roman. I am convinced that his soul has found
its place next to Mars and Jupiter in the heavens.*

*Thank you also for the update on Nerva. He certainly
has my loyalty, but he has not asked for help against
the Praetorians. I know Casperius and cannot imagine
he would involve himself in a plot against the emperor.
But I cannot judge the resentment among his men. In
a way, I even understand them. They fought many
wars with Domitian. He treated them well. Many have
fought for his Divine Father and his brother Titus. The
men want justice. I believe they don't know whether
Nerva himself was involved in the plot, but I can tell
you that the plot was initiated by the Senate. And if I
know that, the Praetorians likely know that too...*

*As to my troops, there is nothing to worry.
Remember, Domitian campaigned with them
unsuccessfully. They don't hold him in high esteem.
The Rhine Army commanders have no problem with*

Nerva either. I am in constant touch with them.
I would love to be in Rome with you when it
gets cold here, Pompeia. But I may not be able to.
We shall see. If I can force the Suebi to make a
final stand and achieve a great victory, it might be
possible. Pray for us and sacrifice to the gods.
As to Hadrian, is he thinking of marriage?
How about Sabina? Is she interested? I would
not want her to be unhappy. You know,
she is near and dear to my heart.

Love,
Trajan

Plotina was stunned that Trajan had known all along where the plot against Domitian had come from - the Senate!

It made sense. The conspirators had likely given Trajan a heads up so he wouldn't intervene, and he hadn't - despite his loyalty to the Flavian House. She wondered, how many other governors and senators had been in on this. Ingenious - they had made it look like a palace cabal...

And darn, Trajan had not given her much of a hint whether he would approve of a marriage between Hadrian and Sabina. As the official guardian for both of them, he would have the final say.

Chapter 29

On a windy day in late fall – the gale swept the last remaining leaves from the oak trees in the Domus Tiberiana – Nerva was sitting in his study with his secretaries and worked on more progressive legislation. He had decided not to move into Domitian's monumental new palace and instead resided with his staff in Tiberius's old palace. Domitian's mansion was now public property and used for events only.

Nerva's health had improved and he was feeling better. Best of all, the dreaded succession talks had died down.

While dictating to his scribes the emperor heard angry voices erupting in the palace courtyard. Before he could send someone to find out what was going on, the door to his study flew open and a group of furious Praetorians, headed by Praefect Casperius himself, paced into the chamber, hands on their swords.

Nerva looked at the soldiers aghast. "What-"

Casperius cut him off. "We demand the immediate execution of Domitian's murderers Pantherius and Petronius! Where are the knaves?"

Shaken but undeterred, Nerva resisted. "Over my dead body! Go back to your barracks and leave these matters to the Senate."

The officers laughed at him.

"The Senate? If we wait for the politicians, we'll wait forever," Casperius hissed. "Where are the scoundrels? Tell us now!"

Nerva shook his head and pulled down the collar of his toga to expose his throat. "You would have to cut me down first if you dare!"

Casperius smiled at him wryly. "Search the palace. You will find them somewhere around here."

It didn't take long. They returned with both men, manhandling them with contempt. Wide-eyed, their faces chalk-white, Petronius and Pantherius stared at the guardsmen.

"You are the most disgraceful officials that have ever served the Roman People," Casperius accused them.

Without warning, he drew his sword and skewered Petronius with a lightning-fast blow. The former praefect cringed and fell on the floor with a loud thump. A puddle of blood formed around him.

Pantherius screamed and begged for his life, but the officers tore his tunic from his body, cut off his testicles and stuffed them in his mouth. Using a leather-belt, they strangled him to death in front of the helpless emperor and his scribes.

"Justice has been served. We are done here," Casperius said at the end. They swung round, leaving the two bleeding corpses behind.

Nerva sunk back on his chair, choking. Then he headed for the door but stumbled on his way, vomited and fell on the beautiful mosaic floor. His whole body was shaking. The clerks were frozen at their desks, didn't move, didn't talk. Nerva cleaned his mouth with a toga fold and pulled himself together. "Take away the bodies," he croaked. Slowly, life returned to his men. They dragged the dead corpses out of the study, bloodying the ornate mosaics all the way to the entrance.

Nerva tumbled back to his desk and wiped the cold sweat from his face. *They almost killed me too - their superior!* His rule was dangling on a thin thread: He was completely at the mercy of the Praetorians.

Nerva's stomach was still upset. He was throwing up once more as Casperius returned to the study, eyeing the emperor kneeling on the marble floor. "Now, now. You don't look very imperial, Marcus Cocceius, do you? Pah, you disgust me!

I came back to tell you we expect a public thanksgiving ceremony today where you will declare your gratefulness for our deed. It was about time those wicked men were put to death."

Several hours later, the Praetorians forced Nerva to stride to the Forum with them and render solemn thanks to *Jupiter Optimus Maximus* for the punishment of Domitian's murderers in front of a puzzled crowd.

At night Nerva was finally able to meet with his advisors behind locked doors. "Our worst fears have come true," Antoninus gasped. "The Guard took revenge - a mutiny! If the Praetorians can give orders to our emperor at will, he is no emperor. This is a disaster, Marcus Cocceius, the collapse of your authority."

Some councilors argued Nerva should resign right away. The arguments went back and forth, but he resisted, and they dropped the idea. Still, it was undeniable that his position was unsustainable. To restore his authority, he needed a strong force to back him up.

"That can only be the legions," Priscus expressed the obvious. "Marcus, you need to cow the Praetorians with a general they fear and respect."

Soon thereafter, Traianus died in his sleep in his house on the Aventine. When the news reached Trajan in remote Pannonia, he was devastated. How much he would have loved to see his beloved father one more time...

Victory had been elusive. Now, he had a hard time concentrating on the task at hand. He suspended military operations for two weeks and ordered public offerings and sacrifices on Carnuntum's drill field to *Mania*, the Goddess of Death. The rituals helped him overcome his pain.

In Rome, the city was grief-stricken. Nerva ordered a state funeral with consular honors. The procession was miles long. Thousands of men and women participated, including many senators, officers of Guard and Army, and Nerva himself.

For a moment, the competing factions put their differences aside and showed the People of Rome how to honor a great citizen. Traianus was carried in a lavish casket from his house on the Aventine to the pyre in the Forum Romanum, accompanied by his extended family. There, Nerva in his role as *Pontifex Maximus*, held the eulogy, after which Traianus's body was cremated and his soul released to the heavens.

Will I follow soon? Nerva knew he was on borrowed time himself.

Soon, the dire realities of a mutinous Guard dominated the conversations in the Senate again. In this somber mood, encouraging news reached Nerva from the East. A routine message sent by his governor in Syria contained an amazing bit of information: Roman army scouts east of the Parthian border had almost made contact with an army of the Sinae...

The soldiers said they had met with some natives, who told them that Roman troops had missed a Sinese army by only a day's ride! The Bedouins claimed the Sinae were pursuing the remnants of a Hun army they had defeated in the western parts of their kingdom. There was a lot of fighting along the silk route, they added. They even mentioned the Sinese leader's name, Gan Ying.

Nerva was thrilled to hear that. His people had been importing silk goods from the Far East for centuries. They were popular among the wealthy. The Romans knew that the material was not manufactured where the merchants acquired it in the eastern Mediterranean and that it came from much farther east, transported via caravans through Bactria and eastern Parthia and by ships circumnavigating the subcontinent of India. Rome did have a seaport on the Indian west coast that was maintained in exchange for a hefty concession fee, but no Roman had ever reached the Far East and met with the fabled Sinae...

How awesome would it be, Nerva pondered, if they could trade with the Sinae directly and didn't have to go through Parthian and Armenian middlemen. But how?

Another bit of news from the northern frontier was even more important and caught Nerva's full attention. A laurelled wreath signifying a military victory arrived in the city and was brought to the ailing emperor. It came from Trajan. In his attached report he reported a crushing victory over the Suebi and their unconditional surrender. The war in Pannonia was over!

Nerva called his Council. He had an idea. "*Amici*, isn't this the opportunity we have been waiting for? Trajan was successful. He is now Rome's most celebrated general. I want to adopt him!"

The room fell silent for a moment. Then the councilors talked all at once. Nerva couldn't understand a word until they calmed down.

"A perfect choice, Marcus," Antoninus cheered. "The Praetorians won't dare to challenge someone like Trajan. You would be out of trouble."

But Tacitus cut in, "This is surrender to the military. Yes, the Praetorians will no longer be our problem. But instead of Casperius, we would be at the whim of Trajan. We would only replace one evil with another."

"What is the alternative?" Priscus asked. "Tell the Guard they have to obey the consuls and the Senate? Or accept a Praetorian candidate that would most certainly be a Flavian loyalist, maybe Casperius himself? Ridiculous!"

Tacitus defended himself. "Of course you are saying that. You are Trajan's ally. Everybody knows that. I am too! I was close to his father, a great Roman. But this is not the time to support one's friend. The Roman world is at a critical juncture that will decide our future government. We need to think it through *sine ira et studio*, carefully and without bias."

Antoninus supported Priscus. "I disagree, Publius. Our only option is an emperor backed by the power of the legions. The time of the Republic is over. Face it! Now, which general should it be? Let's see here:

Who commands a large and war savvy army? Trajan.

Whose command is the closest to Rome? Trajan's.

Who is Rome's greatest warrior? Trajan.

Who is Rome's most popular general? Trajan.

There is not even a competitor out there. Rufus is dead and Frontinus, Vespasian's old marshal, is too old.

Who has widespread connections across the empire and among key factions in the Senate? Again Trajan: by birth, marriage and military allegiance. Nobody compares, my friends.

Yes, I do support Nerva's idea. In fact, I think it's brilliant. It will neutralize the monster Casperius. He may even embrace it because he fought with Trajan's father in the Jewish War."

"There is another problem," Tacitus interjected. "Adoption only means Trajan would become Nerva's testamentary heir. We are not a monarchy. Only the Senate can approve his nomination as Nerva's successor. It has to bestow on him the dual privileges of *tribunicia potestas* and *imperium maius*."

"I don't see a problem with that either," Antoninus countered. "Trajan is a smart man. His bills will be wise and beneficial to all. Nor would I fear his veto power. To protect his life he has to enjoy sacrosanctity. As to the *imperium maius*, he is used to vast military powers and has never abused them.

I say, Trajan is the right man. Nerva, you need to make him your imperial colleague. I know he can't be *Pontifex Maximus* yet, but the Senate can take care of that later."

The discussion went on for a long time. In the end, the Council supported Nerva's plan.

"It is agreed then. I will send Trajan my diamond ring as a token of his adoption and proof of his legitimacy," Nerva announced.

The next morning the emperor took Trajan's letter and his laurel wreath and made his way down the Palatine Hill to the Forum Romanum and up the Capitoline Hill. There he entered the majestic Jupiter Temple, dedicated Trajan's letter, put it into the lap of Jupiter's huge statue in the temple's inner sanctum, the *cella,* and offered burning incense.

After that, he returned to the Forum and mounted the *rostra*, Rome's traditional stage used for proclamations. He declared to the crowd, "May great luck and happiness always be with the Roman Senate and People. I hereby adopt Marcus Ulpius Nerva Trajan as my legal son and heir."

Then he strode into the Curia and repeated his announcement among the cheering senators. Trajan was co-ruler now and designated to succeed Nerva after his death. The old emperor's satisfied gaze swept the senatorial ranks. Yes, this would work. They had the protection of the Army now. His ring was under way to Pannonia.

Chapter 30

The news hit Plotina like a hammer. She felt depressed and elated at the same time. What would the future hold for her and her husband now? How would their lives change?

The rest of the family was single-mindedly exuberant, however.

"If only my husband had lived to see this," Trajan's mother exclaimed.

"Trajan will be so happy," Marciana chimed in.

They hugged each other and danced. A gold pitcher full of delicious Falernian red made the rounds in the Traiani household.

Plotina didn't join the revelers. She was still absorbing the incredible news. Will this elevation change Trajan, perhaps corrupt his goodness? Will he become another Domitian?

The lives of every member of the family would change too, and his friends'. They would benefit in many ways although Trajan was not the nepotistic kind. Merit would hopefully remain his guiding principle. And how about Hadrian? Trajan's ward and cousin would immediately be perceived as a potential successor – and therefore inevitably be drawn into imperial politics...

The uncertainties scared her, but she was happy for her husband. He deserved it. He had put his life on the line for the empire many times. Trajan would be an excellent ruler. Plotina shook off her doubts and fears, at least for the moment. *It will be all right. Trajan and I will MAKE it all right.*

"Sabina, the pitcher," she shouted at Matidia's daughter. Then she lifted it up high with both arms so all could see her. "This is brilliant," she screamed. "Today I am going to get drunk!"

An icy wind clutched Trajan's bones as if he wore nothing. He pulled his scarlet cloak closer, shivering. Snow would hit Pannonia soon, but so far only dense fog covered the banks of the Danube. Standing on the watchtower of a temporary camp he had set up outside of Carnuntum Trajan could barely see the Suebi recruits on the drill field below him. The general had built several such boot camps for his new Germanic auxiliaries.

After the victory in September, fortuitously timed just before the end of the campaign season, he had worked on the details of a peace treaty with the different Suebi tribes. Despite their unconditional surrender he went through great pains to arrange a fair and lasting compact so that the Suebi problem would be solved once and for all. This Germanic confederation had pestered the border long enough.

The agreement included tributes, hostage arrangements and other safeguards to ensure compliance, but Trajan also put in incentives for the Suebi to live in peace with their Roman neighbors. The treaty's annual tribute would not deny the Suebi the harvests and livestock they needed for their own sustenance, but the compact required their Chiefs to send royal hostages Trajan intended to translocate far away from their own land. He hoped the young men and women could be romanized and would become more inclined to live the Roman way of life. As a practical matter, the hostages would tie the chieftains' hands and deter them from invading Roman territory. If they upheld the other parts of the compact, after ten years they would get the hostages back. If they didn't, they would never see their loved ones again.

And then there was the conscription article. The tribes had to offer up five percent of their male population between eighteen and twenty years of age for service in the Roman auxiliaries.

Right now, Trajan was inspecting the progress of some two hundred Suebi recruits. They were not very enthusiastic in their efforts, but the Roman centurions did not let them off the hook. Who didn't perform was yelled at, reprimanded or beaten on the spot with the dreaded vine stick. It was harsh, but not any harsher than what legionaries had to endure in their own boot camps.

Trajan had seen enough. It would take all winter to make them into decent soldiers. He sighed. At least, it would keep them busy. The general climbed down the watchtower, jumped on his horse and cantered to the drill officer in charge.

"Tribune, don't forget the river exercises. None of these people can swim. We have to teach them. Can you do that?"

"No, Governor. I need more instructors."

"You will get them. After all, we don't want them to drown when crossing a river in Caledonia, do we?"

The officer chuckled. "Certainly not. It would be a shame."

Trajan planned to establish five Suebi auxiliary cohorts for deployment in Britannia. Those recruits would never be allowed to come back to their home country. Instead, they would fight the wild tribes of Britannia's uncivilized north. Auxiliaries were rarely stationed close to their homelands. In Britannia they wouldn't have any relationships with the enemy. Instead, they would benefit from the perks of Rome's Army.

"Something else," Trajan added as he reined-in his skittering horse. The mustang neighed, eager to gallop and warm up in the nippy weather. Trajan wheeled the unruly mount around the tribune. "Latin classes are as important as the drill lessons. What good would it do us if we have new troops that can't understand our orders? Schedule class every day. I will send you some teachers. They are on the army payroll so treat them well."

The officer saluted.

Trajan nodded and went easy on his reins. The mustang darted off as if a mythic monster from the underworld was chasing him. Trajan laughed loud. The gallop was exhilarating, but soon his thoughts circled around today's scheduled negotiations with Pannonia's duumvirs. Many of their villages had suffered from the Suebi attacks. Not so much through loss of life – the people had found sanctuary in the fortified towns and army camps – but through loss of crops, housing, livestock and personal belongings. Many provincials had lost everything except what they had been able to carry on their bodies.

Trajan planned to compensate them with Suebi reparations. Still, the details weren't trivial. He had instructed his clerks to carefully examine all applicants. The general would not tolerate cheaters.

Some thirty magistrates were waiting for Trajan in Carnuntum's refectory. The talks with the governor had barely started when a side door opened and Callistus paced into the room.

Trajan looked at him irritated. Ignoring the annoyed magistrates' faces, Callistus scurried to Trajan and whispered into his ear, "Master, I need to talk to you right away - in private. A senatorial courier has arrived with a message from the emperor. It is most important."

"What is it about, Callistus?"

"Outside, Dominus. I cannot talk you here."

"Callistus," Trajan insisted. "What is it about?"

He didn't want to leave the conference. The duumvirs had come from far away and deserved his respect.

"Please, Master. Let us step outside."

Callistus's face was obsequious, but he stayed firm.

"It had better be important," Trajan said gruffly.

He excused himself and followed Callistus out the room. After the secretary closed the door behind them, Trajan asked Callistus again, "So what is it, my friend?"

The faithful secretary lifted his gaze to the legate and took a deep breath. "Master, the emperor has adopted you as his son... You will be emperor when he dies."

"What???"

Trajan was thunderstruck. His jaws went slack, and he looked at Callistus in disbelief. Then he closed his mouth and swallowed hard. A myriad of thoughts raced through his head. He had to lean back against the closed door. "If this is some sordid joke, Callistus..."

Callistus shook his head. "No joke, Master. It is the truth, Dominus. I swear!"

Trajan stared at his secretary. They had gone through much together.

"Where is the letter? I need to see it at once. And send for my laticlavian tribune. He is familiar with the issues of this conference. Tell him that I need him to chair the meeting. Tell him I will talk to the duumvirs later. But I want the conference to proceed."

"*Sic, Dominus.* The Senate's courier is waiting in your office."

"Thanks. Go now, Callistus."

Trajan hurried to his office. When he entered, a messenger was sitting on the visitor's chair. He immediately rose to greet the governor. "*Salve, Legatus.* I bring great news. Marcus Cocceius Nerva has adopted you as his son. Here is his dispatch." The man handed Trajan a sealed scroll. "And here is something else I am supposed to give to you."

Trajan frowned while the courier pulled a small object from his pocket. It was a box. Its clasp was covered with Nerva's imperial wax seal. "Both items are for your eyes only," the man said. "This box contains Nerva's personal diamond ring. It is a token of your adoption and proves its legitimacy. The ring is yours now, and yours alone."

Trajan didn't know what to say. He almost forgot the courier's presence until the man cleared his throat. "Hmm, Legate?"

"Ah, yes, yes. Excuse me. You are dismissed. Ask the quartermaster for a place to sleep tonight and be ready tomorrow to canter back to Rome with a letter of my acknowledgement."

The man saluted and left the office.

Trajan was alone now.

Him - emperor?

What was happening in Rome? He had heard about the appalling incident with the Praetorians and sent an inquiry to the Rhine Army asking them about their thoughts on this matter. Spurinna had answered they were considering to remove Aelianus from his office. Dispatches had been sent back and forth, but no action had been taken. Trajan himself had been in the middle of the Suebi campaign with no opportunity to do anything about it one way or another. Now this!

Nerva must have come to the conclusion that his position was under such pressure that he needed the backing of the Army. And he had picked him to be his counterweight to the Praetorians...

Trajan had never thought of himself as a candidate for the principate. Yes, he was a successful military leader, but he was not of ancient Roman nobility. The Traiani hailed from Spain after all, even if their ancestors had emigrated from Italia during the wars against Carthage three hundred years ago.

Pompey, Rome's most revered general in his heyday, had never become First Man because he had lacked aristocratic heritage and been forced to share power with the Patricians Crassus and Caesar.

But times have changed, Trajan pondered. The Claudio-Julian emperors had killed or exiled many prominent members of the Famous Families. After them, the Flavians had shown that the emperor did not have to be a Patrician.

I have to talk with Spurinna and the generals on the Rhine to make sure they don't have a problem with this - if I accept the elevation at all.

He picked up his letter opener and broke Nerva's seal. Then he opened the scroll and read the dispatch.

From: Marcus Cocceius Nerva, IMP CAESAR AUG
To: M. Ulpius Traianus, Legatus Augusti pro Consule in Pannonia

Dear Marcus:

Congratulations to your superb victory over the Suebi. Well done! Nothing is more important than a secure border with the barbarians. Their incursions were disruptive to trade and commerce and terrified the local population. To show our gratitude the Senate grants you a second Triumph and bestows upon you the honorific title 'Germanicus'. In addition, you are to be hailed Imperator.

You must know what the Praetorians under Casperius Aelianus did to me and the dignity of my Office. I am the legal ruler of Rome, and yet I cannot trust my own bodyguard... The Guard cannot get over Domitian's assassination. Even now that they have killed Pantherius and Petronius, they resent me and my government. Casperius thinks I am old, fragile, and incompetent. He may even have ambitions on the throne himself. The Senate is scared and legislation is stalling.

In this emergency and to prevent any further destabilization of the government I have decided to adopt you as my son, Marcus Ulpius Nerva Trajan. I ask for your protection and look forward to working with you next year as my partner in the consulship.

The Senate has agreed to endow you with all imperial prerogatives except Pontifex Maximus. You will be Caesar Imperator. I will be Augustus Imperator. We will rule jointly, under my leadership.

Trajan, I want you to succeed me when I die. My health is fading. The empire needs stability. You are the man that can give us that. Effective immediately, you are holding both imperium maius and tribunicia potestas. And you are appointed commander-in-chief of the whole Roman Army. Your word is the law of the land – as long as you act in agreement with the Senate.

Specifically, I ask of you the following:

Now that the Danube border is restored, please relocate to Colonia Claudia and secure the allegiance of the Rhine Army. I have sent a letter to its commanders with instructions to give you their support.

I am confident they will comply, but you need to go there in person and assert yourself. Messengers announcing your elevation were also sent to all imperial legates and governors. Additionally, I understand work needs to be done to consolidate the Rhine-Main border. We need to extend our fortifications on the right banks of the Rhine and maybe even establish a new defense line by linking the rivers Main and Neckar.

I leave the details up to you and the local commanders, but I do know from this year's dispatches that the tribes east of the Rhine and north of the Main are wanton, harassing unprotected Roman settlements on the northern banks of the Main. There is also trouble with the Chauci and Frisii on the Lower Rhine. I am confident you will sort it all out. You have commanded there before.

I leave it up to your judgment what you want to do about the Praetorians. Casperius is no stranger to you. He may fall in line because he served both Vespasian and your Father in the Jewish War. I do expect him to back off, but it is of the utmost importance that you restore the dignity of our high office and the discipline of the Guard.

Your Father,
Nerva

Trajan put down the scroll. This was no joke indeed. He was Nerva's legal son and heir now - and co-ruler of the Roman world…

Next, he opened Nerva's ring box. There it was - the golden diamond-studded ring, proof of the adoption's legitimacy. Trajan held it up against the sunlight with his fingers and was dazzled by the diamonds and the reflection of the polished gold. Awed, he put it back in the box.

The responsibility... Would he be up to it? What would change? Would he have to reside on the Palatine Hill and not see the legions anymore?

He cringed. Never. He did not want to become a bureaucrat. Maybe he should decline Nerva's wish. After all, that's what Rufus had done. But then again, how else could the emperor stabilize the volatile situation in the Capital?

Fortunately, he didn't have to go to Rome straight away. There was appealing work for him in Germania, and he would not have to deal with questions of authority or squabbles with rival commanders.

What to do with the Praetorian Guard? How about Casperius and the other mutineers? Their conduct was unacceptable. Funny, he was barely Caesar and already thought of the things he needed to do as emperor though he had not even accepted his elevation yet. Nerva seemed to think this was a no-brainer, but it wasn't to him.

He was certain he wouldn't get carried away with the powers he was going to wield. The emperorship was an office like any other; yes, it was the most powerful office on earth, but still an office to serve the people and the interests of the empire. The power that came with it had a way of tricking the mind, making its wielder feel impervious, invincible even. He would have to stay aware of that. Sure, he would have the power to kill and destroy at will. In fact, he would have more power than any human being ever in the history of the known world. He swore to himself he would use it wisely, with caution and purpose. He would not abuse it - not him, the son of Traianus. Somebody had to succeed Nerva. Emperor and Senate had spoken. Who was he to defy the will of the gods?

He did have one concern. The Army life he was so fond of would have to make room for diplomacy and government. But what was the alternative? Watch Aelianus take over? Stay on the sidelines of on-going disputes in the Senate and among military commanders? There would be no uncertainties if he agreed to this elevation.

Trajan sighed. Maybe nothing would change. Perhaps he would be better able to do the things important to him - augment Rome's glory and bring peace to the long and daunting frontier with the uncivilized world.

The touch of a smile formed around his lips. He called for Callistus.

Chapter 31

Hadrian hated the drizzle and clammy winter mist on the Lower Danube. It fit right in with his appointment today, he ruminated. *Just my luck!*

Surly stroking his coiffed curly beard that covered his handsome, but pox-scarred face, Hadrian kept striding down the *cardo maximus*, the main artery of downtown Oescus. He was wearing a thick hooded wool *paenula* over his purple-stripped tunic that signified him as the laticlavian tribune of the Fifth Legion *Macedonica,* stationed in Lower Moesia Province. The poncho was impregnated with tallow to make it water-proof, but it left his uncovered legs exposed to the dank cold, allowing the spray of every puddle he stepped in to add injury to the insult of the weather.

The tribune stopped in front of a representative-looking house and knocked at the ornate ash door. A hatch opened, and the doorkeeper gawked at him.

"What's your business?" he grunted.

"I am here to see your Master," Hadrian said.

"What is your name?"

"Hadrian. Quick. Let me in. The weather is terrible, can't you see?"

"Does my Master expect you?"

"Yes. Open the door!"

Instead, the porter disappeared and slammed the hatch shut. Several minutes later, the door opened. The scowling porter reappeared, led Hadrian into the villa's *triclinium* and returned to his station.

Hadrian looked around and sat down on one of the sumptuous sofas. Its mattress was wrapped in an embroidered forest-green velvet sheet. Tasseled pillows cushioned the elevated end. Here he was - in the lion's den.

The *triclinium* was nicely decorated, at least for a town in this remote part of the world. The frescoes were painted in brilliant colors and depicted scenes from Roman and Greek mythology. They were quite good on first glimpse, but Hadrian's schooled eyes noticed they lacked the elegance and beauty you would find in a similar house in Italia.

Finally, the door opened and the merchant Homullus entered the *triclinium*. He was some fifty years old, a big man with a belly so extensive he was hiding it under a toga the size of the Flavian Amphitheater. Homullus wore a conspicuous amulet around his neck, and his fingers were studded with gold and diamond rings. *Preposterous.*

Homullus welcomed his visitor with feigned affection.

"*Ave*," Hadrian replied with no enthusiasm, nervously touching his beard. "I have received your letter."

"Great. So you have the money?"

"No. I need more time, at least another week."

Homullus's unctuous smile froze. "You don't have the money to pay me back? Why are you then wasting my time?" His puffed up face turned red like a ripe tomato. More like the crest of a rooster, Hadrian corrected himself.

Homullus grabbed a chalice from a side table and smashed it on the stone floor. "You think you can come here, enjoy my hospitality and not pay your debts?" he screamed.

Hadrian kept his composure and bowed to the man. "I have sent for the money, but it hasn't arrived yet. It comes from far away, you see. Maybe something happened to the courier. I am investigating this," he said.

Homullus kept ranting and whining. "You promised you would pay me on time! It's been a year now since you started borrowing from me. My patience has run out. You have no more credit, do you understand? And I will complain to your commander, yes! You are a disgrace to the entire legion."

Great, that's exactly what I need. Hadrian rose and crossed to the door. "You will be paid, Homullus. Don't worry."

"Yes, I will be, and I am doubling the interest you owe me from this day forward," the angry merchant hissed.

Several days later, Hadrian was in the legionary commander's office when Homullus splashed in, red-faced once more and out of breath. The door sentry tried to hold him back, but Homullus ignored him and paced forward with his three hundred pounds even while the soldier was pulling back his toga folds, exposing the merchant's hairy chest. In vain. Homullus didn't stop until he reached General Julius Marinus's desk from where he pointed at Hadrian. "This man is a liar, a thief and a debtor. He owes me five hundred dinars!"

Marinus pulled up his left eye brow. "And you are?"

"Homullus, Eminence. My name is Homullus. I sell the finest silk and wool in all of Moesia…"

"And you think you can crash into my office like a Sarmatian invader and harass a Roman officer?" Marinus cut him off.

Hadrian gave the legate a thankful look, but he was embarrassed.

"But, but…" Homullus stammered and pointed his index finger at Hadrian again. "This officer of yours, Hadrian, hmm, excuse me, the laticlavian Tribune Publius Aelius Hadrianus, owes me money. I demand repayment."

"How much do you owe him, Publius?" the general asked Trajan's cousin. "And what for?"

"I hosted a boar hunt when I arrived here a year ago. That included a sumptuous dinner and associated festivities. I also borrowed money for other events and religious rites."

"Ahh, I remember the boar hunt," Marinus said. "I was there. You still have not paid for it?"

"No, Legate," Hadrian said, blushing.

Marinus shook his head. "You must have done quite some entertaining. One can buy a beautiful female slave for this amount of money. Five hundred dinars is not exactly pocket change."

Homullus grinned at Hadrian with glee while a centurion entered the office, announcing the arrival of a courier from Rome. Marinus waved him in. "Homullus, excuse us."

The merchant howled. "I will not leave this room until I get paid by this sinister and unsavory character! If I don't, there will be no wool shipments for the garment makers to produce army *paludamenta*, I swear by the gods."

"Are you threatening me, sutler?"

The derogatory term the general used to address the rich merchant told Hadrian that Marinus's patience was wearing thin. Before Homullus had a chance to justify himself, the courier entered the room. He was visibly exhausted from the ride. Dust, sweat and grime covered his face. He grabbed a sealed scroll from his leather bag and handed it to the general. Marinus and Hadrian arched their eyes.

"The Imperial Seal," Hadrian shouted. "It's from Nerva."

Marinus nodded. "Out with you, Publius! I will deal with this later," he barked.

Hadrian left hesitantly. Homullus had to be pushed out by the guard and kept arguing in the hallway. Hadrian was still in the Praetorium when he heard Marinus call for him. Homullus lingered not far from the general's office at the other end of the hallway. Ignoring the obnoxious merchant, Hadrian scurried back into Marinus's quarters. "Legate?"

"Come in and close the door," Marinus told him. "I have incredible news for you. Emperor Nerva has adopted your cousin Trajan as his son. He made him his heir and co-ruler. Trajan will be sole emperor when Nerva dies..."

"What?" Hadrian couldn't believe it. "You are not yanking my chain, General, are you? That would be astounding... I mean... fantastic! My cousin - Emperor..."

Marinus's serious face told him that the governor was not joking.

"Incredible... But it makes sense. Rome needs a military man at the top. Nerva wouldn't do, and Trajan is our best. The Army will love it."

"No doubt. Everybody respects Trajan. He is a great and unpretentious soldier, and he will make a great ruler."

"Yes, he will, Legate!"

Marinus gazed at the young officer portentously. "Hadrian, your life will change forever."

"Maybe." Hadrian knew Marinus was right, but he didn't want to sound cocky. "Time will tell. For now, I am your faithful tribune, not more and not less."

Marinus smiled. "I know. You are a good man, but fix the problem with that moron outside. You owe it to your *dignitas*."

"Yes, Legate. I will."

"As far as Trajan's elevation goes," Marinus continued. "I want you to travel to Pannonia and convey to your cousin the acclamations of the Moesian legions. I believe, as his kinsman, you are the right man for this task."

Hadrian's face lit up. "It will be my pleasure."

In Carnuntum, the news had spread fast. Wherever Trajan went, soldiers addressed him as Caesar or Germanicus, and congratulated him. He cautioned them each time that he had yet to accept this elevation, but they were certain he was only being humble. Everybody expected him to accept the Purple.

Many letters arrived from Rome. One of them came from Pompeia.

From: Pompeia Plotina
To: Marcus Ulpius Nerva Trajan

Dearest husband:

I am sure you have received Nerva's ring by now.
I cannot tell you how happy I am for you! If there ever
was a man in the empire ready for this honor, it is
you, Marcus, and you alone. Hail Trajan Caesar!
But I know you. Don't even think for a moment that
you can dodge this or that you are not good enough or not
noble enough. It is the will of the Senate. Please do accept
your adoption and elevation to Rome's highest office.
You and Nerva will be ordinary consules
next year. You will have to come back to Rome
in January. I can't wait to see you!
Dearest Trajan, our lives are going to change.
I want you to know I will always be at your side
as humble as before. I will not let anything come
between us, even if our lives as Emperor and Empress
will expose us to temptations and challenges.
I am not concerned that you would become a tyrant.
As a successful general you have been granted a Triumph

*- remember what the state slave riding on the chariot with
you ritually whispered into your ear that day? 'Memento
mori - remember you are mortal'. It's the same being
emperor. If you keep that in mind, you will retain your
humanity, dignity and honor, and all will be good.*

Please send a dispatch so we know when to expect you.

Love,
Plotina

The letter affected Trajan deeply. Pompeia was an incredible woman, and wise. But she couldn't possibly know of Nerva's orders. He would not return to Rome anytime soon. Nerva had appointed him *consul ordinarius* only to symbolize Trajan's status as his equal. By endowing him with the proconsular *imperium maius* he had also given him supreme authority over the Roman magistrates and the Roman Army as a whole. This had priority now, particularly for his mission in Germania.

Trajan wrote his wife back, telling her he would not come home for a while. He thanked her for her encouragement and loyalty and asked her to extend his greetings to the whole family, particularly his mother and his sister, Marcia and Marciana.

His attention then focused on the upcoming trip to Colonia Claudia. It was early December, and he wanted to arrive on the Rhine before the end of the year. Most importantly, he wanted to meet with Spurinna, the senior general there. Trajan sent him a dispatch with a proposal to meet in Argentorate.

He had his own plans with Spurinna. He didn't doubt his loyalty, at least for now, but Trajan didn't fully trust him either. Spurinna had shown too much interest in political affairs before Nerva's ascension. He had been one of Nerva's kingmakers and held back information at the time. Trajan couldn't say what exactly bothered him about Spurinna, but he wanted the general to relinquish his command.

Chapter 32

After putting his second-in-command, General Pompeius Longinus, in charge in Carnuntum, he left for Argentorate with six cohorts of infantry and several detachments of archers. They marched along the Danube on the main road to Raetia Province. Near Guntia, they left the Danube valley and trekked straight west through the Agri Decumates, arriving in Argentorate in the middle of December.

"Hail Caesar!" Spurinna greeted the emperor-designate with a perfectly executed military salute.

"You are quick to adjust, Vestricius," Trajan answered stone-faced. "*Ave.* But I am not Caesar quite yet. The journey was long and I am tired, but first I want to sit down with you and discuss the situation. You have seen Nerva's orders, I take it?"

"Yes, I have."

"So, what do you think of all this?"

"I sincerely belief it is good for the empire. Remember our conversation in Aquileia? I told you Nerva would be an interim ruler only. Of course, I didn't know it would be you to follow him, but you are the natural candidate. I embrace Nerva's choice."

He shouldn't have said that. Those that brag the loudest have the most to hide.

"That is good to hear. Thank you, General. It makes things easier. How about your officers?"

"Likewise. They were fine with Nerva, but they are even more satisfied with you. You are a solder after all whereas Nerva is just a civilian."

"Good. And what are your plans? Do you want to stay in Germania under my authority? You would be second-in-command?"

"I could – if this is what you want. But I could also be deployed elsewhere. I am not tied to this post."

"That makes my proposal straightforward then. I would like you to go back to Rome and hold a suffect consulship. It is hard enough to become Consul, and even harder to do so twice. Is that agreeable?"

Without showing any emotions Spurinna replied, "Perfectly agreeable, Caes-hmm, excuse me, Trajan."

Trajan clapped his shoulder. "It's all right. I guess I will have to get used to my new title."

The next morning Trajan and Spurinna ordered a parade of Argentorate's legion and proclaimed Trajan's adoption to the troops. It wasn't a surprise for the men and they cheered enthusiastically. Then Spurinna left for Rome and Trajan set out for the Lower Rhine. His first stop was in Moguntiacum.

Julius Servianus, Governor of Upper Germania Province and through a lucky coincidence Trajan's cousin-in-law (he was Hadrian's sister's husband) was already waiting. Trajan had notified him via courier that he would visit him on his way north.

Servianus welcomed him with open arms. "I hope you had a good trip, cousin. Great tidings I hear, great tidings!"

"Indeed, Julius. My life is in for a change, but I am also playing with fire. It's wonderful to be with family in such times - I need you now."

"I am flattered, Trajan Caesar. How can I be of assistance?"

Trajan shook his head. "You too. Everybody calls me Caesar now or *Imperator* or *Germanicus...* I am not used to it."

Servianus laughed. "You will get used to it, Trajan. You will."

"Anyway, I need your help to assert my authority in Germania's border provinces. Let us orchestrate a parade of your legion during which I will accept the acclamation of the troops. I have done that with Spurinna's men in Argentorate, and it went very well. Then I would like you to travel to Vindonissa and hold another ovation there without me. Tell the men I will visit them in person as soon as I can, but right now, my presence is required on the Lower Rhine.

Tomorrow I will leave for Colonia Claudia and plan to spend the winter there. This will give me the time and opportunity to develop a field strategy for next year. We need to consolidate and reorganize the borders along Main and Rhine."

Servianus nodded. "Certainly. I am happy to go to Vindonissa. The rankers of the Eleventh *Claudia* are good boys. They will understand. I don't expect trouble with the officers either. I should be back in Moguntiacum by mid January. Would that be all right?"

"Of course. In any case, we will stay in touch."

While they continued their discussions and parsed the governor's intelligence reports from across the frontier a visitor was announced. It was Hadrian.

"Avete, Legati," Hadrian greeted them in military pose, hitting his cuirass with his right fist, stretching his arm and pointing the opening hand at the generals. He avoided their baffled gaze by focusing his eyes on some imaginary object behind the two men. "I am bringing the acclamations from the Danube legions, Caesar," Hadrian exclaimed and nodded at Trajan. He lifted his gaze to his cousin for a split second and added, "This is an official dispatch from General Julius Marinus who represents the Moesian troops in this matter."

Hadrian made a taut step forward and dropped a sealed army scroll on the table. Then he retraced his step and stood to attention again.

His relations with his guardian had not always been the best. Hadrian felt on edge not knowing know how Trajan would react to his sudden presence. He had been looking forward to this moment. Now that it had arrived, he felt awkward and lost.

Trajan and Servianus were still staring at him. At last, the governor responded. "At ease, Tribune, and thank you. Please sit down and tell us everything."

Hadrian hesitated, waiting for an encouragement from his cousin. Finally, Trajan too smiled at him. "By all means, Hadrian, join us. And thanks for traveling all the way from the Danube to bring us this important document. Marinus picked the right man for this mission. You are my ward and cousin after all."

Hadrian managed a weak smile. Servianus picked up the scroll and passed it on to Trajan who opened and read the dispatch at once.

"How was your trip, brother?" the governor wanted to know.

"Fine. Long, but it went mostly well. My horse fell sick; that was all. I had to commandeer a replacement from civilians in the area. Arriving at the next posting station I asked the *Cursus Publicus* official to compensate the civilians for supplying me with a new horse. I understand it's the law now, isn't it? Nerva changed that, I believe. We can no longer requisition without compensation, right?"

"That is correct, Hadrian," Servianus commended him. "You acted in compliance with regulations."

"Everything else went well?"

"*Sic, Legatus.* I am so glad I am finally here. I wasn't sure where to find my cousin. In Carnuntum they told me to go to Upper Germania."

Trajan put down the scroll and chimed in. "You did well, Hadrian. Thank you! This is a very important dispatch. Now I know that the undivided loyalty of the Danube Army and its commanders is mine."

Hadrian eased up. "Of course, my Lord. You are most welcome."

"Servianus," Trajan said. "Please arrange quarters for our young relative here."

"Sure thing."

"We will talk some more tomorrow, Hadrian," Trajan added. "For now, you are dismissed."

After servants shut the door behind him, Trajan commented to Servianus, "This is excellent. All I have to do now is to secure the loyalty of the legions of Lower Germania and come to terms with the Treasurer of both Germanic provinces. When that is accomplished, I will need to determine next year's key office holders in Rome with Nerva. It will require some horse-trading, and be assured, Servianus, you will be on the list."

"I am not worried," the governor replied. "But please keep me posted."

"In terms of Hadrian, Marinus tells me in his letter that Hadrian's tribunate in Oescus is complete. He is leaving it up to me what to do with him going forward. Julius, I would like to keep him in the army a while longer. He has served as tribune twice now and should start his civilian career now, but the army is good for him. Marinus tells me he is a debt-ridden spender. There is a lot of money in the Hadriani Estate but still... I am convinced living in Rome would tantalize him to spend even more. The hard frontier life on the other hand might be a 'remedy', don't you think?"

"That is up to you, Trajan, but I would agree. I could retain him with the Twelfth Legion *Primigenia*. But do realize there is always an opportunity to burn money – anywhere."

"You could do that?" Trajan was thrilled and ignored Servianus's cautioning remark. "That would be fantastic. The current laticlavian tribune would not be miffed?"

"I don't think so. He has been here for a year and a half already."

"Good. It is agreed then. Hadrian is better off being close to me now – and far away from the Capital."

Trajan was concerned about his kinsman's safety. His adoption would not go undisputed. There was always the chance for a cabal. Any plot would target both him and his cousin, but here at the frontier they were both safe.

"And Servianus, please keep an eye on the young man. Treat him like any other tribune. Don't let him get away with conduct that you wouldn't tolerate from the other officers. If you find out that he is running up a lot of new debt – I don't know how that would be possible here in Moguntiacum, but you never know – challenge him and make him aware that it's a bad example for the staff. Keep me apprised and tell him that you will keep me apprised. If all else fails, send him to me. Being the future emperor's cousin might get to his head, you know what I mean?"

"I will do my best."

Chapter 33

Trajan left Moguntiacum in the morning. On his way down river, he received many more congratulatory messages from throughout the empire, mostly from the western provinces. It would take more time for messages to arrive from the remote eastern provinces like Syria or Egypt.

Pompeia sent letters again, and he received correspondence from his sister Marciana.

From: Marciana Ulpia Traiana
To: IMP M. Ulpius Trajan

    Dear brother:

    So much is going on in Rome right now that
I don't even know where to start. The family is
still bewildered, but we are very excited. Myself, I
am joyful and concerned at the same time!
    Be careful, Marcus. I talked with Arrius Antoninus
the other day, who reminded me how dangerous it is to
be emperor. He said he would never want to hold this
highest of offices. Especially the transition period could
be a problem. What if some commanders won't go along?
What if they try to assassinate you? You and Nerva,
and even Hadrian could be targets. What if some self-
aggrandizing aristocratic drone conspires against you? And
what about the Praetorians? They were never consulted...
Admittedly, they know you are a soldier and you have
the legions at your disposal. But don't forget, the Guard
murdered Caligula many years ago, and only the gods
know who was involved in Domitian's assassination...
    Maybe you can trust Casperius Aelianus. He
served with Father and is supposedly a friend
of the Flavians, but I say, trust no one.
    Excuse me, dearest brother, I am babbling. Please be
careful. Only trust your next of kin. Maybe you should make
Hadrian your aide. Test everybody's loyalty before you rely
on them. Callistus is dependable of course and I like Sura.
    I am certain others keep you posted about what's
going on in Rome so I don't want to be redundant.

Just one thing, Nerva's health is truly bad. He had a
fever the other day and missed an important session
of the Senate. Be ready for what is certainly coming.

Love,
Marciana

Another dispatch came from Nerva. It contained a list of candidates for the suffect consulship. Attached was a discussion, how and why he had picked the men. Trajan suggested some changes in his reply but he was confident they would come to terms.

The most interesting message came from the Praetorian Praefect.

From: Casperius Aelianus, Praefect of the Praetorian Guard
To: Marcus Ulpius Nerva Trajan, Caesar Germanicus Imperator

Your Excellency:

I would like to take this opportunity and send my
most sincere congratulations to your adoption. It fills
my heart with the greatest joy that you, a good friend
of the Flavian Family, were chosen to be emperor.
I have served with your Father in the Jewish War
and I will serve you with the greatest pleasure.
The whole Guard shares my enthusiasm. We
are fully committed to guaranteeing your safety. At
last, Rome will have a strong and competent leader
again. We cannot wait for your arrival in the City.
If there is anything I can do, please let me
know, and I will do it. The situation in Rome is quiet
and peaceful. Your elevation is undisputed.

Yours sincerely,
Casperius Aelianus

Hmm, Aelianus thought he was returning to Rome. Clearly, Nerva and the praefect didn't talk to each other. No surprise there. But Casperius was mistaken - Trajan had no intentions to go into the lion's den. Instead, he wanted Casperius to come to him.

At long last, Trajan and his military escort arrived in Colonia Claudia, capital of Lower Germania Province, in late December. The eventful year was drawing to an end with the winter solstice festival, the *Saturnalia,* the most fun of all Roman holidays.

When the general and his men entered the city, snow was falling in a windless night, wrapping the soldiers in a surreal pallid coat and transforming them into ghost-like silhouettes trotting in formation, with Trajan at the fore. A blanket of thick snowflakes muffled the air and transfigured the town.

Trajan didn't mind snow or cold. In fact, he deemed the landscape rather picturesque, spectacular even. It reminded him of his time in Colonia where he had been in command after Saturninus's revolt.

Despite the weather, many people were on the streets, bundled up and wearing soft felt caps. Some carried packages and rushed to and fro without paying much attention to Trajan's troops. Others stopped, however, cheered at the troops and wanted to know the latest news from up river.

The packages they carried were of course presents for relatives and loved ones. *Saturnalia* was a time of joy and merriment, an occasion to light candles and enjoy a fabulous meal with friends and family. People were grateful that the shorter and shorter days were coming to an end. If they propitiated well, Saturn would be on their side next year and help them sow flourishing seeds for the critical summer harvest.

In all the frolicking even the slaves got time off. Many households, including the Traiani, allowed them even to be masters for one day. In a whim of nostalgia Trajan's thoughts returned to the Domus Traiana. The family would always pick a mock king or queen to preside over the mirthful festivities. If he just could be home now... Harpenna would be the queen and make him laugh imitating his father's idiosyncrasies - how he used to rearrange his hair by running his thumbs behind his ears and sweeping his hair back with the other fingers although there was barely any hair left to sweep, and how he would droop and sway while doing so. How funny this spoof always was.

Trajan's lips broke into a smile. His father might be dead, but he was with him in spirit.

Shortly after they had settled in at the gubernatorial palace a visitor arrived - Lucius Licinius Sura.

"Lucius, old friend! So good to see you. Sit down and rest from your demanding journey."

"You called for me, Trajan. Here I am. I rode as fast as I could. You don't want to come to Rome, eh?" Sura rattled. "You would rather stay in this gods-awful place?" he added with arched eyes.

Trajan chuckled. "That's the plan. I am happy you heeded my calling. It will take a great burden off my shoulders. I want you to take over as Governor of Lower Germania and command the three legions here. This will allow me to concentrate on the border and develop a campaign strategy for the spring - and to prepare myself for my duties as emperor. I understand Nerva is very ill."

"Can you believe it, Marcus?" Sura shouted, sawing the air with his arms. "Has it really sunk in on you? You will be emperor! Emperor..." He paused.

"Do you remember our time together in Syria when we solved the world's problems in an army tent at the Syrian frontier? How 'expertly' we evaluated the cabals at the Parthian Court? And now you will have your own court, the Greatest Court the world has ever seen. You will be the Master of the whole civilized world. And as I know you, you will add more lands, maybe even Parthia itself. You could become another Alexander the Great!"

"Hold the horses, Lucius. I am not even emperor yet. The gods are fickle. Don't count the chickens before they have hatched. First, we have work to do here in Germania.

But of course I remember. How could I not? I am so glad we met then. Now we can change the world together!

Oh, yes, Rome... I have no time to go there for a while, but what do I need to know about the situation there that is not covered by the official dispatches?"

"As you said yourself, Nerva's health is frail. Sometimes he has better days, sometimes it's so bad you'd think he's going to drop dead any time now. It doesn't matter. The Senate respects you, even the Republican faction headed by Tacitus do. They all need you against the Guard."

"Tacitus doesn't like me?" Trajan said concerned. "Though he was a good friend of my Father's."

"It's not about *liking* you. He likes you just fine, even compares you with his capable father-in-law Agricola who fought great campaigns in Britannia. To Tacitus, it's a matter of principle. He does not like the emperorship, period. I defended your elevation, and he seems to back off – for now."

"That's good to hear. Lucius, read this. Praefect Aelianus sent me a letter pledging his loyalty."

"Aelianus of all people," Sura replied with narrowed eyes. "He's got to say that - you are his superior. But don't even think of trusting him, Trajan. He is a mutineer and an oaf. I hope you know what to do with a man like him."

"I think so," Trajan said, glowering.

"Now, do you want me to help you organize the acclamation of the legions in your province? We should follow Servianus's example."

Trajan sighed, looked the other way.

"It is important. You know that, Marcus." Sura put on his most serious face, but then his cheeks tugged his lips into a wide grin. "Do you have any plans for tonight? Let's roll some Falernian. Is the kitchen well stocked?"

"I believe it is. Let me send for Callistus." Trajan was glad for the distraction.

They spent the evening indulging in nostalgia - first in the bathhouse, then over dinner in the triclinium. At midnight neither of them was sober. Callistus needed to help Trajan find his way to his chamber. For the first time in many weeks, Trajan relaxed. He fell asleep right away.

In late January, Nerva had another bad day. He broke a cold sweat and started to shake all over his body. Cursing his health, he sent for the doctors again. The Praetorian Guard was providing him with their best medics now. Much had changed since Trajan's adoption; everything had become easier. Even Aelianus was now polite and respectful to him. Nerva didn't see him much, but state business made it often unavoidable. When he did Aelianus was friendly, even proclaiming concern for his health, but Nerva snubbed him. He could afford to and still wanted him punished. Forced to lie down, his mind wandered back to the beginning of the year - when he was well enough to preside over sacrificing the White Bull as consul and *Pontifex Maximus*. The animal had been immaculate, and the sacred ritual had gone well, resuscitating Nerva's hope that the gods might give him another lease on life. But now he was sick again... It was high time to appoint a trusted man suffect consul.

Nerva was satisfied with his accomplishments. He had avoided a debilitating Civil War and resurrected the rule of law in the difficult time after Domitian's death. But peril had been with him all the way. He had survived conspiracies and a near-death experience with the riotous Praetorians. How stupid of him to appoint Casperius Aelianus, but how could he have known? If he had kept the previous praefects in office, a mutiny would have broken out right away.

By the time the physicians and medics arrived at his villa in the Sallustian Gardens, a third of a mile away from the Castra Praetoria, he was running a steep fever. They gave him a herbal medicine and ordered absolute bed rest, instructing his staff not to let anybody into the emperor's chamber.

Awake on and off, with aching bones and heavy lids, Nerva waited for his friend Antoninus who had promised to call and discuss with him Trajan's nominations for suffect consul. The emperor had his notes ready, but Antoninus didn't come. Instead, late in the afternoon the commander of his detail, a centurion named Regulus entered Nerva's *cubiculum*. "My Lord, I have this wax board with a message for you. Senator Antoninus left it behind when he came to visit you this morning."

"Came to visit me? By Rome's holy trinity, Regulus, why did you not let him in? Do you not know Arrius Antoninus is one of Rome's most eminent senators? He had an appointment with me!" Nerva's face turned red in anger. He coughed hard, again and again.

"Your Excellence, I had instructions not to let anyone into your room - not clients and not even senators. I apologize, but the doctors were very strict about this. Here is the board."

Nerva's coughing got worse. Regulus frowned and after a long glance at the ailing emperor, he stepped out of the chamber. Nerva was gasping for air. The bed was spinning underneath him, faster and faster, like a wagon wheel on a cartwright's bench. Darkness engulfed him and he felt no more.

When Regulus returned with the medic on duty, the emperor was dead.

"The fever has overwhelmed his old heart," the medic muttered, closing Nerva's eyes. "Call the praefect."

Chapter 34

Amessenger from Rome arrived in Moguntiacum after dusk. At the Praetorium they told him to ferry across the river, canter on to the spa at Aquae Mattiae and report to Governor Servianus there. Late at night he finally stood before the general and handed over a senatorial dispatch.

Servianus was in his night robes. A slave adjusted the wicker of the oil lamps in his office so he could more easily read the letter. The governor didn't wait for him to be done but paced through the message at once. Then he put down the scroll smiling at the courier. "We have a new emperor - my cousin Trajan! Isn't that something..."

"*Sic, Legatus.* I know. My orders are to ride to Gaul and notify the governors there. It will be up to you to inform the army of both Germanic provinces – including Trajan himself."

"No problem. I can't wait to do just that. I will send a trusted *decurio* at daybreak. You are dismissed. The quartermaster in Moguntiacum will take care of you and your horse."

By the time the courier returned to Moguntiacum, it was midnight. The air was clear and cold on this day in February; the stars were out in full force, sparkling brightly. The messenger's mare neighed and tossed her head with urgency. Tired and hungry, she desired to be stabled. The soldier couldn't wait himself. He gently stroked the horse's neck. Soon he dismounted in front of the quartermaster's office and handed off his mount to the stable slaves. An orderly of the garrison assigned his quarters and had him sign the paperwork.

"How about the taverns around here? Anyone still open?" he asked the enlisted man.

He chuckled. "At this time? I don't know. Maybe the Dragon's Lair."

"Is the food any good there?"

"It usually is. Of course, I don't know about a meal this late..."

"Where do I find this tavern?"

The orderly gave him directions. Then he asked, "What is your business up here in the middle of winter if I may ask?"

"You may. I have been so busy riding back and forth across the river that I haven't had a chance to spread the news yet, and the governor needed to know first. Anyway, it's not a secret anymore, but it will be news here. Nerva is dead! Our emperor died from a fever two weeks ago."

"Now you are telling me," the orderly exclaimed. "I can't believe that! Incredible - Nerva is dead..."

The courier nodded. "Yes, but I am tired now. See you in the morning."

As they were talking a small group of inebriated officers passed them by. One of them must have overheard the orderly's words. He stopped and pulled away from his colleagues. "What did you just say, man?" He eyed the two men. Then he pointed his finger at the courier from Rome. "You are not from here. This is a Roman city cohorts' uniform, isn't it?"

"*Sic, Tribunus.*" The messenger stood to attention and saluted the unknown ranking officer.

"Did I hear this right – Nerva is dead?"

"You did. The emperor is dead. I just informed the governor."

The tribune swung round to his colleagues. "Listen to the news here, my friends! Nerva is dead! This man here is a courier from Rome."

They stopped as if hitting a wall, turning to the other three men. One of them stepped forward, squinting at the courier. "I am Hadrian, the laticlavian tribune of this legion. Is it true?"

The courier stood to attention again and saluted the newcomer. "Yes, Tribune. It is. Emperor Nerva died from a fever - about two weeks ago."

Open-mouthed, Hadrian stared at the courier. "What else do you know?" he slurred. "What is happening in Rome?"

"I don't know all that much. Nerva has been in bad health for a long time. The Praefect of the City Cohorts ordered me to ride north and inform the Rhine Army. That's all. Governor Servianus will send a detail to Colonia Claudia tomorrow to inform Trajan and the other generals." The courier saluted again.

The officers looked at each other surprised. Suddenly the other tribune shouted out loud, "Long live Trajan!"

They all chimed in. "Long live Trajan! Trajan *Imperator!*"

Hadrian scurried to his room, his mind racing. Need time for myself now, need to think. The ramifications...

What should he do? Servianus would inform Trajan, but was that right? Should he not tell his cousin himself? After all, he had come all the way from Moesia to bring him the Danube Army's acclamation. They had sent him because he was Trajan's kin. Now, his cousin was not only designated emperor, but emperor in fact. Should he not tell Trajan himself?

Hadrian made up his mind. He would command a detail tomorrow and ride to Colonia Claudia. Trajan would expect him to. It was his duty!

He had a hard time finding sleep and tossed and turned all night. His slumber was shallow; he dropped in and out of disconcerting dreams. An hour before dawn, he was glad the night was coming to an end. He got up, put on his armor and went straight to Servianus's office. The governor was still in Aquae Mattiae, but Hadrian didn't have to wait long.

When Servianus and his escort arrived at the Praetorium, he frowned at

Trajan's cousin lingering at the entrance door. "What are you doing up so early in the morning, Tribune? Let me guess. You heard the news last night and want to go to your cousin right away, is that not so?"

"You read me well, Legate," Hadrian said stiffly. "Yes, indeed. I am asking for your permission to convey the news to my cousin and guardian in person. I would like to leave within the hour."

"Ah," Servianus said coldly. "Permission denied. This is state business. I will send a gubernatorial delegation representing the ranking officers of Upper Germania."

Rubbish. You are jealous, want to bask in the glory yourself and, more importantly, you want me not to.

"I respectfully disagree," Hadrian protested. "I am Trajan's kinsman. It was me who the Danube Army sent to convey their acclamation. It should therefore be me once more to tell my cousin that he is now emperor. I carry the trust of the Danube legions and I am happy to represent your legions as well."

"Don't be insolent, Hadrian," Servianus snarled. "I am the ranking officer and I am ordering you to stay here, and that is that. Now, get out of my way."

Hadrian shook his head but kept his mouth shut. He turned and left the premises in front of the Praetorium.

Knowing his sister's husband all too well he had not expected anything else. Hadrian hurried back to his quarters, picked up a travel pouch he had packed beforehand and rushed to the stables. His squire had his horse ready and was waiting for him. Hadrian thanked the boy, took the steed's reins, swung himself onto the horned saddle and spurred off. He was hell-bent to beat Servianus's men and didn't care about the consequences.

The severe winter weather forced Sura to invite less numerous detachments from the provincial legions to Trajan's acclamation. Each legion contributed six hundred soldiers, mostly rankers, and half its officers. Trajan's Pannonian cohorts including the archers who had escorted him to Lower Germania completed the congregation. Sura and the two other legates lined up the total of three thousand troops on Colonia Claudia's forum in front of the city's holy shrine, the *Ara Agrippinensium*.

Colonia Claudia was a Roman colony where Nero's mother Agrippina had been born fifty years ago, the daughter of the General Germanicus and second wife of the Emperor Claudius. In the following years the Romans had rebuilt the town, originally a port on Ubian territory. Due to its convenient position at the intersection of the main Roman roads on the Rhine it had become the capital of Lower Germania Province. As such, it had attracted settlers and grown to twenty thousand inhabitants. Solid stone ramparts surrounded the town on all sides to protect its citizens and the governor's residence. No legion was stationed here. The garrison, reinforced with town militia, was deemed strong enough to defend the walls until help would come from heavy infantry stationed in camps to the north and south.

The Germanic shrine had been converted to honor Agrippina, the famous female descendent of the Divine Emperor Augustus.

Sura sighed. *Not a bad place, but no replacement for an inauguration in Rome itself.*

The troops now filled the space between shrine and the semi-circle portico that housed many offices of the Roman administration. Thousands of civilians watched when three thousand army throats roared their allegiance to Nerva's adopted son under the eagle standards of the legions of Lower Germania, and hammered swords on shields in a deafening cacophony. Had it not been for the muffling effect of the snow on the ground, the din would have been heard even across the majestic river.

Chapter 35

Trajan applied himself to fully studying the geo-strategic situation of this distant outpost of Roman power. Weeks after his acclamation snow and frost still prevented him from making extended trips in the area, but he was able to sail downriver and visit the legionary camp at Vetera. The old fort had burnt down in the Batavian revolt. Because of its key location at the confluence of Rhine and Lippe, his predecessors had built a new camp not far from the old site. Trajan was impressed by the location and vowed to take advantage of it.

He studied military reports and maps, talked with many locals and traveling merchants returning from deep inside the free parts of Germania, hosted tribal leaders at his residence and picked the brains of his senior officers and their scouts. Often he would sit down with Sura to get his take on the situation, enjoying the brainstorming and massaging of ideas.

One day Trajan muttered with raised eyebrows, "I have thought about this long and hard now. It seems to me the Flavians did the right thing by conquering southwestern Germania, the Agri Decumates, even if it was a tough struggle with hardy natives. This makes it much easier for us to shuffle troops between Rhine and Danube. Founding Roman colonies and forts at key locations along the rivers has worked out too. We are well entrenched. The issue at hand is consolidation. Nerva, the old fox, recognized this. That's why he wanted me to reorganize the frontier."

His friend studied a large map they had unfolded on Trajan's desk. "Agreed, but what is your plan?"

"Before we get to that, let me ask you this, Lucius: Do you believe that the Rhine frontier is more exposed to unrest or less than the Danube?"

"Less."

"I agree. I say, much less. But we have six legions stationed here - why?" Trajan took his hands from the map and stepped back, frowning. He paced up and down the room, his hands clasped behind his back. "We have done much to bolster the Rhine since the Varus disaster, and two wars with Domitian have debilitated the most dangerous of the western Germanic tribes, the Chatti, who live just on the other side of the river. They are a shadow of their former past. And I might add killing Valdomarus hasn't hurt..." Trajan cleared his throat and grinned at Sura.

"By Mars Ultor, absolutely," Sura shouted approvingly. "That was something else. I wished I could have been there."

"The next powerful tribe east of the Chatti, the Hermunduri, has traditionally been a reliable Roman ally - a great diplomatic achievement. But several years ago, the powerful Bructeri, against whom I have fought as a young tribune many years ago, was destroyed by an alliance of their neighbors. They were annihilated in a series of engagements. This couldn't have been better; the lower Rhine is now safe from invaders. The remaining tribes are busy distributing the spoils of war or fighting each other – with no end in sight.

Now, the tribes in the northern lowlands and along the lower Weser, the Frisii and Chauci, are good warriors but disorganized. It is difficult for them to attack because competing tribes are stacked between us and them, and they have no good reason for war because their lands are sparsely populated and there is no lack of crops. What we still have to deal with is the occasional Chatti raid on distant outposts and hamlets in the Main valley.

Lucius, I see no reason why we need three legions in Lower Germania, likewise in the South. Vindonissa and Argentorate are no longer frontline cities. Since we conquered the Agri Decumates, the upper Rhine no longer marks the border."

Trajan stopped pacing, waiting for Sura's comment, but his friend kept quiet. The emperor resumed. "I like Domitian's policy of building palisade walls and watchtowers along the new *Limes* border. The palisades help monitor the commercial traffic between our provinces and the rest of Germania and slow down potential raids. Taking advantage of that, my dear Lucius, we need less infantry and more cavalry. Given the enormous length of the *Limes*, this is the way of the future.

Unless we try to push the border out all the way to the Weser River - and I can see absolutely no reason why we would do that - we are in great shape, but not so on the Danube. Yes, there is always glory in conquering new lands, but Germania's endless bogs and woods yield no returns. We know that from Drusus's campaign. The tribes are primitive, superstitious and even less civilized than their western brothers.

Still, work needs to be done. To increase our presence here I want to found a colony near the camp at Vetera to contain the Frisii and Chauci. We shall call it Colonia Ulpia Traiana. To secure our settlements along the western Main let us take advantage of Chatti weakness, expand the *Limes* barrier into their land and occupy the heights of the Taunus Mountains.

Additionally, I would like to close the gaps in the palisade walls between Rhine and Danube and establish one continuous wall with watchtowers and intermittent cavalry camps in its rear. We would have to make the western north-south section of the Main River into the new border and patrol the river with vessels from the Rhine fleet. The area between Main and Rhine would become a buffer territory within Upper Germania Province. Am I making sense?"

Sura met Trajan's gaze fondly. "You do, Marcus. We have talked about this before. We should involve Servianus in our planning now because he will get his hands full with this."

"Of course. I will brief him. For now, we have plenty of time; the snow has yet to melt."

"So no bold campaign deep into barbarian lands?"

Trajan laughed. "No. Valdemarus was an exception. My time in Pannonia showed me the Danube frontier needs my full attention even after the victory over the Suebi. Don't forget, the Dacians destroyed a whole legion once.

The Suebi is a numerous, but loose federation of several Germanic tribes, most prominently the ferocious Marcomanni and the cunning Quadi. The Dacians, their eastern neighbors, are a more advanced people. Originating from Asia Minor, they are not barbarians at all, Lucius. And they have been in touch with Greek Black Sea settlements for centuries. The Dacians have real cities and fortified strongholds. They are led by an ambitious king and funded by extensive hoards of gold that they dig in the mountains not far from their Capital Sarmizegethusa. A capital, Lucius! These people have a capital like we do. Their government collects taxes like us. Have you ever heard of a Germanic tribe doing such things? Those people don't even have a written language!

Anyway, that's what we know, and it's not enough; I want to learn more. When I left Pompeius Longinus in command of Pannonia, I promised him more troops for this year's campaigning season. I will keep my promise, Lucius. He will need them. Who knows, I may have to go there myself."

Sura nodded. He looked at a Danube map and counted the Roman troops stationed there, comparing their number with their counterparts on the Rhine. "Eight legions," he remarked. "Pompeius has eight legions of which he can only use four to fight the Dacians. On the Rhine, we have six legions in total. We could shift at least two of them to the Danube frontier."

"That's what I am thinking," Trajan said. "Perhaps even three. By the way, did you know that Domitian had planned to conquer all of the Marcomanni and Quadi lands? Amazing, isn't it? Domitian... What a strange man. He was a bad ruler, but his foreign policy was not so dreadful. He had intriguing ideas. Maybe that's what I liked about him. Maybe that's what held me back and not just my loyalty to the Flavian dynasty.

Unfortunately, paranoia got the best of him. He wasn't able to handle the nobles, didn't include the Senate in his government. A shame. Anyway, Lucius, I am telling you, he was onto something. Longinus thinks so too. If we had conquered the lands north of the Danube and made our allies, the Hermunduri, into a client kingdom, we would have one straight border line today from Dacia to the Rhine, with the Main river and Marcomanni lands east as the northern boundary. It would have confronted the Dacians with

Roman territory on both their southern and western borders.

The problem was and is still that the Marcomanni and Quadi are impressive fighters with a seemingly endless supply of men. I have seen that in the war last year. Their lands are vast, mountainous and thickly forested. Despite defeating them in battle, I believe full-scale annexation would take many years, cost many lives, too many, and deplete the treasury for no good reason other than glory. I will rather concentrate on the Dacians. Mark my word, Lucius. I have a feeling we will hear from them no matter what we do."

Trajan was in his element. He could not wait for winter to be over, but other obligations kept him busy enough. He received missives from senators in Rome, from generals like Pompeius and Marinus and from aristocrats and administrators all over the empire. They all wanted to get in touch with the designated emperor and consult with him on matters of State or policy.

He was most responsive to Pompeius and Marinus because he needed their cooperation for his Danube plans, but Sura pushed him not to neglect his contacts in Rome and the nobles whose support in the Senate he needed to maintain. Trajan also sent detailed letters to Nerva to keep him abreast of his activities and submit his strategy for approval. But no word came back from the emperor. He received letters from Pompeia instead, complaining about his continued absence.

When the politics and family obligations were getting too much Trajan sometimes dropped everything and shifted his attention to local military matters like recruiting more horsemen for his Personal Guard. He had taken over trusted men from the previous governor's unit and he could always count on his Pannonian crack troops. However, he needed to send them back to Longinus in the spring.

Traditionally, the horseguards of the Roman governor of Lower Germania were recruited from the Batavian tribe, but they had rebelled and fallen in disgrace after Nero's death. Despite that, Trajan had noticed Batavians in the governor's Guard. One generation after the awful events leading to the destruction of many frontier towns and forts in the revolt, the Batavians had apparently rehabilitated themselves.

For his recruitment effort Trajan also tapped into auxiliary cavalry from the allied Frisiavones and Ubians. He interviewed their best horsemen in person, assessing their military skills through tournaments and competitions all winter long, and signed up hundreds of men.

Chapter 36

Hadrian had been riding at a canter for three hours. The weather was sunny, but the winter air was bitter. Snow covered the landscape around him as far as his eyes could see, interrupted only by forested stretches of gray and black in the distance. He was getting hungry and his panting stallion needed a rest, but the tribune pressed on. He wanted to reach the next posting station. The road was in good condition because slaves of the *Cursus Publicus* had shoveled most of the snow to the sides and piled it up on the shoulder. Nonetheless, he never took his eyes away from the surface ahead, scanning for black ice.

Trajan's ward cantered on the main Roman road, parallel to the Rhine. It followed the river's western shore where possible but was never close enough for him to see the water. He had memorized an army map before his departure which gave him a good idea of his progress. The map was in his pouch now, and he didn't want to stop and waste time looking at it again. There was only one road along the river and only one relevant direction for him - north!

He had passed through several villages without a break. The locals had gawked at him. They didn't see a laticlavian tribune every day riding a horse at the double like a lowly emergency courier.

Rejoicing, Hadrian reached the courier station and inn. Reining in the horse he barked at the servants of the *Cursus Publicus*. "Quick! Feed my horse and give him water. Don't let him just stand; walk him under a warm blanket so he can wind down. Then wipe off his sweat, brush him and let me know when you're done."

He patted the stallion's neck and whispered soothing words into his ears. Then he walked into the building and wolfed down a quick meal: split peas and hard-boiled eggs, bread dipped in olive oil and vinegar, some fruit, water and a beaker of diluted wine. He also ordered a lunch bag, which he intended to eat on horseback. That way he would not have to stop again.

An hour later, rider and horse were rested and refreshed enough to continue the whirlwind trip. Hadrian was careful not to overdo it though. He couldn't afford the stallion to fail him on the long day trip to Colonia Claudia.

His mind was less at ease than the cantering horse, worrying about Servianus. Certainly, the governor would have discovered his absence soon and was cursing his imprudence by now. Riders would be on the way to catch up with him. Hadrian was determined not to let that happen. If he wasn't the first to inform Trajan of Nerva's death, his trip would serve no purpose. On the contrary, he would only be in trouble: Servianus would charge him with disobedience and Trajan would not see much value in protecting him. His cousin would value Hadrian's 'sacrifice' only if he achieved his goal. Or would he? Hadrian didn't even know that for sure, but he believed Trajan would appreciate it.

It was afternoon now. Hadrian looked back over his shoulder again and again to see if any riders were catching up to him. *Epona knows, faster horses than his might be on their way to intercept him. Jealous Servianus would try everything.* He couldn't fathom why his sister had married the ambitious governor. Now he had to compete with the man for Trajan's favor. *Almighty Jupiter, what is in store for me?*

On he pressed through the Germanic winter wonderland in the pale late afternoon sun, spittle flying from the cantering horse's mouth. Sometimes he tormented himself with the prospect of Trajan reacting differently than he expected. What would his guardian do? Hadrian could never go back to the Thirteenth *Primigenia.* Not anymore; he had disobeyed a direct order!

Once in awhile he would see a rider dash out from a hostel or house behind him. It scared him each time, but it was only local traffic, errand runs for impatient masters or a magistrate on a schedule.

Shortly after passing through Bonna – the sun was very low now - the stallion lost speed and started favoring his right front leg. Minutes later he was limping and fell from canter to trot. Concerned, Hadrian stopped and examined the horse's limping hoof. He could not see anything wrong with it, but he was not a veterinarian. Probably nothing serious but painful enough to hurt the animal. Galloping or even cantering was out of the question. The stallion flung his head up and neighed as if to say 'I will be ok, don't give up on me!'

"It's all right," Hadrian whispered in his ear, hugging the horse's sweaty neck. "Epona will take good care of you. All you need is a good day's rest."

But he didn't have a good day. Hadrian grabbed the bridles and started walking. The stallion followed without hesitating. They would have to do it the infantry way. The last 'leg' of his trip would be literally that: a march on foot. He strode as fast as he could, hoping to reach another posting station soon so he could recruit a new mount. Unfortunately, they had only passed one milestone since leaving the hostel. He knew Colonia Claudia wasn't far, but he would still have to tramp at least for an hour, maybe longer.

The sun was setting now, and the temperature plummeted. Nobody was on the road. Hadrian cursed his bad luck, shivering despite the fast pace of his strides. He kept craning his neck to watch out for riders. The visibility was not great in the twilight, but a crescent moon shed some light on the lonely road, allowing him to make out the road behind him for at least a quarter mile.

Hadrian became more and more nervous. The longer he was handicapped like this the more Servianus's riders would catch up. He had no way of knowing when they had left Moguntiacum or how fast their horses were. Finally, the tombs of Colonia emerged from the dark on either side of the road and the city walls became faintly visible in the distance. The tribune passed several glass and terracotta factories, which filled the space between the road and Colonia's port facilities. They were closed now, the furnaces silent and shut down. Everything looked bleak and abandoned, but he could see smoke billowing up from Roman bath houses behind the city walls. Civilization was beckoning!

It took another half hour until he reached the south gate of the city. Blisters from the forced march made every step painful now. He was exhausted but didn't grant himself any rest. Without further explanations, he handed the reins to the startled guards. They recognized his rank, obliged him. Hadrian ordered them to take good care of his horse and commandeered the only mount they had available at the gate. There was still no sign of other horsemen. Reinvigorated and certain he had prevailed, he galloped off to the governor's residence.

He had to ride across town and past the shrine in its center because the residence was located at its northern end. At the entrance he reined in hard, jumped off the horse, picketed it and ran as fast as he could into the building and past the startled guards. Inside, he announced himself to the steward. After a short while the official led him to the *triclinium*.

Trajan and Sura were reclining over dinner when Hadrian trudged in, begrimed and disheveled.

"I hope you have a good explan-" Trajan said perplexed.

"Oh my guardian and protector!" Hadrian interrupted. "*Legatus*, my cousin, you are Emperor!!!"

Trajan's cousin fell on his knees, heaving. He took off his red plumed helmet and put it down on the gorgeous mosaic floor. Tears ran down his sweaty cheeks, still glowing red from the cold air outside while he untied his army scarf. "I have ridden all day long to bring you the news, oh my cousin." Hadrian sobbed, still out of breath. "Nerva is dead! He died from a fever two weeks ago."

Trajan dropped the spoon he was holding. It fell into the soup bowl with a splash, but he barely noticed. His jaws went slack.

Sura was expressionless at first, but then a smile creased his face. He looked at Trajan's sobbing cousin with sympathy and helped him up. "Get up, my friend, and sit over here. There is no need to kneel."

Sura walked Hadrian to the free sofa while hundreds of thoughts flashed in Trajan's mind. So it had happened after all... Much sooner than he had been hoping for. Should he travel to Rome right away? What should he do with his command in Germania? What were the Praetorians doing, the Senate? Questions over questions. Only one thing was certain:

His life would never be the same.

He composed himself. "Tell me more, Hadrian," he asked his ward. "What else do you know?"

Hadrian shook his head. "Not much. The messenger from Rome arrived last night. Servianus is supposed to inform you, but I wanted to bring you the news in person. I am your kin!"

"What do you mean by 'supposed to inform me'? Hasn't he done so by sending you?" Trajan asked stupefied.

"Ah... well... Not exactly. He didn't want me to go. He wanted to send a detail of officers with a personal letter from himself, I guess."

Trajan gulped. "Are you telling me, you rode off anyway?"

"Yes, Caesar!"

"I can't believe you did this. You violated his orders?"

Hadrian held Trajan's gaze defiantly. "He is jealous, Trajan. He doesn't want me to be on good terms with you. Servianus wants your favors for himself!"

Trajan turned his head to Sura. "Did you hear that? My cousin does not need to follow orders anymore because his cousin is an emperor now..."

"Don't mock him, Marcus," Sura said sharply. "Listen, I understand Hadrian. He is your cousin - and your ward. Look how fast he made it here. From Moguntiacum to Colonia Claudia in one day in the middle of winter, all alone. That's impressive! Kinship is kinship. What matters is that you now know that Nerva passed away - the gods bless his soul – and you, Trajan, are emperor. You are our new lord. This is the best news I have ever heard in my life - thanks to your brave relative here who risked his career to bring it to you so fast!"

Trajan still didn't know what to think. He was mad at Hadrian for ignoring Servianus's order. At the same time, Hadrian's courage and the lightning-fast ride impressed him. And what a body...

"Thank you, cousin. Thank you," he finally said. "Don't think I don't appreciate what you have done. We will talk about military conduct another time. But now, do you want to eat with us or take a bath first?"

Hadrian looked down at his disheveled uniform. "I am hungry, but I need to take off my armor and get out of the messy uniform first – if you don't mind."

"Of course not." A gentle smile appeared on Trajan's face. "We don't, do we, Lucius?"

"No, certainly not," Sura concurred. "Take a quick bath, Hadrian, and join us for dinner afterwards."

He clapped his hands and a cupbearer entered. Sura ordered him to take care of the young tribune. Hadrian nodded at the two men and followed the servant out of the room.

Chapter 37

"**B**y Castor and Pollux, it's getting cold in here," Sura cursed as they resumed their meal.

An attentive slave hurriedly left the *triclinium* to complain to the hypocaust supervisor.

"Save the Deities of Salvation for more important purposes," Trajan admonished him. "We may need them soon."

"You are right, Marcus," Sura conceded. "But it IS cold in here." As if to prove the point he scratched his arms with his hands.

Trajan shook his head. "I should send you on a winter expedition into the land of the Suiones. That would remind you what cold is."

"Oh no, my friend," Sura shouted. "There is no need for that. Come on, what are the steam cavities under this floor and the hot tubes behind the walls for? Let me have a bit of Roman civilization. Let me whine a bit; I am tired of the chilly weather in this gods-forsaken place."

Trajan fell silent. His mind was consumed with the tidings from Rome. Emperor now... But he didn't want to return to the capital; the frontier still needed him. Could he afford to stay?

Sura interrupted his thoughts. "You are so quiet, Marcus. Are you not looking forward to being Caesar?"

"I don't know, Lucius. I guess I should, but I have no illusions. It will be a huge task. We both know that."

"Sure, but I also know that you will be the best emperor ever. Historians will compare you to Augustus and Julius Caesar. The world will remember you as the epitome of courage and excellence. I am sure of it, and I am not saying this to flatter you. You know that, don't you?"

Trajan didn't hear Sura finish his sentence. The comparison with Augustus and Julius Caesar upset him. He thundered. "Caesar? Augustus? Are you saying I measure up to a Julius Caesar?" He scowled at his friend. "Lucius, are you comparing me with Caesar - Gaius Julius Caesar?"

Sura only returned a blank stare.

"Caesar was a phenomenon, a force of nature that swept away the decay of a dying Republic. He was a genius like there had never been before and never will be again! A giant like that is only born once in a thousand years.

Yes, my new title will include his name - and rightly so because it makes us remind ourselves of his greatness. But Lucius, the comparison is humbling, depressing. Caesar is the incarnation of all that is good and right and just in humanity, all that is competent and capable, all that ignores hardship and one's own petty interests for the good of all. Caesar saved the Republic by destroying it; he had no choice. The corrupt Senate and its egotistic millionaires obsessed with power, who called themselves *Optimates*, the 'Best' though they were the worst, ruined the commonwealth and everything our forefathers had accomplished for centuries.

We were close to self-destruct in endless civil wars because avarice had gotten the best of our leaders! I don't even want to think of Caesar as a general. He conquered all of Gaul within eight years. Imagine that, Lucius. Within eight years... Do you have any idea how incredible that is?

It took us one hundred years to conquer Hispania, and Gaul is larger than Hispania and more populated. At Alesia, he defeated three hundred and fifty thousand Gauls with an army of maybe seventy thousand legionaries. Imagine the odds. That, my friend, was Caesar. Compared to him I am nothing, a dwarf, a beetle at best."

"Now, now," Sura protested with a smile. "You make it sound like you are street beggar."

"Not at all. I don't lack self-confidence, as you know. But I have yet to prove to the world that I can rank among men of the caliber of a Caesar or Augustus," Trajan insisted.

He lifted his eyes to the beautifully vaulted ceiling of the *triclinium*. When his gaze met Sura's again, they were glistening wet. "As to Augustus, he was very different from Julius Caesar, yet he was truly great also. Augustus was not a military man, but he knew how to pick a brilliant general: Agrippa who became his right hand man. With Agrippa running the Army Augustus brought peace to the world, dispatching the decrepit Republic at the same time. His genius was to keep the institutions of the State alive while at the same time foiling the destructive warring of the nobles. He outmaneuvered the Famous Families, and is probably still laughing at them in the heavens. But it was not only a smokescreen. He in fact allowed the Senate to keep governing some provinces like Greece and Hispania and appoint proconsuls and propraetors there. But these provinces didn't billet the legions and were secondary in importance. Where it mattered, he kept the reins close to himself or ruled through trusted family members like Drusus or Tiberius. After his death forty-five years later, senatorial government had become an artifact, and he had established an empire.

But you know what, Lucius? It was Tiberius who finished the work of both Caesar and Augustus. Had it not been for his valor, steadiness and wise decision making, Senate rule would have returned. I am convinced of it. The bickering would have resumed and the reckless efforts of the Famous Families to grasp power at the expense of everyone else would have sprung up anew.

Yes, Lucius, it would have been a return to the time of Marius and Sulla when Romans fought Romans and the government was unjust and weak, perverted and rotten. Did anybody thank Tiberius for that? No, nobody. Tiberius is as unpopular today as Caligula and Nero because it is the historians who write history books – and to be a historian you have to have money. To have money you need to be a senator. And senators hate emperors because they crave power for themselves.

Emperors on the other hand don't have the time to write history books; they have work to do. Tiberius was appalled by the politics, horrified by the backstabbing, even in his closest circle. Think of the treacherous Praefect Sejanus. After the wretch's plot Tiberius lost trust in humanity altogether and retreated to the isolation of Capreae. Despite his disappointment he ruled wisely and competently until his death. I have much sympathy for him. I can relate - and I have seen it too - the human beast." Trajan sighed. "Thankfully, Pompeia balances me and so do you, Lucius. You give me empathy and endurance. Tiberius didn't have a Sura or a Pompeia. He had no one he could trust. I am certain, if he had been married to someone like her, he would never have gone to the island. His isolation and becoming a recluse invited rumors that he was a bloodthirsty, debaucherous monster. But that is another story."

The *triclinium* went quiet. Both men dwelled on their thoughts. Then Trajan called out, "By Jupiter, I talk too much, Lucius. Let us have more wine."

"Where is Hadrian?" Sura asked. "He still hasn't come back."

"My cousin is likely more tired than he thought he would be. He may have fallen asleep. Don't worry. The servants will take good care of him."

The cupbearer stepped forward and refilled their goblets.

"I hear you, Marcus," Sura responded to Trajan's long monologue. "But listen to me: You will be a great Caesar. After what you just said I believe in it even more."

Trajan was flattered.

So much to think about. He would not find any sleep tonight.

It was late at night when the steward knocked on the door and announced the arrival of Servianus's representatives. They were quickly admitted, but Trajan cut them short. "I already know. Hand me Servianus's dispatch and leave us. The quartermaster will assign you rooms."

"Thank you, Caesar. Hadrian has beaten us, huh," one of the officers said, pulling up his left eyebrow. Trajan didn't answer, grabbed the scroll with Servianus's seal and dismissed the men. Then he opened it. *Caesar they call me now, Caesar...*

The letter contained the governor's congratulations and a complaint about Hadrian's conduct, but he deferred to Trajan as to whether or how Hadrian should be punished.

Trajan still didn't know what to do about that. A smile appeared on his lips when he thought of how ferociously Plotina would defend his cousin, but other things were more important now. Tomorrow, he would dictate a letter to the Senate. They rightfully expected his assurances.

Early in the morning Trajan called for Callistus and informed him about Nerva's death. The faithful secretary and friend boxed the air with his fists and cheered. "I had an inkling," he shrieked. "When I told you about your adoption that day in Carnuntum I was thinking this might not be a long transition period. And here you are! Emperor Trajan... Splendid! Will you keep me around though?" He looked at Trajan with anxious eyes. "I have heard stories that emperors have so much correspondence they need an army of secretaries..."

Trajan laughed. "My friend, you have nothing to worry about. Of course, you will stay in my service."

"You are serious?"

"Yes, I am."

"Dominus, dark rings surround your eyes. You didn't get any sleep last night, did you?"

"Is it any wonder? It's too much to digest in one night. Callistus, I called you because I have some urgent letters to dictate. Get ready."

Callistus pulled a fresh scroll from a pigeonhole behind Trajan's desk and sat down. He picked up his reed pen and dipped it into the inkwell on the desk.

"Write this," Trajan said and started pacing back and forth in the office.

From: M. Ulpius Nerva Traianus, Consul Ordinarius, Son
of the Divine Marcus Cocceius Nerva, IMP CAESAR AUG
To: Senatus PopulusQue Romanus

Senators and People of Rome:

It is my sad duty to acknowledge the death of my
Father, the late Imperator Nerva. May his soul ascend to the
heavens! Though still in awe, I am honored to take his place.
Let me affirm the inviolate principle under my
rule that no senator or any other citizen will be sent
into exile or executed without due process. The days
of terror are over and will not return as long as I am
Princeps. Long live the liberty of the Roman People!
As a first step, I am requesting you to approve
the deification of my Father, the late Marcus Cocceius
Nerva. Please grant him the obsequies customary for a
legitimate Emperor of Rome. After the traditional five-day
public waking period there shall be a State Burial with

procession and pyre in the Forum Romanum. Nerva's
apotheosis shall include the erection of temples in his name
throughout the empire, with associated priests, altars
and the installation of the Cult of the Divine Nerva.

Dear Senators, I am looking forward to working together
with you in a spirit of amiable consultation and cooperation.
Like Augustus, I am only a Princeps, First Man of Rome, and
not an absolute ruler detached from People and Senate.

As Consul Ordinarius and in my absence,
I hereby call the Senate into session, asking
it to formally confirm my succession.

I will travel to Rome as soon as the circumstances
allow and cannot wait to meet with you all in the Curia
and elsewhere to discuss the well-being of the State.

For now, my first duty is the safety of the empire. To this
end I am reorganizing and reinforcing the northern frontier
in Germania. Expect ongoing dispatches on this matter.

Roma Aeterna Est – Rome Lasts Forever.

Trajan
IMP CAESAR AUG

Trajan dictated many more letters: to key individual senators, to his mother Marcia, to his sister Marciana and of course one to Pompeia. He told her about Hadrian's willful ride and asked for her advice. One thing was clear: He could not send Hadrian back to Servianus. Maybe it would be best for his ward to serve in a province that he had never seen before. Perhaps he should serve directly under him. Or should he send Hadrian to Rome and have him start his civilian career?

Trajan decided to keep him in Colonia Claudia for the time being and assigned him to Sura's staff as *Comes Augusti.* That way Sura could use him in different roles without having to replace his own laticlavian tribune. It was obvious to everyone that Hadrian had a special relationship with Trajan, and Hadrian would be relieved for not having to go back to his post in Moguntia-cum. In a way though, the new assignment recognized his defiant ride. Trajan felt a punishment was still appropriate to make him understand the importance of military hierarchies and to send a message to the other officers that, kinship or not, Trajan expected everyone to follow orders. Maybe a tough first assignment could take care of that.

Chapter 38

In the following months Trajan paid close attention to recruiting trusted men for his Personal Guard. Presently, he only had the five hundred gubernatorial horseguards of Lower Germania Province. As emperor he needed more, not only as a matter of station but out of necessity. After all, the Praetorian Guard was in Rome while he was up here on the frontier.

To distinguish his Guard from the Praetorians Trajan renamed the horseguards *Equites Singulares Augusti*, Elite Imperial Horsemen. To double their number he would recruit qualified men from the province's auxiliary cavalry. He asked his commanders to nominate their best soldiers, but limited the number to no more than two thousand candidates from whom he would select five hundred.

Trajan didn't mind that none of them was Roman or at least a Roman citizen, but they needed to be fluent in Latin. He even liked men of provincial Germanic stock. They wouldn't have vested interests in domestic politics. As long as they were motivated and well paid they would be a reliable force, loyal only to their paymaster – him. This system had worked well for the Julio-Claudian emperors. The Praetorian insubordination had disgraced the Flavian model of sticking to native Romans only.

As soon as the candidates arrived Trajan put them through their trials. He designed thorough tests himself and interviewed every man in person, looking for excellent riders and formidable spearmen. Tournaments would examine and verify their ability levels and endurance. Trajan also held mock fights with wooden swords to test their fighting skills both on horseback and on foot.

Watching the men fight on the compacted snow of Colonia's drill fields reminded him of his youth – when he had carved his own wooden swords and played with Quintus in the woods of Hispania. Unfortunately, he had lost touch with his boyhood friend. The news of Trajan becoming emperor would likely knock his sandals off. Life was constant change; only family had staying power. He missed his family, most of all his father. How much good advice old Traianus would give him now...

Following Governor Paulinus's request the new emperor sent most of the Pannonian cohorts back to Paulinus; only the Syrian archers stayed in Colonia. Their shooting ranges were located adjacent to the main drill field. Trajan had them hone their skills with the composite bow every day. Each shootout increased the distance to target. The round plates with the bull's eye in the middle were soon so far away that the soldiers called the range a lottery. But the best bowmen were able to hit the targets over a distance of up to four hundred and fifty feet.

All the while Trajan directed his staff to execute his border expansion and fortification plans. Work also started on the new city of Colonia Ulpia Traiana. The weather had warmed up enough for the snow to melt. Traces were still visible on scattered shaded spots, but Trajan's pioneers could now fan out with their *gromae* and survey the site of the new colony. The layout would follow the ubiquitous rectangular grid of intersecting streets at ninety-degree angles.

The Governors Sura and Servianus were Trajan's administrative pillars, but he also needed a commander for his Personal Guard. Who would be the right man for this? A valiant and experienced soldier certainly and someone he could trust. Sura! But no, he corrected himself, Sura was already stretched thin with supervising the extensive border reorganization.

Meanwhile, delegations arrived from the legions to pledge their loyalty. They came from Britannia, Gaul, Hispania, North Africa, Egypt, Syria, Palestine, Cappadocia, Thrace and Illyria. A delegation also pulled in from Pannonia, sent by Pompeius Longinus, who let him know he was about to engage the enemy again. Marinus sent a detachment from Moesia. Both generals requested the emperor's presence. They pointed to a tough campaigning season ahead, confirming Trajan's own thoughts on this matter. He would have to wrap up the affairs in Lower Germania soon and march off. Rome would have to wait.

The only legion that did not send a delegation was the Praetorian Guard. Instead, Praefect Aelianus sent a letter, offering to come to Germania and take his rightful place at the emperor's side to guarantee his safety and reinforce his military presence in Germania. Trajan accepted one part of the offer and allowed Aelianus indeed to visit him, but he put restrictions on the size of Praetorian delegation: no more than twenty officers, no rankers.

Then there were the many letters arriving from the administration and courts in Rome, from provincial city officials and imperial governors –congratulating him and requesting guidance for their affairs. Trajan was stupefied by the amount of the mail. He and Callistus needed help. Julius Caesar had supposedly dictated five to ten replies all at once. But he wasn't Caesar, and Callistus was drowning in correspondence.

The Senate sent a dispatch to confirm Trajan's accession. Its leaders signed the declaration, putting their seals underneath: Arrius Antoninus, Julius Ursus, Annius Verus and Neratius Priscus. The Senate also elected Trajan *Pontifex Maximus*, Chief Priest, the only imperial office he had not already held together with Nerva. This made his elevation final and sacrosanct, but the senators went beyond that. They awarded him the title *Pater Patriae*, father of his homeland. Additionally, they honored Marciana and Plotina with the title *Augusta*.

This horrified Trajan. He wrote back that he would accept being *Pontifex Maximus* but refused to be called *Pater Patriae*. Nor did he want the titles of *Augusta* for his sister or wife. He argued they needed to earn these titles and that he would be happy to reconsider that in the future but under no circumstances now.

Trajan was still upset over the Senate's accolades when Sura entered his office. "What is going on, Marcus? The soldiers can hear your distress out in the hallway..."

Trajan grumbled. "I can't help it. Politicians! They are all politicians - opportunistic and eager to please. That's not what I want. Rome will need to learn dignity and integrity again."

"What happened?"

Trajan filled him in.

"I can't blame them," Sura said. "This is how it's been for almost twenty years - throughout Domitian's reign. It will take them time to adopt a different mindset, but once they do they will never go back to the old ways. You will be an agent of change. Don't forget, not pleasing the emperor in the past could have meant death or exile. Nerva turned things around, but the incident with the Praetorians made them jittery again. Many senators don't know you that well, they are cautious. Some even associate you still with the Flavian House, and that included Domitian."

"I didn't realize Domitian had corrupted the political culture so much. Perhaps Tacitus is right. Maybe the whole concept of monolithic rule has outlived itself. I wouldn't know how to replace it though."

"That's exactly it. What is the alternative? Senate rule? Thank you very much. That greedy crowd ruined the Republic with their ambitions and machinations. Rome needs a strong but benevolent hand - you." Sura's grin was infectious.

"My friend, your trust in me is flattering. I hope I will do this high office justice."

"You will. By the way, Marcus, did you hear that Tacitus is writing a monography about Germania? He sent me a letter saying your presence here has resulted in much interest in this part of the world. Many Romans think it must be important. Tacitus is committed to educating them. He did time in the Rhine Army and is well connected. I am convinced he will write a fascinating book. People will be amazed how many different and dangerous Germanic tribes there are.

The book will be good for you too because you won't have to explain why you are not coming home. Have them read Tacitus's book. He calls it 'Origin and Geography of the Germanic Tribes'."

"When will it be published?"

"I don't know. Tacitus is determined to wrap it up by the middle of summer."

"Perfect. I have a feeling I will be on the frontier all year long."

"Marcus, we were talking about a successor for Aelianus the other day, remember? I had one of my freedmen do some research on this by looking into the military archives. After studying his recommendations I like Attius Suburanus the best. As procurator of Belgica Province, he is the paymaster of the Rhine legions. Servianus and I can always rely on him. And he never abused his power." Sura paused. "I think he is your man."

Trajan nodded. "I have thought of him too. Attius is an experienced governor and a good man. But will he be up to this particular task? It will take courage, cunning and stamina. You realize, he would not only command the newly formed *Equites Singulares* but also the Praetorian Legion in Rome, a scary bunch."

"I realize that, Trajan, but I believe he is up to it. Suburanus is clever and knows the mindset of the soldier, including the Praetorians. But how about Aelianus himself? What are you going to do with this ghastly fellow?"

"I don't know yet. I actually met him here in Germania many years ago, during the revolt of Saturninus. He helped Domitian quell the revolt." Long wrinkles creased Trajan's forehead. "Very well, I will have the procurator come to Colonia. Suburanus offered to visit us anyway. In his latest dispatch he joked it would be fun to see where his money is going. 'His money'... It made me laugh."

On an overcast day in late March, the Praetorian Praefect Aelianus and his men arrived in Colonia Claudia. The snow was gone, and Colonia's citizens were out and about, cleaning up the streets, repairing winter damage on their terracotta roofs. Squalls roamed the fields outside the city walls, planting seeds for the summer harvest.

Trajan's Personal Guard admitted the caparisoned Praetorians to the imperial residence and steered them to the stables where ostlers took care of their horses. From there, the officers strutted to the Praetorium, expecting to meet with their new master. The doors in fact opened, and Trajan stepped out on the drill field, flanked by Sura, Suburanus and Callistus. Several centurions of his Guard stayed behind, lingering under the canopy of the entrance doors.

Aelianus recognized Trajan right away though he had filled out and grayed a little since he had last seen him ten years ago. "*Ave, Imperator,*" Aelianus saluted. "We have come to join and protect you in your endless efforts for the good of all."

His gaze swept about Trajan's entourage and then fixed the emperor. His men stood to attention behind him wearing their best uniforms and helmets. A s*ignifer* held the Praetorian standard with his trademark lion's skull strutting on top of his burnished helmet. The animal's hide was hanging down the man's back. The huge paws were crossed over his chest. The soldier's staff was littered with silvered and gilt bronze plaques and figures. One plaque depicted the scorpion, the Praetorian Guard's heraldic animal. Another plaque displayed the name of the new emperor Trajan, engraved in gold.

Trajan frowned at the *signifer.* "I see you have already adjusted to your new master," he shouted at Aelianus, pointing at the plaque with his name.

"Yes, my Lord," Aelianus replied unctuously. "It is our sacred duty. You are our master, the legitimate ruler of Rome. We serve you and only you." His throat was dry. He swallowed hard. "It is good to see you again, Trajan. It has been many years..." The praefect formed a fist with his right hand and struck his chest with it to underscore his loyalty.

"Is that what you told Nerva?" Trajan asked him sharply.

Aelianus froze. A pang of fear gripped his heart.

"Will you also push me aside and kill men in my service?" Trajan glared at the praefect while pointing to Suburanus, Sura and Callistus at his side. "Maybe the patrician Sura here or wispy Callistus?"

"*Imperator,* we never meant to be impudent. But we had sworn an oath to defend the Flavian House-"

"Well, you failed at that as well," Trajan interrupted him. "You - all of you - are a disgrace for the empire! You have violated your sacred oath, the oath of loyalty and obedience. You are scoundrels and mutineers, trying to save your necks. Instead of coming here you should have resigned and taken your lives in honor."

Aelianus's mind was racing. He had miscalculated the situation. The House of Traianus and the Flavian House had been allied for so long. As a young tribune he had even served with Trajan's father. He and Trajan had worked together during Saturninus's revolt. But that was a long time ago, and obviously, it didn't matter.

Aelianus turned half-way and eyed his officers. They were nestling their belts, looking at him for leadership in this unexpected confrontation. Casperius motioned his face back to Trajan. He tried to swallow, but his mouth was so dry it hurt. He coughed, cleared his throat. *By Minerva, what can I do to save us?*

He raised his head, determined to brave Trajan's unrelenting glare. They measured glances for a seemingly unending moment.

"Are you calculating the odds, Casperius?" Trajan mocked him now. "We are only three plus four. You have twenty men with you!"

Aelianus was no fool, however. They had no chance against the whole garrison, and Trajan looked prepared. On top of that he was a skilled fighter. The praefect fell on his knees. "I apologize, Dominus! We are all here to pledge our allegiance. No Praetorian will ever raise his sword against you!"

His men kneeled with him. Some nervously fondled the hilts of their swords.

"Good," Trajan said magnanimously. "Apology accepted. Rise."

Then he lifted his right arm, and out of nowhere a detachment of archers surrounded the Praetorians, their boots crunching the snow with thick leather soles. Aelianus shuddered. His men huddled closer together, eyes flickering, glances darting in all directions. As officers they carried no shields. Forty pinewood and hazel arrows with sharp iron tips were pointed at them on strong Persian bone and sinew bows - death at close range...

They started to scream, to beg, to argue, but Trajan's arm went down. The arrows whipped forward with a hiss, hitting their targets one by one. Aelianus felt the terrible impact in his throat. Once, twice, punching him like a boxer in the Olympic arena. He reached up, tried to pull the arrows from his neck. A gusher of warm blood ran down his trembling hands. Casperius couldn't speak or shriek or even croak. He whirled around, hoping to defeat the pain somehow. Instead, he lost his balance and fell on the white snow. The arrows twinged his neck and head, making the pain even more unbearable. Aelianus rattled. Aghast, he stared at his blood that was soaking the snow everywhere around him, turning it crimson red. Then he felt no more.

All Praetorians were impaled in throat and neck by two missiles; they couldn't even yelp. Trajan had not taken a chance: two archers for every officer, sealing their fate the moment their horses had trotted onto the imperial compound. The rigorous training had paid off.

The emperor left the scene without looking back. Sura and several centurions of Trajan's Guard remained on the drill field to supervise the cleanup and removal of bodies.

In his office, Trajan addressed Suburanus. "Attius, you have your work cut out for you. Not only do you need to forge my horseguards into a cohesive fighting unit, but you will also have to clean house at the Praetorian Guard in Rome. We have killed the leading officers today whom I consider the ringleaders of last year's mutiny. That is a deterrent, but you don't want terrified soldiers, you want motivated ones. It won't be easy." Trajan paused, hesitated. "And one more thing." He took off the sheathed sword and shoulder belt from a hook on the wall behind him and handed it to Suburanus. "Here. Take this sword. Use it for me if I rule well and use it against me if I don't!"

BOOK V

THE WARS OF NECESSITY

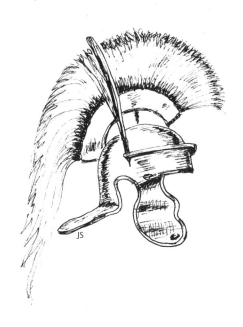

Chapter 39

Three years later (99 AD), Rome

Trajan could see from far away that Rome was not like on an ordinary day. Everywhere people clambered on rooftops, aqueducts and arches to see him. Throngs crowded the defunct ramparts of the Servian Walls Rome had long outgrown; the legions gave the city the protection it needed. All wanted to see the new ruler today. After all, Trajan had not been to Rome since he became emperor.

From his distant viewpoint the people looked like swaying ants, but as Trajan and his entourage came closer he could make out details and hear the jubilant clamor. His lictors and Praetorian horseguards, all dressed in civilian tunics, approached the Flaminian Gate now, the portal marking Rome's northern boundary on the Via Flaminia. The crowds took aim at them right away, pressing through the open gates and pushing against lictors and horseguards. Men and women alike reached out with their hands, trying to touch the emperor somewhere on his shiny white and purple toga. "Trajan! Trajan! *Salve, Imperator!*"

Many attempted to break through the cordon surrounding the emperor. Keeping them at bay was difficult without *pila*, but the lictors hooked their elbows together and formed a determined human shield wall that kept the crowd from overrunning the emperor and his companions.

Trajan was walking on foot to demonstrate he was but a citizen like them, a man of the people and for the people, who enjoyed being in their midst. His hair was cut short in military fashion, his garment but a plain senatorial toga. Only the laurel wreaths his lictors had attached to their *fasces* indicated his status as *Imperator* - victorious general.

Trajan smiled, waving at the multitudes around him. "*Avete, Quirites!* It is good to be home. Home at last!" he shouted.

Inside the arches of the Flaminian Gate, the Praetorians opened a pathway into the crowd through which the senators and knights of Rome, assembled behind the walls, could stride to welcome the emperor. Close-by, droves of ordinary citizens lingered to watch the imperial procession.

Trajan recognized many of his clients and the sons of senators and knights, who were hoping for political advancement. Callistus and Titinius Capito, a secretary he had added to his staff last year to help Callistus, walked beside him, flanked by Praetorians and their detail commander, all wearing civilian clothes to emphasize the civilized character of Trajan's reign. Of course, the tunics were belted and had *pugiones* attached, just in case. Somewhere behind him followed Hadrian and other ranking officers. Trajan did not award Hadrian any preferential treatment, such as letting him enter the Eternal City at his side. Cousin or not, he wanted Hadrian to earn it.

The first official to salute Trajan on sacred city ground, inside the *pomerium,* was Praefect Suburanus, who had done a fabulous job over the last eighteen months reforming and cleansing Casperius's old Guard and integrating many of Trajan's *Equites Singulares* into the Praetorian ranks. Without his success Trajan could not have returned to the Capital. Having the unconditional loyalty of the Guard was an absolute requirement for his safety. Today, Trajan's column of horse troopers, waiting behind him, would add another twelve hundred men to the Praetorian Guard, raising the total number of *Equites Singulares* in the Guard to two thousand.

After Suburanus, Trajan greeted the two suffect consuls and leading senators: Antoninus, Ursus and old Frontinus, water commissioner under Nerva and his designated consular colleague next year. With Sura, Priscus and Longinus in command on the northern frontier he was looking forward to Frontinus's experience and advice in the Imperial Council.

Trajan shook hands with many more senators and knights and also his private clients against the backdrop of the jubilating throngs lining the streets near the Flaminian Gate. When Trajan finally lifted his arm, tubas were blown to indicate his departure from the Gate and his ensuing procession on the Via Flaminia to the Forum Romanum. Slowly and gently, the lictors clawed their way through the crowds. Loosely screened by his troopers, Trajan followed his escort, smiling and waving at his people.

When he peered at the rooftops up above he saw them so packed with men and women of every age and class that some of the roofs were dangerously sagging. Loose mortar was falling on the ground and some terracotta tiles. Alarmed, Trajan sent his soldiers to remove people from those roofs. *The City Cohorts should have managed this better.* To his relief, the pressure was relieved before anyone was hurt.

Then the procession resumed its march to the Forum Romanum. It had been a long time since his last stay in Rome, Trajan mused. Rome seemed not to have changed much though he had yet to see Domitian's preposterous palace.

Trajan yearned to see Pompeia again. His poor wife had unremittingly complained about his long absence. Now he was back. What would she say? How was she? And how was his sister Marciana? And her daughter Matidia and the two grandnieces, one of whom Pompeia wanted Hadrian to marry?

Callistus and Capito also beamed and waved at the crowd though Capito's smile was well contained. Trajan sometimes wondered whether Domitian had made Capito a cold and apprehensive man. Nerva had retained the man's service after Domitian's death and recommended him even before Trajan was looking for an experienced administrator to assist Callistus. And Capito had in fact exceeded Trajan's wildest expectations. He turned out to be a capable and efficient secretary and worked well together with Callistus.

Trajan enjoyed seeing the myriad of garlands people had decorated their houses with. As he passed by, women emptied buckets of tufting rose petals and showered them on him and the whole procession. Revelers on the street snapped them up and tossed them in the air again. The emperor was basking in a sea of red exuding the finest rose scent he had ever smelled. What a welcome! Only one thing bothered him: He would miss the Army, and he was afraid he would miss the army life very soon...

Awhile later the procession reached Rome's hallowed center: the Forum Romanum. Trajan's heart beat faster as he saw the lictors in front of him turn right, passing the Forum of Julius Caesar to their left. On the right, he glimpsed at the ancient State Prison, the Mamertinum. Then the column reached the Via Sacra and the forum plaza between the two court houses, the Basilica Aemilia and Basilica Julia. To the left, smoke billowed up from the Vesta Temple as always, filling Trajan's heart with joy and awe. Ever since the foundation of Rome many centuries ago the six Vestals have been tending to the hearth of Rome, making sure the sacred fire would never go out - a ritual honoring the importance of fire to the well-being of all and a permanent and heartening reminder of the stability and peace Rome had bestowed upon the world.

The procession marched on to the Treasury, located in the towering Saturn Temple, and passed the temples of Concord and Vespasian in front of the Tabularium, seat of the public archives that connected the two hillocks of the Capitoline Hill. Then it pressed on between the temple of Concord and the *Rostra*, the oratorical platform on which Nerva had announced Trajan as his son and successor. Then it passed the new colonnade of the *Dei Consentes* and started its climb up the left side of Capitol Hill to the massive Jupiter Temple, Rome's biggest. Trajan raised his eyes at the humongous building containing in a dedicated chamber each the statues of Rome's supreme gods: the trinity of Jupiter, Juno and Minerva.

The time of reunion was at hand. Plotina and the whole Traiani family were waiting in front of the temple at the stone altar of *Jupiter Optimus Maximus*. He could not see them yet because the street meandered up the hill and took two sharp turns until it connected to the temple square.

Finally, there stood the Empress Plotina, dressed in a stola made of the finest emerald silk, fixed to her waist by a jewel-studded belt and expertly draped to form stylish pleats. Over the dress she wore an oversized golden chain necklace crossing over breast and shoulders. Her hair, dyed copper-blonde, was artfully piled on her forehead in a fanciful assembly of towering curls and gathered in an elegant bun over the nape of her neck. She looked beautiful and yet austere.

Their reunion reminded him of how they had met for the first time, here in Rome, on a stormy winter day in the house of a friend of his father's, who had introduced her not without pointing out her impeccable ancestry. Offended and embarrassed by this blatant act of 'brokering' a wife, Trajan had stayed away from her. But she had drawn him in with her wit and many interests - and the rest was history. Their bond had weathered many storms, even his disaffection with the female body. Pompeia was nothing short of a miracle - now they would be the imperial couple.

Plotina stood reverently by the altar and was flanked on either side by a Vestal Virgin. Behind them was the imperial family and Rome's assembled priesthoods.

As Trajan stepped closer, Pompeia and the two Vestals bowed before his lictors. They stopped and parted to allow Trajan to greet the empress. Trajan's pace accelerated until he stood right in front of her, hugging her with pleasure. "Pompeia, dearest Pompeia. The wait is over. Here I am..." he whispered.

She beamed. "You look wonderful, Marcus. Strong and tall as always."

"I missed you. I am so glad we are reunited."

Then he turned to the Vestals and ceremonially kissed their hands. They stepped aside and he crossed to his family to hug Marciana, Matidia and his nieces.

His sister chirped, "It is so good to have you back, little brother. I was afraid we'd have to find a new *Pater Familias!*"

Trajan put on a glib smile. "Right... Is there someone specific you have in mind?"

"Just joking," Marciana assured him. "But we did miss you with all that happened: Father's death, the unrest in the city and so forth. It is most unusual for a new emperor to spend so much time in barbarian lands. Your place is here, in the Eternal City!" She pointed down to the Forum with both hands.

"Well, I am not your normal emperor, you know," Trajan replied with a wink. "The safety of Rome demands a sacrifice at times." He caressed her cheek and returned to the altar, which was now surrounded by Jupiter's High Priest, the *Flamen Dialis*, and the Vestal Virgins.

"Speaking of sacrifices - we have all convened here to do just that. *Flamen*, proceed!" Trajan ordered.

The Priest of Jupiter paraded around the altar on which his assistants had started a small crackling fire. The altar was cut from ashlar and painted in a bright blue, like the frieze on the Great Temple itself. The stone masons had chiseled it to look like an open scroll. Its left edge resembled the stud of the scroll's wooden core. *So we can read the book of the* gods... Ceremonial fires had blackened the countertop over the years. Paint was only left in specks on the sides.

The *Flamen Dialis* handed Trajan a blessed piece of meat and *mola sals*a, roasted wheat flour with an extra pouch of sacred salt. Then he turned to the altar and lifted his arms up to the mighty columns of the Jupiter Temple. He intoned with a baritone voice, "Dearest *Jupiter Optimus Maximus*, we have gathered here today to render our gratitude for Trajan's safe return to our beloved city. Please accept the gifts he is offering you as a token of his and the People of Rome's appreciation of your benevolence."

He shifted to Trajan and signaled him to go ahead with the Sacred Act. The emperor tossed the meat into the fire with a bang. Sparks flew in all directions. Then he took the *mola salsa* and dropped it onto the flames. Finally, he opened the bag of salt and emptied it into the crackling fire. With his act complete, Trajan kneeled down in front of the altar and watching the flames he prayed silently while the *Flamen Dialis* continued the holy procedure with ritualized verses.

Trajan rose and remerged with his lictors. They picked up their *fasces,* and the procession headed back down the forum valley and over to the Palatine Hill. This time Plotina walked by his side, followed by the imperial family. After some final cheers the senators and knights scattered, but the Praetorian Guard remained to screen the imperial family from the pressing crowd in the Forum Romanum, caparisoned with vibrant garlands on all sides. The procession passed the Curia and Basilica Aemilia to the left and then marched on the Via Sacra past the temples of Castor and Pollux and the Deified Julius Caesar to the right.

The gilded trim of all the public buildings basked golden in the soft light of the afternoon sun. Peeking between the two temples, Trajan could see the monumental arcades and colored marble façade of their new home soaring in the background, the Domus Tiberiana, Rome's imperial palace dating back to the days of the Emperor Tiberius.

The din of the hooting crowd destroyed any attempt for a conversation between him and Plotina on their way. So they just smiled at the people. At last, they arrived at the entrance hall of the towering palace. Praefect Suburanus had gone ahead so he could welcome them once more at the threshold to their new home. He smiled at the couple. "Welcome, *Augustus* and *Augusta*. It is my supreme honor and duty to host and protect you in these hallowed halls."

Trajan was going to enter the building, but Pompeia held him back. "Wait," she whispered, glancing at the lofty marble fascia of the palace. "There is one thing I want to say to you, husband." Her index finger pointed at the magnificent edifice. "I don't want it to change me, Trajan. Please promise that you will tell me if it is changing me. You know what they say, power corrupts and absolute power corrupts absolutely..."

Trajan nodded at her stern-faced. "It is true. And I promise - I will tell you. But it is not going to happen. We will remain who we are. You will see!"

Pompeia's eyes hazed over. She took a big breath. "I swear," she said with her voice shaking. "I swear by all that is sacred and holy that I will remain who I am: Claudia Phoebe Pompeia Plotina Piso - empress and all!" Then she grabbed Trajan by the hand. "Let's go and be worthy of this place. At least it's not Domitian's ostentatious monstrosity!"

Trajan chuckled and they entered the vestibule. Inside, they crossed the somber entrance hall with echoing steps on the Egyptian marble floors. At the back of the vestibule, railed switchbacks constituted a ramp to the main building upstairs. Suburanus showed the way and guided them to their quarters. Along the way Trajan admired the elaborate stuccowork on the ceilings and the gorgeous mythical frescoes on the walls. Arriving on the top he realized that the palace's main building was enclosed in all directions by lush gardens. Three of these courtyards formed terraces overlooking the upper and lower Forum Romanum, and one even extended down the hill in the form of a hanging gardens.

Trajan had seen the shrubs from the Via Sacra, but he realized he had never been up here before. Vespasian and Titus never resided here, and Domitian had gone ahead to build a new and much larger palace in the middle of the Palatine Hill. Nerva was the first emperor to move back into the Domus Tiberiana, and Trajan deemed it proper to do the same.

It was on these terraced lawns where Suburanus had arraigned the palace staff to salute the imperial couple. Pointing at the many men and women he said, "Before I walk you to the imperial suite I would like to introduce you to your staff."

Plotina and Trajan nodded. He was glad to see that Callistus and Capito attended the assembly. But where were Marciana and his niece and the grandnieces? After all he had asked them to move into the palace with him. There. They came rushing up the ramp behind them, and the praefect ushered them alongside the Imperial couple. "Now that we are complete, may I direct your attention to the members of your staff?"

To start with, he presented the members of the imperial administration by rank: the all-important commissioners of the water and bread supply, the praefects in charge of Fiscus, City Cohorts, Fire Brigades and the Night Watch, the procurators of the *Cursus Publicus,* Games and the Mint, adjunct accountants and treasurers, petition officials, palace librarians and many more.

Trajan shook hands with each and every one of them. Some had served under Domitian, some under Nerva and some were new appointees, signed by Suburanus. Continuity was important to Trajan because he didn't want to lose precious expertise, but at the same time he was resolved not to employ officials, who were too closely associated with Domitian's acts of terror.

Suburanus then pointed at the Lord Chamberlain, who bowed to his new masters and introduced them to the household staff, the *Palatini*: the chamberlains and chambermaids, scribes, secretaries and stenographers, cooks and confectioners, tasters, cupbearers, janitors, porters, caretakers, carpenters, metal workers, physicians, vets, nurses, midwives, dressers and hairdressers, masseurs, barbers, landscapers, florists, druggists, perfumers, page boys, scullery boys, ostlers, couriers, goldsmiths, blacksmiths, shoemakers, tailors, dyers, embroiderers, seamstresses, saddlers, waterers, grooms, waggoners, carters, stable-guards and others.

At the end, Trajan signaled to the praefect that he wished to address the assembled men and women. He raised his hands. "Attius, thank you for the introductions. *Palatini*, before Pompeia and I settle into our new quarters – and I know the move-in will be a lot of work for all of you – I would like to talk to you about myself and my expectations." He glanced at their mum faces. "You all know I am a soldier. I have simple needs and simple requirements. All I expect from you is honesty and dependability.

In the palace you won't see me as a soldier or as a general. I will not have you parade or beat you like a centurion sometimes pounds his recruits with his vine stick. This palace will be a place of civility, dignity, sincerity - and fun I hope!

I know some of you have served under Domitian and Nerva, and you have seen huge differences between the two. Myself, I will be more like my adoptive Father, but more casual than he was. Still, I share many of his values. He had to be careful and sometimes aloof to save his neck. I can afford to be different because I have the support of the Army, the People, the Senate and the Guard - a great advantage for us all." Trajan paused. "I will be an accessible emperor," he continued. "You can come to me at all times. There will be no chamberlain in your way. I will abolish arcane court rules and certainly those that would restrict access to me. If you have a concern therefore or want to share something with me, please, do not hesitate. Come and see me! You can approach me in the hallway, in my office, at lunch or in the morning hours after I have received senators, equestrians or clients of my family. And don't be surprised to find me on the streets and other places by myself, sometimes with a Praetorian escort but never in a litter. I prefer to walk and will ride a horse only when I am in a hurry.

At any rate, I would like to establish a spirit of fellowship behind these walls and encourage you to keep your doors open like I will and help each other in your assignments. The better you work together the more you will get done and the happier you will be – and make me."

Abruptly, he raised his voice, glaring at them. "I will not tolerate intrigue and the playing of games in my house!" Then he smiled again and concluded his speech. "Now you know where I stand and what I expect from you. I am confident we will get along fine."

The Palatini clapped politely, and Trajan turned to Suburanus. "Attius, our quarters?"

"*Sic, Imperator.* Follow me."

Chapter 40

Trajan eased up to Pompeia in their *cubiculum* where she was standing at the window, eyes cast down on the Forum below. "What are you pondering, dearest?" he asked.

"Oh, not much, Marcus," Pompeia said with a heavy sigh. "It's just... I thought I would never be here. But low and behold, at my feet is the political center of the civilized world." She met his gaze with a peculiar mix of surprise and contentment.

"Will you miss the Domus Traiana?" he wondered.

"Not at all. The Domus Tiberiana is fabulous, and I have all the people here with me that are dear and near to me. What more could I ask for?"

Trajan kissed her hair and gave her a hug. "I am glad to hear."

Plotina looked at him as if she had seen something strange.

Trajan frowned. "What is it? Is something wrong?"

"No, nothing. I am so glad you are back, grayed and all-"

"Oh, I can have that fixed."

"No, no, no," Plotina hurried to say. "It gives you an extra aura of *gravitas*. You are only forty-two, young for an emperor. The gray hair looks good on you."

Trajan still wasn't quite sure whether this was a compliment or not. "They are not all gray – yet," he quipped.

"It is fine. Don't worry."

She eased closer. "I missed you," she whispered and touched his muscular chest.

Trajan froze, looking away from her. "Pompeia," he said softly. "In the last couple of years - while we were so far apart, I always looked forward to your letters, your sound advice and your thoughts. I did. You are so wonderful, but..." He hesitated.

Pompeia lifted her gaze to him. "Yes..." she said.

"I can only be your husband," Trajan croaked, feeling terrible. *Why did it have to be that way? Was that Claudia Aemilia's spell?* "Pompeia, you deserve more. Have a man - I would not object. Or divorce me. I can handle the gossip."

"Never! I am no adulteress. My place is at your side - even if we cannot..." She didn't finish the sentence. She couldn't. Such a man – and yet... He was not hers to have. "I love you," she whispered. "I will always love you."

Trajan stared at her in despair, opening his mouth.

"Shhhhh," Pompeia admonished him. "Don't say anything. Shh, shh." Then she hugged him and pressed his face hard on hers.

Trajan just stood there, feeling like the greatest failure in the whole entire empire. He would never be her lover or, for that matter, any other woman's lover. He was not attracted to the female body. There was no way around it. "I adore you, Pompeia," he managed to say. "I cannot give you what you deserve, but know this: You have my friendship, always." He swallowed embarrassed, dropping his eyes on the floor.

"I know, Marcus. It's all right. I will manage."

"What do you plan to do with Domitian's wretched informers that we have in custody and with those who are guilty, but we haven't caught yet?" Julius Frontinus asked.

The other Council members peered at Trajan with probing eyes, but his face gave nothing away. Instead, he asked, "What would you do, Julius?"

"Hm, hm... I don't know. That's a tricky question, but I would say that those who have admitted their crimes and were sentenced by the courts should be punished as a message to all that you don't put up with despicable behavior. Those on the other hand whose guilt is unproven should be indicted as soon as possible. The plaintiffs have been waiting for your arrival to file their cases, I am sure."

"And what about corrupt procurators still holding office, who have not been charged because nobody dares to?" Arrius Antoninus questioned.

It was a month after Trajan's advent in the Eternal City. He had attended several sessions of the Senate and familiarized himself with the top political issues but so far had made no decisions. The Council was getting apprehensive. He could tell from the way they looked at him.

Only the splash of the water fountains outside the Council chamber and Callistus's reed pen scribbles were audible in the room. Trajan's secretary was recording in short hand every word spoken in the meeting and would later distribute copies to the attendees.

Suburanus chimed in. "Certainly, your Majesty has pondered these weighty matters. We would like to hear your thoughts. Now that you have paid the Army's *donativum*, issued the *congiarium* to the eligible residents of the City, struck coins to commemorate both events and announced Public Games to celebrate the new rule, these constituencies are taken care of. It may be time to take the next step, Trajan, and address the more complicated issues."

"You are right," Trajan answered. "As a matter of fact and as some of you know, I spent a lot of time thinking about these matters. But it's not like the courts haven't worked on this already. Ever since I sent Attius to Rome to take over the Praetorian Guard the courts took up many cases that were hung because the Praetorians had intimidated the juries. We have many sentences on the books today, some of them death sentences, some of them exiles.

What is left to do is the execution of those sentences.

And this is the problem I have. I don't want to begin my rule with executions. I want to usher in a new era, a civilized era, an age of liberty and opportunity. Executions don't go with that. Justice must of course be served and evil-doers be punished. I cannot tolerate crime. These felons altered wills, seized properties, usurped the positions of their political enemies and worse. They deserve to die, but there will be no executions."

The Council members frowned at Trajan with wrinkled foreheads.

He continued. "Plus, they are too despicable to waste money on execution tribunals. I have a much better plan. At the end of the next gladiatorial games we will parade them on the floor of the Flavian Amphitheater. Let them walk on the blood of other criminals that will have died killing each other in front of their eyes. Let the people yell and howl at them, and pepper them with rotten eggs and tomatoes. Let us scare them, make them believe they too are going to die – and then lead them away, march them to Ostia, force them to board a ship with tied hands, set the sails and let it drift out to the open sea. May Neptune decide their fates – not me!

If they die, so be it. If not, then the god of the sea decided otherwise and they can live out their wretched lives on some distant shore. But they cannot return and will never again hurt innocent people."

"Brilliant," Antoninus cried, and other Councilors applauded in support. "What a great idea!"

Trajan added, "Men that have not been indicted or caught yet, shall be brought before a jury now. I will leave it up to the magistrates, but if they are condemned they shall suffer the same fate as those that we have dealt with before.

Now, the problem of corrupt procurators and governors installed by Domitian is entirely a court issue. I will not press legal charges myself. In prominent cases I am happy to serve as the presiding judge, and I will certainly encourage prosecution where appropriate.

In critical tax disputes between the government and its wealthy citizens I will institute a new lottery system to appoint the judges from the bench of fiscal praetors. This will make it impossible to lobby for the 'right' treasury official favorable to one's cause. If the Treasury loses, so be it. At least nobody will be able to say it wasn't fair."

Pompeia was ecstatic. "I am so proud of you, Trajan. The people love you, rich and poor – even the capricious senators. When you start your third consulship next year you will be the most popular emperor since the days of Augustus!"

"Now, now," Trajan played it down. "Not true. Titus was popular also and his father Vespasian."

"Titus does not count," Plotina argued. "He only ruled for two years. And Vespasian, yes, they respected him, but they LOVE you, husband."

"It didn't hurt that I threw extravagant Games for them."

"Yes, I heard the gladiators were terrific though I don't care about that sort of thing. It's barbaric."

Trajan shrugged. "Maybe, Pompeia, but it is very Roman and necessary masculine education. It inspires young men to become fighters themselves, shows the glory of victory. Wars are far away these days. The populace must not think they don't exist. They do, and we need courageous soldiers that don't shy away from bloodshed."

Pompeia sighed. "I guess. You like a good fight because you are a warrior. That I understand.

But back to your public standing - aren't you happy how well things are going? People realize a new age is dawning in fact, a time of freedom and stability - created, guaranteed and fostered by a gallant monarch – you."

"Of course I am happy, Pompeia. But remember what we said when we moved into this palace? Let's stay humble. I don't want this to go to my head. I want to concentrate on the important tasks, namely agricultural reform in Italia and a potential war with Dacia. And I want to embellish Rome, to visibly underpin the new age. Almost every emperor since Augustus has built a forum of his own. I want to add mine and I want it to be both beautiful and practical. I have sent for the best architects and engineers in the whole empire."

"Don't worry, husband, I will stay grounded. It's just so nice to be in such good standing, supported by the aristocratic networks, provincial governors and the Senate here in Rome. The Army downright worships you."

"You are right – we are blessed. I enjoy it as much as you do, but I am not naïve. Even with all that support, there will always be dissatisfied elements, envious of my power. One knife in my back is all it takes to undo everything we have accomplished.

I have founded an agency on the Caelian Hill. It will use the infrastructure like couriers, horses, posting stations etc. of the grain supply agency to keep an eye on what's going on among the nobles. The agents will tell me who meets with whom and so forth. I believe that's better than a massive bodyguard presence around my every move."

"You are going to have your own spies in the city?" Pompeia shouted out.

"No." Trajan wiggled his head. "Not at all. In my view, they aren't spies. I won't use them to do harm. All I will use them for is to gather intelligence with discretion. Liberty needs claws too, you know."

Chapter 41

One night Pompeia woke with the urge to go to the bathroom. Turning to the other side of the bed she saw that Trajan wasn't there. *Oh the wine*, she sighed, slipped into her nightgown, left the *cubiculum* and trudged to the latrines on the other side of the hallway. There she got a glimpse of her husband, as he and the pageboy Pulcher entered one of the imperial guest rooms together. She gasped and quickly hid behind the closest marble pillar so they couldn't see her. The door closed, and they were gone. Sadness engulfed her and a tear rolled down her cheek. *Oh Trajan...* Why does it have to be that way? She swallowed and scurried to the toilets. Back in the *cubiculum*, she kept crying on the tasseled velvet pillows of the imperial bed.

Her mood brightened in the morning when Hadrian came to visit. "It's so good to see you, Publius! What can I do for you?" She hugged him, firmly pressing him against her breast.

"Oh, nothing, my Lady," Hadrian said and gently pulled back from her embrace. Glances darted from his eyes in all directions. "Is Trajan around?"

"No, he is not. My husband is meeting with the architect Apollodorus of Damascus on the Capitoline Hill. They are discussing plans to build a new forum between the Julian and Augustan Forum. The Jupiter temple gives them a good viewpoint, even better than this palace. After the meeting Trajan wants to decide which builder will get the contract. Apollodorus is a likely candidate."

"Of course he is. The Syrian is the most distinguished architect in the whole empire. They say he is a genius with concrete and has experimented with groundbreaking vaults of dazzling dimensions, grander than anything we have ever built."

"Well, there you go." Plotina smiled. There wasn't much Hadrian did not know about. "What are you up to these days?" she asked him. "Your days in the legions are over, aren't they?"

"Yes, my service is complete, and I am getting ready to pursue my public career. I will be up for quaestor soon. The *Cursus Honorum* is demanding in its own right, you know. At this point, however, my focus is on my father's inheritance. I have come of age and I am a ward no more. As you know, Attianus and Trajan have relinquished their guardian duties. I am my own man now."

"I am happy for you!"

"Thank you, Pompeia. It is very exciting. In the spring - when it is safe to sail - I will visit my father's vast estates in Hispania, particularly the olive plantations in Baetica."

A pageboy came by and bowed in front of them.

"Yes?" Pompeia asked him annoyed.

"Majesty, this young lord's sorrel horse is picketed in front of the vestibule. Should we take it in and give it a spot in the stables?"

Plotina looked at Hadrian. "How long are you going to stay, Publius? I am more than happy to have him take care of your horse."

"No, that's all right," Trajan's cousin replied with a salacious glance at the pageboy. "I won't stay long, Empress, but we can have a quick chat."

"You heard him," she told the boy and dismissed him. "Please, Publius. Sit." Pompeia pointed at the sofas of the reception area. "A glass of wine for you?"

"Please."

The empress signaled the cupbearer standing-by. He scuttled off.

"Hadrian, I was thinking - now that you are no longer a ward, you will be expected to get married and have children."

Hadrian pressed his lips together. "I guess so."

"Have you looked around?"

Plotina knew Hadrian wasn't ready. At the same time she didn't want him to lose the opportunity with Trajan's grandniece Matidia Sabina.

"No."

"I have an idea, Publius."

"You do?"

"Yes. How about Sabina, Matidia's daughter?"

"You mentioned her before, Pompeia, I am not interested."

"This isn't a matter of what you are interested in! It isn't even a matter whom you love or don't love, Publius," Plotina lectured him. "It is a matter of prudence. You are related to Trajan and you should seal this bond by joining the Traiani family through marriage."

"Trajan doesn't like the idea," Hadrian cautioned.

"He will come to his senses. My husband doesn't want anyone to marry his darling niece. One day he will realize she needs to get married to someone and he knows you are the natural candidate. The family likes you; everybody in this household likes you! Best of all, Sabina likes you too. It's easy and it's time."

"Fine. We shall discuss it later." Hadrian took one last sip from his goblet and rose. "Pleasure seeing you, Pompeia," he said without a smile.

The empress hugged him good-bye. "You will see. It will be all right."

She accompanied him to the Palatine portal of the Domus Tiberiana. Gatekeepers opened the heavy oak doors for the visitor, and an ostler brought up his horse. Hadrian swung himself on the steed and wheeled her around. "Pompeia, what's that pageboy's name again?"

"Pulcher. Why?"

"Oh, nothing. I like men that take the initiative and use their brain on the job. Commend him for me."

A week later, on the eve of *Saturnalia,* the imperial couple hosted a state dinner. Hadrian was looking forward to it. The weather in Rome had been damp and cold, the days short. This would be a great distraction. The empress had praised the event as merry and colorful, featuring dancers, acrobats, flame-throwers, musicians, pantomimes and other entertainers. The festivity would be private, but a similar event would be held for the public in the new palace built by Domitian. *Winning favors – the name of the game in politics,* Hadrian thought.

When he arrived at the Domus Tiberiana the event was in full swing. As before in the Domus Traiana, Harpenna was appointed mock queen with the power for one evening to order anyone around. She visibly enjoyed being at the center of the attention. Imperial slaves swarmed all around her like court jesters, dressed like their masters, who occasionally served them and refilled their glasses as per the ancient Saturnalia custom. Falernian flasks flowed freely, lyres and flutes were playing, exuberant dancers skittered in exotic costumes everywhere. Guests lounged on their sofas and chairs masquerading as craftsmen, cooks, fullers, soldiers, sailors and members of other professions. Some had even dressed up as real or mythical animals.

A werewolf approached Hadrian, growling at him. He almost didn't recognize her, but it was Plotina! A smile tugged Hadrian's lips. She had a bushy tail attached to her derriere, wore a furry wig and had stuck false teeth into her gums.

"I have never heard of female vampires, Pompeia. What's up with that?"

"I am not a vampire," Plotina corrected him. "I am a werewolf!"

"Ah. I thought you were a vampire from dark Dacia, trying to make us familiar with our enemies."

"Interesting thought but tied too much to reality. Tonight, we will forget all about that, I hope!"

Hadrian grinned. "Sounds good to me."

"It's a shame you didn't dress up too, Publius" the empress chided him.

"I never do." Hadrian craned his neck seeing Marciana from the corner of his eyes. "Excuse me please, Pompeia," he said and hurried to greet Trajan's sister. She enacted a centurion, wearing colossal padding underneath the *pteryges.* A fine leather cuirass simulated an abdomen rippling with muscles.

"Marciana! You look hysterical. If it weren't for the long hair, I could mistake you for my cousin!" he joked with a generous smile.

She laughed back at him. "Not bad, huh? After all, I am the sister of a warrior and need to keep up!"

Hadrian went on bantering with the other members of the imperial family but shunned Sabina. He was mingling with guests from the equestrian order when he ran into a group of pageboys including Pulcher, who was wearing the Lord Chamberlain's tunic and had painted his face to look like the official.

Hadrian remembered him right away. "You may look like the Lord Chamberlain, but you are Pulcher, the boy with the beautiful eyes, aren't you?"

Pulcher blushed, pulling up his eyebrows. "*Ave*, young Master. I am happy you are here. All good times," he slurred.

Hadrian decided to catch up with him quickly. He lifted a decanter full of wine from a serving table nearby and filled his and the boy revelers' goblets. "Drop that word 'Master' tonight, Pulcher. Tonight, you are the Master and I am the slave!"

Pulcher giggled. "*Sic*, Mas- ahem, Hadrian."

Trajan's cousin joined Pulcher on his sofa and they spent the next couple of hours together as if they were old friends - blabbing, drinking, joking and savoring the mirth around them.

Hadrian enjoyed himself thoroughly, and Pulcher became more and more inebriated. Having served in the legions Hadrian could handle vast amounts of alcohol. *Perfect.* After several hours he dragged Pulcher away from the others and walked him to an empty chamber in the upper level of the Domus Tiberiana. "You can have me," Pulcher purred.

And I will.

At the end Pulcher fell asleep and Hadrian left the *cubiculum*. Exhausted, he decided to go home and snuck out of the palace in the cover of the night.

The next day Marciana dropped a casual remark in Trajan's presence. "Oh Marcus, did you see Hadrian and Pulcher last night, all cozy and sharing one sofa?"

Trajan frowned. "Yes."

"I saw them disappear into a guest room together..."

"You did? You are certain it was them?"

"I swear!"

A feeling of envy clasped his heart. He called for Pompeia. "It seems Hadrian slept with Pulcher yesterday! Your favorite relative is out of line – again. And this is the one you want to marry my Sabina? Out of the question! Who does Hadrian think he is? He is just a distant cousin, and I don't share lovers!"

"She is not 'your' Sabina, husband," Pompeia countered. "Stay rational,

Trajan, please! He is the right man. I know it and you know it."

Trajan paced up and down the atrium floor of the Domus Tiberiana. Around them imperial slaves were still cleaning up from yesterday's event. "Hadrian is an ingrate! He is insolent, jealous and can't control his penis."

"We don't know that. Marciana has only seen them enter the room together. What happened in the room is conjecture, some kissing maybe. Trajan, they were both drunk. Hadrian may not even have recognized Pulcher. The pageboy was dressed like the Chamberlain after all. I will ask him. If he crossed the line, I will scold him, don't you worry!"

"Of course he crossed the line. 'Not recognized him…' Bah! You don't seriously believe your own gibberish! The Chamberlain is fat and flabby whereas Pulcher has the perfect body."

"Well, you must know all about that," Plotina said sarcastically. "In any case, I insist, he may not have recognized him. And who says they slept together? I doubt it. Hadrian knows his limits."

"You doubt it - I don't!"

"You are jealous because you think he touched your pageboy. Admit it. Then you dare come to me and complain about it – to me! The very person you SHOULD touch…"

Pompeia's shoulders were shaking now. She sobbed and pulled out a fine silk handkerchief to blow her nose.

Trajan backed off. "Fine. I understand. I will take care of this on my own."

"You will not," Pompeia shrieked. "Don't you dare. This is our issue, not just yours."

"Exactly," Trajan said, striking a more conciliatory tone. "Ours. Think of the scandal: 'The emperor and his cousin get it on with the same slave.' Unthinkable… This is the imperial family. We must stay above the fray!"

"And we are," Pompeia claimed. "Nothing happened. We will tell Hadrian not to see Pulcher again, and that's it. He is not stupid, likely regrets it already."

Mind awhirl, Trajan was still pacing back and forth on the marble floor of the atrium portico. "What if he bragged to other people about it?"

Plotina tried once more to assure him. "Why would he boast cuckolding you? That makes no sense. You are not married to Pulcher. Pageboys are an imperial prerogative. Everybody knows this. It's in compliance with your status. Other noblemen do it. In Greece everybody does it. It's not a scandal as long as you are not the receiving party – and I know you never are. Plus, everybody knows you treat the boys well, and they are consenting. THAT is what is important. Plus, they get an excellent education and have great prospects in the imperial administration. It's a very Roman 'quid pro quo'. I have to live with it, but that's a different story.

Hadrian cutting it too close for your taste is annoying but harmless really. Don't blow it out of proportion, husband. So, by the gods, keep it together, Marcus, and make sure your sister doesn't prattle."

"She will do what I tell her to. My sister only wanted me to know so it doesn't become a problem later on. She doesn't care - as long as everybody gets along."

In the afternoon Pompeia implored Hadrian to keep his hands off the imperial pageboys. "You can't afford to strain your relationship with Trajan, Publius. Trajan will sulk for a while, and let's hope he will get over it. Keep a low profile now."

Hadrian was mortified. "I will be contrite, I promise," he pledged. "No one will know, and, by Apollo, it won't happen again. I don't believe Pulcher remembers anything. He was far too intoxicated."

I've got to be more careful, he scolded himself.

Chapter 42

"Faster, faster! Go get him, Trajan," Callistus shouted as he watched Trajan struggle to catch up to the competing rower in the other skiff, Claudius Livianus, the new Praetorian praefect. Callistus jumped from his stool on the Tiber banks to cheer the emperor on. Trajan was in fact steadily inching closer and closer. When the two contenders passed the final race marker Callistus couldn't tell anymore who was first - a draw.

"Hurrah, hurrah," Callistus shrieked. "Now we have two winners!" He scurried down to the pageboys who were waiting for Livianus and Trajan to help them out of their skiffs, but the two men were too exhausted to move. They barely managed to paddle their vessels to the riverbank where the pageboys grabbed either skiff and hung on to them so the current wouldn't carry them off.

Livianus and Trajan slouched forward, panting. "I can't believe you caught up with me at the end," Livianus rasped with a groan. He was an army officer from Greek-speaking Lydia Province whom Trajan had come to appreciate over the last couple of years. When Suburanus had retired from his post as praefect last January to become a senator, Trajan had appointed Livianus new Praefect of the Guard. They spent much time together, appreciating each other's company, including competitive events such as this one.

Trajan was still breathing hard but managed a faint smile and croaked, "That was close, but... You know, I hate to lose." He looked at his faithful secretary who was holding the skiff now. Callistus turned his head and grinned at him. "A spirited fight, Trajan," he said. "And a nice finish!"

Trajan nodded, still gasping for air. They spent several more minutes recovering in the skiffs until they finally climbed out. The pageboys helped them out of their sweaty tunics and had fine olive oil ready for them, which they slathered on their bodies. Then they used sickle-shaped scrapers to remove the oil and sweat from the skin. Finally, the boys doused buckets of fresh water on the two men and dried them with the finest Egyptian towels.

It was a nice fall day. The leaves were starting to change color, turning ruddy, yellow and brown. Trajan's day had been pleasant and uneventful: client meetings at dawn, an inspection of the City Cohorts after that, a trial in the late morning, imperial correspondence over lunch. After the race with Livianus he was scheduled for supper with his Council.

"I truly enjoy drills like this, Claudius," Trajan muttered. "It keeps me in shape. Emperor or not, as commander-in-chief of the greatest army in the world I cannot afford to grow a belly. And it's always a pleasure to do it in a fun way with you." He met the praefect's gaze. "Isn't it ironic? When I was little I didn't want to learn Greek or any other language for that matter. And here I am - having a great time with a Greek-speaking Roman like you. I am glad my Father persevered and forced some Greek down my unwilling throat. If it were not for him, I couldn't even converse with you in your native tongue - although I am the first to admit that my accent is terrible."

"Not at all, *Imperator*. I understand you perfectly well. And I am always happy to duke it out with you. The race was terrific. Next time, let's play *harpastum*."

"Great idea. I am itching to snatch the ball from you and score. You won't catch me even if you were *Mercurius* himself!"

"Not if I steal his wings," Livianus countered and chuckled.

Trajan laughed with him. *Nothing beats good old-fashioned male rivalry*, Trajan thought fondly.

Meanwhile the pageboys under the supervision of Callistus dragged the skiffs on shore and hauled them onto an extra-long army carriage. Now fully dressed, Trajan and Livianus strode up the river bank to their horses. Praetorian troopers held them ready when an imperial trooper arrived behind them in full gallop. His mount snorted and tossed his head as if the stallion was annoyed at the exertion. Sweat was gleaming on his withers. The courier reined him in hard and saluted the emperor. "I have a message for you, Majesty," he said, dismounting. He handed Trajan the brown parchment case of an army dispatch, saluted again and stepped back to attention.

Furrowing his brows, Trajan removed the scroll from its case and broke the seal. It was from Sura. He reported he was on the Via Flaminia on his way to Rome and would be here by nightfall.

"Claudius, send someone to General Sura. He is going to arrive tonight. I want him to join us for dinner. Tell the trooper to hurry. I don't want Lucius to make other plans and spend another night outside the city walls."

Livianus acknowledged and sent the courier off with Trajan's orders.

Sura arrived at the Domus Tiberiana before sunset. He and Trajan fell into each other's arms with great delight. "I am so pleased to see you again, Lucius," Trajan exclaimed and hugged the general with the brawn of a bear.

"Likewise, dearest Trajan," Sura roared. "Likewise! It's been more than two years, and I heard great things. You are righting many wrongs and you uplift the people. Your gladiatorial games are breathtaking, they say. Best of all, everybody I have talked to on my way here is raving about your efforts to support the common man in Italia, poor peasant families in particular. Buying land with public money, renting it to low-income tenants and helping towns to raise orphans with the interest raised - what a neat idea!"

"It just made sense," Trajan played it down. "I am only resuming the work that Nerva – the gods bless his soul - has started. There were limited precursors to the orphan alimonies I created, but nothing on my scale. The new initiative is rather pervasive. It will hopefully improve the state of Italian agriculture. I want our small farmers to be healthy and strong. Only then will they be great soldiers. The small landowners have gone through several years of bad weather, lousy harvests and financial hardship. I hope the measures will make a difference, Lucius."

"They will," Sura shouted. "At least from what I can tell. Even the big landowners seem to like it because they provide an incentive for other citizens to lease land from them. Despite their vast slave manpower the *latifundia* owners are hit hard by a shortage of tenants although I have to say I was surprised you didn't run the bill through the *Comitia* like Nerva did. Any reason for that? You of all emperors, the people's hero…"

"It's a waste of time, Lucius." Trajan shook his head. "The People's Assemblies are an anachronism. To a large degree they were even in the days of the Republic. The wealthy could always muster a majority if they were united. Today, the people like what they see without having to go through meaningless elections. No, I don't want to go that route, but I am aware that some senators disagree with me on that, Cornelius Tacitus for example. But the Republic of old is gone. We live in a different age, an age of enlightened leadership. At any rate, I keep the Senate fully involved in the government of the empire, don't worry."

"I know you do," Sura agreed.

"I believe I convinced them I am one of them - the only difference being that destiny picked me to lead them. I am no authoritarian, just the First Man of Rome, not more and not less, *primus inter pares* if you so will: first among equals."

"Of course, Trajan, of course." Sura was happy to see that his friend had slipped so well into his new role, carrying the burden well. "No need to persuade me."

"Many guests have not arrived yet. Let's sit down and catch up, would you?" Trajan picked up a decanter of Falernian red and filled both their goblets. "First of all, thank you for the regular flow of dispatches. They always kept me abreast of the situation on the Rhine frontier. You have been busy consolidating and expanding the *Limes* border, built walls, palisades and forts, yes? And Priscus took over as planned?"

"Yes, he did. Thanks for sending him. The situation in Germania is solid now. The tribes are quiet or busy with warfare against one another, but I am also bringing news from the Danube. The situation there is rather volatile. Longinus's scouts report that King Decebalus is using Roman torsion artillery to protect the passes in the Carpathian Mountains. Remember, he stole them when he defeated a Roman legion ten years ago and he received more from us when Domitian cut a hasty armistice after we defeated Decebalus because the Suebi were attacking our provinces. The Dacian king is increasing the number of his warriors and fortifying his cities with tradesmen we accorded him in Domitian's cursed treaty.

At any rate, General Longinus keeps a close eye on the Dacians. He has four legions and an equal number of auxiliaries at his disposal and should be able to handle any possible intrusion into our lands."

Trajan nodded. "The Dacians worry me. Decebalus runs a tight ship and has forged alliances with the Roxolani and the Bastarnae, even with some Germanic tribes to the northwest. I spent the whole summer last year to secure our positions, rebuilding auxiliary forts in stone on the Danube's left riverbanks. I also renewed the critical towpaths for up-stream cargo traffic and cut a canal to protect our vessels from the rapids.

Anyway, we will discuss this more over dinner. Frontinus and Ursus will be there, the generals Senecio and Palma, the new Praetorian Praefect Livianus whom you have not met yet and the commander of our Moorish crack cavalry, Lusius Quietus."

"Ah, Rome's elite commanders, all present tonight. I cannot wait. I guess this will be the men you intend to send to the Danube next year?"

"I don't believe 'send' is the right word, Lucius. But yes, they will see action there," Trajan confirmed.

Sura studied his friend's face. He suspected Trajan was up to something but didn't want to probe him any further - for now. Instead, he asked, "Suburanus is no longer a military man?"

"That's correct. I helped him get a seat in the Senate. That was long overdue."

"I guess so. How about Servianus? Is he staying on as Governor of Pannonia?"

"Yes," Trajan answered. "But I will add him to my general staff once we make our move."

"What about me? I am sure you have recalled me for a reason."

Trajan smiled. "I want you on the Danube."

"In what role?" Sura pressed on.

"All in good time. We will discuss it later." Trajan's voice made it clear that he really didn't want to talk about specific plans now.

Sura changed topics. "What else is new in Rome? Has Hadrian married

Sabina yet?"

"No, but Plotina has been working me for months."

"I know. I have been in touch with her. We both think it would be proper. Think about it, Trajan. Your cousin is a good man. He is strong, smart, a competent soldier, knowledgeable and loyal. He doesn't have many flaws. You just don't like his love for luxury and everything Greek, but that pales compared to what he brings to the table. That's what I think. Do what you want, but don't blow it. Don't give Sabina to a toady."

"I would never do that!"

"Well then. There aren't many choices among the families close to you. I see some decent officers, but Sabina needs to marry someone who is a candidate that can succeed you one day. Hadrian has what it takes and he fulfills the imperial criteria. He would not fail you."

"It is way too early to think along those lines, Lucius," Trajan snapped. "Do you want me dead?"

"Of course not! But it is always a possibility, especially if you are going to take the field against Dacia."

"We shall see. I have not taken the field this year, but I did 'campaign' in other ways. As you might have seen upon your arrival, construction is going on everywhere in Rome. Crews are performing extensive maintenance work on bridges, aqueducts and sewers. I also had the Tiber banks resurveyed and started work on a relief channel to better contain flooding. The river inundated the Campus Martius again last year. It's still a mess there in some areas because the water had nowhere to go. I also commissioned the Circus Maximus to be rebuilt in stone, adding bleachers on the Palatine side, and one of these days work will start on monumental new Baths adjacent to the Flavian Amphitheater."

"By Jupiter, an even bigger Circus? It is already holding one hundred and twenty thousand spectators... I heard rumors of a grand new forum too. How do you want to finance all that? Didn't you just cancel a lot of debt and lessen the impact of the inheritance tax on foreign immigrants?" Sura asked.

"Yes, I did. But you know what, Lucius? People have largely dodged those taxes because they were onerous. I strongly believe reducing assessments will make the Treasury more money in the long run. We will make it up through increased economic activity."

"Interesting," Sura admitted. "Maybe, but it's a gamble. What if it doesn't work out?"

"There is another way to enhance the Treasury," Trajan added ominously. "The new forum in particular will require enormous funds. I have no idea how to ever finance it. So, don't hold your breath. It may never happen."

Sura was puzzled and wanted to hear more, but the door opened and the Lord Chamberlain strode in, announcing that all guests had arrived and dinner was ready to be served. Trajan asked Sura to go ahead and join the assembled generals and members of his Council.

"Tell them not to wait for me. I will join them later," he said. "First, I want to read Longinus's detailed dispatch. Thanks for bringing it down with you, Lucius."

Sura nodded. He was sure now - they would definitely talk about Dacia tonight.

Chapter 43

Claudius Maximus wondered what in the world he and his men were doing on this side of the Danube as he gazed at the soldiers of his patrol behind him. Like pearls on a string, the eight men had been leading their horses out from the thick undergrowth of the forest, one after the other, and were now lining up before him on a slanted meadow, holding their horses' reins.

He ordered them to remount and trot down to a familiar precipice from where they could see their small but well fortified river fort below. Spread out behind it, on the other side of the Danube, were the flowing hills of Upper Moesia Province.

At this time smoke was billowing up from the fort's bakery. The fort, big enough only to accommodate two squadrons of Roman auxiliary cavalry, had been built right at the shoreline and was connected to a wooden dock where three patrol vessels were laid up.

"Centurion," one of the men said. "Mighty inviting, isn't it?" He pointed to the fort. "Are we done for today?"

"Yes, Chlorus. Isn't that obvious?" Maximus snarled. Then he barked his orders. "Cavalrymen, resume mounted line formation. We will return home now, trot only. Watch for loose pebbles on the ground and wait for my signal."

The men saddled up, and Maximus raised his arm. He dropped it as he pushed off and steered his horse down the steep slope. His men followed suit, keeping a good distance between each other.

Maximus didn't like the current military situation. His unit had been ordered to build this fort on the northern side of the river, on Dacian land. It was one of many such fortifications that were strung along the border to keep a close eye on the enemy. For his taste too close. He would have liked to see the river not behind them but between them and the Dacians, as it was the case for the civilian settlements on the southern shore. *Nobody lives on the northern shore, nobody but us. Madness.*

Patrols like the one he was wrapping up today were supposed to prevent surprises, but Maximus knew better. The vast thick woods along this stretch of the river hugged the Danube on higher ground and were close to the fort. A whole army could assemble in there and they wouldn't notice.

At least the weather was good. The leaves were falling off the trees. The breeze was warm and gentle, the skies blue and clear as far as the eye could see. Maximus was looking forward to the end of fall when the foliage would be gone and the trees became less menacing, improving their vision when on patrol.

Upon arrival at the fort's Porta Praetoria the guards asked for today's password. "Yellow Vampire," Maximus answered. As the fort's ranking officer he selected the password every morning. The centurion had a knack for conjuring up words that fit the circumstances of their deployment. Dacia was famous for its vampires and werewolves, and the foliage was turning yellow on many trees. Hence 'Yellow Vampire'.

Inside the Castra, Maximus was the first to drop off his steed at the stables and paced to his office, curious of new orders they might have received. As he rushed by the barracks he ran into the duplicarius of the 2nd *contubernium*. The man seemed irritated when he saluted his superior officer. "Centurion, my unit is in charge of supper tonight, but supplies have not arrived. Shall we send a hunting party to shoot some deer?"

Puzzled, Maximus asked, "What do you mean by 'have not arrived'?"

"Well," the duplicarius shrugged. "The merchant's boat did not come yesterday and hasn't arrived today either. As you know, we buy our meat from him, but now we have neither beef nor pork, only what is in store pickled and salted."

"I see. It's too late now to send a hunting party. Make some porridge instead. I saw the bakery in action. We should have plenty of fresh bread."

The duplicarius saluted and headed for the bakery.

In his office, Maximus inspected the new-mail pigeonhole, but nothing was lodged. Odd. The fleet courier had been due at noon, and even if no dispatch from Upper Moesia's capital Viminacium was in the package he always received some other mail, but there was no mail at all.

It was getting dark. Maximus called for his second-in-command, the Duplicarius Crassus. Ausonius Crassus was a hulk of a man and didn't talk much, maybe because his Latin had a distinctly eastern accent. But he was a reliable officer and a competent quartermaster.

"Yes, Maximus?" Ausonius grumbled. "The courier from Viminacium has not arrived today? He might come later tonight. It wouldn't be the first time. Sometimes Governor Longinus is late with his dispatches. Then his couriers have to wait and get on the boats late at night. We are always last to get our orders out here, you know."

"Fine, it's just..." Maximus didn't finish the sentence. He scowled.

"What is wrong, Centurion?"

"Nothing," Maximus hurried to say. He didn't want to upset the other officer.

"You are worried, aren't you?"

"It's probably nothing, my friend. But see, the merchant has not arrived either. It could be a coincidence, but in any case double the guards tonight and ready the scorpion. Bring it up on the rampart to protect the main gate."

Ausonius looked at Maximus with probing eyes. But the centurion's face was well composed and didn't give away any clues. Crassus saluted and left the commander's office.

The pitch-black moonless night started out quiet. They only heard the loud chirping of thousands of crickets. They could hear, but they couldn't see. Maximus slept fitfully in his room when he woke up to the smell of fire. He jumped from his bed and ran to the door. As he threw it open a flaming arrow barely missed his face, drilling into the doorpost next to him. He cursed, pulled out the stalk and tossed the arrow on the ground. Quickly, he put out the lingering fire with a blanket. *By the gods, we are under attack!*

Looking out the window he could see many flaming arrows whipping over the palisades. The guards on the ramparts screamed, "Alarm! Alarm! Grab your weapons. We are under attack!"

Tubicens blasted their instruments and soldiers poured out of the barracks, putting on chainmail while they ran to their posts. Ausonius was buckled in full kit as if he had slept with it. He held a flaming torch in one hand and barked orders to organize the defense. Maximus couldn't understand his words in the chaos.

Ffft, ffft. More flaming arrows whipped over the walls like lightning bolts. *The enemy must be close. The night be damned. We can't see!* To his left, a roof over the stables was catching fire. Maximus had seen enough. He ran back to his quarters to get his weapons: shield, helmet, javelin, sword and dagger. *No time to put on the body armor.*

When he made it out again, he saw his men returning fire with salvos of their *pila.* The heavy javelins whistled through the air, raining down on the enemy on the other side. Most of the action seemed to be at the Porta Praetoria. Maximus aimed for it as fast as he could.

Then fighting broke out on the ramparts. *Dacians!* Maximus could easily recognize their uniquely shaped apex helmets. They had mounted ladders on the outside walls and were trying to overwhelm the defenders on the battlements. Roman resistance was fierce, but in man-to-man combat the sickle-shaped *falx* often found its target, wreaking havoc on Maximus's men. Inside the fort, one *contubernium* was busy extinguishing the stable fire. *A shrewd enemy. That's how they are draining manpower away from the ramparts.*

He changed direction and scuttled to the men. "Stop it! Ignore the fire. Get up the walls. We need to keep the enemy out at any cost! Quick, quick!"

The men gave him dazzled looks but aborted their effort and dashed off. Inside, the horses and mules whinnied in panic. Ostlers tried to calm them down and doused the flames with buckets of water.

I need to find Ausonius, Maximus thought, as he ran up the rampart staircase on the west side of the parapets. There was no skirmish there. Then he darted to the *Praetoria* side to join the fighting where Ausonius was directing the scorpion crew. His men had mounted torches on either side of the big torsion engine so they could better see the enemy down below. The crew was firing bolts in rapid sequence, but Maximus could still not see at whom. He hadn't reached that side of the walls yet. From his view point he could only see Dacian cavalry closing in on the fort.

Suddenly, a Dacian warrior climbed over the wall right in front of him, but he didn't see Maximus in time. The centurion dispatched him with a quick blow of his sword. He pushed the man aside and resumed his run. Ausonius and his men were still firing the terrible scorpion, but the soldiers at their sides struggled hard to keep Dacian intruders away from the engine. The Romans used their big rectangular shields to deflect the enemy and pushed them down the ramparts or back over the walls. Many Dacians had died and were piling up underneath the scorpion platform. Inside the fort, Maximus could see Dacians roaming. They had been overrun!

Finally, he reached the *Praetoria* battlements and could see what the scorpion crew was firing at: hundreds of Dacians assembling around a ram that was approaching the gate.

Five hundred men at least! More than five times our own...

The scorpion bolts inflicted horrendous losses on the enemy. He saw droves of Dacian dead in the ditches in front of the walls. The *Praetoria* side trench was slowing down the ram, but hundreds of dead enemy fighters piled up in there. *To our detriment!* The enemy tossed in stones and small boulders as well that they must have brought with them for this night attack. The trench was filling up with boulders and corpses in one spot that the Dacians evidently wanted to use to push the ram carriage across.

The scorpion was a huge boon, but it wouldn't prevent the inevitable. They were simply outmanned. Maximus pressed on, but he couldn't get to Ausonius. Wearing his red-crested helmet, the Dacians recognized him as the commanding officer. They howled in fury and went after him. Fortunately, the parapet gangway was narrow and the Dacians could attack him only in pairs of two. Additionally, the scorpion battlement was now crowded with clusters of fighting Romans and Dacians.

Maximus pushed forward like a maniac, slaying several Dacian infantrymen that aimed to kill him. The enemy's blows rattled his shield arm. A *falx*'s near miss tore through the copper frame. He almost lost his balance. From the corner of his eyes he could saw a Roman soldier fighting two Dacians at once. The man kept one fighter at bay with his shield and fought the other with his *spatha*. But the Dacian at his sword side managed to land a fierce blow on the Roman's head. The *falx* struck his helmet with a terrifying CLUNK and cut it open as if it was made of papyrus. Blood and brain pulp gushed out. The Roman went down with a gasp. It was Chlorus.

He was dead before he hit the ground.

Maximus shrieked in rage. He smashed another Dacian warrior down the parapet. Then he lifted his shield and nailed the Dacian who had killed Chlorus to the parapet with so much force that the man spilled his guts on the floor. A split second later the centurion rammed his sword into the other Dacian's chest. He yanked out the bloodied sword and looked around.

Next to the scorpion, Ausonius was fighting for his life. He had joined the soldiers who protected the engine from Dacian attackers. They were at the brink of being overwhelmed by sheer force of numbers.

Maximus shouted, "Ausonius, there is no point! The scorpion is only buying us time, but we don't have enough men!"

At this moment the Dacian ram reached the gate and struck it hard. The blow was so fierce that the parapet above was shaking as if struck by an earthquake. Exasperated, Maximus looked down. He could see details now: The ram was a Roman design! A standard equipment legionary ram, hoisted on a two-axle carrier and protected by a pointed roof covered with sheets of bronze. Maximus could see it was old. The wheels' nails had bled plenty of rust. It struck him! This was a captured engine from Fuscus's legion, the one Decebalus had destroyed in the reign of Domitian many years ago. Maximus had served in General Tettius's legion as a standard-bearer at the time and knew exactly how powerful this ram was. He had seen it in many training drills.

"Ausonius, they have a Roman ram! It will smash the gate within minutes. Look how many they are. We need to retreat!" The centurion didn't wait for an answer and ordered a *tubicen* beside Ausonius to blow his trumpet. "To the boats, everybody. To the boats! Ausonius, stop firing the cursed scorpion. There is no use!"

Ausonius nodded and shouted orders of his own. Maximus couldn't hear them, but the scorpion crew stopped and tumbled down the last open staircase. The other Roman defenders and Ausonius disengaged from the enemy too, although it was not easy because the Dacians pressed forward hard. At last, the Romans killed or disabled the immediate attackers and were able to scurry toward the river along the ramparts and down the staircase on the south side. Everywhere in the fort the men left their positions now.

Maximus watched the orderly retreat and hastened down the parapets himself. His men had taken heavy losses, but at least half of them would reach the boats. The guards opened the Decumana gate and the fleeing Roman troops hurled themselves through it to the dock, but alas, the patrol vessels were gone. They were cut off...

Chapter 44

Trajan arrived for dinner when it was half over. Plotina shot an angry gaze at him which he chose to ignore. He stopped at each sofa, shaking hands with his officers and advisers, apologized for being late and lay down at last on the empty ranking sofa in the center of the banquet. The palace chef entered the hall and bowed in front of the imperial sofa. "Your Highness, do you want me to serve the previous courses for you now?"

Trajan shook his head. "No, I will eat whatever is coming next. That will be plenty for me, but bring enough Falernian."

After exchanging niceties with Sura, Frontinus and others who were seated close to him, the emperor addressed the assembled dignitaries. "My dear friends, thanks for coming. Of course, I did not call you here only to socialize. You know me. It wouldn't be my style. I have asked you to come because we need to discuss a critical foreign policy matter: our relationship with the kingdom of Dacia." Trajan paused. The conversations of his guests ceased. He had their full attention. "King Decebalus is a proud and dangerous man. Some years ago he has defeated a Roman legion and killed two of our generals. He was only mildly punished for that. Yes, Tettius had defeated him in battle, but then Domitian hurried an ignominious peace because Germanic tribes assailed us elsewhere. Decebalus didn't have to return the captured artillery. We even sent him tradesmen to help with his construction projects and have payed him off to this very day."

Trajan thundered the last sentence. "Needless to say, I am not pleased. After reading the latest dispatch from the Danube it is quite evident that the Dacians have no intention to desist from raiding our lands. They interpret our passivity as weakness. As a consequence, Decebalus's pride and power is rising. He is fortifying his strongholds and forging alliances against us. This has to stop!

We need to redeem the Roman name once and forever and bring him to terms, hopefully without bloodshed. But war is an option.

I will stop making any more payments. Additionally, I will ask the Dacian king to cancel his anti-Roman alliances and pay back the tributes he received from us. Dacia can be a friend of Rome and enjoy client status, but it cannot stay what it is today: a dangerous, powerful and well-organized state funded by Roman money and the precious metals in its soil. It is an insult, it has to end!

Do you agree with me?"

The cavalry general Quietus bellowed, "I do. Let's quash them!"

Amidst grumbling sounds of agreement from the other officers, Frontinus asked the emperor, "What is your plan, Trajan? Do you want to stare him down with diplomacy and a display of strength or do you suggest a Roman offensive no matter what the Dacians do?"

"A good question, Julius," Trajan replied. "What does this Council think?"

They weighed in with different ideas, arguing back and forth. Some were in favor of diplomacy, but most wanted military action. Dacia had been a sore spot for Roman pride for a long time. Trajan raised his arms to take the word again. "Let us launch a punitive campaign then, in the spring, complemented with offers for Decebalus to come to terms. If he does, we will cancel the offensive. Again, I do not want to conquer Dacia, I want to tame it. For the same reasons I don't believe we will need to recruit additional troops. The available legions should do, but I will reinforce them with two Rhine legions from Vindonissa, led by Quadratus Bassus. Governor Servianus will join the campaign as well and I hope many of you in this banquet hall will also.

Legati, I am asking you to sit down with Julius Frontinus, our most senior marshal, and plan this campaign with him. You have all winter to prepare for the operation. Pick a seasoned quartermaster for logistics and baggage train, select our best vanguard units and scouts, conduct war drills among the legions that will be deployed, hire surgeons and medics, study armor requirements and issue new equipment.

Livianus, I want the whole Praetorian Guard to deploy as well and I will involve myself into the planning. My foremost concern is the ferocious Dacian *falx*, a vicious close combat weapon. Its hardened bent tip has split many a helmet. We may have to reinforce the Roman standard issue helmet to make it strong enough to deflect a *falx* blow. Anyway, I am already losing myself in details. You get the picture." The emperor was in his element, fired up about a campaign against a formidable foe.

Livianus had another idea. "Why don't we issue a coin with the inscription 'Mars Ultor – Mars the Avenger'? That would be a nice message for the Dacians and at the same time let the people of the empire know that no one gets to oppose our might unpunished."

"Excellent, let's do it!" Trajan said. He was encouraged by the excitement in the room. It would be a unanimous effort.

The Roman auxiliaries were making their last stand on the fort's dock. Nobody knew what had happened to their vessels, but Maximus was certain that before attacking the Dacians had cut them loose in the cover of darkness. He and his men were fighting for their lives. For every Dacian they killed three others pressed forward. The *falx* inflicted terrible wounds on his men. Pushed back ever more, Ausonius and Maximus were in the last cluster of Romans resisting the onslaught. Meanwhile, Dacian cavalry cut off all potential escape routes on either side of the fort. The only way left open to them was the majestic river itself, glistening gloomy and black behind them.

Maximus had not put on his body armor. Now it would be an advantage – it was time to act. He shouted at Ausonius, "Friend, into the river. Take off your armor!" Maximus stepped forward to shield his comrade and take on the next wave of thrusts against both of them. Dacian *falces* hit his oval cavalry shield with blow after blow after blow, but he wielded his defensive weapon wisely, moving from side to side fast so that their blows never achieved maximum impact, allowing his friend to hold his ground. Ausonius used the reprieve to untie the laces of his chest armor and took off the plated jacket. He shrieked, "Ready!" when an arrow hit his face with full force, and his heavy body tipped over in slow motion. Maximus could see the horror-struck eyes of his friend in the night as he collapsed to the wooden planks with a loud thump.

"Noooooo!" Maximus screamed in despair. He tried to hold Ausonius, prop him up but couldn't. He had to let him go to save his own life - the attackers were closing in. Maximus whirled round, hurtled to the edge of the dock, tossed shield and sword into the water, pinched his nostrils shut and leaped into the river. Upon impact he immediately dove off as deep and far away as he could as Dacian missiles pierced the water all around him. Pfft, pfft... He almost panicked but kept diving upstream with mighty strokes assuming the Dacians would suspect him to do the opposite. When he couldn't possibly stay under water any longer he came up to the surface, gasping for air. He had covered thirty yards. The Dacians were lingering on the dock, howling and still looking for him in the water. The pitch black night was his savior, but he had to be careful. Part of the river was dimly lit by fires from the burning fort. He took a deep breath and dove off again, aiming for the other side of the river. The Dacians kept shooting into the river hoping for a lucky hit, but they were off target. Intermittently coming up for air, he soon covered one hundred, then two hundred yards. Gradually the enemy disappeared from his sight, but not so the burning Roman fort behind them – a haunting reminder of this disaster. Tears rolled down his cheeks now. His fort was taken, the garrison killed or taken prisoner – if the enemy took prisoners at all. Maximus shuddered.

The centurion kept swimming away from away from this place of horror. The river god be thanked the water wasn't cold. Still, Maximus was eager to reach the safety of the opposite shoreline – Roman territory - and alert the next village. He was still in a state of shock. Why were they attacked? Why them, a minor river fort, one of many? Why here, not far from the provincial capital? Of course! They wanted to show off, demonstrate their power. The Dacians aimed to terrify his fellow Romans with the message, 'We can strike close to you, anytime and anywhere.'

It had been well planned. The enemy must have intercepted both the fleet courier and the merchant's boat. He needed to be vigilant; Dacian skiffs might operate on the river right now. It was hard to see anything in the moonless night, but he hoped he would hear any approaching vessel. The oars would give it away, but only if it was coming upstream.

He swam on. Water and land were blurring together. After a while Maximus couldn't tell anymore where the shore was and where the water ended. He did know the crooks and turns of the river in this area and kept swimming toward what he deemed the southern shoreline. Half a mile from the fort he reached its banks at last. Maximus clasped the sprawling bough of a willow tree with his fingers and slowly pulled himself out of the water. Miraculously, he had reached land... Gasping from exhaustion he drooped on the muddy ground.

After a short rest he took off dagger and belt and dragged the soaked army tunic off his wet body. He dropped it behind the willow's thick roots and re-cinched the belt around his naked waist. Then Maximus hunkered down again, thinking. Which direction was the closest village? He would have to first reach the Roman road and from there make it to the villagers. Determined, he trudged off. It didn't take him long to find the road. He patiently followed it to the next hamlet several miles upriver. An hour later and very tired he walked up to the first house in his path and knocked on the door. Exhaustion overmanned him and he fell on the ground. A bright light hit his eyes. Then darkness swallowed his mind.

Chapter 45

Maximus woke up on soft woolen sheets in a cozy bed, propped up by supple pillows behind his head and shoulders. A Roman officer was sitting next to him on a chair. On the other side of the bed a maiden beamed at him. "He is awake," she shrieked excited.

"Where am I?" Maximus croaked. A pounding headache was milling around in his skull.

The officer answered softly, "In safety, soldier, in safety. What's your name?"

"Maximus, I am Claudius Maximus, centurion of the Fourteenth and Fifteenth *Turmae* of the Second Auxiliary *Ala* of the-"

"Claudius Maximus? Never heard of you. You are auxiliary cavalry and yet your rank is centurion? That's impossible."

"It is not," Maximus protested weakly. "I am a Roman citizen. They detached me... I am thirsty, so thirsty."

"Bring water and some hearty food for this hero here, maiden," the officer ordered. "I will need to notify the governor. This is amazing. There is a survivor after all..."

He turned to Maximus. "Which fort are you from?"

Maximus told him.

"You are the commander of one of the forts that were destroyed last night?"

Maximus looked at him aghast. "There were more attacks? How many? Are we at war? And where am I now?"

"Many good questions, and I have only a few answers," the officer said. "You are in Viminacium. Villagers brought you here earlier today. They said you had walked in on them in the middle of the night, naked and banged up. Seeing your haircut, belt and dagger they thought you must be a soldier. They took you in, cared for you, gave you clothes, put you in a warm bed and in the morning on a coach. Now you are in the hospital of Viminacium. Governor Longinus wants to hear about you. And yes, yours was not the only fortified camp that went up in flames last night. We lost two more, both downstream of yours.

By Jupiter, none of this is good. It could mean war, but get some sleep now. I will be back later." The officer touched Maximus's shoulder with a soft clasp of his hand and left the room.

Longinus! Maximus realized he would soon meet the governor himself. Scary thought. Would Longinus blame him for the disaster? Maximus cringed. Again, the image of Ausonius Crassus dying on the dock crawled back into his consciousness. He trembled. Crassus's death was personal and painful.

231

No matter what would happen to him, he swore revenge. By *Mars Ultor*, Decebalus would pay for this.

In Rome, Trajan received the senator and ex-consul Publius Cornelius Tacitus, now a prominent representative of the Republican faction in the Senate. "What can I do for you?" Trajan greeted him in the imperial audience chamber.

"Oh, I am not asking for favors," Tacitus replied. He lowered his eyes, fidgeting with his belt.

"What do you want to talk about, Publius?" Trajan asked him.

The nobleman hesitated. His gaze was still fixed on the beautiful Carrara marble floor. Finally he lifted his head and said, "I don't know how to say it, *Imperator*. You see, I have always been a loyal member of the Senate, and like so many other senators I suffered from Domitian's tyranny. You also know I am a writer and... hm..." Tacitus struggled for words again.

"Yes, my dear Publius," Trajan encouraged him. "I know you are a writer. I have read your biography of your father-in-law Agricola that's telling the story of his great deeds as governor of Britannia. It is good reading, and people still talk about the insightful book on Germania that you published two years ago. I was there at the time, organizing the frontier defenses. Many people in Rome were wondering what it's like in that remote part of the world and what kept me there. They were dying to know all about the Germanic tribes and the geography beyond our northern borders. Your book became quite popular."

"*Sic*, my Lord, certainly, but my new book is very... hm... different and a bit – how can I say – sensitive..." The senator looked like the unhappiest man in the empire.

"How so? Tell me, what is the book about?" Trajan asked innocently. He had no idea what the problem was.

"It will be a book that covers the history of Rome under the Flavians."

Trajan squinted his eyes. He still didn't understand the problem. "That's wonderful, Publius. We need an account of the period. Don't forget to include my father."

"Certainly, my Lord."

Finally, it dawned on Trajan and he burst out. "You are worried about censorship."

"Well, not censorship in its strict sense, but can I in fact write what I want?"

"Absolutely you can," Trajan assured him, seizing Tacitus's shoulders. "The era of tyranny is over, Publius Cornelius. Once and for all. You can write what you want and cover history as you see fit."

Tacitus was visibly relieved. His gaze met Trajan's who didn't shy away from it. "There is no censorship while I am First Man of Rome," Trajan reiterated.

"Good then, Princeps. That is all I wanted to know."

"However, I would like you to be objective and fact-oriented."

"Certainly, I will not distort the truth," Tacitus said, holding his head high.

"I know you are a Republican at heart," Trajan continued. "But please realize that the Republican form of government worked only as long as Rome was small. It failed us when Rome became an empire. Great wealth corrupted the politicians. Greed and avarice created social disparities and misery and resulted in a century of Civil Wars. I am in power only because there is no alternative to unified leadership - or do you think the Senate could take over again?"

"A tough question indeed. My heart says yes, but my mind agrees with you. As much as I would like to go back to Republican rule it would be a challenge, but it's not entirely out of the question."

"Yes, not out of the question, but realistic? For every Frontinus there is a Verres, for every Ursus there is a Catilina, for every Caesar there is a Brutus," Trajan maintained. "The Senate would splinter and enrich its pockets at the expense of everybody else. Individual senators would exploit their position and loot the people. Then they would start fighting against each other to loot some more and draw the whole country into their messy disputes. Maybe not right away, but at some point."

"On the other hand," Tacitus countered. "For hundreds of years the Senate ruled wisely and effectively. Just think how we became Italia's dominant power, how we integrated the different peoples of Italia, how we heroically dealt with the Samnite and Punic threats. All this happened under the leadership of the Senate. And there are more examples.

Trajan, you have to agree that conceptually it is the right way: The people should determine themselves who rules them. The orders of society should elect representatives that then elect the country's supreme leaders."

"True, but isn't that what happened under me and under Nerva before me?" Trajan responded triumphantly. "Informally at least."

Tacitus shook his head. "Perhaps, but Vespasian came to power based on his military might. That is wrong. The Assemblies should have elected him. The state needs to have checks and balances that we used to have in the Republic - through independent courts, assemblies and public officials that are elected for a limited time and who are subject to the Law like everyone else."

"But Tacitus," Trajan argued. "We have all that. The Republican system is at work today. I declared again and again that even I am subject to the Law like any other citizen. I do not interfere with the courts and the work of the Senate. The cities in Italia freely elect their magistrates and *duumviri* as they have done for hundreds of years.

I only skip the ancient Assemblies, and my term is unlimited. The senators are still independent, and it will stay that way. Yes, I coax them sometimes to legislate in the interests of the State, but I am a threat to no one."

"That works fine because it is you who is in power, Trajan," Tacitus concurred. "But what happens if a monster like Domitian ever comes back? If an emperor's term was limited, an ogre couldn't terrorize the commonwealth forevermore."

"I do carry a heavy burden, Tacitus," Trajan admitted. "I must do no wrong. I must be just and fair and balanced, but I know I am, and my successor will be the same. My plan is to follow Nerva's example and adopt the most competent man in the empire before I die. That man will act like me, and so will his successors and so forth. That way Rome has the best of both worlds, enjoying benevolence and efficiency. That is what I am striving for, Publius."

Trajan eyed the historian with a long, penetrating glance and added, "But you agree with me on one thing, Publius. The Senate is at this time unable to rule the country. You will surely give me that, right?"

After a long pause Tacitus nodded grudgingly. "Probably. That is why it's so important that you are a good ruler, preserving the liberties of the Republic: free speech, the right to assemble, the right to initiate legislation. Do you recognize that?"

"Yes I do, and that is what matters most, Publius. We can have it all and we do have it all."

"I praise your wisdom, my Lord," Tacitus exclaimed. "I feel better now. You seem to be a good man who is watching out for the interests of all and who respects due process. But who is watching the emperor when things go wrong? *Quis custodiet ipsos custodes*, Iuvenalis would say, 'Who watches the watchers'? More importantly, who or what guarantees a smooth transition to the next great man? We have no good answer for that. Maybe there is none. But at least we should strive for the best possible solution."

"Indeed, Publius. It is up to me to assure a successful transition."

The historian nodded. "Thank you, Trajan. I like what I heard.

By the way, your cousin Hadrian deserves advancement. I have met him several times. He is of the same mold as you." Tacitus squeezed out a shy smile and stood up from his chair. "But let me get back to my desk now. A book is waiting to be written."

Trajan was speechless. *Another Hadrian fan...*

Chapter 46

At the end of the year Trajan finally consented to the marriage of Hadrian and fourteen-year old Sabina. Both Plotina and Sabina's mother Matidia expressed their gratitude, and in early spring he adlected Hadrian into the Senate when his cousin reached the required age limit of twenty-five, appointing him quaestor - Hadrian's first public office.

But the spotlight of the emperor's attention was on the far away Danube. Moesia's Governor Longinus had kept Trajan abreast of the developments at the Dacian border all winter long. His reports were filled with attacks on Roman military installations – a major embarrassment that confirmed Trajan's gloomy assessment of the situation. At the end of March, after half a year of preparations, he set out to the frontier with his *Equites Singulares* and the entire Praetorian Guard. Decebalus's answer to his demands had been unambiguous: He had executed Rome's messengers, cut off their heads and thrown them over the walls of the fortress at Viminacium - the empire was at war.

Trajan and his troops arrived in Viminacium in April where he conferred with Longinus and his officers, Hadrian among them, right away.

"Our forces on the north Danube shores were spread too thin," Longinus said. "Our presence did allow us to protect the vital river traffic and keep an eye on the enemy, but it didn't work as a deterrent. On the contrary, it provoked the enemy. They attacked our fortifications with mixed success. Taking advantage of the local geography they were able to destroy several encampments not far from here. I believe we built them too close to the forest, allowing them to sneak up on our men."

Trajan was outraged. "Pompeius, abandon all the forts on the northern shore and have the garrisons join the new expeditionary corps that will soon enter Dacia proper."

The officers in the room grumbled disagreement. Trajan arched his eyes in surprise. They were conferencing on a windy day in Trajan's office in the Praetorium of Longinus's Moesian headquarters. Outside the walls, the citizens of Viminacium were witnessing the greatest concentration of military might in Roman history: over fifty thousand men assembling in one place and readying to cross into Dacia on twin-pontoon bridges that had just been built for the purpose of this campaign. Another fifty thousand men were being distributed along the border to protect the two Moesian provinces all the way to the Black Sea and thwart Dacian or Sarmatian counter-attacks.

Half the troops were heavy legionary infantry, composed of nine legions. The other fifty thousand were non-citizen auxiliaries plus a small number of specialized ethnic levies from around the empire, most importantly Quietus's irregular Moorish cavalry and five hundred Palmyrenian archers from Syria.

Trajan was glad he didn't have to worry about Pannonia Province. An alliance with the Jazyges, Dacia's western neighbors, was keeping the peace there, constraining Decebalus's forces.

"It's not what you think, my friends," he appeased the officers. "We will still use the forts as forward-bases along the Danube, but I want the auxiliary troops there to join the campaign, replacing them with the levies from Britannia and Cantabria that arrived here in the last several weeks?"

A murmur went around the room, and some men nodded in agreement. They seemed to welcome his clarification.

"Now, this is going to be a punitive expedition, not a war of conquest. There will be no enslaving of the Dacian civilian population. Do I make myself clear? Wherever I can I want to keep the populace out of this. This also applies to your Moorish cavalry, Quietus. Make sure they behave. You don't want to attract my wrath. It isn't the Dacian people's fault that Decebalus is our enemy.

Here is my plan: We will march in a straight path toward the Dacian capital, Sarmizegethusa. Hopefully, on our way Decebalus will realize he cannot possibly win and sue for peace. Our terms will depend on the degree of his resistance and our losses. I hope that the bloodshed can be limited." Trajan looked at his men. "Questions?"

Manlius Felix, the quartermaster, lifted his hand. "How should we assign the auxiliaries' torsion engines? Every two *turmae* share one engine, a much higher ratio than is customary, and only because each cavalry fort on Dacian land required a scorpion for protection. Should we redistribute this artillery among the expeditionary corps or leave them behind for the new garrisons?"

"A good question," Trajan praised him. "Redistribute them. The auxiliaries currently manning the forts will join the main host, but they are cavalry after all. The engines, which have to be transported on mule-drawn carts, would slow them down. Assign the engines to the auxiliary infantry within the attack corps, Manlius. That reminds me. Senecio, please provide the quartermaster with a complete engine inventory, allowing him to send detailed dispatches to the affected commanders. Hurry. I want the engines here within a week."

After the meeting Trajan dismissed the men. Only Callistus stayed behind to discuss the organization of imperial correspondence for the duration of the campaign. "Master, I have secured enough supplies of papyrus, parchment, wax, reed pens, styluses and ink," he reported.

The emperor smiled at him. "Excellent. I will not only want to send letters and dispatches but want you to help me write a detailed account of the whole operation, akin to Julius Caesar's 'Commentaries on the War in Gaul'. I intend to publish them in book form, likewise-titled: 'Commentaries on the War in Dacia'."

"What a great idea! The readers in Rome will devour it, but I have a question. I thought we don't intend to conquer this land. Doesn't your book imply we do? After all, Caesar's 'Commentaries' describe a war of conquest."

"A good point, Callistus. I don't think it implies that. It's just... I have a feeling this campaign will not be easy and I don't think Decebalus will back off – as much as I would like him to. The Dacians will not budge. Therefore a detailed account of the events makes sense. Anyway, I have no plans to make Dacia into a Roman province. It would be hard to defend because the country lacks natural borders with its barbarian neighbors. We shall see."

A week later the scorpions arrived in Lederata, the Roman crossover point at the confluence of the Csernovec and the Danube. Trajan's host was now assembled and ready. General Senecio's infantry units gladly added the additional artillery to their baggage train. Without further delay Trajan ordered the army to cross the river. It took the fifty thousand men and their horses, carriages, carts and wheeled torsion engines a whole day, but everything went like clockwork. On the other side, the emperor ordered the traditional *suovetaurilia*, the sacrifice of bull, ram and boar to Mars, the god of war. As *Pontifex Maximus*, Trajan presided over the religious ceremony himself. Then the army started its long march up the Csernovec valley, the shortest route to the Iron Gates Pass. Thirty miles behind and east of the pass they would find Sarmizegethusa.

The march was arduous because Dacia had no paved roads. The men could not cover more than twelve miles a day, but the pioneer units did their best to clear the way of obstacles, smoothen the trail and build small bridges to traverse creeks or ravines.

They marched six to seven hours every day. A vanguard of scouts and cavalry units under General Longinus would set out first to secure a suited location for the night's camp, designed to protect them from ambuscades. These units were allocated to both the head and rear of the column. While the campsite was secured the main host started to march to that site. By leaving at cockcrow the first units could reach the camp by noon. The last units, however, did not get there until sunset. The rearguard then would leave first thing in the morning of the next day, and the previous day's vanguard would become the rearguard.

The vanguard units were drawn into daily skirmishes between them and Dacian light cavalry, but by and large the Dacians only observed the invading army, putting up no meaningful resistance. Sometimes Roman cavalry would forage and meet local villagers. They interrogated them but didn't learn much, not even when they thought they had finally picked up one of Decebalus's scouts. He did tell them that Decebalus's army was waiting for an opportunity to strike.

To Trajan's relief the Dacians didn't destroy the country's crops. They were evidently aware that the Roman army had plenty of supplies with them and only collected burning wood. The invaders left the villages and small towns alone. In turn the Dacian warriors stayed out of their way. This 'arrangement' lasted for several weeks and Decebalus kept his entire army out of sight.

Over time the hilly and thickly forested land put Trajan and his commanders rather on the edge. They didn't like to be clueless on the position of the enemy's troops. There was one silver lining: Not staging a war of attrition, Decebalus at some point would have to fight them head on. Therefore, Trajan believed, the Dacian warriors were always close to the Roman host, but far enough away to stay hidden from his roaming scouts. They had to be prepared for an attack at any time of day or night.

Trajan and the Praetorian Guard traveled in the center of the army. He would have much preferred to march at the head of the column, but that was too dangerous. Hadrian helped his famous cousin with command-and-control duties and directed the scout commanders on Trajan's staff.

They still had not encountered any resistance when a scout galloped to the Praetorian column and reined in his horse in front of Hadrian. The courier saluted and handed him a dispatch from General Longinus. It read:

> *Dacian warriors ahead to the southeast, about*
> *twenty thousand men, cavalry and infantry. It seems*
> *they are intent on preventing us from going any*
> *further. We are clearing the ground for battle. Senecio*
> *and Quietus need to be ready to engage. I recommend*
> *keeping the legions in reserve. They can start building*
> *the night camp when they arrive at the site tonight.*
> *Unless the Dacians change their location the battle will*
> *be no more than two miles from our chosen campsite.*
>
> *Longinus*

The scroll included a scribbled map and directions to both the battle site and the camp. "By Apollo!" Hadrian exclaimed. "Follow me," he ordered the courier. He wheeled around his steed and they both dashed off to Trajan's closed carriage. The emperor was outside it, marching and bantering with Governor Servianus and his friend Sura, who commanded the two legions of Lower Moesia.

"What is it, Hadrian?" Trajan shouted at the incoming riders. He could tell from their crazy speed that the news was important.

"Trouble, Caesar," Hadrian yelled. "I have a dispatch from Longinus. Looks like the Dacians are getting ready to do battle." He stopped before his cousin and handed the scroll down to him.

Trajan browsed through the dispatch, then he lifted his head, meeting Hadrian's gaze. "I am not surprised. Well then. No parley. Let us first have them feel Roman steel. Ride to Senecio and send someone to Quietus. Order them to fall into battle formation, and have Callistus in the carriage here copy this map so both commanders know where to go.

I agree with Longinus, Hadrian. The legions should stay behind. Sura, you take command of them. Livianus and Servianus will assist you. We will handle this engagement with the auxiliaries, under my direct command. Archers and slingers stay with the legions. If I need them or heavy infantry for that matter, Lucius, I will let you know."

Sura bowed in acknowledgment.

"And I want Quietus to join the regular auxiliary cavalry. Where is my bodyguard? I need to join Longinus right away. Questions?"

They had none. Hadrian vaulted off his horse, tied the reins to the slow moving imperial carriage, opened its hawthorn back door and clambered in. Inside, Callistus was surrounded by piles of correspondence.

"Here is a map, secretary," Hadrian said. "My cousin wants you to copy it. It contains directions to a likely battle site."

Callistus whistled. He set his scrolls aside and grabbed the map. "No problem, but I have to jump off. I can't draw in the rattling carriage." He picked up his ink well, a reed pen and an empty scroll and hopped out of the trundling coach, Hadrian right behind him. They sat down on the side of the path as endless rows of soldiers in glistening plate armor and rumbling wagons of the baggage train wound by them like the links of a miles-long viper of metal.

While Callistus went to work, many thoughts raced through Hadrian's mind. *Would he see battle? How would it go? How bloody would it be? Would they win?*

He was yearning for glory, but Trajan would likely have him shuttle back and forth and coordinate the battle couriers from a safe location. Alas...

He had a question for Callistus. "Have you seen our new helmets? They look strange, don't you think?"

"Don't distract me now, Hadrian. I need to get this done."

"I know. I just hope that the monstrous cross-brace that we riveted to our helmets can withstand the blow from a *falx*."

"It will. We worked hard on it," Callistus assured him as he feverishly copied message and map. Without looking up he added, "Many of our legionaries have vambraces and greaves to protect their arms and legs from the *falx*, almost like gladiators. But army steel is much stronger."

"Yes," Hadrian sighed. "We went through a lot of trouble to prepare for this." Up ahead he watched Trajan assemble his bodyguards, then they cantered off. Livianus and the Praetorians were under Sura's command now. Servianus and his two Pannonian legions would stay behind as well - Servianus... Three years ago he had hated the man for giving him a hard time in Moguntiacum, but they had both realized there was no point obsessing over Trajan's favors. His cousin was hard to manipulate. He had treated them both equally - at least most of the time.

In the far distance over the horizon to the east Hadrian suddenly saw dark grey clouds rolling in. The wind was picking up too. *A thunderstorm?*

Finally, Callistus was done. Hadrian stuffed both Longinus's original dispatch and Callistus's copy into a tallow impregnated parchment cover and stood up. He had his work cut out for him.

Chapter 47

When Trajan reached Longinus's hilltop position Roman skirmishers were already engaging the enemy frontlines. On Longinus's hill, a battery of scorpions was aiming a combination of darts, arrows and rocks at the center of the enemy host. The auxiliary infantry under Senecio was waiting in the nearby woods for the order to engage.

Trajan conferred with his generals. "You were right, Pompeius, about twenty thousand hostiles. I think I can even see Decebalus's position on the side – see those flags there?" The emperor pointed to enemy cressets and dragon standards in the far distance, fluttering on a hilltop similar to their own. "He is going to watch the battle from there." Trajan turned to Longinus. "Is the ground clear?"

"Yes, my Lord. We are ready."

Trajan could see the pride in the governor's eyes. "Great. Fire the scorpions. Then, at my mark, send in the bulk of your cavalry, at least ten *alae*. They are to rout the enemy flanks and then attack the Dacian infantry from the wings."

The scorpions started their terrible pounding with a screeching whirr, creating bedlam in the enemy lines. Trajan looked into the sky. It was overcast everywhere now, and he could hear rolling thunder. "Stop firing," he bellowed. "It's going to rain soon. We need to act quickly before the ground becomes too wet for the horses. Longinus, unleash the cavalry. Quick!"

Longinus saluted. A squire brought the governor's horse. He flung himself on it and galloped off with his senior attendants to direct the auxiliary cavalry wings in person.

Minutes later the Roman offensive was fully under way. The din from thousands of hooves hitting the valley grounds was deafening. The Roman cavalry hit the Dacians hard as ordered. Outnumbered three to one, the enemy cavalry panicked and surrendered the battlefield. The Roman wings moved on to hammer the Dacian infantry host on either flank. Even the long-stalk *falx* was no match for the furious waves of Roman cavalry hitting the Dacian fighters. Roman *spathae* took a terrible toll, but the Dacians didn't give up, fighting hard to prevent the Romans from enveloping them.

Trajan issued new orders, this time to Lusius Quietus. "General, take your Moors and find Decebalus. You have seen those banners. It will be difficult in the rain, but if you are successful we might be able to shorten this conflict. If you do find the king, take him prisoner and bring him to me alive. Be careful. What we have seen from the distance might be a decoy, maybe even a trap."

"With pleasure, *Imperator*," barked the stocky moor. "Don't worry, I will send scouts before going in closer."

After Trajan realized his cavalry was not numerous enough to encircle the resisting Dacian host he ordered Senecio to launch his light infantry. The centuries deployed in battle formation, and their front lines opened with barrages of *pila*. Seeing the Roman frontal assault on foot the Dacians picked up speed and pushed forward against the approaching Roman infantry and the hail of sky-darkening *pila*. The missiles flew through the air with a howling whistle caused by a little hole in their tips. The impact of thousands of *pila* killed hundreds of Dacians before they could make contact with the Roman lines. Most of them had no body armor, only thin birch shields with hemispherical bosses and bronze helmets - useless against a direct hit from a *pilum*. The heavy spears easily pierced their shields, killing or maiming the men behind them. Worse, once a shield was punctured the iron *pilum* tip bent over, entangling itself with the enemy shield and could not be pulled out, forcing the surviving fighter to throw away his only protection. Nor was he able to pick up the Roman weapon and hurl it back.

Senecio's tuba blows ordered his men into a formation of multiple wedges. Then they charged, running the last sixty feet. The following pandemonium was hair-raising. Fifteen thousand Roman auxiliaries crashed into not quite twenty thousand Dacian fighters that also had to fend off the persistent wing attacks from Roman cavalry. The initial clash drove the Roman line ten yards into the clustered Dacian host. The momentum allowed them to press on using their mighty rectangular shields. The Roman *gladius* stabbed and killed wherever it found Dacian skin.

Rain was falling now, first only a slight drizzle, but soon a full gusher, drenching friend and foe alike. Low clouds enveloped the hillsides, and Trajan could not see much of the battle any longer. He had to rely on messengers now to track the progress of his men. Even the battle noise was eerily muffled. Lightning sprang up around him. He could hear a tree crashing down in the distance. Boisterous thunder followed without delay. The storm plunged the whole valley into a jarring twilight, but the battle went on.

After the successful first charge the Roman attack had lost momentum. The Dacian defenders were standing their ground, seemingly unbreakable, ferociously slashing at the Romans with their scythe-like *falces*. The Romans had to be careful even behind the protection of their almost man-high curved shields. The vicious fighting went on. Dacian losses were mounting as fatigue took its toll. Wielding the *falx* was a lot more tiring than the Romans' opportunistic *gladius* stabs from behind the cover of their shields. The enemy fighters were slowly being pushed back.

Would Decebalus allow them to be butchered?

There! Dacian horns filled the air, and the enemy started disengaging.

242

Trajan rejoiced, but there was still no word from Quietus... On horseback, he cantered down from his position on the knoll with his bodyguard and moved closer to the action in the valley below. The Dacian rout wasn't pretty. Some Hibernian auxiliaries were cutting off the heads of Dacian wounded, grasping the hair of their ghastly trophies with their teeth and moving on to kill other fleeing fighters while the blood-dripping heads of their victims were dangling from their jaws. Seeing that, the remnants of the Dacian host tossed everything, swords and shields and *falces*, and ran and stumbled off the soaked battlefield as fast as their tired legs could carry them.

Trajan didn't condone the Hibernians' acts, but there was not much he could do. Employing auxiliaries from different lands had its downsides. He had to respect their war customs if he wanted to keep them in his service.

After the battle the Romans buried their dead and attended to the wounded. The soldiers reveled in their victory – despite the torrential rains that soaked them now. Only the wounded were disheartened, being in grave pain as they were – an excruciating reminder of their own mortality.

Trajan visited the infirmary tents, stopping by at every wounded soldier. It wasn't pretty: One man's gash to his hip was as deep as the Tiber River in the spring. Another man's arm had been amputated above the elbow and his bandage was blood-drenched. He was biting on a cloth-wrapped piece of softwood, his body mired in sweat, blood and dirt. Medics cleaned him up and poured wine down his throat to keep him inebriated.

Even in his delirious state of mind, he recognized the emperor, eyes glowing with satisfaction. Trajan wrapped his hand around the soldier's healthy arm.

"We won, didn't we?" the wounded rasped.

"Yes, *Optio*. Mars was with us today. What's your name?"

"Rufus. My name is Rufus, Caesar. *Optio* in the Second *Ala* of the-"

"It's all right, Rufus. I am proud of you. Your valor and gallantry will be a model for generations of Romans to come!"

Tears filled the man's eyes. "Thank you, *Imperator*. Don't give up on me. Please! Don't release from your service. The Army is all I have ever known. It's all I have ever wanted. I can still fight with my healthy arm, can't I? And who needs a shield anyway?" he quipped with a wry grin.

Trajan kept his composure, but he was weeping inside. No success in this war, not even all the gold in the all the world would ever make this man whole again.

He left the infirmary determined to hunt down Decebalus without mercy. There was still no word from Lusius Quietus. Trajan was getting anxious. After his men cleared the battlefield he allowed the Dacians to retrieve their dead and wounded. Then the Romans settled down for the night.

243

Trajan was in the command tent with his staff when Lusius Quietus at last returned. Soaking wet, he resembled a black cat that had been thrown into a river – and no, he had not found Decebalus. His scouts had not even been able to localize the escarpment where the Dacian king's pennants had guttered in the wind before battle. The rain had washed away all remnants of Decebalus and his entourage.

The bad news didn't blow the good mood among the officers. Thanks to the courage and discipline of the auxiliaries the battle had gone well after all. Communications had worked perfectly in spite of difficult conditions on the ground, thanks to Hadrian. Only Quietus had reason to grumble - and the legionaries under Sura, who had not seen any action. Trajan consoled the legionary officers, assuring them heavy infantry would be needed rather sooner than later.

The battle had been successful, but Decebalus had cleverly broken it off in time to save his army. They had not been able to pursue the fleeing enemy because of the inclement weather. Though the Dacians had lost several thousand warriors the Romans also mourned several hundred dead.

Late at night, Trajan dictated the notes for his 'Commentaries'. Callistus scribbled them dutifully on a papyrus scroll. The emperor was content but not euphoric. The war was far from over.

Chapter 48

The army resumed its march to Sarmizegethusa at the crack of dawn. The rearguard had not left camp yet when a group of unarmed *Comati*, Dacian longhaired noblemen, approached the Roman vanguard, asking to see the emperor. Trajan knew from the preparations for this expedition that the *Comati* were the lowest-ranking nobles in the Dacian hierarchy. Either Decebalus had not sent these men himself or he had sent them with no serious intentions to parley. And in fact, nothing came of it. They had gifts for Trajan and politely asked him to leave Dacia. The emperor dismissed them and pressed on.

Later in the day Dacian warriors began harassing Roman foragers and vanguard units. Whenever the terrain was suitable they launched rocks down on the marching column, slowing down the Roman advance. Bad weather and continuing rain were another problem. The terrain was muddy everywhere. The wagons got stuck in the sludge and had to be unloaded so that the oxen were able to pull them out of the muck. Although the pioneers tried to clear the way as best as they could and even put down planks to support the wagons, carts and the all-important wheeled engines, the army could not cover more than four miles a day. The terrible weather bogged down even the scouts, and Trajan had to wait longer and longer to receive his reports.

His diaries became rather monotonous. At least he had many good friends with him: Sura, Servianus, Livianus, Senecio. He even found Hadrian more and more to his liking. His cousin was charming and fun at supper. Not unlike Trajan and Sura, he enjoyed a long evening spiced up with delicious Falernian.

At last the emperor had enough of the harassing assaults. To put a lid on the Dacian guerilla activities he ordered retaliatory attacks on their strongholds and villages. Some of the hamlets and towns were protected by strong turf walls, and it took his men weeks to vanquish them. Sometimes they found Roman prisoners after a skirmish, tortured by Dacian women with clubs and spikes. Trajan became very angry. Why did the Dacian king allow this? What good would it do? He didn't understand. The generals explained it away as the sordid ways of barbarians. But Trajan knew Decebalus was no barbarian. He was the king of a well-organized state that over the past centuries had learned much from Greek city-states along the Black Sea. Torturing Romans was supposed to send fear into the hearts of his men, break their determination - and extract the emperor's plans from the prisoners, but there wasn't much to hide. The army's destination was plain enough.

Sometimes the Romans found half-empty villages with only women, children and elderly men left. Trajan took great pains to move them out of the way - much to the chagrin of his soldiers. After burying many of their own in a tortured and degrading state the men lusted for revenge. The generals had to work hard to keep them in line and prevent retaliatory acts.

By August they still had not reached the Iron Gates Pass. Instead, news from the Danube indicated that Dacian troops under a leader called Susagus had attacked Roman forts there in great numbers, even crossing into Moesia Province.

"Decebalus wants to open a second front," Trajan explained to his staff. "He can have it."

"What?" Sura burst out. "You want to allow a distraction? That's exactly what he wants you to do! Isn't that a bad plan? Haven't you always taught us to do the unexpected and not what's good on face value?"

"Hold it, Lucius," Trajan countered. "In a way I will, and in a way I won't. I do plan to go south with several legions to relieve the pressure on the border, but after we're done we will make our own pincer move and march to the Iron Gates Pass from a different direction. The rest of the army stays here and presses on, systematically destroying as many Dacian installations and outposts as it can. Don't forget, the summer harvest is coming up. Let's sting them and lay waste to the countryside. This will hamper their operations and create unrest among Dacian villagers. They will be torn between attacking us and protecting their fields.

Anyway, within a moon both armies will reunite at the Iron Gates and attack Decebalus on either side of the Pass. After that we will march on Sarmizegethusa and lay siege before the campaigning season is over."

They deliberated some more, but the emperor's words were final. He set out with the Praetorian Guard and two Moesian legions plus Quietus's Moors and hurried back to the Danube in forced marches. Servianus took command of the main host.

To make good time Trajan had the men march at the double, cantering up and down the long column and impressing upon them how important this effort was for the success of the campaign. One night Quietus's scouts discovered a camp of Roxolani cavalry. The Roxolani were Dacian allies, famous for their fast steeds and effective bowmen. Unaware of the Roman troops, they were taken by surprise at night and destroyed. Again, Trajan insisted on leaving their non-combatants unharmed.

In the morning – the Romans were still cleaning up and interrogating prisoners - a delegation from Decebalus himself arrived. This time he was sending *pileati*, members of the high nobility wearing Phrygian-style hats called *pilei*, which indicated their social status. The hats were forward-shaped and curved like a Dacian army helmet but made of felt.

The negotiators offered parley with Decebalus. They said he would bow to the will of Trajan and obey his orders. The emperor was skeptical. *Too easy, too obvious.*

The Dacian king was still not in a bad position. His army was not defeated yet, the main cities unconquered. He could not possibly have any motivation to give in to Roman demands. Still, Trajan decided to give peace a chance. He sent Livianus and Sura to meet with Decebalus, but they came back empty-handed. Decebalus had chosen not to meet them, sending intermediaries once more. Disappointed and angry, Sura and Livianus had broken off the talks and returned to the Roman camp. Trajan shrugged and decided to go back to the original plan and clear the Danube from enemy infiltration.

They swept into Moesia as far as Nicopolis to chase Susagus out of the Roman province. Ominously, he did not put up much of a fight and quickly retreated over the river. Trajan reinforced the Danube garrisons with small detachments from his legions, turned north and rushed back to the Iron Gates Pass where Servianus was waiting.

It was late September now. The campaigning season was soon coming to an end. They needed a victory soon or somehow force Decebalus to surrender by other means. The good news was that both Roman armies were presently threatening the Iron Gates Pass, 'knocking' on the gates of Sarmi-zegethusa. Would Decebalus fight? The answer came when the king appeared with his army, offering battle near Tapae. Tapae! There was great meaning in this location. It was at Tapae where Tettius had fought a great victory over Decebalus in Domitian's reign – a good omen? Fidgeting with the general's ribbon on his cuirass, Trajan scuttled from his command tent and ordered battle formation. He signaled Servianus to follow suite, determined to end the conflict here and now.

The two Roman armies took the field at the same time, presenting a sea of burnished armor and menacing siege artillery. But the emperor's eyes were fixed on the enemy troops. By Mars, what a host! Over one hundred thousand men covered the plains before him like swarming locusts, directed by standard-bearers blowing into serpent-shaped tubas and waving dragon standards with attached wind catchers stiffened by the squall. The Dacians, mostly infantry, wielded spears, battle-axes and *falces* and carried oval shields that were richly decorated with floriated or geometric patterns.

Trajan's mind was racing. His men were outnumbered two-to-one... Yet, Julius Caesar had often been outnumbered five-to-one, and had carried the day. Roman skill, discipline, equipment and training would have to make the difference – if led properly. He would have to split up the Dacian host, draw it apart with his two smaller Roman armies.

The emperor ordered the skirmishers forward. Then his archers and scorpion squads rained thousands of *pila,* arrows, bolts and rocks on the Dacian warriors who, being confronted with two Roman hosts at their flanks, started pulling in two directions to take on the enemy.

This time Trajan held the auxiliaries back. This set-piece battle was perfect for his heavy infantry, forming up now. After the barrage of missiles he deployed them forward. When the Dacians hurled their spears at them they halted, raising shields over their heads in *testudo* formation to deflect the volleys. The javelins' impact on the copper-reinforced Roman shields was earsplitting, but the missiles bounced off without doing much harm. Down came the shields in one fluid motion, and the legionaries pressed on. Hurtling forward in the mean time, the Dacians had almost reached the Roman lines, and both sides clashed with great force.

Trajan ordered Quietus's irregulars and Longinus's light cavalry to attack the enemy's flanks. He also sent Palmyrenian archers and Balearic slingers up the hills to shoot volleys into the center of the Dacian host on Servianus's side. Meanwhile the front line clashes were in full swing. The legions pushed hard with their shields, stabbing at the enemy from intermittent gaps between the men's interlocking shields, killing many opponents. This was successful but happened unevenly. The Roman frontline had careened into the Dacian lines, forcing the legionaries to fight the enemy both up front as well as to the side. This hampered their formations and enabled the Dacians in some areas to take on the legionaries one-on-one. They wielded their *falces* to great effect in hook fashion, grappling a legionary's shield and pulling it forward while a second fighter would wait for the Roman soldier to be exposed and then slash his face with the *falx.* Though Roman vambraces, greaves and reinforced helmets reduced casualties the Dacians were able to slow down the Roman charge. Fighting intensified and went on for half an hour, stalling.

In response, Trajan shifted some of his cavalry back to support the legionaries on the ground. Roman horse troopers, particularly the swift Moors, penetrated the Dacians' rear and inflicted terrible losses, but the enemy knew what was at stake and would not cede any more ground. Sarmizegethusa's fate depended on their valor.

The number of Roman injured in close combat mounted so fast that the medics could not supply sufficient bandages to stop the bleeding and make poultices fast enough – maddening Trajan. He had sent them into battle - their blood was his blood! He cursed, vaulted from his stallion and tore off strips of fabric from his own tunic and the purple cloak. "Here! Make more bandages," he yelled at the *lictor proximus,* his senior attendant, and ordered him to tell the medics to cut up the clothes of all non-combatants and lightly injured men. "The doctors have to intensify their efforts. I don't want to hear of anyone dying because we couldn't stop the bleeding of his wounds. Make more bandages!"

Then there were the dead: More and more corpses arrived behind the lines, and nobody had the time to put them down properly. Tears glistened in Trajan's eyes. *My brave men, I will honor your greatness. Rome shall never forget this day.*

After hours of fighting, the Dacian host, under severe pressure from all sides and unable to fully deploy its multitudes, buckled at last, first on Servianus's side, then on Trajan's, and collapsed. In a free-for-all the Roman cavalry dispatched thousands of fleeing Dacian warriors.

Chapter 49

Decebalus had lost. At least thirty thousand Dacians littered the ground, but he had exacted a great toll on the Roman army: Trajan's losses numbered hundreds and hundreds of men. Trajan ordered to regroup and perform an exact count of Roman casualties while the remnants of the Dacian host retreated behind the strong walls and battlements of Sarmizegethusa.

Trajan supervised the cleanup himself, visiting the scattered infirmary tents filled with thousands of wounded soldiers. Many had suffered terrible gashes. Even the medics had endured some bad contusions from extracting the wounded from the battle field. The emperor was everywhere, spending time with the men, cheering them up, promising them he would take care of their families, making them chuckle with raunchy jokes that reduced the vast hierarchical gap between him and the soldiers.

He was watching in pain as the medics perform their grisly duties. Often he would ask them about head injuries, knowing they were often deadly despite the daring surgeries some doctors performed.

One doctor was just wrapping up his operation, washing his bloody hands in a bucket of fresh water when the emperor entered his tent. "Can I ask you a question, *medicus*?"

The doctor peered at Trajan with intelligent but tired eyes. "Of course, my Lord."

"How are the head injuries?"

"Not too bad. I mean... Not worse than after any other battle," the *medicus* clarified.

"Hm. That's good news, I guess," Trajan mumbled. "The *falx* has not roughed us up too badly?"

"No, it hasn't. I have not seen any split helmets. I think the new design works well, but we are dealing with many other gashes to our men's arms – despite the vambraces the legionaries now have. After I am done here I will count such injuries and compare them with the gashes amongst the auxiliaries, who mostly don't possess vambraces or greaves for that matter. I will need to talk to your officers, Excellency, to learn the exact circumstances under which the various units fought."

Trajan nodded. He liked the man. "What is your name?" he asked him.

"Crito. I am Titus Statilius Crito, chief medic of the Fifth *Macedonica*."

"I am glad we met, Titus. Please send me a report when you are done. My commanders will give you all the information you need. If there is a problem, do not hesitate and see me in my tent."

"Thank you, *Imperator*. It is a pleasure serving you."

They shook hands and Trajan headed back to his bivouac. The bloodshed was tormenting him. He would have to work harder to finish this war through cunning, not combat.

After studying his officers' reports and tallying the dead and wounded with Sura and Servianus he resigned to the fact that that he would not be able to subjugate Decebalus this year. "Decebalus, the *mentula*, lost a battle and many of his men, but he bought himself time. We cannot take Sarmizegethusa this year. Many of our units need to be consolidated, new *contubernia* formed. The men have to get acquainted to new combatants in their midst, train with them. And winter is knocking on our tents. The gods be cursed!" Trajan scowled at the visitors in his tent. "As soon as the dead are honorably buried and the wounded can be transported or march on their own, we will return to Viminacium.

But not to worry, my friends, we will be back in the spring and have dinner in the Royal Hall of Sarmizegethusa, I swear by the gods of the holy Capitoline trinity! I will stay in Moesia in person to prepare for next year's campaign."

The army insisted on congratulating their victorious commander and hailed him *Imperator* for the second time, his first as emperor. Trajan sent Hadrian, Servianus and Sura back to Rome. As the imperial quaestor it was Hadrian's duty to report the emperor's acts to the Senate. He would submit a detailed account of the campaign. Sura and Servianus deserved a reward for their loyalty and military accomplishments. Trajan designated them as the Ordinary Consuls for the coming year.

Sura didn't want to leave his best friend, but the emperor insisted. "I need you in Rome, Lucius. You have served me well for so long. It's your turn now to be Consul and lead the government back home. You and Servianus get along well. With both of you in charge in Rome I don't need to worry about the politics in the capital and have my back free to concentrate on the war. It will get even harder next year. The Dacians know we mean business and are determined to thumb their noses at us. We have killed many of their warriors. Their families are lusting for revenge and Roman heads to lessen their pain. Even Decebalus's grudging allies will hold still and line up behind the king."

Lucius grumbled, but Trajan stayed firm.

The two generals and Hadrian left with an escort of auxiliary cavalry from Viminacium. Trajan's cousin carried a sealed letter from the emperor for his wife.

Dearest Pompeia:

*I cannot tell you how much I miss you. It pains me
to tell you I will not be back for at least another year. We
have not been able to force Decebalus into submission
- despite achieving great victories on the battlefield.
Hadrian can tell you all about the fighting. He outdid
himself handling communications. He is a good soldier.
Your assessment was right. You will love to hear that,
and I am not ashamed to admit that I was wrong.*

*I will stay here on the Danube all winter long to
get the army ready for next year's campaign. Callistus
and I are working together to complete the first chapter
of my 'Commentaries' on this conflict. I will send you
draft copies as well. Let me know what you think.*

*I made Sura and Servianus Consules Ordinarii. Hadrian
will join them on their trip to Rome. After finishing his
quaestorial duties he has my permission to move on with
his cursus honorum. I wish him well. Fortunately, Livianus
has capable men on his staff that will take over for him.*

*How are you holding up? How is the family?
Please send me tidings – and your latest take on
Rome's politics. I always appreciate your insights.*

*Pompeia, I will defeat Decebalus. I will come home
after that, and we will celebrate a Triumph together!*

Trajan

Trajan's advisers on the Danube were now Praefect Livianus, the Governors of Pannonia and Moesia Bassus and Longinus, respectively, and the three army generals Senecio, Laberius and Quietus.

After an assessment of how many warriors Decebalus would field in the spring – Trajan estimated some seventy thousand Dacians complemented by some ten thousand allied cavalry recruited from different Sarmatian tribes – he concluded it would be wise to increase next year's expeditionary force from forty-five thousand to sixty-five thousand men. He planned to arrange them in separate columns to attack Dacia via three different routes: the Iron Gates Pass, the Vulcan Pass and the Red Tower Pass. This would hopefully both surprise Decebalus and force the king to divide his forces. Each Roman column would have to number at least twenty thousand combatants to have a chance of success.

By November the general staff in Viminacium had honed the new strategy enough to start start recruiting. They sent dispatches to commanders throughout the empire in an effort to determine where to levy the additional troops. In the end, Trajan ordered the entire Eleventh *Claudia* and significant detachments from three other legions to the Danube. He also enhanced the auxiliary corps with troops from Britannia and vexillations from Gaul, Noricum and Asia Minor.

In April Trajan was ready. He lost no time: Two massive columns fanned out from Lederata to make their way through the South Carpathian Mountains - one via the Iron Gates Pass under Trajan himself, the other via the Vulcan Pass under Lusius Quietus. The remaining third column shipped downriver to Oescus, under Laberius's command, and launched an attack up the Olt valley targeting the Red Tower Pass.

Chapter 50

"Quiet! Quiet!" Burebista barked with his booming voice. "The king will speak to you now." Decebalus's right hand man stood beside his king on the dais of the *Pileati* Council Hall of Sarmizegethusa. In front of them Dacian nobles were seated at two long parallel tables connected to each other at the far end with a shorter one. The long tables measured sixty feet and accommodated twenty men each.

Decebalus himself was sitting on his Royal Chair. The king was a small and slender man with a scruffy gray beard and a thin sputtering voice. He preferred to let Burebista do the heavy lifting in the Council, at least when it came to command silence in the Hall. In all other ways he held him – and Dacia as a whole - in his tight grip.

After the chamber fell silent Decebalus addressed the nobles with his high-pitched voice. They could barely hear him - his way to enforce complete quiet in the Hall. "*Pileati* of Dacia, I have called this war council because our nation is facing the greatest challenge in its history. Our very survival as an independent country is at stake. As we speak, Roman soldiers are invading our homeland in large numbers, destroying our crops, raping and enslaving our women, killing our men, stealing our gold and silver, putting fire to our villages-"

He stopped abruptly as if by the very shock of what he had just said and swept the audience with fiery fast twitching eyes. Decebalus was a man of unlimited energy. He had been king for decades, amassing great riches through mining, raids and invasions. His acts had bought him many favors, and over time he had filled the *Pileati* Council with loyal supporters, but the king was realistic enough to know that only success would keep him on the throne – and alive.

Decebalus sighed gravely. "I have come to this venerable Council today to ask you and your clans for great sacrifices. I need every male from the age of fifteen to the age of fifty to join our warriors. I need every blacksmith to produce nothing but weapons and armor - spears, helmets, battle-axes and most of all *falces*. I need every carpenter to make shields and nothing but shields. I need every village to defend our fields and hide our stores from the enemy.

In other words, I need every possible effort to protect the homeland."

The *pileati* stared at him. Many of them had lost a friend or two in the war last year. Would they comply? "Furthermore, I need messengers to ride out and ask for help from-"

Suddenly, a disheveled warrior dashed into the hall. The begrimed man looked exhausted and afraid.

Decebalus eyed him with repugnance. "How dare you intrude these hallowed halls?"

The warrior prostrated himself on the floor in front of the Royal dais and croaked, "Forgive me, Great King. I am bringing tidings from the Danube. The Roman army has crossed the river as we expected, but after crossing they have split up in two mighty columns, at least twenty thousand men strong each. Our spies cannot say where they are going yet. All we know is that one column is marching toward Sarmizegethusa, led by Trajan himself. No one knows where the other one is headed. The directions seems to be east."

For a moment it was dead quiet in the Council Hall. Then the nobles hurled questions at the soldier. Decebalus lifted his hand, and again Burebista commanded their attention. "Quiet! You will be quiet. Listen to the king."

"This is confirming my worst fears," Decebalus declared. He was absolutely calm. "The Romans will attack us everywhere, but we need to find out where they will cross the mountains and which pass they have picked for their invasion. Their approach is cunning because they are forcing us to split our forces, but, by Zalmoxis, we will defeat them – if I have your full support. *Pileati*, I have to go."

"There is more," the messenger whined.

Decebalus transfixed him with an icy glare. "What?" he hissed at the man.

"Another Roman army has left Viminacium on boats, sailing downriver."

The Dacian king showed no emotions, but some of the princes in the Hall shrieked in open distress.

"And..." Decebalus encouraged the courier.

"We don't know what they are up to, but they are also part of the invasion..."

"Don't panic, my friends," Decebalus shouted at the *pileati*. "We will handle them!" He stood. "There isn't anything else for me to say. You heard the courier. We are under attack. My aides will contact you to discuss the military situation on the river, but I am asking you to send heralds to the villages right away and call your men into battle. Do stay in Sarmizegethusa yourselves until I have had a chance to talk with everyone of you in person and give you my instructions."

The king turned to the courier who was still kneeling on the floor. "Get up, wretch, and come with me. I need to know everything."

The soldier scrambled up and hurried to the dais. Decebalus and Burebista left the Hall with him, leaving behind some very distraught *pileati*.

The Roman troops made good progress, especially the light cavalry under Quietus. Dacian resistance on the way to the Vulcan Pass was disorganized and scattered. Quietus's moors gladly killed many natives and destroyed their villages. In the process they made thousands of prisoners of all ages and both genders. The great influx of prisoners was slowing down the Roman advance, as it took more and more men to guard and feed the mounting number of Dacian prisoners. Irritated, Quietus sent dispatches to Trajan to ask for instructions.

The emperor himself was not so lucky. The path to the Iron Gates Pass was fiercely defended. It was the direct route to Sarmizegethusa, and the area was swarming with Dacian warriors. Decebalus had ordered most of his troops to defend this pass and protect the Dacian capital at all cost. Still, the Roman army pressed on. Ignoring Decebalus's incessant hit-and-run tactics, Trajan attacked every Dacian stronghold along the way and reduced it to rubble. As his men pushed deeper and deeper into the mountains and as the peaks grew higher and higher, it took longer and longer to destroy the Dacian forts. Painfully slow they moved from crest to crest in adverse terrain, from peak to peak, stronghold to stronghold.

One day General Senecio entered the emperor's tent. "*Imperator*, our men have uncovered a hidden lair on the mountainside not far from here," he reported. "It is heavily defended and..." Senecio hesitated, clearing his throat. "The Dacians are attacking us with Roman artillery darts."

Trajan was electrified. "What are you saying?"

Senecio tossed his head up and down vigorously. "Yes, yes, my Lord."

"If you are thinking what I am thinking..." Trajan muttered, stretching the words.

"Then we have found Fuscus's engines!" Senecio finished the sentence for him.

"Very well," Trajan said. He had recovered from the shock. "Let's find out for sure. I will set the Guard into motion. Call Livianus. And your men too, General. But let us be careful. This could be a trap."

The Praetorians set out right away. While marching uphill with Trajan in their midst Senecio's cavalry protected their flanks. The main host stayed behind under Longinus.

When the terrain became too steep for the horses Trajan ordered Senecio to stay behind and the Praetorians into attack formation. They were on their own now. At least Senecio would watch their backs.

Century after century of Praetorian infantry ascended the hill, stacked together in tight wedges, the men interlocking their shields. Not too soon. Heavy fire soon engulfed them, pounding their bronze-reinforced shields. The barrage slowed them down, but didn't stop their assault.

Trajan was surrounded and shielded by *Equites Singulares* from his personal guard, wearing full armor but without the purple imperial cloak. It would be too easy a target for a Dacian sharp shooter. Ahead of his men Trajan could see many Dacian fighters crouching behind trees and boulders, thrusting spears at the advancing Roman shield wall. Behind the fighters a hole was visible in the rock-faced hillside - the entrance to the enemy lair. From there, battle-darts were fired at them in rapid sequence, some of them punching a hole through a Roman shield, instantly killing the man behind it. It was imperative to storm the hole and stop the artillery fire.

Trajan jotted down instructions for Praefect Livianus and his front commanders and ordered them to concentrate the Roman attack on that opening in the hill. He handed a wax tablet to his *lictor proximus,* and flanked by body guards, the man scuttled off to Livianus, intermittently ducking for cover from the ferocious dart fire. The praefect was directing the attack up ahead from within the Second Century, at the spearhead of the column. Trajan could see his crimson plumed helmet in the distance.

Livianus read Trajan's tablet and waved back at the emperor to confirm. Then he issued new orders, and his centurions redirected their men toward the mysterious opening in the rock.

As the legionaries pushed closer Dacian warriors sallied from behind their covers and hurled their bodies against the disciplined Roman lines attackers. Careful not to tumble, the legionaries used their shields to absorb the wave of attackers. Then they resumed the uphill push. Some Dacians now whipped forward, slashing *falces* against the crimson red Roman shield wall, perhaps hoping to scare the Praetorians and achieve some kind of avalanche effect, making the Romans soldiers tumble down hill. But Trajan's soldiers quickly opened small gaps in their formations, let the enemy fighters pass through and finished them off behind the front line one by one.

Soon the Romans could see details inside the hole they were targeting. Dacian-operated scorpions were rapidly firing at them, but as they came closer the enemy crews halted their fire in order not to hit their own men. When the defenders' lines were thinning out due to heavy losses at the hands of the Praetorians the engines fired again. The legionaries sped up their pace, running at full speed now and stormed the entrance to the cave. Trajan could see them disappear inside.

Anxious to catch up with them, Trajan accelerated his own pace. He had to cross through an area of tall fir trees and lost the cave out of sight. On his way up a messenger from Livianus arrived telling him that the fighting inside the lair was over. They had overwhelmed the defenders after a short but intense fight. When Trajan arrived on site Livianus was waiting for him. His soldiers had re-ignited the torches on the walls that had gone out in the bedlam of fighting. Trajan saw dead Dacians all over as well as shackled prisoners and injured legionaries treated by their medics. Livianus asked to join him deeper into the lair. Their suspicion had proven correct: Here they were - Fuscus's long lost siege engines.

They also found the eagle of the Fifth Legion *Alaudae.* It filled Trajan's eyes with tears: the pride of every legion, its Golden Eagle, the incarnation of Roman military might. They had recovered it. Roman honor was restored.

The gilded bronze eagle lay on the ground, scuffed, dull and dirty but undamaged, reminding him of Crassus's Eagles, lost at Carrhae against the Parthians. Augustus had recovered them after many years of haggling with the Parthian king of kings. "This is a great day, Claudius," Trajan said to the praefect. "It's not just a military victory because we have recaptured these scorpions. It is also a moral victory. The men will like it. It will lift their spirits and show them the enemy is vulnerable."

Chapter 51

General Laberius and his three legions had come a long way. After sailing down the river they had marched up the Olt valley and engaged the enemy at Buridava, simply pushing it out of the way. Now they were fast approaching the Red Tower Pass, unchecked by Decebalus's forces.

The steep mountain tops to either side of the rugged trail looked dark and menacing. The muggy air felt heavy. Thunder rumbled far away, muffled by the hills around them but audible like drummers practicing their rhythm in the house next door.

The trees in this gods-forsaken place had the appearance of grotesque mute statues, suffering from old age like people, Laberius mused. There was absolutely no wind and no rustle in the trees. Maybe they used to be people, punished by the Medusa... He scolded himself: The Medusa's glance was petrifying, not lignifying and by the way, why should he believe such hags' tales?

Still, the trail seemed devoid of life. What was going on - and where was the enemy?

The eerie quiet was disconcerting. No bird was flitting in the air or picking on seeds on the ground. No brook could be heard trickling in its banks. Laberius shuddered. The Dacian gods were protesting the Roman intrusion into their land. Or more likely, he corrected himself, nature was scared by the inevitable battle in its domain. Perhaps Trajan should have co-opted the Dacians' Supreme God, Zalmoxis, and built him a temple to gain his favor.

"I don't like this," he spoke to Callidromus at his side. The Bithynian freedman was his adviser, scribe and clerk all in one. "It's too quiet. Nature is holding its breath - for something. I can feel it."

Callidromus rubbed his chin. "Admittedly, this is a scary place, Master. But we don't know this part of the world. It may mean nothing. Perhaps it's like this here all the time."

"Oh, it means something. We just don't know what. Better be prepared than sorry," shouted Pompeius Falco.

The commander of the Fifth *Macedonica*, a legion raised after the destruction of the Fifth *Alaudae*, had picked up the last comments of their conversation as he was catching up to them on his checkered stallion.

"So you agree with me, Pompeius," Laberius asked the newcomer. "Something's amiss."

"Definitely. I propose we order the men into battle formation," Falco suggested. "I believe it is so calm here because the animals have run away from a Dacian host ahead of us."

Callidromus disagreed. "What tells you it's Dacians they are running away from? It could be just as well us."

"It could," Falco acknowledged. "I just don't want to take the chance."

Laberius concurred. "Battle formation it is. Issue the order, Legate."

It wasn't a moment too early. As the *cornicens* blew their horns, up ahead the Romans noticed a billowing dust cloud. It was too far to recognize details, but Laberius had an inkling: Dacians – and many of them.

While the legionaries dropped their travel kit in favor of shield and *pilum* scouts returned from the vanguard units and reported they had made contact with the enemy. A Dacian host was descending from a turf-walled stronghold on the foothills of the Red Tower Pass to their left.

"That's it," Laberius shouted. "We have reached the pass, and they are defending it."

He issued orders to double the pace to assist the men of the vanguard. Soon they could see the skirmish ahead. The light-armed vanguard was falling back, trying to disengage from the Dacians. Anxious for blood, the rankers in the frontline didn't hear the heavy Roman infantry approaching on the other side of the hill and kept pounding Laberius's vanguard. Too late. The legionaries punched through the Dacian lines, wreaking havoc. The enemy fighters fled back to the main force head over heels, and Laberius chose not to pursue them. He called for Falco.

"Pompeius, I will lead my two legions over the pass while you take the Fifth and engage the Dacian host. The fleeing enemy will show you the way. Destroy them and take their stronghold. We need our backs free during our passage. I will not stop until my men have safely reached the lowlands on the other side. Keep me informed via dispatch. When you are done, follow us. I will send scouts with our exact location. Good luck!"

Laberius wheeled his horse around before Falco could acknowledge his orders and darted off to the head of his column.

Three days later an express rider arrived from the Fifth reporting to Laberius in camp on the north side of the pass that they had taken the fortress after heavy fighting. He added that the legionaries had taken a noblewoman prisoner who Falco's Dacian mercenaries identified as Decebalus's sister. She was on her way here with a mounted escort. Hearing that, the legate decided to set forth himself right away to see and interrogate her. He left camp with two cohorts. The Dacians had been pushed off the pass, and they met up with Falco's prisoner squad without difficulty.

After a quick report from the *turma* commander Laberius ordered the princess off the horse. "Look who we've got here. What a pretty find," he teased her with glee.

They arraigned her before him with hands tied behind her back, but as he strode up to her she spit into his face glowering. Infuriated, Laberius wiped her spit off his face with a fold of his cloak. "How uncivilized," he hissed. "Gag the bitch, shackle her legs with chains and tie her hands to a steed's tail. I am convinced a walk behind the horse's ass will do her good."

The men chuckled. "Shall we tear off her clothes while we're at it?" one of them asked the general.

"Spicy thought, *decurio*," Laberius answered grinning. "But no - she is leverage for us. Trajan would not approve. Don't touch her. Just make her stretch her legs a bit. It will make her more agreeable to the presence of a Roman commander."

He climbed back on his horse and ordered his best scouts to locate Trajan's army and bring him the good news.

Laberius was not ready for what he saw when he returned to camp. Dead corpses of Romans and Dacians alike were scattered everywhere on the ramparts and on the grounds. The buildings were disheveled, the palisades blackened from fire. The timbers were plastered with arrows and spears and resembled cornered hedgehogs rather than austere Roman fortifications.

Quartermaster Felix greeted him at the entrance on foot. "*Salve*, Legate. As you can see," he said, pointing his thumb over his shoulder. "We were attacked."

"What happened?" Laberius asked enraged.

"A Dacian host under Susagus paid us a visit. Remember him? The man commanded the invasion of Lower Moesia Province last year. I guess he thought with the two cohorts gone we would be short on manpower. Well, he was mistaken, and we fended them off, but not without casualties: Seventy men are dead, over two hundred wounded, some of them badly - *falx* wounds…"

They walked about the camp so the general could assess the situation.

"This is terrible, Felix. Susagus might come back. I only hope Falco will join us soon so we can leave the area," Laberius said.

"There is something else," Felix pointed out with a low voice.

"What?" Laberius scowled. "What is it?"

"They took a prisoner."

"A prisoner? Whom?" Laberius shook Felix' shoulders. "Whom did they take? Tell me!"

"Callidromus."

Laberius let go of the quartermaster, mouth hanging. He stumbled away from Felix. Poor Callidromus! They would torture him. He would never see him again, certainly not alive – unless… "Maybe there is hope. We could offer Decebalus's sister!"

Felix looked at him appalled. "You have to clear that with the emperor," he cautioned. "Her capture could end this war, you know…"

Eighty miles away, Trajan and Callistus reviewed the account of today's events for the emperor's 'Commentaries' in the dim light of a flickering oil lamp. The makeshift compound around them was bustling with activities. Legionaries were feeding their horses and mules, greasing their torsion engines, repairing wheels and bearings, grinding wheat for tomorrow's meals. Many fireplaces lit up the camp, providing the men with warm porridge and the occasional pig roast. Guards patrolled the palisades.

Longinus, Senecio and Quadratus Bassus had assembled in the command tent's anteroom. Trajan and his secretary could hear their muffled conversation through the canvas partition.

"What do you think? Am I concise enough?" Trajan asked his faithful aide.

"Julius Caesar would be pleased," Callistus assured him.

"Writing these accounts is quite difficult," Trajan admitted. "I am glad you and I will have the winter months to refine the vernacular. Without you, Callistus, I couldn't do it. My Latin is not good enough." He sighed. "I wished I had listened to my father. He always told me not to neglect my schooling, but, by Jupiter, I had no interest in reading or writing whatsoever!"

"It's all right, Trajan. You are a great soldier. Don't be too hard on yourself. You need not also be a great writer."

"Caesar was."

Callistus smiled.

"So they say. But that was Julius Caesar and this is you. You are your own man - with your own attributes, your own greatness. Don't worry. Posteriority will revere you."

Trajan wasn't convinced.

"Your 'Commentaries' will be well received. Cheer up, Master. The topic is to your advantage. Just don't write any love poems," Callistus admonished him with a wink.

Trajan laughed.

In the anteroom the officer's conversation all of a sudden stopped. Trajan heard a courier enter the room and salute the generals. Curious, Trajan pushed aside the partition and crossed into the room. The messenger was one of Quietus's express riders. When he saw Trajan he saluted the emperor. "*Salve, Imperator.* I have a dispatch from General Quietus for you." He handed a sealed scroll to Trajan, who opened it on the spot. While he was reading the dispatch the Moor showed no emotions, standing to attention.

"This is good news, my friends," Trajan finally said, putting down the scroll. "Quietus crossed the Vulcan Pass with barely any losses. He will reach

Sarmizegethusa one week from now and is awaiting further instructions. Excellent."

"Have we heard from Laberius?" Longinus asked.

"No. As you know, his legions are the farthest away. I don't expect any news for a while." He paused. "But let me get back to you, soldier," Trajan said and turned to the Moor. "Ride back to your unit. Take some of our scouts with you – they know shortcuts you may not be aware of - and tell the general that I want him to ride to the hot springs at Aquae. We will meet him there. Tell him to be very, very careful. The enemy is lingering in this area, and tell him to stay away from any Dacian stronghold. I don't think they will attack unless Lusius provokes them. If they do, I want him to retreat and go around them. I want no engagement. Is that understood?"

The Moor nodded.

"Good. Go to the backroom. My secretary will put this into writing and seal the dispatch for you."

Callistus had been listening in through a gap in the canvas. Now he crossed to the express courier, greeted him, and the two men walked to the backroom together.

Trajan looked at his generals triumphantly. "The campaign is going well. We have conquered many Dacian fortresses, taken many towns, recovered Fuscus's artillery and his legion's eagle. Quietus got his cavalry across the mountains, inflicting heavy losses on the enemy. He is sending a whole army of prisoners to Moesia Province for leverage. We will join forces with him soon.

Now we only need to wait for Laberius. Once he arrives, the noose will drop on Sarmizegethusa."

"Do you expect another battle, Trajan?" Senecio asked.

"I hope not. We have defeated another Dacian host last week and demonstrated with our *testudo* formations that no stronghold is safe from Roman ingenuity and perseverance. If we succeed - and let me repeat that - if we succeed in merging our forces, Decebalus has no choice but surrender. After all we are only several days away from his capital facing a combined Roman army over fifty thousand men strong."

"So he can either try to defeat us in battle one more time or attempt to hold Sarmizegethusa, but hopefully he surrenders. These are his options, aren't they?" Bassus summarized.

Trajan nodded. "Yes. But again, we have not heard from Laberius. The enemy may have obliterated him. Who knows? Let's not count our chickens before they hatch."

Several days later the uncertainty lifted. Laberius's scouts found Trajan's camp and gave a detailed report of the successful events on the Red Tower

Pass, including the capture of the princess and, sadly, Callidromus's abduction. The emperor's instructions were swift. He ordered Laberius to meet him at Aquae, adding that he was sorry for his loss, but under no circumstances was he to trade the princess for his aide.

It was the middle of August when the Roman armies reunited twenty miles from the Dacian capital. In the Roman camp Decebalus's sister had turned into a celebrity, but Trajan allowed no one to touch her.

Scouts reported that Decebalus's men were outnumbered and exhausted, had nothing left to give. Trajan put the army in motion, apprehensively waiting for Decebalus's reaction. What would the Dacian king do?

Decebalus again sent a delegation of *pileati*. Trajan stopped his advance and parleyed with the embassy. Their leader was Burebista.

He stepped forward, removed his *pileus* and kneeled in front of the Roman emperor. "Marcus Ulpius Traianus, Master of the civilized World, please hear me. I speak for the great King Decebalus and the whole Council of Dacia. I also speak for our allies in this unfortunate conflict," Burebista droned.

Trajan signaled him to go on. His throat was dry with anticipation.

The Dacian noble continued. "I am authorized to let you know that the Dacian people are willing to surrender without conditions and are ready to accept your terms."

It was over!

"I congratulate the Dacian people to their wise decision and I am happy to avoid any more bloodshed," Trajan answered exulted. "Here are my terms: Surrender all arms, stop all fighting, return all prisoners. Return the Roman arms we know you still possess, return any Roman deserters and foreign craftsmen. Destroy all your forts. Relinquish all territories we have captured at this time - all the lands between the Danube and the Carpathian Mountains, including the Banat.

Become a Roman ally, make our allies your allies and make our enemies your enemies. Do not enlist any Romans or Roman allies into your forces and refuse to give refuge to any deserter. Finally, accept Roman garrisons in the lands north of the great river that are now ours.

In return, we will release all our prisoners and make you a client of the Roman People.

In other words, be our friend or perish!"

Burebista bowed before the emperor expressionless and said, "Agreed. There is but one minor request. May we have our princess back?"

Trajan shot him a sharp glance. "After you have returned all Roman prisoners – yes."

"You are most generous, Caesar," Burebista replied with a relieved smile.

On the next day Decebalus himself entered the Roman camp to sign the treaty with an entourage of Dacian nobles. He cast aside his weapons and prostrated himself in front of Trajan, asking for forgiveness.

The emperor was pleased, but looking at the man he could not escape a sense of dismay. *He is a weasel*, he thought. *We will have to keep a very close eye on him.*

There was another man who attentively watched the surrender cere-mony: the Centurion Maximus. He had sworn revenge and at last he was able to set eyes upon the man guilty of ordering mass murder and treachery - the scoundrel who had ordered his men killed without mercy. Maximus trembled with rage, but there was nothing he could do now but memorize Decebalus's face. His time would come.

Chapter 52

Standing together under the arches of Livia's Portico on the Oppian Hill in Rome, Hadrian and Trajan enjoyed the shade as they were facing the massive Flavian amphitheater, but their attention was caught by the hustle and bustle of a vast building complex under construction right in front of them: Trajan's new Baths.

"Note their size, Hadrian: three times bigger than Titus's," Trajan remarked with pride.

His cousin could barely hear him against the raucous din extending from the site. "Certainly, Trajan" he said. "Apollodorus likes big, but will it be beautiful?"

Trajan sneered. "Don't be jealous. Just because you don't like the architect doesn't mean he is not doing great work. In fact, I believe he is a genius. Think of the great ashlar bridge he built across the Danube. Some people call it the Eighth Wonder of the world. The bridge isn't just an engineering feat. It also buttresses our forces in Dacia, enabling us to take reinforcements across the river at any time no matter the weather conditions."

"I am only saying I would design some details differently," Hadrian backpedaled. He knew how much Trajan appreciated the skills of his architect and didn't want to hurt his feelings.

"You can't stand Apollodorus," Trajan accused him. "Why, cousin? That's so strange... You are hard to please, yet anxious to shine. Loosen up, Hadrian, you are not in a competition with the man from Damascus. Your zeal is unbecoming of a praetor of the Roman People."

Hadrian winced. Trajan usually called him 'cousin' when he intended a criticism – as if to say, 'You are no good, in high station only because you are my relative'. Hadrian sizzled with resentment but knew when to back off. Trajan was in no mood to discuss the merits of Apollodorus's design without bias. Hadrian clenched his teeth, swallowing the ready answer on his angry tongue.

Evidently, the emperor wasn't waiting for one. He pushed off the portico stairs and headed to the construction site, Hadrian trudging after him.

After roaming the complex for a while they found Apollodorus near the outer walls. "*Avete*, my Lords," he welcomed them waving his big hands. He shuffled forward to shake their hands and pointed at the site behind him. "What do you think? Looking good, eh?"

"Absolutely, Apollodorus," Trajan praised him. "You have made great progress since my last visit. But tell me one thing - what are those semicircles along the rim walls?"

"Ahh, those... Well, they are called *exedrae*. They are for looks only, to break up the long walls. We don't want the Baths to resemble a fortress, do we?"

"I see," the emperor said. "Yes, this shall be a place of fun and joy. It is bringing back fond memories in me, from my childhood – when I used to go to Italica's bathhouse with Father. I always had a great time there. Alas, the great man is long dead. He would have enjoyed seeing the sheer size of these Baths!"

The three men discussed the building some more, ambling around on the sprawling site. A steady stream of ox-drawn wagons was arriving from kilns outside the city, supplying the edifice with brick to face its bulky concrete walls. The artificial stone itself was made on site from quicklime, pozzolanic ash and an aggregate of pumice, combined with water and poured into forms via chutes and shafts. Apollodorus explained the different activities all around them.

They had nearly reached the other end of the edifice when Hadrian turned halfway, pointing with his index finger to the center of the site. "Apollodorus, why don't you erect a big dome to enclose the Bath's *calidarium*? Wouldn't that give the whole complex a nice focal point?"

The Syrian architect pulled up his eyebrows. "Too risky," he muttered. "I don't want my building to collapse and kill the people inside. The thought alone is revolting..."

"But why?" Hadrian insisted. "I have talked with some engineers about it, and they told me our novel ways of making concrete should allow the construction of domes one hundred feet tall or higher."

"What do you know about these things, young man? You go back to your pumpkin domes and play yard models. Serious people don't entertain such foolish ideas!"

Hadrian had a sharp reply on his tongue when Trajan intervened, "I think it is fine, Apollodorus. Excuse my young relative here. He is full of enthusiasm for new ideas, the privilege of youth, I might add," the emperor said diplomatically. His voice indicated, however, that he wouldn't tolerate any more of Hadrian's criticism.

Frustrated, Hadrian bit his tongue again. *They don't get it.*

The imperial company strode on to the main entrance where not much had been built yet. All they could see were slaves pouring the concrete foundations. Apollodorus outlined his designs when a loud shriek suddenly filled the air. Whirling around they saw a Nubian slave lying on the ground on the other side of the semicircle that was to later enclose the Baths' park between the outer rim walls and the main entrance. The man must have fallen from his scaffolding. Several other slaves were standing around him.

Trajan and Hadrian rushed to the spot, followed by a gasping Apollodorus, who had a hard time keeping up with his more athletic visitors.

Distracted by the injured slave, the other workers didn't recognize the emperor of Rome - only wearing a plain toga - in their midst. When Hadrian reached down to the injured man, he saw that his arm was standing ajar from his body - broken or dislocated or both. The Nubian's head was bleeding. He moaned loudly.

"We need a medic," Trajan shouted.

Hadrian grabbed the shoulders of the next best man in the throng. "You heard the emperor. Call for the medics."

The man gasped, nodded obediently and ran off.

"Where are the medics?" Trajan asked Apollodorus.

"They should be close. Accidents happen every day, you know, with so many people working here," he answered. "It won't be long."

Hadrian felt bad for the Nubian. Holding his head he tried to make him more comfortable. "It will be all right," he encouraged the man. "We will give you strong wine. A *medicus* will pop your arm back in place. I believe it's dislocated at the elbow if you know what I mean. Don't worry. You will be fine."

The shocked slave put on a brave smile. "Thank you, Master," he managed. "But please, don't let them cut off my arm!"

"No way, son," Trajan assured the worker, drooping over him with a friendly smile. "There is no need."

Soon, the medics arrived with a stretcher and examined the injury. They confirmed Hadrian's assessment and were about to snap the man's arm back into place when Trajan intervened. "Are you crazy? You have to give the man some wine first. This will hurt bad!"

The medics looked at the emperor perplexed. One of them said, "Master, he is just a slave. Don't worry, we'll take care of it."

"No, you won't," Trajan insisted.

He waved at Hadrian and said, "Get an amphora of strong red wine. These people don't know how to treat a human being."

Apollodorus stifled a sigh but didn't say anything. Hadrian could tell he was baffled by Trajan's behavior. "You heard the emperor," he barked at the medics. "Wait for the wine."

Trajan turned to Apollodorus and pulled him aside. "Slaves or not, I want you to treat your workers humanely, do you understand? Only motivated men work well." He pointed at the injured Nubian. "This one will take time to recover. He has a dislocated arm, maybe broken also," Trajan lectured the famous architect. "Grant him leave until his arm has healed."

Servants were now arriving with a big amphora full of undiluted red wine. The medics had the injured worker drink liberal amounts with big gulping slurps.

At this moment a Praetorian courier cantered up to the imperials with a message for Trajan. To Hadrian's surprise, the scroll was not a routine dispatch from Praefect Livianus, but a letter from Pompeius Longinus, commander-in-chief of all Roman forces in Transdanubian Moesia Province, the part of Dacia Rome had retained after the war. Trajan broke the seal on the spot, rolled out the scroll and paced through the letter. Then he handed it to Hadrian. "We have to go, Apollodorus," he said. "Immediately. Keep up the good work."

Hadrian read the letter himself. His jaws went slack when he had finished. "Decebalus is at it again," he stammered.

"Indeed. I had hoped the king had better senses. What is it with him? Doesn't he know he will be destroyed? Doesn't he care about his people? Anyway, let's hurry back to the palace and consult with Sura. I am sure Livianus will be waiting for us."

They rushed down the Hill, striding past the many cheerful and sometimes shrill noises of men, women and children splashing in the Baths of Titus. They passed the gigantic Flavian Amphitheater with its almost blinding sheets of gilded bronze glittering in the sun light on top, and pushed up the Via Sacra.

"I am stunned," Trajan went on. "How could the Dacians get into the Banat in such numbers? We have two legions there that should have blocked them. Pompeius apparently needs help. I was aware that Decebalus had been violating the Treaty's terms for months now. He had rearmed, been busy hiring mercenaries, but I didn't think he would dare raid Roman territory!"

"On the other hand," Hadrian reminded him. "Not long after the armistice he annexed Jazygian territory because they had fought on our side. That should have told us he wouldn't stand still behind the mountains."

"That's what the legions near Sarmizegethusa were for though! They must be in trouble, either wiped out or pinned down. There is no other explanation why they didn't come to Pompeius's aid. We have to call in troops from Pannonia - Decebalus... I loathe him!

I will have the Senate declare Decebalus an Enemy of the State. Legally, he is still our ally if I don't. We have to rescind his status before going to war. It's already May – the bastard knows that. By the time we get legions into the field, it will be fall and we won't accomplish much."

"Nonetheless, we need to secure the border," Hadrian stressed.

"Sure. I will lead the effort myself."

On their final ascent up the Palatine Hadrian pondered the ramifications of another Dacian War. What would it take? How long would it be? What should they do with Dacia afterwards? He also mulled his own future. He was supposed to preside over several marquee trials this year. After that, Trajan wanted him to administrate the *Ludi Romani.*

Trajan interrupted his thoughts. "You know, Hadrian, what the irony is? I had planned to circulate my 'Commentaries on the Dacian War' any time now. My publisher is coming up from Puteolis next month to discuss the details. Now I will have to first write some more chapters... Thank Jupiter that Decebalus is striking now - imagine I had published the 'Commentaries' with the Dacians on the attack again! I would have been the ridicule of the whole city."

Trajan's acute awareness of his *dignitas* made Hadrian smile. "My Lord, there is always a good thing to a bad thing!"

Chapter 53

"**B**y Epona, what are we doing in this gods-forsaken place?" the *Duplicarius* Spurius Carbo cursed. He had lost more than twenty men of his vexillation over the last couple of days and had wounded his left arm. His troops' spirits were in the ditch, and the misty weather didn't help. Carbo missed the good life his unit, the *Prima Ala Hispanorum Veterana Equitata*, had enjoyed in the flatlands of northern Macedonia. Being sent to the Danube had changed everything.

His right-hand man, the *Decurio* Petronius Scaurus, shrugged. "The generals say, 'Offense is the best defense.' We were sent here to be the eyes and ears for the garrisons along the river. Problem is we aren't welcome here. The Dacians and the Roxolani want us out." Scaurus pointed at the crop fields in front of them. "And they want to destroy the wheat and barley our people have sown in the spring. Much easier to burn than to harvest," he added.

"Of course. The protection of these crops cost us many men, and the campaigning season is only beginning. I have sent dispatches to Novae asking for reinforcements, but nothing is forthcoming. Decebalus is on the attack everywhere, not just here in Oltenia but also in the West. The governor promised troops from Noricum. But even if they were set in motion right away, it would take them another month to arrive. We are on our own. What's the latest strength report, Scaurus?"

"One hundred and twenty men, *Duplicarius*. We have only one hundred and twenty left, down from one hundred and sixty when our four *turmae* left Stobi. I don't have the number of the rest of the *ala*, but they are likely not faring any better."

Carbo rolled his eyes. "That means we have only sixty men to protect the fort."

And only sixty more to protect the fields, he added in his mind. To make matters worse, some of the soldiers were wounded and not in fighting condition. Being stretched thin, it was no wonder the Dacians picked off his men one after the other.

The *duplicarius* looked at his injured arm. Every movement hurt. *Cursed are the generals, cursed be the emperor! Why didn't they send reinforcements?* "How many Dacian warriors do you think we are dealing with in this area?" he asked his *decurio*.

"That's hard to say. The scouts are guessing three to four hundred, but it could be easily twice as many," Scaurus answered.

Carbo nodded. "Likely an understatement, Petronius. The only good thing is that we kill three Dacians for every one of ours. I pray to the gods though that they won't overrun us like they did the castra farther up the Olt."

His thoughts meandered back to the cozy life of his Macedonian base in Stobi: the baths, the women, the blessed pleasures of military indolence.

While the two officers talked, men with Phrygian caps wearing baggy trousers appeared on the other side of the crop field. Carbo raised his hand to alert his *turma* behind him. The men tucked in their shields closer and drew their *spathae*. Carbo and Scaurus scurried back to their horses and flung themselves on the horned saddles.

"Dacian *pileati!*" Carbo shouted. "Three of them and who knows how many warriors. Can anybody tell?"

The man with the sharpest eyes piped up. "There are throngs of men in the undergrowth behind the noblemen on either side, at least fifty warriors. I can see *falces*."

"By Jupiter," Carbo shrieked. "Get ready to charge."

They were about to attack when one of the Dacian nobles stepped into the open. He cupped his hands on his mouth and called out the Roman leader in broken Latin, "Spurius Carbo, I have a message for you from King Decebalus!"

Carbo arched his eyes. *How did they know my name?*

"My name is Burebista. I am speaking for the Great King himself. I have an offer to make."

Carbo gestured his men to stay put. His horse jousted with a snort. Annoyed, he reined it.

"We hold no grudge against you and your men, Spurius Carbo. You are only following orders. But we want you to leave this land and return it to its rightful owners, our allies, the Roxolani. If you do, we will pay you the equivalent of twenty thousand dinars in gold and another twenty thousand if you switch sides and fight for us in the war. And every man in your unit will receive five thousand dinars!"

Five thousand dinars - the lifetime stipendium of a Praetorian... An amount the men could never make in a lifetime. Twenty thousand for him... He would never have to fight again, risk his life for the benefit of the generals or rot away on the cursed northern frontier. Twenty thousand dinars and a guaranteed life in luxury...

Carbo hesitated. His mouth dried up, and his healthy arm, still raised for the next signal, came back down on his thigh. His mount whinnied. *A sign from Epona that this was an offer too good to ignore?*

Carbo turned halfway to watch his men. Some appeared confused, others were visibly disgusted and spit on the ground. Others yet seemed to entertain the idea. He peered at Scaurus.

"You are not seriously entertaining this proposal, *Duplicarius*, are you?" the *decurio* said with his voice low so that the enlisted men wouldn't hear him. "It would be treason," Scaurus added.

Carbo made up his mind. He made his mount lunge forward and with a skilled blow of his *spatha* he lopped off Scaurus's head. It dropped on the dirt, blood gushing into the soil. Adrenalin rushed through Carbo's body. He whisked his horse around Scaurus's – his headless body was still oddly perched on his stallion, somehow held in by the four-pommeled saddle - and bawled at the detachment from his skittering horse, "It's your call, soldiers, but I intend to live it up!" Carbo wheeled around and cantered off to Burebista.

Some of the men cursed him. Others followed their leader, but the majority did not. When Carbo reached the Dacian lines, he could see them riding back toward their base.

Hadrian and Trajan rushed straight into the gilded palace atrium and helped themselves to some gargantuan glass decanters always on hand by the water-filled *impluvium*. Plotina must have heard the shuffle and strode in to welcome the men, joined by one of Trajan's court favorites, Pylades, a former pantomime who had charmed the emperor with his body and skills.

The man reminded Hadrian of the dreary time under Domitian when pantomimes were not allowed in Rome. Pylades had changed all that because the emperor was smitten with him. As Hadrian expected, Trajan hugged the ex-pantomime most cordially. Then he kissed Plotina on her cheek.

"We've been waiting for you," Pompeia said. "Livianus told us the news. He and Sura arrived a short while ago."

"They are in the *triclinium*," Pylades added, pointing at the gleaming bronze doors.

"Great," Trajan exclaimed, still breathing from their forced walk. He guzzled another goblet. Although a pageboy dutifully offered him a towel of the finest linen, he declined and instead wiped the water off his mouth with the back of his hand. Hadrian grabbed the towel instead to dry his beard. Then they entered the *triclinium*.

Sura and Livianus hailed them with somber faces. *Was Sura possibly jealous of Pylades?* Hadrian wondered amused. The general seemed to ignore the artist though he welcomed everyone else. But then again, Trajan and Sura's friendship had long gone past physical attraction. Hadrian shook off the thought and focused his attention on the lively debate that ensued.

"Looks like our victory celebrations two years ago were premature," Sura summarized the obvious with a smirk. Trajan ignored his sarcasm, scowling.

"On the bright side," the general continued. "We are well prepared. I'll warrant our fleet still controls the Danube. We are entrenched in southern and western Dacia and have a chain of reconnaissance forts in Oltenia and in the lands of the Roxolani. And we have reinforced our forces last year – when the trouble on the river commenced."

"Lucius," Trajan warned. "Don't fool yourself. What about Longinus, what about the two legions in the heart of Dacia we haven't heard from? What about the steady losses we have been taking in Oltenia and Moesia Inferior?

Decebalus is striking with all he's got. According to this latest dispatch, he has even sent word to the Parthian king to enlist his support or at least tie our troops up in Syria. This could be a ploy, but it's forcing me to take extra precautions along the eastern border that I can ill afford."

"Should I alert the Praetorians?" Livianus asked eagerly.

"Yes, you should, Claudius," Trajan confirmed. "I want us to leave Rome as soon as possible. You and the whole Praetorian Legion will go with me, and I will send word to General Senecio to meet us in Brundisium. We will set sail from there and cross the Adriatic. Hadrian, it is time for you take a command. I will give you the First Legion *Minervia*, but for now, work on the fleet logistics at the port in Brundisium. Make sure enough galleys and transport ships will be ready to ferry us to the other side of the sea. My goal is to reach the bridge at Drobeta within two months."

Sura whistled. "Not bad," he said. "You are not losing any time, Trajan, but be levelheaded. Mobilizing the legions in Moesia, Pannonia and Noricum will take time. Realistically, we will not have a big enough force at Drobeta before the campaigning season is over."

"This may well be," Trajan acknowledged. "But it is always good to push the limits. We will cover the distance in forced marches. I expect the same from all commanders. Maybe we can get to Decebalus before the winter. If not, we won't get bored in winter camp. I will also launch a frenzy of diplomatic activities to buy off the tribes with uncommitted loyalties, call in favors from our allies, and most importantly, break Decebalus's allies away from him as much as I can, maybe the Dacian nobility itself. They cannot all be suicidal!"

Hadrian rose his hand. "After all is said and done – and I have no doubt that we will defeat Decebalus – what do you intend to do with Dacia? Are you considering annexation?"

"It will depend on the war: how bad our losses will be, how much damage we will take and so forth. But, yes, if I come to the conclusion that the Dacian people are beyond hope and will likely continue to follow nefarious leaders after another defeat, chances are that I will eliminate Dacia as a country once and for all."

Hadrian nodded pensively but argued, "Despite the difficult geographic position we would be in?"

"It's an issue but not insurmountable. I realize Dacia has no natural borders to its north, west or east. We would have to fashion another *limes* and build *clausurae* to slow down potential invaders. Not pretty, but doable if we have no choice. Listen, there may be no other way but to subjugate the Dacian people and make the land a Roman province. Certainly, we would have to raise two more legions to hold the country in the future.

It is true, Hadrian, I did not intend that when I took up arms against Decebalus two years ago. But I also didn't know how dangerous and stubborn he would be."

"Will I come with you?" Pylades blurted.

"No, my friend," Trajan looked at his beautiful body and smiled. "Too dangerous. You will stay. I don't want to lose you."

"But-" the ex-pantomime protested.

"No. This is my final word, Pylades," Trajan said firmly. "Only Livianus, Senecio, Hadrian and Callistus will join me - and Crito, the *medicus*. No one else. By the way, where is Callistus?"

"In his office I believe," Plotina said. "What about me? Can I come with you, husband? Please!"

"Pompeia, I would love to have you by my side, but it is too dangerous even for you. Do not underestimate the hardship of campaigning and the ordeal of spending winter on the harsh northern frontier." Trajan kissed her forehead and stroked her hair. Then he stepped back and asked, "Why don't you summon Callistus and Capito? I need to dictate some letters for Longinus and the other Danubian field commanders."

"We will crush Decebalus once and for all," he added with grim determination. "If I am not mistaken, we can field twelve legions - this reminds me, Lucius, I need you to send letters to the governor of Hispania Tarraconensis. He needs to start recruiting another legion there, just in case. Hispania hasn't seen war in a long time; it is time for them to make a contribution.

Claudius, we should also raise a legion here in Italia. Work with the municipalities on this. I want you to form both these legions from seasoned frontier troops. The Danube army will have to provide us with detachments of bloodied legionaries and officers as the core for the new legions, who will train the new recruits from Hispania and Italia." Trajan swerved around. "Where are my secretaries?" He was in his element remobilizing the Roman war machine.

Chapter 54

Strong earth and timber walls and steep ravines on all sides provided Sarmizegethusa with great protection. The city had only one gated entrance, accessible on a steep narrow slope alone. Waiting on horseback in front of this gate beside Burebista, Carbo gauged the effectiveness of the fortifications. Yes, it would be hard to take, but he knew how formidable Trajan's siege craft was. The Dacians would not be able to hide behind these walls forever.

The renegade officer had rationalized his actions to himself and was glad not being the only rebel. Eight men had joined the new cause. By throwing their lot in with him, they had nowhere else to go, assuring him of total loyalty - a virtual bodyguard, he convinced himself. He didn't trust the Dacians, however. So far, they had kept their end of the bargain and made the promised payouts. Now Carbo and his men were even invited to the king's palace.

He was hoping Decebalus would give them land they could call home and provide women for their amusement. Carbo desired to stay close to the amenities of the Dacian capital. It would also give him protection from Roman wrath. As deserters, he and his men had forfeited their life and were subject to prosecution everywhere in the empire. They could never go back, not ever...

At times the *duplicarius* toyed with the idea of escaping to Parthia. They would be safer there because of the imminent war with Rome. If his countrymen overran Dacia, he would have to flee north – into the unknown, to lands that had not even seen money before, to people so savage they still relished cannibalism... He shook off his gloomy thoughts and concentrated on Burebista, who reined in beside him.

The Dacian noble looked pleased. Carbo's betrayal and the ensuing paralysis in his cavalry unit had given the Dacian warriors easy access to the crop fields along the river Olt. With Carbo's help they had laid waste to them all and forced other Roman garrisons in the area to retreat to the Danube.

After recognizing the new arrivals, the Dacian guards opened the mighty oak gate for Burebista and his Roman companions. The *pileatus* turned to the Roman mercenaries with a smile and pointed to the lowered hanging bridge. "Enter, my friends! Welcome to Sarmizegethusa. Quarters are ready for you. Follow the guides behind the gate. They will show you around and later pick you up to join me and the High King for a splendid welcome feast in the Great Hall of our capital."

Burebista himself hurried straight to the palace to report to Decebalus.

"Good work, my friend," the king praised him, hugging his faithful support-er. "Your operation has served us well, but you know my goals, Burebista. If we are lucky, Carbo and his ilk will become even better pawns in our game. Keep pampering them. Show them all Sarmizegethusa has to offer. Send the most beautiful females to their quarters. Have them indulge, and they will eat from our hands when we need their service.

By the way, the gold transport from the Royal lair has arrived. It will be more than enough to advance my plans."

"How is the war going?" Burebista asked. "Have the Roman legions in Dacia surrendered?"

"It is going well, but the legions have not surrendered - yet. They are pinned down in their bases, however. Don't worry. They cannot help their friends in the Banat. The smaller Roman units there are taking heavy losses. We are holding the countryside and performing raids deep into Moesia. Ru-mor has it that the news of our attack has reached Rome. Trajan will take the field again. He is on his way to Dacia, they say. As expected, I might add. He will be duly welcome," Decebalus said with a smirk.

The next day Decebalus prepared himself for another *Pileati* War Council meeting in his palace suite. He was kneeling before an effigy of the supreme deity of the Dacians. "Almighty Zalmoxis, all powerful God of the Dead, of Heaven and Earth, I implore you. Grant me success in my holy strife to main-tain the freedom of my people."

The king wasn't much of spiritual leader, but every endeavor needed a degree of luck to succeed, and luck was a quality only the gods – if they existed - had possibly control over. It was therefore only logical to ask for their consent. "I vow to you, Zalmoxis, that I will send you a messenger as part of the Rite of the Spears in case you grant my wishes!" Decebalus knew this was a turning point in the history of his people. Would they be able to preserve their independence, maybe even recover the lands they had lost in the last war? Or would they be exterminated and entirely forgotten by future generations?

He believed it was nobler to die than to live as the vassals of a powerful empire gobbling them up. Of course, had the Dacians not invaded Roman land, nothing might have ever have happened to them. But he was a proud king and his was a proud people. He and the nobles had craved glory and conquest, riches and spoils. Decebalus didn't find anything wrong with that. The Romans after all were conquerors themselves and always had been. The king refused to be the cowering leader of a people of shepherds and farmers just tilling the lands and fending for themselves. He thought of himself as a warrior king. That was the way of life of the Dacian nation. It had always been that way, and it would always be so Rome notwithstanding.

He had great hopes his people could persevere and outfox the Romans as they had done before with other Roman generals, even with the Emperor Domitian himself, and recently with the new Emperor Trajan. Gullibly, the Roman had called off his invasion with complete victory so near. His stupidity would cost him.

Decebalus stood with renewed determination and left his chamber. The *pileati* were already waiting. Several noblemen asked for permission to speak and present their views of the military situation. It turned out some favored peace negotiations. Others proposed bold ambushes against the approaching legions. Susagus was to speak last. The nobleman carried much clout in the Council after his daring raids into Moesia and even Macedonia in the first war with Rome. His clan was rich and fielded Dacia's finest warriors.

The hall was dead quiet when he took the floor. "Noblemen of Dacia, Great King, I am honored to be here with you and help determine the future of our proud nation. We have regained so much of our strength thanks to the great Decebalus. We were able to punish the Jazyges for siding with Rome, and I applaud our cunning hit and run tactics that have undermined Roman morale. Great King, you deserve our gratitude!

But we also have to be wise and consider the ramifications of another war. We cannot defeat the Roman army over the long term. We just can't. I wish we could, but it is a folly to think so. There are limits to our power. What I am hearing today does not reflect this unwelcome fact. *Pileati*, fighting the legions is madness!"

He paused, and the nobles ogled him, puzzled and with apprehension it seemed. Many fixed their eyes on Decebalus, trying to gauge his reaction to Susagus's unexpected words. But the king stayed aloof, his glance directed over their heads to the other end of the Hall.

Susagus continued. "We are facing a Roman army of twelve legions and auxiliaries, one hundred and twenty thousand men, maybe more, led not by some run-of-the-mill commander, but by the Emperor Trajan himself, a competent soldier who has never lost an engagement and who has defeated us before.

Nothing is different this time. Once the Roman army crosses the river and begins its march on Sarmizegethusa - and you all know they have built this incredible bridge at Drobeta, which allows them to enter our country at will - once they invade, all we can do is hang tight in our hill forts and defend each and every one of them against a force many times ours. The Romans have terrible siege engines and will patiently take the strongholds one by one. We have seen it before. Only unconditional surrender saved us then.

Pileati, listen to me. If we fight this war, we have no future: Our men will die on the battlefield, our women and children will be sold into slavery and our riches taken by the invader. Noblemen of Dacia, I implore you, do not follow Decebalus!

There is still a way out. We can repent for the treaty violations, parley with the Roman generals and negotiate an armistice so by the time Trajan arrives the situation would have calmed down and we can buy the Romans off with gold and silver from our lairs. It can be done! Not on the cheap, but it's ten times better than being dead, enslaved or a fugitive in foreign lands."

Decebalus was fuming. What was this cowardly gibberish? Had Susagus lost his mind? Finally, he couldn't restrain himself anymore and cut in. "Parley you are saying? You want to parley? Armistice? Surrender? Selling out? What kind of prattle is this?" he thundered. "Susagus has lost his wits, Councilmen. He is shivering in his boots at the sight of Roman soldiers. Maybe it is them who bought him, not the other way round!"

Susagus shouted back at the king. "How dare you say that? It is you who brought these dire straits upon us. Instead of putting blame on me you should ask for forgiveness and leave this place."

A murmur went through the ranks of the *pileati*. Stunned, they kept listening.

"Oh, now it is my fault," Decebalus hissed. "It was only a matter of time until a culprit had to be found. Well, watch what you are saying, Susagus. I am ashamed that a Dacian *pileatus* like you is rattling in this Council like a woman. You be cursed! Your clan should expel you. You are a traitor!"

Now the councilmen were yelling all at once, some accusing the king, some siding with Susagus, including his brother Telerion. Burebista's booming voice outshouted them and the tumult slowly subsided.

Again, the king spoke, "Susagus may be right about one thing: This is a time of the utmost importance and it will determine our fate for generations to come. The Romans want our land and they want to get rid of us. They will kill everyone who is in the their way, everyone who does not submit – as if that was a viable option to escape oppression - and when nobody is left, they will call it Peace, *Pax Romana*, ha ha ha!

Now is the time to stand up to them. Brave leaders of Dacia, let us not fall into bondage and toil our lives away in the mines while the Romans sleep with our women and children. Instead, rise to the occasion, stand up to the invaders and maintain the freedom of our People." His furious glare swept the audience. "Rise we shall! Rome has stomped on our feet long enough!

Can anyone in this hallowed hall give me one, just one example where the Romans did not enslave a people once they had set foot on their land? What happened to the proud nations of Britannia, the Silures and Atrebates, the Dumnonii and the Iceni, the Trinovantes and the Catuvellauni? What happened to the Germanic tribes along the Rhine, the Treveri and Chatti, and to the Cimbri and Teutoni when they tried to find a home after their land had been devastated by a terrible flood? What happened to Carthage and Egypt? What to the Illyri, the Thraci and the mighty Macedoni?

Even proud Greece had to bend and is a Roman thrall now! So is Gaul - a degenerate Roman vassal!

I could go on and on. The Romans always thirst for more. More plunder, more slaves, more gems, metals and goods of all kinds so that their women can dress in the finest silk they import from fabled lands.

The Romans will never stop! The only language they understand is the language of force. Now is the time to use it, to resist, to cave in no more and - like the heroic Germanic tribes under Arminius - to defeat them so soundly that we will never hear from them ever again!

Is it not curious that no Roman army has ever set foot over the Rhine after losing three legions in a crushing ambush a century ago? This is the glory awaiting us! Freedom will triumph over slavery, happiness over misery, valor over greed. Death or glory! I'd rather die than be Trajan's puppet!"

Without waiting for their reaction Decebalus left his station and scurried across the hall. He stopped in front of Susagus and shouted, "For Dacia!" Then he drew his *falx* and drilled its bent tip into the surprised Susagus's chest, ripping him open like a slaughtered hog. The nobleman's eyes bulged from their sockets, and he fell on the expensive maple floor with a loud thump, blood and bowels spilling on the polished wood. Susagus's brother Telerion yelped and dashed for the king with his own *falx*, but Burebista and the guards blocked his way. They manhandled him and twisted the weapon from his hand. It pounded on the floor with a loud clang.

Decebalus swept a cold gleeful gaze at the nobles, now all standing by the long tables. Yes, fear was gripping them now. Good, they would fall in line, but he would have to be careful. Not all of them were on his side

Chapter 55

The village was burning everywhere. A gruesome stench of corpses and carcasses of livestock hung in the air. Trajan looked at the mayhem in anger, gripping the ornate brass hilt of his *gladius* so hard that his knuckles turned white like chalk. The emperor had seen many spills of blood in his life, but this hit him harder. It was senseless, and the dead bodies in this ruined hamlet weren't soldiers paid to fight and risk their lives. The disfigured and mutilated corpses were innocent men, women and children, Romans and Moesian provincials alike, caught off-guard by a Dacian surprise raid deep into the Upper Moesia Province. He would never forget these images.

A dream from his childhood reared in his head: He had been a boy standing on a vast plain all alone, assaulted and then run over by an army of barbarian warriors with the cut-off heads of Roman soldiers dangling from their belts. Would this dreadful nightmare become a reality? Was this Jupiter's way of saying 'Thou shalt perish'?

Hadrian interrupted his brooding thoughts. "They must have come here on skiffs," the young general said pointing toward the Morava River.

"Why were they not evacuated?" Trajan snarled at the other man standing beside him, an officer from the garrison at Naissus whose unit had arrived here before them. His men were cleaning up the village, torching dead animals and sanitizing the site of bloodshed. They were also setting up sacrificial altars and piles of wood to cremate what was left of the dead provincials.

"We don't know," the soldier answered. "We had sent heralds a week ago to notify the settlements in the area, instructing the peasants to leave their homes and relocate to Naissus for protection. The couriers either skipped this hamlet or the villagers here didn't obey the order. I am still investigating, *Imperator*. If they did receive the order and stayed put any way I can only guess that they didn't expect Dacian raiders so deep inside the province. Maybe they had heard that Roman troops were reinforcing Moesia and felt safe despite the warning.

In any case, seventy-five are dead now, mostly the men. The Dacians took the women and children with them, probably in the same vessels they had arrived in, and they pilfered the people's belongings." He glanced at the emperor with a mixture of guilt, sadness and determination. "Someone will pay for this, Excellency. I swear."

Trajan's eyes narrowed to a small, mean slit. "I know who - Decebalus!" Trajan lusted for satisfaction. These poor people had done nothing to deserve this; they had done the Dacians no harm. The emperor was resolved now more than ever before to capture the Dacian tyrant, hopefully alive so he could be paraded before the Roman people in a humiliating triumph before being executed in the Tullianum.

Trajan was resolved to crush anybody standing in his way, *pileati* and lowly fighters alike. If necessary, he would reduce all of Dacia to rubble. These people had no honor. They had attacked, killed and stolen without warning, without provocation and without discrimination.

He and Hadrian strode back to the Praetorian detail and climbed on their horses. "Let's return to camp," Trajan ordered. "I want to reach Naissus tomorrow. There is nothing we can do here."

The month was July, six weeks after leaving Rome. The Praetorian Legion had transferred over the Adriatic as planned, and they had hurried north after their arrival in Greece, but bad weather had slowed them down.

Meanwhile Roman forces were on the move everywhere in the Balkans. Pannonian reinforcements had crossed the Danube to relieve Longinus. Most other Danube legions assembled at Drobeta, but not without making sure that all the castra they left behind were sufficiently garrisoned and the provincial countryside adequately secured. Hadrian's legion, the First *Minervia*, and thousands of mounted auxiliaries had pitched camp near Naissus and were waiting for the imperials.

Upon his arrival in the city Trajan devoured the latest dispatches. Longinus reported intense fighting everywhere in the Banat but said the tide was turning and he was repelling the attackers. There was still no word from the two legions deep inside Dacia.

Naissus was not big enough to accommodate a host of twenty thousand behind its walls. The troops and their tents spread out on the fields and meadows all around the town. The First *Minervia* had built the customary protective palisade wall and ditch around this tent city, allowing the Praetorians to settle in fast. Trajan had refused nicer accommodations in the city; he wanted to be with the troops, and Hadrian was wise enough to follow his example. He, Crito and Callistus, now Trajan's *lictor proximus,* were sharing the command tent with the emperor. Praefect Livianus, the generals Sura, Senecio and their aides were lodged in another bivouac abutting Trajan's.

At nightfall, the night was lit up by thousands of campfires. It was a warm and lush evening. The soldiers were in good spirits, itching to strike back at the cruel enemy. Both the First *Minervia* and the Praetorians had experienced heavy fighting in the last Dacian war, and the men desired to finish what they had started. Thousands of auxiliaries from all over the Balkans were assembling as well, as in the previous war under Senecio's command.

Trajan and Callistus were working on the emperor's 'Commentaries' after supper when the Praetorian Guard on duty opened the tent's curtain. "*Ave*, Caesar. Outside is a *duplicarius* with two of his men. They would like to address you on a matter of the utmost importance, they say. Are you willing to admit them?"

Trajan had a strict open-door policy with his troops, one of many other reasons for his popularity with the troops. Anybody, independent of rank, could come to him and express a concern or ask for a favor, but at the moment Trajan frowned at the distraction. He wanted to commit today's visit of the destroyed village into writing without delay – before fatigue would get the best of him. "Did he say what's so important?"

"No, Caesar. He did say it is so important that he wants to talk about it only to you and nobody else."

Trajan sighed at Callistus. "This is really not a good time, but when ever is?"

The secretary smiled. "Never, Trajan, never."

"Let him in," Trajan ordered the Praetorian.

The guard saluted and left. Then the curtain opened again. In walked a scruffy *duplicarius* with a salute that was subtly casual. Trajan greeted the man and asked him to sit on the visitor's chair in front of his desk. Callistus ignored the visitor and scribbled on.

"What's your name, *Duplicarius*?" Trajan asked.

"I am Spurius Carbo, *Prima Ala Hispanorum Veterana Equitata*, from Stobi, Macedonia," Carbo answered in a stilted manner.

"I see. Where are your men, Carbo? My guard said there are three of you."

"*Sic*, your Excellency, but the guards didn't let them in. Protocol, they said."

"Ah. That's true. I guess you can easily speak for them, can you not? But if you want them to speak with me too, I can have it arranged."

Carbo' eyes twitched, glances darting in all directions but Trajan's. "That's all right," he said. His voice crackled with nervousness.

"How can I help you?" Trajan went on.

Carbo rambunctiously talked about terrible events in Oltenia he had endured. While he rambled on, Trajan remembered a scroll he had forgotten in the back room. He lifted his arm to interrupt Carbo and asked Callistus to fetch the papyrus for him.

"Sorry about that," the emperor apologized. "But I don't want to forget about it. Go on, *Duplicarius*."

Carbo watched Callistus leave the anteroom. Then he abruptly stood, pulled his sword and tried to ram it into Trajan's chest, but the emperor was faster. As soon as Carbo made his move he had sensed the danger, surged from his chair, sidestepped the sword and lunged backward to grapple his own *gladius* on the wall behind the desk. "Guards," he shouted. "Alarm! I am attacked. Callistus, stay where you are!"

Carbo pulled back his *spatha* to regain his balance and scuttled to the short side of the desk. Trajan parried by darting to the opposite side where he stayed put. *Can I throw him off somehow and capture my shield?* He decided to wait for the right moment. "Guards!" he yelled again, but there was no response. Instead, he heard fighting erupt outside the tent, the clashing and clattering of swords and shuffling of feet.

"Your brothers in arms, I guess," Trajan calmly addressed the assassin. "Who is sending you? Decebalus? Did he send you to kill your own Lord? How much was I worth? Ten thousand dinars? More? Less?"

He was hoping to distract Carbo, but the *turma* commander did not answer or move. Trajan knew that time was working against the intruder. His two accomplices outside the tent would soon be outnumbered and killed. Carbo would have to finish this fast.

At that moment Callistus appeared from the backroom. He froze at the threshold, staring at Carbo in disbelief.

"Go back, Callistus," Trajan yelled at his aide. "Now!"

Callistus was unarmed, and Trajan didn't want him to get hurt by the assassin. The *duplicarius* attacked again, and their swords collided in midair with a clang. Trajan swiftly counter-rotated Carbo's *spatha* and struck it from the rebel's hand. It fell down on the ground. Trajan quickly stepped on it and pointed the tip of his *gladius* at Carbo's jugular. "Speak, scoundrel," he thundered. "Who sent you?"

Carbo glowered, saying nothing. Finally, several guards and Trajan's doctor dashed into the tent, screeching to a halt when they saw Carbo at Trajan's mercy.

"Take him away," the emperor barked. "What happened with his accomplices?"

"They are dead, Caesar," Crito said. "They attacked the two men guarding the entrance to your tent and wounded one of them, but the noise alerted the camp's soldiers. The assassins were killed in the fight, my Lord."

"Well, we still have this one here. Ready him for an interrogation," Trajan ordered.

The Praetorians gripped Carbo's arms hard and yanked him out of the tent. Crito wanted to examine the emperor to make sure he was unharmed, but Trajan pushed him aside. "I am fine, *medicus*. Really." He crossed to Callistus and gave him a long heartfelt hug. "You are shaking, my friend. Don't worry. It's over. As you can see, Decebalus does not hesitate to fight dirty. He must be behind this attempt to take my life. Who else has a motive?"

Callistus swallowed. "Puh. I am glad we are alive, Master!" The secretary wiped off the sweat on his forehand with trembling hands. "I am not a soldier.

Thanks for saving my life, Trajan."

"My pleasure. Rest now. I will question the traitor. We will resume our work on the book tomorrow."

Outside the command tent Livianus and other officers had arrived. Trajan took the praefect with him to Carbo's interrogation. Under the threat of torture and hoping to save his life he admitted that Decebalus had promised him ten pounds of gold if he brought him Trajan's head. He and his companions had traveled through Moesia until they learned of Trajan's location from soldiers on their way to Naissus. They had followed them and arrived last night. It was not hard to blend in with the many soldiers camped around the city.

Despite Carbo's desperate pleads to spare his life, Trajan ordered his immediate execution. A centurion severed Carbo's head with a precise blow of his *gladius.* The by-standing soldiers intoned, "Death to Decebalus! We will kill Decebalus!"

Chapter 56

In early August Trajan pulled in at Drobeta, bustling with military activity. Fresh detachments, siege engines, baggage train units, mobile barricades and supplies arrived from the Roman Danube provinces every day and assembled on the northern bank of the river. Sura and the army quartermaster coordinated logistics, assisted by a staff of well-trained *librarii* who tracked and assigned goods and equipment. This host was even larger than the one Trajan had drawn together in the last conflict.

Apollodorus's mighty bridge served the effort well. Not only did it prevent transportation bottlenecks, but it also sped up the transfer of men and provisions as it was three times wider than the old pontoon bridge at Lederata. The ashlar viaduct comprised twenty piers of squared stone and cement, each one hundred and fifty feet high and sixty feet wide. The piers were set in intervals of one hundred and seventy feet and connected by huge wooden arches. The total length of the bridge was over three thousand five hundred feet, enough for the width of the river at this location. Still, its construction had been risky because of the torrential waters and the muddy bottom the piers had to be placed upon.

Trajan took in the sight with pride. Yes, this was the buttress of Roman power in the North. *Alone among nations we can come and go across great rivers at will.*

"You know what I like best about this masterpiece, Lucius?" he asked Sura beside him while tidying the ribbon on his iron muscle cuirass. "We can cross the Danube on this bridge even in winter when the river can freeze and in early spring when floating ice makes crossing by boat a daring gamble. It's a miracle – and the longest bridge ever built…"

Sura patted the *pteryges* on Trajan's broad shoulder blade. "It is, but we always have to make sure the enemy doesn't use it from the other side."

"That's what the legions are for," Trajan countered with a rumbling chuckle.

While they watched the endless flow of chariots, carts, wagons, carriages and soldiers crossing back and forth a Praetorian courier cantered up in great haste. He handed Trajan a dispatch from Livianus. "The praefect is asking you to read this message immediately, Caesar."

Trajan grabbed the scroll and broke Livianus's seal. The Praetorian remained seated on his saddle, waiting for the emperor's orders.

Trajan and Sura read the dispatch together. When they were done Trajan lowered the scroll in disbelief. "Is the Dacian messenger still in town?" Trajan barked at the horse trooper.

"No. He left right away."

Good, Trajan thought. *Livianus let him go unharmed.*

"Ideas, Lucius?" Trajan asked his friend.

"Not yet. We have to think this through carefully. Let's not jeopardize General Longinus's life. Decebalus didn't waste time: As soon as he found out that Carbo's assassination attempt had failed, he must have picked the legate as his next target. We cannot let him get away with it! He wants us to relinquish all of Dacia including the new territories and repay him for the cost of the war. It's blackmail of the worst kind."

"I cannot tell you how much I hate this man," Trajan agreed. "He is full of tricks and evil, like a snake, biting you when you least expect it, but I have to negotiate, Lucius. Pompeius Longinus is near and dear to me. He is one of our best generals, highly decorated, ethical, competent and steadfast. He has stuck out his head for Rome at the frontier for twenty years. We must not lose him!"

"Certainly. Just why did Longinus agree to a parley? The king's men were on the retreat. I don't get it." Sura shook his head. "Anyway, let's outfox the bastard," Sura said.

"Maybe Pompeius wasn't out of the woods yet," Trajan pondered. "Don't forget, Lucius, two legions are still pinned down inside Dacia. Maybe the general wanted to somehow persuade Decebalus to break off the sieges."

He turned to the waiting Praetorian. "Tell the praefect we will return to the command tent right away. Have him gather all senior officers. We need to discuss the situation."

The cave was damp and dark, exuding the musty smell of wet bedrock. Pompeius Longinus tried to make out its dimensions, but it was too dim to see beyond the other shackled Roman prisoners in the grotto. The rusty manacles chafed and cut into his wrists and ankles, and every move aggravated the pain. Pompeius sat straight against the clammy rock, his shackled legs stretched out on the filthy ground. He cursed his gullibility. Not only had he endangered his own life, the Dacians had also taken the whole Roman embassy prisoner. Here they were, one general and ten officers, at the king's whim, a liability for Trajan and the Roman offensive.

Longinus knew the emperor all too well. He would try everything to save their lives. The negotiations would consume time they didn't have. It was already August...

He stiffened - somebody was coming. He could hear the rumble of the boulder blocking the cave entrance. Torch light hit his face. Pompeius blinked. There was Decebalus with a *pileatus* at his side, followed by two *falx*-armed guards. The king held a papyrus scroll in his hand. He stopped at Longinus's feet, drooping over the prisoner. Then Decebalus held out a torch to better see Longinus's begrimed face. He handed the scroll to the nobleman beside him and gripped the general's jowls hard with his free hand as if to see whether they were real. The general cringed. *He is squeezing me like a wine press.*

Decebalus glared at the prisoner. Then he jostled Longinus's head and let go of it with a grunt. He took the scroll again and hissed in broken Latin, "Your master has answered, but I don't know what to think of it. He is offering money, but there is no word on my other demands."

The king dropped the dispatch on Longinus's lap. "See for yourself," he commanded.

Pompeius grasped the scroll with his bruised shackled hands. Decebalus was right: Trajan was offering a generous ransom payment but made no concessions on the war. The general was pleased, but he doubted the king would go for it. "I can make this work," he said. "All is not lost. Let me send a note with a new proposal. There are terms the emperor can accept without losing face."

"Like what?" Decebalus grumbled.

Unveiled loathing, Longinus thought. *This king is watching me like a constrictor snake poised to strike at its prey.* "Our lives for a Roman guarantee not to invade Dacia. But Rome will never return the land it conquered in the last war." Longinus held up Trajan's answer, braving Decebalus's fixed stare.

The king's face showed no reaction. He snatched the scroll and kicked Longinus's thigh hard with the iron tip of his boot. The general recoiled, holding his leg in pain. Decebalus chuckled, turned around and left the cave with his companion.

Hours later, the *pileatus* returned without the king. He hunkered down next to Longinus and whispered in his ear, "My name is Telerion. I hate Decebalus. He killed my brother in cold blood when he spoke out against the king in Council."

Longinus raised his eyebrows. "I am sorry to hear that. But what does that have to do with me?"

"Everything, Roman, everything," Telerion murmured. "How can I get back at the mad king? You may hold the answer. I want the Romans to attack, to kill Decebalus. Any suggestions?"

Pompeius didn't, but he had many questions. "How come you are still alive? Aren't you a liability for the king?"

"Yes, but Decebalus is not stupid. He needs the warriors of my clan. We are the best. By keeping me close he thinks he will always know what I am doing. Decebalus takes me everywhere – even to his prisoners. As you can see, it doesn't work all the time."

"How did you get away from him now?"

"That's none of your business, Roman."

Longinus pondered this unexpected turn of events. *Was there an opportunity?* "Turning tables on Decebalus is too obvious. He would never go to a parley, but let's see here... He has lost momentum, our troops are advancing. I am his only bargaining chip, but Decebalus must pay for what he has done. Trajan won't go after him as long as I am a hostage. This is the dilemma. Perhaps there is a way to give us both what we want: the king's head. Can you come back tomorrow?"

Telerion nodded and left the cave.

The following night was Longinus's longest. He was desperately looking for a solution, but none was palatable. He would have to take himself out of the equation. It was he after all who had gotten the emperor into this mess. For many years, Pompeius Longinus had served the empire. He was in his fifties now, not an old man by any means, but his days as an army commander were coming to an end. He could live the rest of his life in comfort back home in Italia or he could end it all here with a bang and become a hero of his people.

When Telerion returned, he asked him, "Can you procure a deadly poison?"

Telerion frowned. "Why?"

Pompeius waved Telerion closer. Then he whispered, "I am a liability for Trajan - and for the Roman People. Help me die. If I die, Trajan will attack. Isn't that what you want?"

Telerion bobbed his head.

"I will write a letter to Trajan just as I suggested to the king. Decebalus will let me do that, I believe. Nothing in the letter will indicate my plan. All you need to do is get the letter safely to Trajan. Either you go yourself or you send someone you trust. But it is imperative that the purveyor of the letter tells Trajan to ignore the letter and that I have taken my life so that he can move forward with the invasion of the Dacian heartland. Do you understand?"

The general darted a quick glance of regret and sorrow at his unsuspecting officers, manacled twenty feet away from him. *They must not know. Either way, their fate is sealed.*

"I do," Telerion said. "But I cannot trust anyone of the king's men. I will go myself and take my own men with me - to a trip with no return..." Tears swelled up in his eyes. He seemed to feel truly bad for Longinus. "Is there no other way?"

"There isn't," Longinus urged. "Look at me, Telerion. There is NO other way. Think about it. If we succeed, Trajan will kill Decebalus and you will be safe from him. On the contrary, you will become a friend of the Roman

People and your clan will be spared in the war. Believe me, Trajan will not be so generous this time around; he will turn Dacia into a Roman province. My life is unimportant. I give it gladly."

Telerion pulled away from the Roman general. He looked at him one last time, then left.

Two days later he came back and slipped a small vial into Longinus's bruised hand. "I talked to the king. He will remit your letter but wouldn't trust me with it. Don't worry, my fighters and I will intercept his messenger on the way to the Roman lines. We will seize the letter and take it to Trajan and tell him about your noble death." He paused and pointed at the vial. "Swallow this liquid. It will kill you fast, within a couple of minutes. It's painless - almost like falling asleep."

Pompeius closed his hand firmly around it and tuck it away under his torn and sullied tunic. "Thank you," he whispered.

After one last admiring glance at the general Telerion crossed back to the cave's entrance. The guards let him out and the boulder rumbled back into place.

Chapter 57

Trajan was devastated when he heard Telerion's story, but was it true? "Why should I believe you?" he said. "Even if it is true what you are saying, Longinus may have changed his mind or the poison may not work or guards have prevented him from swallowing the venom. Understand this: If I make my move now and Longinus is still alive, he will be tortured in the most barbaric manner..."

"The poison will work. It always does," Telerion insisted.

"I believe him," Sura chipped in. "His story makes sense, Trajan. Longinus is the kind of man to sacrifice himself for the greater good of the empire, no doubt about it. His death would return the momentum to us.

Will he pull it off? That's the only question. And from what Telerion told us, it's very unlikely that Longinus would somehow be stopped."

Gut feeling told Trajan that Sura was probably right. He knew Longinus well and didn't hold this ultimate sacrifice beyond him. But if they were wrong, the general's death from Decebalus's hands would be cruel beyond comprehension. Trajan decided to wait.

Several days later, a disheveled Roman centurion cantered into Drobeta, a man who had been taken prisoner with Longinus. With great distress he confirmed Longinus's suicide. The great general had died shortly after Telerion's visit. The Roman officers had thought he had fallen asleep, but when Dacian guards entered the cave in the morning to bring them rotten food and stale water they noticed the dead officer. The guards called for the king right away, who screeched at the corpse - feeling outmaneuvered, deprived. Seething, he ordered the Roman prisoners all killed, but in the last minute he changed his mind and left some of them alive, including the centurion standing before the emperor now.

Trajan's face turned chalk white. His throat dried up like desert soil in the heat of the mid afternoon sun. *What a loss, what a man...* Interminable hatred reared in the emperor's chest. He picked up a goblet from his desk and smashed it against the mounted shields in his command tent with a bone-piercing scream. "Arrrgggghhhh!"

The officer also delivered a letter from Decebalus. Trajan composed himself and sat down, forcing himself to concentrate on the missive. The king demanded the extradition of Telerion and his men in return for Longinus's officers and the corpse of the dead general.

"Scum, scoundrel, murderer!" Trajan snarled beside himself. "When will you stop tormenting us?!"

In the ensuing war council Livianus and Senecio proposed to heed the king, ranking the Roman officers' lives higher than Telerion's and his fighters. Sura and Hadrian on the other hand passionately advised not to do so. In the end, Trajan sided with the latter two, and did not extradite the rebels. Rome's prestige was at stake, but he hoped protecting Telerion and his men would motivate more Dacian clans to desert Decebalus and convince the neighboring peoples in the region to seek Roman protection rather than siding with a king whom he had defeated before.

Over the next four weeks the Longinus incident did in fact lead to defections among the Dacian nobility and allies and forced Decebalus to call off the sieges of the two legionary fortresses at Berzobis and Sarmizegethusa Ulpia. Telerion's clan left the Dacian war effort altogether. On their march north Trajan's men soon found the decapitated bodies of the Roman prisoners. Grief-struck, the emperor ordered their cremation with all honors. The army hailed him *Imperator* and vowed to hunt down Decebalus once and for all.

Meanwhile the king held assemblies to rally the clans. A combination of persuasion, called-in favors, threats and graft kept them mostly on his side. Then he sent Burebista and other emissaries to alien tribes far and wide, urging them to join his cause. The embassies visited the Roxolani, the Bastarnae and other Sarmatian tribes, the Marcomanni and even Greek cities at the shores of the Black Sea, and implored them to unite with Dacia and help it in its struggle for independence - as they framed it. Their success was limited, but Dacian gold allowed them to buy generous amounts of war supplies from Black Sea armories.

Trajan initiated a round of diplomacy of his own. Time had run out to stage a comprehensive counterattack this year. So he used the remaining time to recruit more allies and keep as many adjacent peoples as possible from lining up with Decebalus, lured by the flow of gold that found its way into the pockets of many chieftains.

Trajan also recalled the two legions inside Dacia. Their provisions would not last them through the winter. The legionaries burnt down their bases and returned to Drobeta to join the main host. Then Trajan tried one last time to save the Dacian people. If Decebalus turned himself in, he pledged to the *Pileati* Council through emissaries, this war would be over and Dacia and Rome could return to the status quo. But Decebalus muffled any dissent. The dice were cast for total war.

Trajan launched the campaign the following year as soon as the weather allowed his legions to set out for the mountain passes of central Dacia. As before, he separated the army into three columns to fracture Decebalus's defenses. One column approached the Iron Gates Pass in the west, one headed for the Vulcan Pass in the center, and the emperor himself commanded the third column targeting the eastern Red Tower Pass.

Trajan moved forward with caution. His troops never entered sketchy trails or narrow ravines in search for a shortcut or fell for tempting stories of hidden lairs or secret passages that Dacian prisoners told the Roman scouts. They avoided anything even remotely ambiguous. Instead, Trajan mocked the storytellers and sent them back to their king.

At the end of each day his troops built the customary palisade wall around camp to be safe from ambuscades. To this end the legionaries carried palisade rods on their backs in addition to other gear such as their shields, assorted weapons, shovels, picks, axes, cooking utensils and more for a total of over forty pounds per man. Mule and ox-drawn carriages pulled the heavy equipment like siege engines or *clausurae* barricades and hauled the food supply and burning materials including pitch to incite flaming arrows.

Decebalus did his best to resist all three columns and slow down the triple advance, but he did not have the man power to challenge any of them in open battle. Last year's raids into Roman territories had taken their toll on his warriors, particularly Longinus's stubborn defense of the Banat. As it was, Decebalus had to retreat to higher ground and seek refuge in Dacia's mountain strongholds. From there his men ambushed smaller Roman detachments or tried to capture some torsion artillery.

Decebalus's war of attrition was beginning to irk the emperor as they drew near the Red Tower Pass. He switched from defense to offense and ordered his heavy infantry, supported by slingers and archers, to take the enemy's mountain strongholds. It was a grueling effort. Every possible approach was steep and fraught with peril as the Dacians defended their positions with tenacity and cunning. The Romans had to repulse sallies all the time, but by applying their siege skills and through head-on *testudo* assaults one stronghold after the other was taken and destroyed. The Dacian warriors fought bravely but could not stem the Roman tide.

Trajan's column reached the Dacian capital in early July where he reunited with the other two armies to prepare for the final assault on Sarmizegethusa. Renegade clans reported to Trajan that the *Pileati* Council was imploring Decebalus to come to terms with the invaders but to no avail. Then word came that the king had fled the city with his family and personal guard and had slipped through the Roman lines before the completion of their siege cordon.

Trajan gritted his teeth. At the same time, he was hoping the *pileati* left behind would surrender despite Sarmizegethusa's formidable walls and its geographic advantage, and in fact within days the Dacians capitulated. The relentless Roman onslaught had been too much for them. In turn Trajan spared the lives of all the citizens living in the capital, but ordered it pillaged and razed to the ground to crush any further resistance and deprive the clan leaders of a place to rally around in the future.

The price of peace was high: Thousands of Dacians, mostly women and children, were sold to the slave traders. A few men were picked up by Roman praetors and earmarked for gladiatorial duty in amphitheaters around the empire.

Trajan himself moved on and ordered the legions to search for Decebalus everywhere in the country. Roman troops soon fanned out in great numbers to the hinterlands of northern and northeastern Dacia where the king was believed to be hiding. Councilman Telerion was in the forefront of this endeavor, still yearning to revenge his brother. The renegade *pileatus* knew many of Decebalus's secret retreats and told the Romans their whereabouts, but alas the king remained elusive.

While the Romans were searching the towns and villages between the Transylvanian Alps and the Carpathian Mountains, fighting flared up here and there, sometimes with great ferocity. In the process, the Roman army captured ever more prisoners including *pileati*. Other noblemen submitted too, but none of them offered up Decebalus's location.

One of these men was known as Bacilis. He had surrendered of his own accord and insisted to be taken to the emperor in person. When they led him to Trajan he threw himself on the ground, begging for his life. "Most noble Lord of the Earth, please hear me. I have something you want to see."

"What could possibly be of interest to me in this unruly place, *Pileatus*?" Trajan snapped. "Unless you tell me Decebalus's whereabouts!"

"Nobody knows that, greatest of lords, but I do know where to find the Dacian Royal treasure..."

"Really," Trajan replied, faking boredom. "Why should I believe you?"

"Because I can lead you there - if you spare my life and let me go unharmed."

Trajan's gaze pierced the man with predator's eyes. "Only if you have committed no cruelties against us or our allies. If you have, there is no deal," he thundered.

"I haven't," Bacilis asserted. "Ask your soldiers."

"I will," Trajan replied stern-faced. "We keep track of every atrocity against our people." He waved Callistus closer and whispered in his ear, "Talk to the generals and have this man's claims verified."

Several weeks passed until the Roman garrison commanders in Dacia confirmed that none of them indeed was looking for one Bacilis. Nor was he indicted in neighboring Moesia or Pannonia. Trajan released him from prison, offering him a *quid pro quo*. "Lead me to the lair and I will restore your freedom. If this is a ruse, be sure you will come to regret it. Dacia has rich gold and silver mines, but I have yet to see the fabled Royal treasure. Maybe Decebalus only mined as much gold and silver as he needed for his household. Have you actually seen this fancy hoard with your own eyes, Bacilis?"

"I have, Excellency, I swear," the *pileatus* said, braving the emperor's probing gaze. "It is beyond your imagination."

"We will see. What about the well-stocked Dacian armories we found? I have a good idea how much they have cost your people - the Royal treasury may be depleted already, filling the pockets of Greek blacksmiths and Sarmatian weapons merchants, don't you think?"

But Bacilis didn't flinch. Soon a troop of Praetorians headed by Trajan and with Bacilis as their guide set out on a trail running parallel to the Sargetias River, downstream of Sarmizegethusa's ruins. After following the river for half a day, the *pileatus* halted his horse and pointed to the currents on their left. "It's right here," he shouted.

Trajan looked at him bewildered. *What a waste of time!* There was nothing to see but a steady stream of water. Before he could respond Bacilis added, "Three months ago Decebalus put Roman prisoners to work here. They redirected the water flow. Then he had them dig a big hole in the wet ground and dumped the Royal treasure in there. Then the prisoners shoveled the muddy soil back over it, five feet deep, and returned the Sargetias to its natural riverbed. I know this because I was there when the work was performed."

Trajan glowered. He didn't know what to think of this outrageous story. "What happened to the Roman prisoners?" he asked the *pileatus*.

"They are dead. Decebalus killed them all so that the location of his treasure would remain a secret."

Trajan swallowed into a dry throat. *Yet another despicable act by the king. The man had no empathy and no conscience - he had to find him!*

"How come you are still alive?" Trajan asked the next obvious question. "Don't you know too much yourself?"

"I am not a Roman. I was a loyal *pileatus*. In fact, I was commanding the Dacian guards when it happened."

"You should have killed this monster your people call king," Trajan reprimanded him. "You should have prevented the slaughter of innocent prisoners!"

"And die myself? I am sorry, Majesty, but that was a trade-off I was not willing to make. I do not condone it and I protested in vain." Bacilis sighed. "Hopefully, you will find Decebalus. Every Dacian knows his face, and many blame him for waging war against Rome, for ruining Dacia. There is more. The king also hid the priceless Royal garments in caves nearby. They couldn't be allowed to get wet. I will show you the location too."

Trajan shook his head in disbelief. What an odd story, but if it was true...

He resolved to call for a detachment of pioneers to try and lift the alleged treasure. They arrived a few hours later and started damming the river with boulders and rocks. In the process they found an empty channel the Roman prisoners must have dug outside the natural riverbed but far away enough to force the water into a temporary new path. Over the next few days, Trajan's men used it to reroute the river a second time. Again, the grueling work was done by Romans but this time not at spear point. Fortunately, it was the end of summer and the water level was low. The pioneers were able to complete the work by the end of the week.

Trajan looked on with great tension when the first troop had at long last removed a long stretch of mud reaching five feet deep. At first they found nothing, but after a while and to Trajan's great surprise his soldiers stumbled on a myriad of mud-covered jars and goblets in the ground. Quickly rinsed, they gleamed and glittered in the late afternoon sunlight. Hundreds and hundreds of items came to the surface, and it took days to recover them all. There was more gold and silver than Trajan could have hoped for in his wildest dreams. Bacilis had kept his word.

Later counts put the total amount to half a million pounds of gold and a full million pounds of silver. The gold weight alone was equivalent to thirty-one and a half million *aurei*, the silver to one hundred and sixty million *denarii*...

"By Rome's eternal gods," Trajan shouted. "I will build the Roman people a forum the likes of which they have never seen before!"

Chapter 58

The manhunt for Decebalus was less successful. Trajan and Telerion sent spies everywhere, looking and sniffing, digging and probing, following every lead. And someone else was lusting for justice: Centurion Maximus. Alas, nothing came of it.

In October Maximus and Telerion met by accident in northern Dacia after an engagement of Roman infantry with fighters still loyal to the king, the last major skirmish of the war. Near the town of Porolissium, Decebalus's faithful had made their last stand and were cut down by two legions commanded by Sura. Maximus's cavalry unit had participated in the fighting, and Telerion was in the area hoping to pick up Decebalus's trail.

The two men came upon one another after the battle during the celebratory feast of officers. At first, Maximus didn't trust the Dacian nobleman. He couldn't even be sure Telerion had not somehow contributed to the fateful raid that had destroyed his unit at the start of the first Dacian War. But as he kept talking to the *pileatus*, he realized the nobleman was unlike Decebalus and when he learned of Telerion's brother's fate he even felt sorry for him. Maximus opened up and recounted his own story.

"You must hate Decebalus as much as myself," Telerion said afterwards. "But we might be able to help each other. I have an idea. We don't know whether Decebalus was present at today's battle, is that not so?"

"True enough. Though we walked all over the battlefield and looked at every dead Dacian fighter, we have found no hint of the king," Maximus answered depressed while stirring his spoon in the lamb stew.

"Not many of Decebalus's fighters have survived. And those who did, don't seem to know his whereabouts. I believe them. They were busy fending for themselves. Besides, the king would not have told them where he is going," Telerion added surly.

"Wait a moment, Telerion. We were told the townspeople left Porolissium and scattered in all directions before the legions arrived. What if some of them were waiting for the outcome of the battle and only left once it was over – once the outcome of the fight was apparent. There is our chance!"

Telerion's eyes lit up. "Maybe the king was here after all and escaped just before the end of the battle. Some villagers might have seen him and fled with him or at least at the same time when it was obvious the battle was lost. These people might know what direction the king took or heard something through the grape vine. Let's set out right away and search the trails connecting Porolissium to the outside world," he suggested and slammed up from his stool.

"I agree," Maximus shouted, pushing back his stew bowl and scrambling up from the table. He wiped off his mouth, and together they hurried back to the tents inside the legionary camp. "In fact," Maximus muttered. "This would explain why the survivors don't know Decebalus's whereabouts. They don't because the king had left before they could!"

"It's conjecture," Telerion cautioned him. "But let me assemble my scouts. Can you persuade some of your men to join us on a potential fool's errand, celebrations and all? I will understand if you can't. They deserve to party after all they've been through."

"I will dangle a nice reward in front of them. If some help me find Decebalus, they can be assured of Trajan's gratitude. Everybody knows how much he wants the king captured."

An hour later they had rallied thirty men, twenty auxiliaries from Maximus's unit and ten Dacian scouts from Telerion's clan. The sundry group departed without delay. It was getting dark, but the scouts found wheel trails pointing east. "The tracks are fresh," they explained. "No more than four hours old."

"Excellent," Telerion shouted. "Let's see who that is."

They galloped as fast as the horses could carry them. Maximus had received Sura's permission for the abrupt departure and urged the general to send more soldiers and search the whole area. Sura had assured him he would do so in the morning. This was just fine with Maximus. He yearned to catch Decebalus himself to get satisfaction for the wicked massacre of his men. Alas, night was falling and they didn't get far. It was too dangerous to push on in the dark. Grudgingly, they camped for the night.

At the crack of dawn they resumed the hunt. By noon they caught up with a group of townspeople on wagon, refugees from Porolissium confirming the king had been in Porolissium yesterday, but they said they didn't know where he was now. Nobody had seen him after the fighting. Some thought they had seen Royal guards heading for the Carpathian Mountains. It was unclear, however, whether the king was with them or not. That seemed unlikely to Maximus. *Why wouldn't Decebalus aim for the Carpathians? They were remote, rugged and provided for an easy hiding ground.*

He and Telerion decided to follow this eastern trail. If they were right, Decebalus would be just ahead of them. *But how far ahead?*

Pumped up, they passed through many villages along the way, some of them entirely depopulated. In one of the hamlets an old man pointed to a hut supposedly accommodating an injured Dacian fighter, maybe a member of Decebalus's Guard. Maximus and his men surrounded it at once and then dashed in, ready for a struggle. The Royal guardsman, however, was too injured to put up a fight. He begged for his life telling them that Decebalus was indeed on this trail, perhaps one day ahead of them. He also said the king had a dozen men with him, plus his concubine, several slaves and his two daughters. If they were able to find him, he would be easy prey. The guardsman believed the king didn't know of their pursuit, but he told them Decebalus paid close attention to his surroundings at any given time and would be hard to come upon.

Maximus sent one of his men back to Sura to call in more troops. Then they started out again, cantering all day, but there was still no sight of the king. *Had he left the trail and veered off into the wilderness?*

The next morning, they reached a township that appeared deserted, but peasants were tilling the fields outside its palisade walls. They told them Royal guardsmen had passed through here only several hours ago. Maximus and Telerion intensified their efforts, forming two parties to scour the trail on either side and abandoning it so as not to give away their approach.

On Maximus's side the underbrush was so thick he and his soldiers had to slow down and walk their horses on foot. The centurion sent one man ahead to reconnoiter. He came back an hour later with even better news. The soldier had located a troop of wagons and riders, almost certainly Royal guardsmen, resting at a creek nearby. Their number matched the statements of the villagers the Romans had talked to earlier. It could be Decebalus...

Maximus was itching to strike, but should he send for Telerion first? He resolved not to, ordered his men to saddle up and follow him, swords drawn, shields ready. At full speed they galloped into the clearing that the unknown men had chosen as their camp site. Maximus knew right away that he had found Decebalus when he saw two toddlers among the strangers, but where was the king? Maximus stayed away from the fighting and headed for the wagons instead. In all probability, Decebalus should be in one of the covered carriages. He reined-in his mount, cantering up and down the wagons, rubbing the bushes and trees nearby while at the same time keeping a steady eye on the fighting around behind him. There! Someone was jumping off the middle wagon. He wore the same kit as the other fighters, but Maximus had never forgotten Decebalus's face when he had prostrated himself before Trajan outside Sarmizegethusa. It was Decebalus! There was no doubt about it.

The king was running fast, aiming for one of the Dacian mares that had taken off when the Romans had burst onto the scene, but Maximus was quicker. He cut off the king's path, wheeled around and galloped straight for his nemesis. Decebalus veered sharply left and started heading for the creek. He splashed through the shallow water leaping from rock to rock, almost slipping on the slippery ground. Maximus had to pull back the reins. If his horse went down now Decebalus would get away. Carefully he guided his stallion across the treacherous rivulet. After arriving on the other side he kicked his heels hard against his horse's underbelly and whipped forward.

Decebalus was running for his life now scampering daringly over uprooted tree trunks in the way. He had gained ground, but Maximus was closing in. Decebalus screeched to a halt against an old aspen tree, gasping for air. His eyes glared at the approaching centurion. "You won't have me, Roman," he shrieked in his broken Latin. "I will not be in your Triumph!"

Maximus was almost there. He reined-in hard, drew his *spatha*, vaulted off the horse even before he came to a full stop and darted toward the king, but too late... Right in front of him and using the tree for leverage Decebalus ran into his own *falx*. Rattling, but smiling he fell on the root-covered sodden ground.

"Nooooo," Maximus screamed in frustration, seeing right away that no force in the world could save Decebalus's life. "You dirty thug," he cursed him. Maximus pulled out the *falx* from the king's twitching body, tore a piece of cloth off his tunic and tried to patch up the king's wound. Decebalus spit at him, but Maximus kept working on him feverishly until he realized that Decebalus's body had gone limp and his eyes were open wide, staring into Hades itself. The king was dead.

Furious, Maximus tossed the corpse aside and stood. Then, with a skilled stroke he lopped off the king's head and wrapped it in his cloak. *It is too bad I couldn't kill him myself, but at least I captured him. I, Maximus, captured Decebalus, King of the Dacians!*

He had exacted his revenge. What would he do now?

Exhausted in mind and body, he swung himself on the horse and cantered back to his men.

The skirmish had come to a quick end. The king's Guard was either killed or on the run. The Royal concubine, Decebalus's children and his slaves were tied to their wagons, destined for Trajan's Triumph in the Forum Romanum. Telerion and his men had also arrived. After hearing the din in the distance they had galloped over as fast as they could.

Seeing the headless corpse of his king Telerion grunted a satisfied sigh. "We were right after all," he snarled. "He was in this area, and now he is dead. Susagus is avenged. He can rest in peace now - I can rest in peace now. It is over. It's only too bad we didn't capture him alive."

"I feel with you, Telerion," Maximus agreed. "Believe me, I tried! But he wouldn't allow it. Decebalus must have been ready for this moment because he didn't hesitate at all when there was no way out for him. He didn't want to give us the pleasure of parading him through the streets of Rome as the Grand Prize of Dacia. At any rate, what matters is that the scum is dead."

On their way back to Porolissium they met up with Sura's troops. The general was elated to hear the news and sent Decebalus's head to Trajan's headquarters in Ranisstorium.

When the king's gruesome face was presented to Trajan mounted on a pole in the presence of his generals the emperor glared at it with great satisfaction. "At long last, justice is done," he exlaimed. "The Dacian monster will never again rear its ugly head and haunt our lands. Callistus, send for the soldiers who hunted him down. I want to award everyone of them before the whole army. They deserve praise, especially the king slayer Maximus. Decebalus won't be part of my Triumph in Rome, but I want the head mummified so we can show his face to the Roman People. They shall see who pestered them for so long before we hurl the skull down the Gemonian Stairs." He winked at Callistus. "My friend, now we can finish the written account of this dreadful war."

He also had orders for Hadrian. "I want you to take this trophy to Rome and report to the Senate. My message is simple: *DACIA CAPTA EST* – Dacia is conquered." He paused, hunching over distressed on his curule chair. "One man's ego has doomed a whole country..."

All Dacian citizens were forced to leave their homeland. Roman settlers took their place. In memory of the four thousand Roman dead, Trajan ordered a gargantuan monument to be erected on the main trade route into the Eastern Europe, in the Danube valley near the new-founded township of *Tropaeum Traiani*. He modeled the memorial after Augustus's own mausoleum on the Tiber, faced it in luminous white stone and shaped it like a drum, one hundred feet in diameter and sixty feet high. It was inaugurated two years after the war, dedicated to *Mars Ultor*, Mars the Avenger, a demonstration of Roman Power directed at the barbarian tribes of the eastern steppes, sending a clear message: ENTER AT YOUR OWN PERIL.

The lavish victory celebrations in Rome were the biggest the city had ever seen. In addition to thousands of gladiatorial fights, wild animals from all over the empire were brought to the Eternal City to be displayed and killed in staged hunts. Elaborate sea battles were enacted with Dacian prisoners of war in a new stadium solely built for this purpose, and delegations from as far away as India arrived in Rome to pay homage to Trajan and receive his assurances that they would not suffer Dacia's fate. The world was at the emperor's feet.

BOOK VI

THE WAR OF CHOICE

Chapter 59

Eight years later (113 AD), Rome

"Trajan is taking his sweet time," Sabina remarked, furrowing her eyebrows.

Her husband barely listened. He readied himself for some delicate policy conversations. It wasn't every day that most of Trajan's Council members were assembled in one place. Hadrian intended to take full advantage.

He could tell that Sabina was getting impatient. She expected to soon catch a glimpse of the new Column that Trajan had commissioned for his Forum. Dozens of dignitaries, knights and freedmen of the imperial administration were huddling with them in the tight space at the foot of the Column between the Latin and Greek Libraries, just behind Trajan's monumental Courthouse and Reception Hall, the recently completed Basilica Ulpia. Throngs of common citizens crowded the plaza between the Forum's temple and the Column, waiting to be admitted after the official inauguration. The free-standing cylinder-shaped pillar itself was still veiled behind a huge piece of white linen that fluttered in the breeze like a galley's sail tethered to its mast.

Trajan was to arrive from the refurbished Temple of Venus after presiding over its opening ceremony. There! *Tubicens* approached, announcing his arrival. The blaring trumpets echoed deafeningly in the enclosure around the Column. The honored guests rushed to put their hands on their ears, but thankfully the *tubicens* put down their tubas immediately after pulling in at the foot of the Column.

Next, the Praetorian Guard swept in wearing elegant white tunics cinched with burnished red leather belts to which *pugiones* in ornate gilded scabbards were attached. The guardsmen took up positions along the walls of the Libraries. Finally, the imperial couple arrived. Trajan and Plotina entered the enclosure together with the emperor's sister Marciana and her daughter Matidia. Praefect Livianus, the reigning consuls and praetors and key senators and generals followed them. Hadrian recognized Palma, Celsus, Bassus, Tacitus and his friend Senecio. He waved at him, but Senecio didn't see him. Admiral Marcius Turbo, commander-in-chief of the western mediterranean fleet, was also there.

"I can't wait to find out what the fuss is all about," Sabina murmured. "They say this pillar is as high as the section of the Quirinal Hill that was excavated to make room for Trajan's novel mall." She chuckled. "That's just like Trajan - boasting how much rock and dirt he moved to accommodate his fancy indoor shops."

Meanwhile, the imperials stopped at the bronze entrance doors to the

304

base of the Column and turned to the invited guests. More than a hundred people occupied the narrow space around the wrapped cylinder now, some of them spilling into the neighboring passageways of the Basilica Ulpia. Several hundreds more were watching from the temple plaza.

Trajan opened his arms to greet the assembled guests, looking splendid in his purple toga and the red *balcei* that enclosed his feet. Fifty-eight years old now, his face had aged, the hair turning gray around the temples, and his cheeks filling out since the Dacian Wars seven years earlier. "Honored guests, dignitaries of our cherished Republic, welcome to the *Forum Ulpium*. I am sure you have all been wondering what the object behind me is all about. Wouldn't the fine Basilica and Courtyard have been enough? Or the Libraries, the Temple and the Markets? You will see why not. The empire's best craftsmen and most renowned artists spent years working on this special monument for a very good reason.

Why behind a veil, you might say. What were they doing? What did the chisels carve into the marble? Why the secrecy? Why the presence of Praetorian guards that wouldn't let anyone sneak in and take a peek? Well, I thought it would be fun to pique your curiosity and then surprise you.

What you are going to see today is a true marvel of the modern age. The pillar behind me consists of hollow drums of Carrara marble put on top of each other. And no, it's not an oversize *mithraeum* as some rumor has it!" He looked about as if he expected the crowd to laugh, but Hadrian knew better. Trajan simply enjoyed watching their curious faces.

What could it be for, he pondered. *Was this Column a watchtower? Or perhaps some mechanical device, maybe a new type of clock to replace Augustus's old horologium?*

"Let me not torture you any longer," Trajan shouted. "I will show you. Officer, perform your duty."

A centurion stepped forward and pulled on a rope that was fastened to the very top of the linen veil. A knot opened at the top and down floated the huge cloth with a whooshing sound. As it dropped down the mysterious structure revealed its colored beauty... Excited murmurs rippled through the crowd, followed by some giggles as huge linen folds engulfed some spectators nearest to the pillar. They had to crawl out from underneath the heavy material to see what everybody else was seeing: A round column covered tip to toe with painted reliefs circling around its circumference in an ever-ascending band. The reliefs were both beautiful and elaborate, depicting an untold number of scenes.

"It's the Dacian War, isn't it?" a man shouted. "It is an account of the war with Decebalus, isn't it? I see Phrygian hats, *testudo* formations, the marvelous bridge at Drobeta-"

Hadrian and Sabina craned their necks to see the pert speaker. It was Senecio; Hadrian had fought in the war with him. Neither of them had been told the 'secret' of the Column – until now.

Trajan answered with a satisfied smile, "That is correct, Quintus. This Column is a visual record of the Dacian Wars, chiseled in stone and painted in life-like colors. I thought it would make sense to place it here, surrounded by the Libraries' knowledge of the world and in the midst of my new Forum that I was able to build from the proceeds of this wretched war. It is true, however, that my original idea was to have the Column merely mark how high we had to cut into the Quirinal Hill to build the Indoor Mall that everybody has come to appreciate, allowing Rome to shop non-stop, at any time, day and night, protected from the weather - a dream come true!" He cleared his throat and added, "Only later did my friend Pliny come up with the idea of transforming this marker into a wider cylinder and putting reliefs on it."

Trajan's words echoed from the walls around the Column. Hadrian could understand him easily.

"Take a look, People of Rome," Trajan encouraged the crowd. "Walk up on the Libraries' staircases and peek through the windows to see all the details chiseled and painted onto this marvel. Or step over to the plaza and look at the reliefs from there. Myself, I will walk up its spiral staircase now and take a look at our beloved city from a brand-new vantage point." He extended his elbow to Plotina who smiled at him cheerfully, hooked her arm into his, and they strutted through the entrance together.

Sabina pushed forward to join the Traiani family who was following the imperial couple's footsteps, but Hadrian had other plans. "I am going to mingle now," he whispered in her ear. "But please, Sabina, by all means, go ahead. I am sure, the view up there will be remarkable!" He kissed her hand and off she went. Hadrian turned around, heading straight for Lucius Publilius Celsus, Rome's foremost magistrate. "*Ave*, Consul," he greeted him. "How do you like the reliefs?"

"*Ave*, Publius Aelius," Celsus answered stiffly. "I do like them. They show Rome at its best - conquering other nations."

Hadrian watched him carefully. Yes, he meant it, a Roman general through and through; no wonder Trajan liked him. He also noticed that the consul addressed him as 'Publius Aelius', adding the family name to his first name. Why so formal? They had known each other for years though never established any rapport.

"How about you?" Celsus asked Hadrian. "Do you approve?"

"How could I not? The reliefs are done artfully and will be admired for centuries."

"I sure hope so," Celsus shouted. "Our veterans will flock to them in droves."

"How is your lovely wife doing?" Hadrian wanted to know, changing the subject.

"Fine. She is doing fine. And Sabina?"

"My wife is well. She joined the imperial family walking up the Column." *Eat this, Lucius. You may be Consul Ordinarius, but don't forget that Sabina and I are members of the imperial family.*

Politely, he said, "What are your plans as consul this year?"

"Oh, there is much to do," Celsus replied. "I wouldn't even know where to start. See for yourself in the Curia tomorrow. The Senate will be in session early in the morning."

"Any military plans?" Hadrian kept poking.

"Maybe."

"I heard the Governor of Syria is reporting discord among the Parthian Royal Family," Hadrian pressed on. "What is your opinion, Lucius?"

"Well, that is always good news, isn't it? As long as the Parthian nobles are busy fighting each other, they won't be a threat. In any case, I am keeping a close eye on it. Perhaps there will be an opportunity. Think of the spoils if we could manage a triumph over the Parthians!"

Hadrian was not surprised, having heard from different sources that Trajan's generals were pondering an invasion in the East. Celsus was likely one of them. They might entice Trajan to fall for it – madness!

Meanwhile, Trajan, Plotina and their entourage appeared on top of the Column. Hadrian could see the party lean against the rails, gawk and chatter and point their arms in all directions, taking in the marvelous views. He was tempted to join them but decided to first mingle some more. He said good-bye to the general and crossed to the Greek Library entrance.

Many guests were leaving the enclosure now, striding to the temple plaza or walking up the stairs of the two Libraries that flanked Trajan's Column.

In the Library Hadrian encountered his former co-guardian, Publius Acilius Attianus, who all his life had been like a father to him. "Uncle," he shouted with joy. "I am so glad to see you!"

"Publius, what a nice surprise! How have you been?"

They fell into each other's arms and sat down at one of the long reading tables on the ground level of the Library. An oversize marble statue of Trajan stared down on them. It was painted so realistically that it looked like the man himself.

"I've been great. How about you?" Trajan's cousin asked.

"I can't complain. Nice day, huh? What a forum Trajan built, don't you think? It's breathtaking."

"True enough. What's new, Uncle? I haven't seen you in a long time."

"Not a whole lot. Business is good. I landed an imperial contract to build wharves for the olive oil trade at Trajan's hexagonal harbor. Ostia is booming also, creating trade opportunities with many ports in the Mediterranean.

How about you?"

"I serve my illustrious cousin in the Imperial Council and attend many Senate meetings, too many it seems. Nothing exciting. I feel empty, lacking purpose. Five years ago I was consul and before that governor of Lower Pannonia. I have plenty of military and administrative experience now, but still don't know what my cousin has in store for me. It's been quiet in Rome – and don't get me wrong, that's a good thing – but I am craving more responsibility, a major governorship maybe. For now, I keep myself busy designing buildings, a passion of mine as you know. Of course, as long as Apollodorus is Chief Architect, none of this will ever come to fruition."

"It may not be so quiet forever," Attianus said with a hushed voice. He bent over to Hadrian and whispered, "I hear war talk..."

"You too? What do you know?" Hadrian shouted - only to regret it right away. The other people in the Library turned their heads disapprovingly. "I am sorry," he apologized. "I will lower my voice now."

"It's all right," Attianus said. "But promise to keep to yourself what I am going to tell you now."

"I will," Hadrian assured him. "I swear by the whole Capitoline Trinity!"

Attianus pressed closer. "You may have heard that Livianus is retiring. Trajan is looking for a successor to command the Praetorians. Get this: he is considering me..."

"You? That is great news, Publius, and no surprise to me. You are close to the imperial family and always have been. Plotina thinks the world of you. What's the holdup?"

"There is no holdup. I am certain I will be offered the praefectship, but Trajan asked me to talk to the generals first so they are comfortable with me. It is a highly influential position after all. For better or worse, they will relay their feedback on me." Attianus chuckled.

"What is so funny, Uncle?"

The knight moved even closer to Hadrian before he answered, "Some of the generals don't like me. They are afraid I might be too much of a moderating force."

"Who?" Hadrian asked point blank.

"Quietus, Celsus and Palma – and Crispinus."

"Crispinus doesn't count, but the others... That's bad. I hate Quietus - he is a butcher. The moor is to Trajan what Labienus was to Caesar: competent but cruel. Some of the things his troops have done in Dacia were downright atrocities. Trajan didn't like it either, but he looked the other way because we needed Quietus's cavalry.

Uncle, I was just talking to Celsus. He didn't want to tell me anything, but I probed and I poked, and I do believe he is considering war with Parthia."

"That is exactly what I think," Attianus affirmed with a grim face. "The generals are getting greedy. There hasn't been a conflict since the fall of Dacia. They are lusting for booty and believe the Parthian empire may be the grand prize." He scowled.

"I am much concerned, Uncle. War against Parthia makes no sense nor would it be easy because of the geography: The Parthians are far away from our borders; hundreds of miles of desert protect them from our wrath – a deterrent for sure, but the generals seem interested anyway. After all, everybody thought Britannia could never be conquered – and we did. After Dacia, they suppose they are invincible."

"I concur. If I become praefect, I will fight this idea tooth and nail. With Trajan's help we can put them in their place. But if he falls for it..." Attianus swallowed. "If he does, there will be war. He has much sway in the Senate. They would authorize anything-" Attianus interrupted himself when Hadrian tugged his head to the right. The knight shifted his shoulders and saw Cornelius Palma enter the Library Hall with his wife Antonia.

"Let's hear it from the horse's mouth," Hadrian suggested and rose to welcome the new arrivals. "*Ave,* Cornelius. *Ave,* Antonia. How are the Conqueror of Arabia and his wife doing today? Do you like Trajan's new Column?"

"Absolutely," Palma intoned. "I wasn't part of the Dacian War, but I heard all about it from my colleagues and from you. I believe this Column is a fitting monument to the war. As you know, Hadrian, I was busy at the time myself, adding the Nabataean kingdom to the empire. The old king had died and it was time for us to take control of the myrrh and incense trade and render the last free patch of Mediterranean coastline a Roman territory. It all came together, and the annexation was peaceful. Let me tell you, their Capital Petra is a place like no other – dazzling canals and cisterns all about and spectacular Greek-style temples cut into a maze of sandstone gorges-"

His wife cut Palma short. "I don't think you want to bore our friend here, Cornelius. He has certainly heard of Petra. Dearest Hadrian, how have you been?"

She seems a nice Lady, Hadrian thought. *As for Palma - the general gloats too much.* "I am doing fine," he replied. "Rome is never boring, not even now with the war celebrations long over and Trajan's building program almost complete. They are still working on the harbor of Centum Cellae, but that's about it."

"Hadrian, it will never stop," Palma patronized. "You know your cousin. As long as there is money, he will spend it. Don't forget the new Via Traiana in the South."

"True enough. Still, I believe things are slowing down now," Hadrian insisted. Then he cut to the chase. "What are your plans, General? Going east? I hear rumbles from beyond the Syrian desert."

"What are you talking about?"

"The Parthians are weakened by internal strife. Shouldn't we take advantage?" Here was the bait...

Palma squinted at Trajan's cousin. "Yes, since the old King Pacorus is dead, his joint successors Osroes and Vologaeses can't agree on anything. In fact, I believe one controls the eastern and the other the western part of their empire. The court in Ctesiphon is paralyzed over this – but what should that have to do with us?"

"Nothing, nothing at all," Hadrian replied innocently. *You don't want to show your hand, old fox,* he thought, *but you know a bit too much about the Parthian situation - it gives you away.* "We should stay alert and watch," he said. "A winner may emerge. Then that's the one we deal with." Hadrian stayed deliberately vague, not wanting to show his hand either.

After some small talk, Palma and Antonia left the Library and Hadrian returned to Attianus who had remained seated in the back of the Library.

"Palma knows the players, Attianus. He never had a clue about the machinations of the Parthian court before. Clearly, he is looking east... It really looks like both Celsus and Palma are up to something though I am not sure exactly what. It is some sort of Roman intervention, maybe even full-scale invasion. Whatever their plans, they will soon make it to the top of the imperial agenda.

Uncle, it is of paramount importance that you are appointed praefect soon. Only then can we keep a lid on their ambitions. We have Turbo on our side, cautious Pompeius Falco and my friend Senecio. They don't crave an armed conflict with the Parthians."

Tired from the talking, Trajan was glad when the reception was over. Before returning to the palace he intended to stop by at Pliny's house. His friend was ill, and Trajan worried about him. The Roman aristocrat from Comum had served him for many years, even in far-away places like Bithynia Province in Asia Minor. There was talk in the city he might not last long. "I need my horse, Claudius," he told Praefect Livianus. "So I can visit Pliny at his house on the Aventine. From there I will return to the palace. Understood?"

"*Sic*, my Lord," Livianus nodded and strode off to issue orders to the commanding officer of the imperial detail.

Trajan, Plotina, Marciana, Hadrian and other friends and members of the Imperial Family were lounging together in the courtyard of the magnificent new Basilica, enjoying the banquet food.

"You still have a callused hand," Plotina called out to her husband. "After all those years…"

Trajan cocked his head. "And? I still practice sword exercises. Who rests, rusts!"

Pompeia didn't answer, rolled her eyes and shook her head, and resumed her conversation with Sabina. Soon a Praetorian approached, holding the reins of Trajan's stallion. The emperor kissed Plotina good-bye and waved at the others. A squire helped him on the magnificent dapple-gray horse and off he trotted, flanked by two horseguards of the imperial detail.

Chapter 60

Pliny was in bed when Trajan entered his room. His family crowded the sides of the divan including his personal *medicus*. "Trajan, my Lord," Pliny croaked. Big droplets of sweat gleamed on his forehead. A maid was trying to freshen his face with a wet cloth of the finest linen by pressing it against the governor's features.

"Your friend," Trajan corrected Pliny with a warm smile. "How are you doing, Gaius?"

"Oh, I have seen better days. I don't know why I am sick again. My body fluids must be out of balance," Pliny said, coughing.

"He is a good patient," his wife praised him. "Takes his medicine and never complains, but we are hm... apprehensive..." Tears glistened in her eyes.

Trajan crossed the room to give her a big hug. "Your husband will feel better soon. It's only a spring fever, I am sure," he consoled her.

After visiting for a while, Trajan begged the family to leave the room. Sitting down at the edge of Pliny's bed he picked up the senator's left hand with both of his own and pressed it fondly. "My dear Gaius, have hope. You are the last living survivor of the Vesuvian eruption - a cataclysm beyond all comparison. You have survived that and you will survive your current affliction!"

Pliny forced a weak smile. "True enough," he said. "I do hope that will never happen again - such senseless and utter destruction! My poor uncle... He died trying to help the Roman people."

"Enough of this gloomy talk," Trajan cheered him up. "Listen, Gaius, I have a question for you. Do you remember Callidromus, the Bithynian? He was a former adviser to General Laberius, then abducted by Susagus and sold into Parthian slavery before the end of the Dacian War and the ensuing prisoner exchange. Several years back - when you were Governor of Bithynia he escaped and was brought before you because his supposed new 'owners' pressed charges. Do you remember?"

"Callidromus?"

"*Sic*, Callidromus was his name."

Pliny frowned. "Callidromus," he repeated to himself. "It sounds familiar. Why are you asking?"

"Remember, you had trouble with his story. You didn't believe he could have possibly been Laberius's adviser in the First Dacian War, and that he was sold to the Parthians as a prisoner of war. Do you recall now?"

"Yes, yes. I do," Pliny rattled.

"What else did he say?" Trajan asked.

"Callidromus... Yes, I saw him in Bithynia, a crazy place. There was this strange sect - the Christians. I didn't know what to make of them. They were unpopular. The people accused them of cruel practices like human sacrifice and that they denied obeisance to your Majesty. You, Caesar, sent me some helpful guidance on this difficult matter. Always fair, always balanced, always brilliant in your judgment." Pliny looked at Trajan with admiration. "Trajan, the people love you because you love them. Their affection makes them loyal citizens even when you are traveling to the end of the world. You know, my Lord, a ruler's affection is forever present, but force is not. Terror only works when its underlying force is omnipresent – which is impossible..." Pliny coughed again and raised his index finger. "Fear turns into hatred, but affection into respect. Never forget that, Caesar, never!"

Pliny's words swelled Trajan's eyes with tears. Embarassed, he dried them with his purple handkerchief. "I will not, Gaius, I promise. You are flattering me. I know that grasping power too strongly is one's own demise. I am just a humble servant of the State. Justice is my purpose, not power. But back to this man Callidromus - I would like to know what he told you."

"Ah yes, Callidromus. Let me see. He said he was captured by Susagus, the nobleman, who later turned against his king. Callidromus said Susagus had sent him to the Parthian King Pacorus as a gift from Decebalus himself. For proof, he showed me a small gold nugget that he claimed he had brought from his labor camp in the Parthian mines. I sent this lump to you, Trajan."

"Yes, you did. But I didn't need proof because I remembered Callidromus. He was telling the truth. We had wanted to get him back at the time, but it had been too late. Susagus's troop had already left the country when the war ended. What else did he say?"

"Nothing." Pliny shrugged.

"Nothing? Think, Pliny, there must be more. What happened during Callidromus's stay in Ctesiphon? What did he do there? What did he see? Why was he sent as a gift? In other words, what did the Dacians want from Pacorus?"

"I don't know. I do remember that he mentioned several audiences his Dacian masters had with Pacorus. He didn't say much else."

"Hm." Trajan sighed. "Audiences... But he didn't attend them, did he?"

"Of course not, Caesar." Pliny chuckled. Then he heaved and the chuckle grew into a long arduous cough. The ex-governor rattled for air, and his shoulders were shaking. Worried, Trajan tried to give him some relief. He pulled Pliny's shoulders forward and stroked his back. Then he picked up the damp cloth at his friend's side and wiped his drenched forehead.

"Why would a Bithynian slave be admitted to an audience with the Parthian king?!" Pliny finally managed to get out, explaining what had amused him so much.

"I realize that, Pliny. It's just... If we knew what happened in those audiences we would know a whole lot more about a possible Parthian involvement in the Dacian War."

"I don't think there was any," Pliny cautioned. "At least nothing substantial. But what do I know? I was focused on judging Callidromus. He was a runaway in my eyes. The Parthian story sounded contrived – dreamed up to get him out of his troubles, but it intrigued me enough to report it to you, Trajan. Thank the gods I did. After receiving your dispatch I set him free. " Pliny's head sank back into the pillows, and he closed his eyes.

Trajan stayed with him for another half hour, his mind racing as he watched Pliny drop into a fitful slumber. Did Decebalus draw the Parthians into the war on his side and if so, did Pacorus heed him and send troops? A request for help seemed likely, but what exactly had the Parthian response been?

Chapter 61

King Exedares's long beard wasn't artfully braided today. The king of Armenia had not allowed his chamberlains to tend to it lately. He deemed spending time with his concubines more important. They liked that of course. Giving birth to a child guaranteed them continued lodging in the palace and preserved their station in Artaxata.

"Stop it," Exedares snarled when his favorite mistress tried to fondle his manhood again. Her eyes glared at him, but obediently she removed her hands. The sullen king was looking out of the window. A dust cloud had caught his interest. He blinked his eyes and yes indeed, what he saw was certainly not of natural origin: An enormous caravan approached the Armenian capital. Caravans had to announce themselves and arrange for accommodations with Artaxata's many inns and hostels through the proper channels – the king. Moreover, they owed taxes for every trade they made in Artaxata in return for protection, water and supplies.

Exedares was not pleased. "Guard," he shouted. "Send for the Lord Chamberlain. I need to speak to him."

The ceremonial guard at the massive doors to Exedares's Royal suite bowed and left his post with swishing robes.

Lord Chamberlain Musa entered the suite thereafter. "At your service, your Highness", he stated submissively.

"Why was I not advised a caravan was approaching?" the king barked at him. "Why did they not send messengers with customary gifts and a down payment on their taxes?"

"A caravan?" Musa asked, arching his eyes. "I don't know of any caravan, Master."

"Look out the window, you useless piece of inventory!" the king denigrated him.

Musa crossed to the window and took a peek. "By Ahuramazda," he shouted. "I will take care of it at once." He bowed and without waiting for permission, Musa scurried to the doors and dashed off.

Exedares shook his head and waved his concubine forward. "You can resume now," he commanded. Outside, he could hear Musa yell instructions at his aides and pageboys and order a detachment of soldiers to the caravan to punish them for their impertinence. Exedares lay back, enjoying the attention of his concubine. The caravan's embassy would soon submit to his wishes.

Hours later – another concubine had taken her predecessor's place – Exedares heard a commotion in the courtyard, followed by angry yelling and cursing coming from the grounds below. Curious, he scrambled from his divan and looked down the court-side window. What he saw was even scar-ier than an impudent caravan. There was his overlord and uncle, the High King Osroes of Parthia and Mesopotamia, clattering into the courtyard with a troop of heavily armed cataphracts. Another member of the royal family flanked Osroes on horseback. One of the king's brothers? Indeed, this was his uncle Parthamasiris.

Their unannounced arrival was terrible news...

Next, he saw Musa running up to the Lords, prostrating himself on the hard brick floor. "Welcome, welcome, your Excellencies," he shouted, hun-kered down on the ground. "What a pleasant surprise!"

"Rise, wretch," Osroes commanded with a baritone voice. "Where is your master? We want to see him right away."

"Certainly, High King," Musa yelped, jumping back on his feet. "Your nephew doesn't know you are visiting. He is not, hm... how shall I put it? hm... prepared to receive guests right now, but I will get him ready for an audience in no time!"

"Audience?" Osroes chuckled. "That's a good one. Audience... You are very funny." Then he abruptly scowled at poor Musa and added in a sinister low voice, "Do not bother, Chamberlain. He does not have to be ready. There won't be an audience. My brother and I will walk straight to him and have a civilized conversation, isn't that so, Parthamasiris?"

"Yes, Brother," Parthamasiris affirmed with a grin. "Indeed."

"What are you waiting for, you mote? Show us the way, Musa," Osroes ordered and dismounted from his caparisoned gelding.

"This way, your Excellencies," Musa shrieked, pointing to the entrance portal of the palace's main building.

The guards, maids, pageboys, ostlers, concubines and everybody else who happened to be in the courtyard stared at the spectacle as the humili-ated Musa led the king of Parthia, his brother and the entire king's detail to their own King Exedares, who now rushed to get dressed. He was still dishev-eled when Musa opened the doors to his suite, Osroes and Parthamasiris prancing in right behind him.

Exedares clapped his hands. "Leave," he hissed at the concubines around him. He struggled to tuck his kaftan into proper shape and obsequiously bowed to his overlords. "My dear Uncles, how good to see you! Come on in. Musa, get us some appetizers, the finest wine and freshest water for our guests. They must be hungry and thirsty from a long trip." Exedares strut-ted to his relatives to hug them, but haughty they remained, arms crossed on their ornate sashes. Ignoring his approach, they strode around him and sat down on one of the many sofas without as much as acknowledging his presence.

The Armenian king turned and looked at them bewildered. "I am sorry you see me like this, but how was I to know-"

"Enough," Osroes interrupted him. "You incompetent excuse for a king, we have come to take you away."

"Take me away? Where? Why? You cannot! I am your nephew, the rightful king. The councils of the empire will never let you do that," Exedares shouted.

"They already have - both the Council of Nobles and the *Magi*. As of today, my brother will take over your realm. Be glad we let you go home; you can even take your concubines. But your rule is over. You will return to Ctesiphon and live there under my supervision. Parthamasiris is the new king of Armenia," Osroes droned.

"You cannot do that," Exedares shrieked, defiantly hitting the chamber's sumptuous Persian carpet with his right foot. "It is illegal. Do you hear me - illegal! Don't forget, the Romans approved me. We have a treaty with them. A king-designate of Armenia can receive the Royal diadem only if the Romans give their blessing. Did they approve of Parthamasiris?" Exedares was confused, desperate and angry.

"I know you would say that," Osroes retorted. "The answer is no. But it doesn't matter. The Romans are far and wide, and Parthia is close. Armenia is our client state. I don't care about a treaty that's fifty years old. I didn't sign it. We have catered to Roman interests long enough - no more."

"Uncle, this is madness! It will lead to war. The Emperor Trajan is a powerful man. He has vanquished anybody resisting him. We are not ready for a war with the Lion of Rome!"

"Trajan is powerful, yes, but he is no fool. A frontal assault on Parthia would be his undoing. The Syrian Desert is our protection; no Roman army has ever successfully crossed it. I am not worried about a Roman invasion."

Exedares did not relent. "Has Vologaeses agreed to this?" He was looking for any angle to avoid his deposition.

"Vologaeses doesn't count. He is not King of Kings - I am. I will consult with him when and if I deem it necessary," Osroes said harshly.

"But if Vologaeses disagrees with you, Uncle, he may send troops and challenge your decision. He may even ally himself with the Romans. This wouldn't be the first time in our history. You would be attacked from both the West and the East..."

"Enough, sassy one!" Osroes snapped. "Pack your belongings and get ready for the caravan. I want you out of here by the end of the day. In the meantime, we are going to enjoy ourselves. Chamberlain Musa, serve up the best your chefs can do!"

Chapter 62

The messenger from Syria did not waste time. As soon as harbor slaves had tied up his courier ship at Trajan's new port, he flung himself on a stallion provided by the local Praetorian detachment and galloped to Rome in great haste. The man arrived at the Palace in merely an hour and demanded to be taken to the emperor without delay. Trajan read his dispatch immediately and acted. Praetorian couriers darted out of the Palace, calling all members of Trajan's Council to the Domus Tiberiana for an emergency consultation.

It was past the twelfth hour when the emperor opened the conference. Numerous star-shaped oil lamps hanging from the gilded coffered ceiling lit the stunning audience chamber. Every imperial adviser present in the city was in attendance: the consuls Celsus and Crispinus, Trajan's secretary Titinius Capito, the new Praetorian Praefect Attianus, Trajan's cousin Hadrian, the generals Falco, Palma and Senecio – and faithful Callistus, who would transcribe a protocol.

The emperor's face radiated a blend of sorrow and zeal when he addressed his advisers. "I have called you here, *amici*," he opened. "To discuss a matter of the utmost importance. The Parthian King Osroes has deposed our client king of Armenia, Exedares, and replaced him with a brother of his by the name Parthamasiris without consulting us..."

At once the loud and excited murmurs of rankled men rose in the chamber, interrupting the emperor and expressing their unequivocal indignation. Only Hadrian, Attianus and Senecio kept quiet, exchanging meaningful glances. *Terrible timing*, Hadrian thought, feverishly calculating the consequences of this.

"Silence," Trajan called them to order. "Silence, my friends. I know it's an outrage, unheard of really. The question, however, is what we should do about it - and what we CAN do about it."

Celsus lifted his hand. Trajan gave him a nod. "Speak, Lucius."

Callistus dunked his reed pen into the inkwell before him, ready to record his words.

"Caesar, the Parthians are feisty," Celsus growled. "This illegal act does not only violate your Majesty and that of the Roman People. It is also a threat to our borders. I say, we ask for immediate reprieve, demand the reinstallation of Exedares, a formal apology from the king and a commensurate fine."

"You know full well that the king of kings will never agree to such humiliation," Hadrian jumped in. "I say, make him undo his mistake, admonish him and be done with it."

"I disagree," Palma flared. "Osroes's act was a criminal violation of the treaty with Parthia. He needs to be punished, not just rebuked. I say, we send the Syrian army into Armenia and take over."

"Not so fast," Senecio cautioned. The veteran general looked disturbed. "I don't think this act justifies going to war. Exedares is not that important. Armenia is a mountain kingdom. What would we gain by going to war over it?"

"A lot," Celsus snapped. "Their merchants are impertinent middlemen, saddling our imports with taxes and tolls only to afford themselves a life-style of luxury and decadence!"

"This may well be," Attianus chimed in. "But short of making Armenia a province this will never change."

"Let's do it then," Celsus demanded.

"Do what? Conquer Armenia?" Hadrian shook his head. "Don't forget Os-roes would get involved. We might as well declare war to the whole Parthian empire. Utter madness!"

"I don't think so. We can defeat the Parthians," Palma disagreed. "Let them attack. They will be easy prey. Look, the Parthians deserve to be thrashed. They helped the Dacians in their aggression against the Roman People - we still have not chastised them for that."

"That's news to me," Hadrian countered. "How exactly did they help the Dacians if I may ask?"

"Dacian *pileati* were in Ctesiphon asking for the king's intervention, and I believe Pacorus indeed sent advisers to teach Dacian soldiers in archery tech-niques. As many of you know, this is Parthia's greatest military strength," Palma patronized Trajan's cousin.

"For one, their greatest strength is the heavily armored *clibanarius* - what they call a cataphract. For two, I participated in the Dacian Wars as all of you know, and have never encountered any Dacian archers, not one," Hadrian responded. "And what is this bogus story about Dacians in Ctesiphon?"

"It is not so bogus, Hadrian," Trajan interjected, joining the discussion on Palma's side. "I have talked to Pliny about this. He confirmed that Dacian noblemen visited the Parthian Capital during the war. The information is two years old, but it seems to me the Dacians did in fact ask for Parthian help."

"And did they receive any?" Hadrian asked him.

"That's what is unclear, but it is certainly possible, even likely. Why else would the Dacians have traveled there while our legions were pounding their homeland? I have tried to verify this claim. We may never know the full truth," Trajan admitted.

"It is crystal clear to me," Celsus maintained. "Parthian archers were seen in our province at the time, riding west - toward Dacia!"

"Even if it were true what you are saying," Attianus said. "Even if it were

- and that's a big if - it proves nothing. They may have been on their way to some Sarmatian people, nomads that could benefit more from archery skills than the *falx*-wielding Dacian infantryman."

"What is all this talk about?" Hadrian asked, drawing his eyebrows to a scowl. "It looks like pretext arguments to me... I don't see any proof of Parthian involvement. But for the argument's sake, even if everything you are saying is true, Lucius, I would still not vote for invading Parthia. Here is why: The country is too far away; our supply lines would be easy prey in the vast desert. Other generals have tried and failed. Think of Crassus, who lost a third of his army near Hatra – what we call Carrhae – and his life. Think of Marcus Antonius. He ignominiously lost even more men – without as much as having one single skirmish! The desert took them... Think of Corbulo, who laid waste to Armenia and still had to negotiate a truce under pressure. Even Vespasian didn't invade Mesopotamia. He was satisfied to consolidate the border and added only Commagene to the empire. Ask our Caesar right here, in this room! He was there when he was a young tribune."

"Well spoken, Hadrian" Celsus said with a thin voice, flicking a glare of resentful disapproval at the emperor's cousin. "Here is my rebuke: Crassus was not an experienced general. He merely had a lot of money and wanted to add military glory to his cachet. The Senate should have never given him a command in the East. As to Antonius, he was a hothead, driven by greed. He committed many tactical errors on his approach to Parthia. By the way, he was not the aggressor. The Parthians had taken advantage of our Civil War following Julius Caesar's assassination and had started pillaging our Asian provinces. They were the aggressor!

As far as Corbulo is concerned, he was hamstrung by an idiot emperor, Nero, who did not allow him to finish the job. And there is not even a comparison between the superb army we have now and the sorry days of Corbulo."

"Plus," Palma added. "This is an opportunity for our beloved emperor to follow in the steps of Alexander the Great and vanquish the East once and forever. The Macedonians did it. So should we!"

Hadrian could tell Trajan was flattered. Despite his successes, did he regret not being able to match Alexander's fame now that he was in his late fifties? "One thing is certain," the emperor muttered. "Parthia has overstepped its limits, requiring an appropriate Roman response."

"If we need to respond," Attianus suggested. "We should remove the usurper from the Armenian throne and install a Roman puppet. And to punish King Osroes we should try and shift the Silk Route away from Parthian territory and ask the merchants to ship their precious cargo via the new province of Arabia Felix instead. Our hero Palma here has conquered Arabia ten years ago. It is the perfect location to receive imports from India by ship. And who knows? The merchants might even like it better than the tedious caravan route through Parthia and Armenia."

"An intriguing idea, Publius," Trajan commended his new praefect. "I will consider it. Thanks to all of you for your contributions. We will reconvene tomorrow. For now, I will send instructions to the eastern governors, ordering them to put their troops on alert, cancel all furloughs, drill the men hard and replenish the armories. Also, I want Lusius Quietus to come to Rome." The emperor stood and left the room, followed by Capito and Callistus.

As the advisers dispersed Hadrian and Attianus walked out together. "Great idea, Publius," Hadrian complimented his ex-guardian. "We should have tried that long time ago. It may not work, but it's definitely worthwhile. I don't like the tolls either we have to pay to the Parthians and Armenians for our silk. But going to war over it? That's shameful!"

"Yes, it is," the praefect agreed. "Cheer up though, my friend. Trajan has made no such decision."

"He didn't, but I know my cousin. I saw his eyes lighting up when he heard Palma mention Alexander's name. Trajan revels in glory. He may fall for this most appealing temptation. And what's to stop him? Certainly nothing we can do or say."

Attianus sighed. "Most likely Osroes doesn't even know what a blunder he made. This diplomatic misstep couldn't have happened at a worse time. Our generals are drooling to invade already, and Trajan is dreaming to follow in the footsteps of his idol Alexander..."

Chapter 63

Several weeks later Hadrian again raised the issue with Trajan over a family dinner in the Domus Tiberiana. "Have you formed an opinion yet, cousin? Rumor has it you are planning to leave the Capital."

"That's just that, Hadrian. Rumors. I have no plans to leave," Trajan answered stiffly.

"But what are your thoughts, Trajan?"

Plotina joined Hadrian's inquisitive glance at the emperor. The silence was palpable.

"You are both staring at me as if I was holding the fate of the world in my hands," Trajan finally mocked them.

"You do. But that is not why we are prying," Plotina said. "We are worried that you might fall for the generals' ambitions. They are egging you on for their own selfish reasons. I hope you realize that."

"Of course I do, Pompeia. But see, our relationship with Parthia needs to be redefined. For centuries there have been two great empires, ours and theirs. The competition is costing us money and energy. It is forcing us to deploy many men at our eastern borders and pay high prices for imports from the Sinae and India. Three hundred years ago, our forefathers fought war with Carthage over similar issues, and we destroyed the Phoenicians. The Punic Wars were a quest to control the Mediterranean. I wonder whether we don't need another quest now to attain control of the world's trade routes," Trajan argued.

"An epic Roman effort or an epic Trajanic effort?" his sister Marciana asked.

"Don't ridicule me, Marciana! There is no difference. I am Rome. I carry the burden to decide what's wrong and what's right. And I have carried it well for many years. None of you ever had to complain, have you? There is no reason to doubt me now," Trajan snapped, perfectly aware what Marciana was getting at. *Is vanity guiding my decisions or good strategic sense?* The accusation hurt, raising doubts in his mind.

"Absolutely! There was never any reason. You ARE Rome's greatest emperor," Hadrian praised him. "It's just that your wife, your sister, your praefect, me and generals like Senecio strongly feel that invading Parthia is a bad idea. That's all."

"Who can tell the future, cousin? Who knows what is right and what is wrong? I am carefully balancing the empire's interests and I believe we have a historic opportunity. Think about it! What if by eclipsing the Parthian empire we can establish direct contact with the Sinae? I would love to found a Roman colony in the Persian Gulf from which to send cargo ships to the Far

East. What is the risk? Who is going to attack us if we do that? No one!"

"I am not afraid of that," Hadrian clarified. "But I am very afraid of a military disaster in the desert."

"Do you really believe the Parthians are our equal militarily, cousin?" Trajan asked him sharply.

"No, but they will use geography to their advantage. Their empire is vast, protected by pitiless deserts through which we would have to supply our troops. It's daring."

"Daring yes, but doable," Trajan insisted. "No more of this talk! You will find out soon."

"Marcus, you are being irrational," Plotina scolded him. "I have never seen you like that. It's as if you were enamored with Sirens singing their treacherous songs... Wake up! Listen to us and not the generals. The gods wanted the East and the West to be separated. Why else would there be an immense wasteland in between? Even reaching the Gulf by boat from Egypt is almost impossible because no water can be found along the Arab Sea to replenish supplies. We are not making this up, husband. These are hard facts!"

Trajan shot a venomous glance at her and said no more.

The emperor held many more State Councils over the summer and didn't make a final decision until the fall but positioned troops early on. Lusius Quietus arrived in the Capital and was instantly excited about an invasion of Parthia, bonding with the likes of Celsus and Palma. Trajan ordered his Moorish cavalry to ship out to Syria in anticipation of a possible Roman move.

A Parthian embassy arrived in Rome, trying to appease the emperor. To keep with the old Neronian Treaty Osroes proposed Trajan to put the diadem on Parthamasiris's head himself in a formal coronation ceremony in Artaxata. The Parthian delegation also brought precious gifts, but he regarded them as thinly veiled graft and merely deposited them in the Temple of Saturn. Uncompromising, he told the diplomats from Ctesiphon that facts, not words determined the relationship of nations.

Preparations for war continued. Trajan made up his mind but didn't say so right away. He first wanted to get Hadrian on board. Many times, they talked about the pros and cons of the invasion. In the end, Trajan managed to persuade his cousin and even put him in command of the initial expeditionary force. Hadrian and Sabina embarked for Antioch in early July.

In late August Trajan's sister Marciana died from a sudden stroke. She was in her sixties. Her brother was beside himself. Against all precedence, he ordered her immediate deification and a State Funeral. To drown his grief he indulged in plenty of Falernian. Every member of his immediate family was dead now - only glory would live forever!

Still mourning, he offered Pompeia to join him on the campaign. This time he didn't want to leave her behind. Plotina was still recovering herself from Marciana's death. The two had been close for many years and always managed the palace household together in harmony. Trajan was hoping the distraction would be good for her. The empress was thankful indeed; she had never seen the eastern provinces. At last she could join her husband on his travels abroad.

They departed in late September and arrived at the end of the year. As ordered, Hadrian had assembled an army of eighty thousand that waited for the imperial couple at Antioch, the Syrian capital.

After checking on the corps's military readiness and not without reminiscing his formative years in Antioch with his father, Trajan and the army left for Satala in April, the designated Roman forward base of operations in eastern Cappadocia. Their first target would be Artaxata. Hadrian stayed behind, in charge of Syria.

Tracking the Roman advance, the Parthians frantically sent delegations to dissuade the emperor, but Trajan called their proposals unacceptable. His army marched on, reaching the Roman fortress of Melitene on the Euphrates River. There, he received a letter from Parthamasiris, who offered to present himself to him and receive the crown from the emperor. Trajan derided the letter as not appropriate. Without answering, he pressed on.

Another dispatch arrived, this time keeping with protocol and diplomatic convention but still insisting on Parthamasiris's legitimate rule. This time Trajan answered and sent ambassadors of his own. In May the army reached Satala and united with vexillations from the Danube army. The combined corps was over one hundred thousand men strong now: nine full strength legions plus auxiliaries.

After some diplomatic back and forth, Trajan and Parthamasiris agreed to meet in Elegeia, an Armenian town one hundred and ten miles east of Satala and one hundred and eighty miles west of Artaxata. Offending the Roman sense of pride, Parthamasiris and his detail came late to the parley. Trajan was left waiting for hours in the southern heat until the Parthian delegation finally arrived. He received them sulking on an elevated curule chair, surrounded by his aides and generals.

The Armenian usurper strutted before him in the finest emerald kaftan and pledged, "Your Majesty, Ruler of the World, I bow to you. Please accept my most sincere apologies for being late to this important parley. We were attacked by marauding supporters of Exedares and had to take a different route. I beg you, ask my men. The fighting was heavy and we took casualties. Fortunately, as we came closer to Elegeia they withdrew."

"Is that so?" Trajan mocked him, seeing that none of the king's guards showed any sign of disheveling, combat or injuries. "I haven't seen any brigands, but go on."

Parthamasiris looked at him irritated. Then he said, "I have come here to pay homage to you, great Caesar. Please be so generous and confirm me as the righteous ruler of Armenia." He took off his diadem and put it on the ground, expecting Trajan to pick it up and put it back on his skull.

Trajan lowered his gaze at the crown. Suddenly, the Roman soldiers and generals about him called out, "*Imperator! Imperator! Imperator!*"

When the soldiers ceased their acclamation, Trajan addressed the usurper. "I do not recognize your rule, Parthamasiris. You are a Parthian puppet. Your regrets are coming too late. From now on, Armenia will be a Roman province."

At these words, armed Praetorians with drawn swords surrounded the Armenian delegation and took the surprised embassy prisoner.

The next day the Romans fanned out in three columns to secure Armenia while Parthamasiris was sent off with an escort of cavalry to be returned to his brother, the Parthian king. Trajan and Plotina stayed in Elegeia with the Guard. The emperor was looking forward to spending quality time with Pompeia in the exotic eastern city, but Plotina was very unhappy. "Trajan, what are you doing? I didn't think you would decide for war. I thought..." She interrupted herself, wiping the tears from her eyes. "I hoped... showing our strength was only a ploy to dissuade any further Parthian aggression. We have achieved that. Rome has saved face. Parthamasiris is rebuked. His overlord knows now we are not going to tolerate his violation of the treaty. I thought we are done here!"

"Pompeia, you don't understand. I want more than reprieve. I want to follow in Alexander's footsteps!"

"You fool!" Plotina shrieked, her voice cracking. "Are you going to have thousands of Roman soldiers killed just to live out your fancy???"

"Not at all, but-"

Plotina didn't allow him to finish his sentence. "Your vanity disgusts me! I despise you, Marcus Ulpius Traianus. You have lost both your wisdom and your humanity. Fine, go ahead, have your petty war, but know this: You have my respect no more!"

Trajan tried to explain again, but the empress turned away and scurried off to the atrium of their residence weeping.

Conquering the new province took all summer as the army encountered heavy resistance in the southern highlands until it was crushed by Lusius Quietus's elite cavalry. During this time Trajan received embassies from all over Armenia and the surrounding countries. Even some Parthian satraps came to Elegeia and pledged allegiance to the Roman emperor. Monarchs visited from as far away as the Crimea and Armenia's northern neighbors between the Black and Caspian Sea.

Trajan enjoyed his stay in Elegeia until news arrived that insurgents loyal to ex-King Exedares had killed the usurper Parthamasiris on his trip back to Ctesiphon. Trajan wrote a letter to Osroes, assuring him he had no involvement in this regrettable tragedy asserting that Parthamasiris had escaped the Roman escort and must have run into Exedares's men somewhere in the countryside.

The Parthian king sent no reply. All other diplomatic efforts were successful, however, and with few exceptions the satraps and kings around Armenia reiterated their loyalty to Rome. Then Trajan sent General Catilius to Artaxata to take over as the first Roman governor of Armenia Province. By the end of the year, the Romans had full control of the country's valleys and river crossings. The last remnants of Armenian resistance were pinned down in the highlands. Unsatisfied, Trajan ordered a network of garrisons and forts to contain a potential insurgency in Armenia's Caucasian hinterland.

Still, Osroes had yet to be punished. The emperor made his move in the spring and launched preparations for a full-scale invasion of Parthia proper. First he had to take Upper Mesopotamia. Again Quietus took the field. Trajan followed with the main host. They crossed the Taurus Mountains, leaving permanent garrisons behind along the way to secure their supply lines and buttress a potential retreat.

Despite his age Trajan always marched on foot at the head of the army as he had done all his life - even when they forded frigid rivers. Despite the physical exhaustion he had never been happier. He so relished being in the footsteps of Alexander the Great – as he called it.

Unopposed on their way south and with time on their hands, Trajan ordered his troops to practice battle scenarios, but Upper Mesopotamia fell quickly. In the fall the Romans swept Lower Mesopotamia with Trajan's trademark pincer move of parallel army columns. The emperor completed the annexation of the whole country and installed another Roman provincial government.

The dual conquests of Armenia and Mesopotamia were the equivalent of an official declaration of war aimed at the Parthian king. Mesopotamia was his land after all, yet Osroes held still. He still had not been able to sign a peace agreement with his rival Vologaeses, forcing him to deploy large numbers of his best troops in the eastern parts of his dominion. The king had no choice but to watch the rapid Roman advance through Mesopotamia.

The military conquests went well, but then riots broke out behind the Roman lines - inside the empire. In Alexandria, tensions flared between the local Greek and Jewish communities. Civil strife had been on the rise for years, and Trajan had arbitrated between the parties in the past. This time, however, there was no holding back. The riots surged into battles on the streets of Alexandria, transforming the inner city into a war zone. The emperor had to send legionary infantry. Egypt's praefect used them to restore order by cracking down on the Jews but also forced the Greek population to apply restraint. In addition, Trajan sent a civilian judge to investigate the matter and find a political solution for the untimely turmoil.

Despite this distraction, in February of the following year and three years after his arrival in Antioch, Trajan completed the transformation of Mesopotamia into a Roman province and sent a laurelled letter to the Senate in Rome. The senators granted him a Triumph and the title *Parthicus*, Conqueror of the Parthians, and ordered celebratory games in the Circus Maximus.

Itching for more, Trajan made his final move: the assault on Parthia's core lands between the lower Euphrates and the lower Tigris. The advance proved lengthy and difficult. The troops had to cross hundreds of miles of bone-dry desert. To manage at all the army marched along the Euphrates River. Parallel to them, a fleet of fifty river galleys and cargo ships sailed down the river, with the imperial couple lodged on the flagship, a huge trireme hoisting an immense sail that displayed the emperor's name and his titles in golden letters.

The Euphrates River emptied its waters into a marshy area before it connected with the Tigris south of Ctesiphon, the target of the Roman expedition. These peaty waters were not deep enough to support the Roman fleet so Trajan's pioneers beached the vessels where the Euphrates was closest to the Tigris, put them on capstan rollers, pulled them over a distance of twenty miles with manpower and camels, and launched them back into the Tigris several days later. Sailing down from there, Trajan reached Seleucia and entered the city without meeting any Parthian resistance.

Trajan was stunned. Though they were close to the enemy's Capital now, the Parthians held still. Why? Praefect Attianus didn't like it either. As it turned out, Osroes had abandoned Ctesiphon and retreated with his troops over the Zagros Mountains. Apparently he did not feel strong enough to defend the capital. Trajan shrugged and gave the signal to advance.

Entering Ctesiphon resembled a triumph procession more than armed conquest. Parthian civilians were lining the streets by the thousands, waving pennants of welcome at the Roman soldiers. It was hard to tell how many people had abandoned the city with their king, but there were certainly thousands and thousands of men and women left. Trajan strutted into the palace with the Praetorian Guard and sank into the Golden Throne in the great audience hall of the king of kings. Osroes's realm was now his - a moment to behold! No Roman had ever managed to do this...

The emperor was elated but also bothered by the fact that Osroes had not put up a fight. He had simply relinquished large swaths of territory. Yes, there had been battles and sieges against him in the North but no encounter one-on-one with the king himself – unlike Alexander who had defeated Darius in person in several epic battles.

Trajan sighed. If Osroes didn't want to fight, he didn't want to fight. There was nothing he could do. He and Plotina were mesmerized by the breathtaking Parthian Capital, captured intact, and the many different colorful cultures and races dwelling here.

The emperor didn't rest long; he had his sights set on the next target, the Persian Gulf. After leaving behind a substantial garrison, the Romans continued their advance down the Tigris, sailing all the way to the Gulf of Persia where the imperial couple set foot in the port city of Charax, the last Parthian outpost. Reaching the docks, they saw a merchant ship sailing off in the direction of India. Tears welled up in Trajan's tired eyes. He flung his arm around Pompeia's shoulders, speaking softly, "If I were only younger, we could follow this ship and sail to the Indi. How much I would give for that..."

Pompeia consoled him. "You have accomplished more than any other mortal, Marcus. In my book, that includes even the great Alexander! Let's not go any farther. Attianus says our lines are stretched thin. Enjoy the moment, but let us not linger here too long."

Trajan gave her a kiss. "Just give me one day. It means so much to me."

They quietly watched the merchant ship as it slowly disappeared on the horizon. "Thank you for everything, dearest Pompeia. Thank you for sticking with me, for being my wife and empress – and friend. You could have left me many years ago." He barely managed to get the words out.

Here was the master of the known world - thanking her, a woman. But all she saw was an old man with gray and white hair, a sun-ravaged face, cracked lips and sagging shoulders, her husband who needed her care and attention. *Yes, why am still with him? What is it about Trajan? Is it his brawn? Or his kindness? Or his unwavering sense for justice? I do not know.*

They had been through much together: Domitian's terror, the volatile reign of Nerva, the Dacian Wars. Yet, she was still here, by his side, his empress, his spouse.

Plotina had always had a soft spot for his better looking cousin. But no one would ever know, not even Hadrian...

Finally she answered her husband, "It was meant to be, Marcus, the god's will. We are the imperial couple, a fixture of Roman society. People will talk about us for millennia to come. How could I run away from that? How could I tarnish your rule with scandal? Never! You are my husband. You always will be. You are the kindest and greatest ruler Rome ever had!" She clasped her hands around his neck, tenderly kissed his lips.

Trajan hugged her even tighter, caressing her hair while they enjoyed the soft touch of the Gulf's breeze.

Chapter 64

The next day the fleet turned around and rowed upriver, heading for the ancient city of Babylon. Located on the banks of the Euphrates, they could not reach it on the big vessels. So they abandoned them, burning the galleys to make sure the Parthians could not appropriate them. The ensuing land route was long and arduous, and Trajan suffered badly in the heat. Crito diagnosed him with dropsy and ordered him to stay on the carriage at all times. The long campaign had worn down his old frame. Pompeia urged him to go slow, but Trajan pressed on.

In the fall they reached the fabled city: Babylon, the cradle of civilization, a ruin town now but impressive nonetheless.

Trajan was eager to visit the chamber in which Alexander had supposedly died. He was awestruck when they found it, feeling more like a tourist than a conqueror. But he could not indulge. Terrible news arrived from the North: The competing Parthian rulers Osroes and Vologaeses had resolved their differences at last and retaken the initiative by appointing another nephew of Osroes, one Sanatruces, as King of Armenia. This nephew showed great skill in instigating revolts all over Armenia and Mesopotamia, expelling or killing many Roman garrisons.

Additionally, Vologaeses's army threatened Armenia, and Osroes was preparing to recover Ctesiphon. Seleucia had already fallen. To top it all off, Jewish unrest, fueled by Parthian gold, had erupted all over the eastern half of the empire now, even hitting the great cities of Cyrene and Edessa. In Cyprus, the mob had overwhelmed local police and coerced Greek and Roman civilians to kill each other in the amphitheater. Arab caravan magnates were joining the uprising in an effort to protect their trade turf, regarding Trajan's invasion of the East as a direct threat to their profits. An incursion was reported in Britannia where Caledonians had invaded the province. And the Roxolani had taken advantage of the depleted Danube legions and invaded the new province of Dacia.

The only dispatch not relating to turmoil and bloodshed came from Rome: Tacitus had published another history book, called *Annales*.

What have I done? What will historians write about me now? How will they rate my military prowess?

Trajan almost despaired. He was at a crossroads now. He HAD TO turn the crisis around, save the Parthian campaign, crush the insurgents. Clearly, the internal unrest had been timed to occur in his absence and the absence of his troops. The Parthian revolt was not a surprise; he had expected them to take up arms eventually. But their timing was a cunning blow to Roman supremacy. He would have to act decisively, deflect their cunning with his own.

First, he sent troops from Syria to Egypt and Cyrene under Admiral Turbo. In Mesopotamia, he deployed crack troops and the Moorish cavalry under Quietus to recover the key cities and expel the Jewish populations to foil their efforts in helping the Parthian counter-attack.

In a sly move, he offered parley to King Vologaeses and arranged an armistice with him in exchange for returning to him the eastern half of Armenia. That gave him the resources to deal with Osroes. Trajan's troops moved swiftly, reconquering Seleucia and burning it to the ground. Then Trajan returned to Ctesiphon and put a renegade son of Osroes, one Parthamaspates, on the Golden Throne, an implicit admission of Roman weakness though because the original plan had been to make Parthia a province, not a client kingdom. At least, it gave him some breathing room and divided the Parthians again. Without Vologaeses's help Osroes was neutralized.

Then the emperor hurried north to squash the rebellion in Mesopotamia. He needed to retake the strategic city of Hatra which controlled the main road between Mesopotamia and Babylon and the grasslands west of the Tigris. Whoever controlled Hatra controlled Mesopotamia.

The Roman troops attacked with determination, but despite several successful wall breaches they were repulsed. Settling for a siege, Trajan and his men dug in. Soon, however, many fell sick, including the imperial couple. The water around Hatra appeared toxic. Only the city itself had access to a healthy perennial spring. All other water sources were filthy. In addition, Trajan's men could not find enough wood to build enough siege engines. They also lacked fodder and food and suffered from a myriad of flies and mosquitoes that spread even more diseases.

With the approach of winter the weather turned bad as well. Thunderstorms and hail hit the unprotected men, rendering the ground muddy. Roman troop movements almost came to a halt. At that point Trajan decided to abort the siege and retreat to Syria. The Parthians had prevailed...

When Hadrian welcomed his cousin in Antioch in February, he was shocked to see him. Trajan's cheeks were hollow; his eyes looked watery and sick. The doctor confirmed Trajan suffered from gout and a weak heart.

Plotina implored her husband to return to Rome. "He has suffered enough," she told Hadrian. "The campaign started like a pushover and ended in a nightmare. Attianus says we should give up our Parthian ambitions. They simply exceed our resources. Given the vicious rebellions all over the empire, I agree with him, Hadrian."

"That's what I was afraid of," Hadrian said. "Not that I predicted the Jewish unrest, but I knew that capturing Parthia would be risky. Now it's a calamity. As a consequence of our invasion the Arab and Jewish merchants are paranoid of losing their trade partners in the East. But I am not sure this is the only explanation for the unrest. Tensions between Jews and Greeks have been brewing for a long time. And maybe it's really a Jewish outburst against the whole Hellenized world, driven by their fanatical worship of an unforgiving single god. No matter the reasons, the timing indicates Parthian involvement." He bit his lips.

"Not all is lost. Trajan made Quietus Governor of Judaea. If anyone can keep a lid on this terrible revolt, it is Quietus - as much as I hate his methods." She paused, looking down on the ground. Then she lifted her head and grabbed Hadrian's shoulders with her hands, shaking him. "Listen to me, Hadrian. Trajan needs you now. It's not the time to say 'I told you so.' Help your cousin! He needs you! The empire needs you!"

Taken aback, Hadrian pulled away. Then he reconsidered, strode up to the empress and gave her a warm hug. "I will, dearest Pompeia," he assured the lady who had always championed him. "I will help him. I will do my part."

Chapter 65

The imperial yacht cruised west at a leisurely pace. Trajan, his elbows propped against the gunnel, was watching the ship's oars swing to and fro on the blue water of the Mediterranean – to and fro, up and down, to and fro, up and down... *How majestic,* he thought. *Order, not chaos. The strength of men combined into one purpose: steady, gentle propulsion.* In addition, the main sail was fluttering above him to aid the men's effort, but the breeze was feeble, having prompted the captain to put in the rowers' muscle power.

Trajan stood at the starboard rail, close to the imperial stateroom, which would be his and Plotina's home for the next several weeks until their arrival in Ostia. The stateroom was cavernous, covering the whole aft of the ship and containing several rooms spread out on different levels and equipped with all the amenities deemed worthy of a Roman Emperor and his entourage.

The yacht itself was a transformed *navis speculatoria*, a fast and elegant cruiser, completely decked over, but with only one row of oars sticking out on either side of the hull. The builder had dyed its two sails purple at great cost to signify the ship from afar as the emperor's personal yacht. A small canvas stretched out in front of the stateroom, providing Trajan with shade and gave his cracked cheeks relief from the simmering heat.

His rheumy eyes studied the treeless Cilician shoreline they had been hugging for days now. It was somewhere on this coast where pirates had captured young Julius Caesar almost two hundred years ago. The Mediterranean at the time had been infested with buccaneers because of the Republican government's unwillingness to empower its admirals and provide an adequate fleet. After all, a successful commander could have become too powerful...

How ironic. Here I am, more powerful than the Republican Senate could have ever imagined. Yes, this is why the Republic had failed. The system of checks and balances had stopped working, leading to paralysis and decay.

Extensive debates he had waged with Tacitus over the years flitted through his mind. The aristocratic-minded historian had admitted that Trajan was right, admonishing the emperor to obey the Law and keep Republican traditions alive. *Tacitus... Will I see you again?*

The emperor's gaze returned to the monotonous coastline. The pirates had hidden young Caesar in one of the countless coves, picking a location far away from the cities but close to their lair. Convinced that Caesar would never be able to distinguish one cove from the other – watching the shoreline now Trajan couldn't blame them – they hadn't deemed it necessary to cover his eyes during the trip. When he asserted he would come back, recover the ransom and punish their crime, they had merely laughed, feeling so safe that they let him go when the ransom was in fact handed over.

But Caesar did memorize each and every cove when his ship sailed him back to safety. Years later he returned with a Roman fleet, caught the buccaneers by surprise and crucified them to the last man.

Ahhh, Caesar, the daredevil... Never afraid, always bold, sometimes reckless – to the very end. A fond smile tugged Trajan's burnt lips. The story was incredible - the stuff legends were made of, almost Homerian.

"Marcus," Plotina interrupted his musings. "You are putting on your nicest smile today. What is so delightful?"

Trajan spun round. "Oh, it's nothing, Pompeia. I was merely pondering how Julius Caesar was able to remember all those seemingly identical coves over there." He pointed to the passing shore on the right. "Do you know how he did it?"

She shook her head.

"He counted them."

Pompeia chuckled. "Really? Unbelievable..."

Annoyed, Trajan raised his eyebrows. "This is not funny. Caesar WAS incredible." He turned back to the gunwale, leaning out over the sea.

Plotina eased up to him, laying her arm on his shoulder. "I am sorry, Marcus. I didn't mean to belittle your idol. It's just that your unbridled admiration sometimes amuses me."

"It's all right," Trajan grumbled. "I know how you meant it. You still get me each time - after all those years..."

They both laughed.

Trajan's limp arm caught Plotina's gaze. "How is your arm today?" she asked.

Since the stroke he had suffered in Antioch some months ago, he had not been able to use it. Pompeia and Callistus were taking care of his correspondence now. Plotina had even learned how to sign on his behold.

"It is unfortunately not getting any better," Trajan snarled. "The arm doesn't hurt, but it pains me to be so incapacitated." He didn't tell her his bowels didn't feel right either. She was worrying enough already.

"I understand, Marcus. We would all feel that way."

He could read the concern in her recessed eyes. *By Jupiter, this cursed campaign has taken its toll on all of us...*

"Come with me," she asked him. "Let's eat. I was told the cook has prepared a delicious meal."

"Fine. Let's go."

Callistus was waiting for them in the galley. "Here you are, Master," he bubbled. "I have asked the chef to prepare your favorite dish today: fresh shrimps dunked in artichoke sauce – as opposed to what the good doctor prescribes you all the time."

Lingering behind Callistus, Crito cleared his throat, responding with the dignified voice of the chief *medicus,* "I am only doing my duty, secretary. Besides, our Lord's health is to be taken seriously." He lightened up with a swift smile and added, "Sometimes, my Lord, it is allowed to follow one's... hm, shall I say... culinary desires?"

They chuckled.

"Shall we?" Callistus asked.

Praefect Attianus came around the corner and joined them. "Here you are," he said. "I thought I would have to eat by myself."

"Not that it would be hard for you," Phaedimus teased him. Trajan's second secretary had joined the imperial party in Antioch and now assisted Callistus with the extensive imperial correspondence. On the ship, he contributed in many other ways, by helping in the galley and by buying goods when they pulled into port to replenish their supplies.

Only Trajan's grandniece Matidia was missing from the imperial company. She was suffering a hangover from last night's supper when she had indulged in the wine too much and expressed no desire to see anyone.

The chef had pulled the shrimps from their shells and minced the meat so it would be easier for Trajan to eat. He dug in with delight.

"Are you looking forward to your Parthian Triumph, Master?" Phaedimus asked the emperor.

Trajan he wiped his lips with a napkin and nodded.

"I mean, it's going to be great, won't it?" Phaedimus said, arching his eyebrows.

Trajan studied the faces around the table before answering. Plotina put on her flat face, braving his gaze. Callistus glanced at the kerchief around his neck with the utmost interest, as if he had never seen such an object ever before in his life. Crito shifted on his sofa, avoiding eye contact with anybody else.

At last, Attianus spoke, "It is going to be a great triumph, no doubt - the greatest ever!"

"Of course I am looking forward to my Triumph, Phaedimus," Trajan finally answered the delicate question. "The Senate has granted it unprompted, and I worked hard for it. No Roman ever sat on the Golden Throne before me. But-" He paused, pointing his good arm at the others. "As you can see from the lackluster enthusiasm in this room, we don't know how well I have succeeded - it is unclear in fact. My Triumph may be nothing more than propaganda."

A pang of uneasiness swept Trajan while he replied, gripping his throat. Lately, courier ships had conferred more bad news. Not one day passed without appalling reports from everywhere. The Parthians were still endeavoring to overthrow their new masters, and no end was in sight for the Civil War-like skirmishes between Jews and Greeks. All sides seemed to have waited for Rome's weakness.

The situation was worst in Alexandria. Marcius Turbo was there now to quell the turmoil. He would hopefully put down the unrest, but the trouble had forced Trajan to give him troops that were desperately needed in Mesopotamia. Then there was Armenia – they had lost half the new province before setting sail for Rome. Now Hadrian was commander-in-chief of the Eastern armies. It was up to him to hold the conquered lands. *Another irony – Hadrian, who had opposed the invasion in the first place! I should have listened to him.*

Attianus spoke again, "You see, Phaedimus, our beloved emperor has not recovered yet from the hardships of campaigning. We are returning to Rome, but the war in the East isn't over. Word has gone around of our troubles, and mischief-makers are trying to take their share of the wounded empire. But we will prevail. We always do."

"What I am really angry about," Trajan added. "Is the treachery of the Jews not only in Palestine but also in the diaspora. They waited until the Parthian invasion and struck when we were most vulnerable. I will never forgive them. Fortunately, they are a minority, and most of the other provincials support our troops. Still, thousands of innocent people have died. Many cities in Egypt, Judaea and Syria have been ravaged. It's a huge distraction for our commanders."

"What about the Parthians, Trajan?" Phaedimus wanted to know. "Do you think they will kick us out?"

"Hard to say," Trajan answered, pensively rubbing his cheeks. "It is possible, but I hope not. All depends on Hadrian."

"He will do well," Plotina said full of confidence. "If it is possible, he will hold them at bay."

Attianus was not so sure. "I don't doubt Hadrian's capabilities whatsoever, Empress, but it will be difficult. And some of his officers are questioning his commitment. Quietus hates him."

"Rubbish," Trajan snapped. "They will follow his orders. His orders are my orders. I made that very clear to all of them, including Quietus."

The old praefect shifted his head. "Excuse me, Caesar. I didn't mean to be impudent. On a different note: Would you mind to conjoin my wounded men tonight? They always relish your company, Majesty."

A century of Praetorian horseguards was with them on the ship. They had protected Trajan throughout the tough campaign. Many of them were suffering from a variety of missile injuries as Parthian bowmen had often targeted the emperor during the siege of Hatra. The arrows had missed their target but wounded several of the bodyguards.

"Of course! It is time for me to make my rounds. I hope their wounds are healing despite the rocking of the ship." *And myself*, he admitted to himself. He needed some healing, too. Something was very wrong. He felt miserable but did not mention anything to the others. Before he shuffled back on deck, his gaze met Pompeia's. She looked at him apprehensively. *Does she suspect?*

Chapter 66

As always, Trajan took great pleasure sharing ribaldries with the men whose tents were pitched amidships. The rankers beamed when he addressed them by name. Trajan felt bad that he couldn't be closer to them on the ship, but Crito had insisted on the comfortable quarters in the stern. *Me in a plush stateroom on a plush yacht – how silly... Getting old is no fun.* Suddenly, he felt a sting in his stomach. He writhed with pain, lost his balance, tumbled and could barely hang on to a rope that was dangling from the ship's mast. He clung to it to regain his footing when an attentive sailor jumped to his aid.

"I am fine," Trajan assured the man. "I am fine, thank you, *nauta,* thank you." He collected all his will power to stand straight and return to the stateroom. Faster and faster he strode despite the discomfort. He needed to get to the latrine at once. *Must have been the food...* He did succeed and relieved himself, but on the way back to the deck the bulkheads spun about him. He tumbled once more and crashed down on the ship's planks. Darkness put an end to it all.

When he woke up, Trajan found himself bundled up in his cot. Every bone in his body was aching. He felt nauseous and was sweating profusely. His skull hurt as if the hellhound Cerberus himself kept hammering a mallet against his forehead.

The emperor wondered how long he had been unconscious. He could tell the ship was still pushing along at the same steady pace. He could hear the drums on the mid deck, dictating the vessel's cruising speed. The oars were splashing on the water at the same monotonous rhythm.

After what seemed an eternity the door opened and Plotina stepped into the room. "Juno be thanked - you are awake!" she cried.

He struggled to keep his eyes focused on her. They felt like they were burning...

Pompeia touched his forehead with the backside of her hand. Trajan noticed the wrinkle lines of sorrow at the corners of her mouth.

"Trajan, you are still running a fever," she muttered. "Crito thinks the shrimp must have been tainted. Phaedimus is sick as well. How are you doing?"

"I've seen better days," he croaked.

Plotina walked around the cot and lifted a cup from his nightstand. "Drink this. It's your medicine. The doctor has made it for you; it will diminish the fever."

She had to hold his cup for him as he slurped Crito's concoction. It tasted bitter, but he would drink sewage water now if it helped. His head fell back and he fell asleep again.

After one last unhappy glance at her ailing husband Plotina returned to Attianus and the others. Crito, Matidia and Callistus were huddling on the top deck with the praefect.

"We should pull into port," Callistus demanded.

"I am not so sure. It would delay our journey, and I don't believe anybody on land can help him any better than our good doctor here," Attianus warned.

"I am flattered," Crito said. "But I am lacking ingredients to formulate better medicine. Let's wait and see how he is doing over the next several hours, but if his condition doesn't improve, we should indeed head to the closest harbor."

"I agree with Crito," Plotina pleaded. "The up and down of the ship cannot be good for Trajan. He had diarrhea; now he is running a fever and is barely conscious. His heart is weak anyway after the cursed war. I am worried. If Trajan were to die now... Unthinkable!"

"He won't die, Pompeia," Attianus assured her.

Plotina could hear the effort in his voice. The praefect tried to spread confidence, but he didn't fool her.

In the end they agreed to heed Crito's advice. Even Attianus.

Trajan did not get better. At sunrise they woke the rowers to make haste for the closest port, the Cilician town of Selinus in southern Asia Minor. Attianus ordered maximum speed. The imperial yacht reached Selinus Harbor after three hours where the Praetorians requisitioned the best inn in town and set up camp for the imperial entourage.

Attianus's men carried Trajan and Phaedimus off the ship on two separate litters and behind closed curtains. Nobody was supposed to see the suffering emperor. Though much younger than Trajan, Phaedimus was also running a high fever. Over the course of the day the two men's condition stayed the same. Neither one was awake much. Crito sent out his assistants to pick herbs he didn't have on board of the ship.

In the evening he sat down with Plotina, Matidia, Attianus and Callistus to give his report in the hostel's dining room. The praefect had cleared the inn off all guests, compensating them generously and instructing them not to talk to anyone about this.

"I am not exactly clear what is wrong with my patients," Crito opened. "I still believe they are suffering from some sort of food poisoning."

"But we have all eaten the same food, Titus," Matidia countered upset.

"We don't know that for sure," the doctor insisted. "They could have been infected in Antioch. Sometimes it takes a while to have an effect on you, perhaps triggered by the rocking of the ship on the waves."

Trajan's niece glared at him.

"Anyway," Plotina said in a brittle voice. She was getting more and more concerned. "Can you help them?"

"I don't know. I am afraid their fate is in *Aesculapius's* hands," he answered.

"What do you mean, *medicus*?" Attianus roared. "Is he going to die? Are you telling us he is going to die from some stupid food poisoning?"

"I am not saying he is going to die at all, but I do believe his condition is serious. It's not just the food poisoning. His body is weak from years of campaigning in the desert, from the stroke he had and, frankly, from old age. I do know his heart is not the best anymore. Also, he is dehydrated after all the sweating and the outbreak of diarrhea yesterday. His stool was bloody and he is running a stubborn fever - another strain on his frail heart. I am trying everything to get the fever down. So far without success, but the new herbs I have will hopefully help.

Look, I don't know what else to tell you. Trajan is suffering a witch's brew of things all coming together at the same time," Crito summarized.

"In other words, Titus, he might die and he might not. You don't know," Callistus said the obvious.

"Yes, Callistus, but cheer up. The human body can be resilient and our Master has been through physical ordeals before. If he were ten years younger, I wouldn't even worry," Crito encouraged them. "Let me go see the patients now. I will watch over them all night and attend to their medication in person."

"How is Phaedimus?" Plotina asked.

"He has the same fever, but he is young. It is strange though that he has not made more progress. Maybe age won't help after all. Hm... Anyway, my assistants will keep a close eye on him."

Crito rose and left the dining room. The others kept poking at their food without much interest. The doctor's words had depressed the empress. After a while Callistus stood and lit more oil lamps. The day was coming to an end, relieving them from the simmering summer heat. Through the windows they could see the busy harbor and the docked imperial yacht. Supplies were being brought to the ship, and Praetorian guards patrolled the port facilities.

"I think I will go for a walk," Pompeia suddenly said. "I need to clear my mind..."

"Take an escort with you," Attianus offered, but Plotina shook her head. "Thank you, Publius. Not necessary. Nobody will come after me, not here in Selinus. I feel perfectly safe."

Attianus frowned but left it at that.

"And I will get back to work," Callistus said with a heavy sigh. "I need a distraction."

Chapter 67

Selinus was not a large town, but its port was an important supply station for ships en route between Greece and Syria. Even now, in the twilight after dusk, slaves and servants scampered back and forth on the docks to service the cargo holds of the moored boats. They also carried fresh food and water to the ships in wooden vats and clay *amphorae*. Night would take hold soon and make their task harder, forcing them to rely on torches for illumination.

Plotina gawked at the hustle in the harbor when she stepped out of the inn. She knew the brimming activities would continue well into the night and the clatter of iron cartwheels on the streets would keep her from falling asleep. She would have to close the windows tight and maybe have the slaves mount bulky drapes as well. But then again, the heat would foil that. Hopefully, Neptune would blow a cooling breeze into the port.

She pushed off and joined the busy street traffic. Her thoughts were circling around Trajan's deteriorating health; she barely noticed anything around her. Closing the windows of his room would be a bad idea, she scolded herself. Trajan's recovery should be her priority. He was sweating more than enough already and would not have an issue with the ruckus from the streets. Crito HAD to break the fever which had Trajan in a merciless grip, tossing him in and out of an agonizing consciousness. *Trajan, my love... You must not die!*

The empress continued to amble on the hectic streets. She nearly misstepped at the edge of a pier, but a sailor grabbed her arm at the last moment and yanked her back to safety. Plotina expressed her gratitude, angry with herself for not having paid more attention to the ground.

She wasn't sure whether the man recognized her. Busts of the imperial couple were of course on display and printed on the coinage everywhere in the empire. If the *nauta* recognized her, he didn't show it. He wished her a good night and scurried off, leaving an exasperated Plotina behind.

She considered returning to the inn but then dropped the idea. *I need more time to calm my agitated mind.* She set out again, heading away from the ships and towards the forum. After a while, she noticed that someone was stalking her. Whoever he was, he stopped each time she did, keeping the same distance to her. Plotina smiled. *Attianus - always looking out for me.* He must have ignored her wish, sending a covert bodyguard after her. The stalker surely was a Praetorian. She had seen his face on the ship though she couldn't recall his name. The man must have gasped when she had almost fallen into the dirty basin water. *Well then, as long as he doesn't bother me.*

After sauntering through Selina's inner city, Pompeia felt calm enough to return. At the inn, she headed straight for Trajan's chamber. Two grim look-ing Praetorians outside the door snapped to attention as she walked in.

Her husband was unconscious. Crito, Attianus and a maid were with him. The skin of his forehead was still burning hot. She could tell the sweat-ing had not let up either. The maid held a wet cloth to Trajan's cheeks to cool him. Crito was sitting at the edge of the bed while Attianus was standing motionless against the wall.

A weak smile tugged the doctor's thin lips when Plotina entered. "*Ave, Pompeia*. As you can see, his condition is unchanged."

"It is heart-breaking," Attianus croaked. "He is burning up!"

Pompeia stared at Trajan's emaciated face with great distress. What should they do? Call for some local priests or physicians? Sacrifice to *Aes-culapius* and all the gods of Eternal Rome? Or should they rush the emperor home by boat as Attianus had suggested? What if he died here? What to tell Hadrian and the Senate? There was no appointed successor...

Pompeia covered her face, sobbing. But quickly she pulled herself to-gether. "Do something, Crito," she implored the doctor. "He is not getting better. Can't you see? Trajan must not die! Do you understand that? He must not die!" Tears rolled down her face as she squeezed Trajan's hand.

"Your Majesty," Crito said with a low voice. "I am doing everything in my power." He bowed and walked out. Attianus strode after him, but Plotina held him back. "Attianus, please stay."

He frowned. "My Lady?"

Plotina wiped down her tears and sent out the maid. Then she said, "We need to talk."

Here they were, Publius Acilius Attianus, Praefect of the Praetorian Guard and the empire's First Minister and Pompeia Plotina, empress and wife of Trajan, ruler of known civilized world, and there seemed to be nothing they could do to save the most important man on earth.

"Yes?" Attianus asked. "What is it?"

"As much as I have a hard time adjusting to the fact that Trajan might, I repeat, MIGHT die, and as much as I hate to think about this, we need to talk about his succession." There! The cat was out of the bag...

Attianus braved the intense gaze in her glistening eyes. "I realize that," he said. "But this is not up to us. The Senate must pick the new ruler."

"Nonsense," Plotina hissed. "The Senate expects Trajan to name a suc-cessor. We need my husband to make his decision when he wakes up. If not, we might run out of time. Ambitious senators and generals will step forward and claim the throne. It is up to us to preserve the stability of the empire."

"Years ago Trajan told the Senate he would give them ten names to choose from. He said it would ultimately be their decision," Attianus reminded her.

"Yes, but Trajan has not acted since then. He didn't feel a need. How could he know he would suddenly fall sick?"

Attianus cleared his throat. "He has been in bad health for a while now, Majesty. I am afraid he may not have made up his mind. He mentioned Neratius Priscus to me as a possible candidate once, yet he recently appointed Hadrian commander-in-chief of the eastern army. I don't know where he stands right now."

"That is why we need to act. I want him to adopt Hadrian and appoint him Caesar, just like Nerva adopted Trajan. I cannot see a better system: A great ruler picks the next great ruler. Adoption is the only way because it grants legitimacy. Attianus, do you agree?"

The praefect turned a long, startled glance at her. Then he tipped his head and said, "I do, my Lady, you have my countenance. Hadrian was my ward as much as he was Trajan's, and I have seen how capable he is. He would be a great ruler."

Plotina heaved a sigh of relief. *He is with me.* "Then we need to make it happen." *Not just Hadrian's career, the well-being of the whole empire is at stake,* she thought shuddering. *We cannot leave it to the Senate; too many players, too many interests. Failure would spawn instability, possibly Civil War.*

She called for the maid and ordered her to be waken up at once when Trajan regained consciousness. Attianus gave her a brief nod and then returned to his quarter. The maid settled on the chair nearest Trajan.

Pompeia opened the windows all the way to let in more air. The breeze felt good on her sticky skin and the sodium-rich air from the sea soothed her lungs. She took several long and deep breaths, forcing herself to relax. Then she lay down on the other bed in the room. Plotina turned on her side, closed her eyes. The breeze from the sea was pleasant and reassuring, but she couldn't find peace. The weight of the world was weighing her down.

On the other bed, dreams of battles and palaces, olive fields and war galleys ravaged Trajan's subconscious mind. He was back in Parthia, admiring the beauty of the Gulf, then he lived through the earthquake again that had almost killed him in Antioch, then he was back in Italica, visiting the Baths with his father, then his childhood friend Quintus appeared, roaming the woods near his hometown with him. They were both playing with mock swords, 'fighting' the enemies of the empire. Then the scene was replaced by a nightmarish one: Barbarians attacked him while he was standing on a desolate plain all by himself. They were carrying the heads of slain Roman soldiers on their belts, screaming and howling as they came closer and closer. He could tell their grimacing faces now – what hatred, what unspeakable loathing. Nooooooo!

Trajan shook in his bed, almost woke up. An old boyhood dream had come back to haunt him again! His eyes felt heavier than boulders in white-water. He tried to pry his orbs open but he could not. Through the hazy layers of his awareness he felt the pleasant cooling touch of the maid's wet cloth on his skin.

Where was he? Was he still on the yacht? No, this cot didn't rock. He was not on the ship. Was he back in Rome? Once more he tried to open his eyes, but his body failed him once more. He dozed off, the slumber overpowered his senses.

Trajan did not know how long he had been asleep when his tormented mind finally gained the upper hand, pushing aside the urge to sleep. Smidgens of firm reality were seeping into his awareness. He was sick! Food poisoning he had overheard them say. Or had someone poisoned him, maybe back in Antioch? Was there a traitor on the yacht? If so, who? Who wanted to eliminate him?

Trajan opened his eyes. He was in a real bed, apparently on land, and he was resolved to overcome this terrible fatigue. There was too much to do. He wanted to enjoy his Triumph in Rome, hold Mesopotamia at all cost, restore the peace in the East and, yes, settle on a successor or have the Senate pick a man of his choice.

He remembered the blissful moment on the pier in Charax, when he was holding Pompeia in his arms and watched that cargo ship on its way to India, on Alexander's footsteps, a dream come true... Alas, he was too old, and they had turned about. But unlike Alexander he would name an heir in time, back home, yes, he would! But he couldn't hold his thought and slipped off again into the realm of nightmares...

Crito and the maid were watching Trajan's struggle in bed, heard him gasp and groan. The doctor counted his pulse every half hour. It helped him stay awake. Trajan's pulse was slowing down - an indication that his heart was losing strength.

After midnight, the emperor surprised them with a rasp. "I am thirsty..."

"He's awake," Crito shouted at the maid. "Quick! Hand me the cup of water." He took it and held it on Trajan's lips. The emperor sipped from it, drinking half the cup. Then his head fell to the side, but he stayed awake.

"How are you feeling, Master?" Crito asked him.

Trajan coughed. "Where am I?" he rumbled.

"In Selinus," Crito answered. "We are in port on the Cilician coast. You passed out on the ship. We thought it would be better to get you off the rocking boat. Here we are. You have been asleep most of the time."

The conversation woke up Pompeia, who had fallen into an uneasy slumber. When she realized Trajan was speaking to them, she surged from her bed and crossed to Trajan's. "Marcus! How are you doing?" Her voice was dripping hope – and apprehension.

"Pompeia," Trajan said. "My poor... faithful... wife. So glad to see you here. I want to go home..." His words came out slow, interrupted by many small coughs. His cheeks were sagging, the eyes had receded deep into their sockets.

Panic flared in Pompeia's mind. She calmed herself down, forcing herself to hold back the tears. "Trajan," she whispered, stroking his cheek. "We will take you home, don't worry." She glimpsed at the doctor. "Isn't that so, Titus? We shall, shall we not?"

"Of course, my Lady," Crito chimed in. "Master, please drink this medicine. I have made it from the best herbs." He picked up another terracotta cup from the nightstand and held it before the emperor. "It will help you get better."

"What is wrong with me?" Trajan asked.

"It's food poisoning. Phaedimus has it too," Crito chirped.

With the doctor's help Trajan drank the whole cup. Then he muttered, "Food poisoning? Maybe. What if it is a real poison? Perhaps someone was trying to kill me." He paused. "Search the ship," he ordered. "Maybe there is a traitor on board. You may even find the ingredients for the poison that camouflages as indigestion and a fever."

"No, no, no," Plotina said, shaking her head. "Dearest husband, there is no traitor. Don't get upset. We have already thought of that and found no indications whatsoever. Attianus can attest to that," she lied, trying to put Trajan's mind at ease. "Maid, call the praefect. Tell him the emperor is awake and wants to see him. Run!"

Attianus was over in no time. Plotina told him of Trajan's concern, subtly shifting her head so he would downplay the issue.

The praefect nodded. "So good to see you awake, my Lord. I hope you will get better soon. You don't need to be troubled. There is no traitor amongst us. I am certain of it."

"He may be sly," Trajan said doggedly, lolling his head.

Afraid he might return to sleep or even die on them now, Plotina decided to put forward the succession issue. "Marcus, we are confident you will recover from this, but I would like you to make your Will now. Whom do you designate as your successor?"

"Successor? Yes, I don't have a successor, do I? But many good friends."

"That's right. Many good friends. Which one of them shall succeed you,

Caesar?" Attianus urged.

"Stop it," Crito shouted. "The patient needs rest. He will consider it when he feels better. Out with you, all of you! You too, Plotina."

Pompeia was itching to disapprove, but he was right. Trajan was in no position to make a decision in the shape he was. "All right," she said. "Let's all leave." She bowed down on her husband one more time and gave him a tender kiss on the forehead, "Sleep well, Marcus. May *Aesculapius* watch over you!"

In the hallway she pulled Attianus aside. "Publius, let's draft a Will for my husband and put Hadrian on it. All Trajan will have to do is sign it."

Attianus hesitated. "We could try," he said.

They walked to Callistus's quarters and knocked on his door. When the secretary opened Plotina gave him a warm smile. "You cannot sleep either?" she asked.

"Of course not," Callistus said. "How could I? How is Trajan doing?" He waved them inside.

"Trajan is not doing well at all, Callistus," Plotina filled him in. "We need to be prepared for the worst."

Callistus puckered his mouth, swallowed hard. "By Jupiter, the cursed Parthian war is killing Rome's greatest emperor!"

"Maybe, hopefully not. We need your help," Plotina requested. "Trajan needs to sign his Will."

"Anything, but there is no Will I am aware of," he answered innocently.

"That is why we need to set one up," the empress clarified. Callistus raised his eyebrows. "I see. How can I help?"

"We will dictate it for you, Callistus," Attianus weighed in. "I will work you through the legal requirements."

"Who is Trajan's successor going to be?" Callistus asked.

Attianus and Plotina stared at each other.

"Hadrian. It is Hadrian," Attianus finally said.

"Is this what Trajan wants? He has never mentioned that to me."

"He has to me," Plotina lied. "It's his wish. Hadrian is his cousin and ward after all."

Callistus shrugged. "It seems right. I like Hadrian. He is a smart man and a good general," he approved and cleared his cluttered desk from the many letters he had been working on. Then he picked a fresh scroll and unfastened it.

They worked on the document until sunrise. Then Attianus and Plotina went to the praefect's chamber. Attianus ordered a page to bring them some food from the inn's kitchen. He came back with fruit, salt cakes, bread, cheese, and a big decanter of water. Reinvigorated, they discussed the situation.

"You realize what we are doing here," Attianus reminded the empress. "It is unprecedented and certainly unconstitutional. Trajan needs to consult the Senate before he can name a successor."

"There is no time," Plotina maintained. "He might be dead before we reach Rome, and then what? Do you expect the Senate to fill the vacuum? Maybe after some time, but until that happens we would have turmoil and unrest in the empire, perhaps even Civil War... Do you think the generals would agree on a candidate? People like Quietus or Palma or Celsus? I don't think so. They will definitely not support Hadrian. And that, Publius, is enough to be a problem. If they don't come to an agreement there will be no acknowledged ruler and rebellions would remain unchecked because Rome would be busy fighting itself. We cannot let that happen! You know that and I know that.

Trajan needs to sign this document. There is no other way. If he signs it, the Senate and the generals will accept it."

"You are probably right, Pompeia. I hope he will, but he needs to have a clear moment. That is not what I have seen last time..."

"I know, Publius. Pray to the gods. We have never needed them more."

The doctor called them in the third hour with good news: Trajan was awake. Exhausted from the long night, Plotina, Attianus, Callistus and Matidia filed into the room. The empress settled nearest Trajan on the bed's edge and signaled Callistus to sit on the chair beside her. Matidia settled into the chair on the other side of the bed. Attianus preferred to stand.

"My friends, I have these dreams," Trajan addressed them with a low voice. "All the time now. They are haunting me. I... have to... shake them..."

They could barely understand him. Pompeia clutched his hand, squeezing it tight. "Marcus, we are all here for you."

"These dreams... I want them to end..."

"They will," Plotina tried to assure him. "Marcus, we need you to sign this document here."

Callistus handed her his reed pen. She dipped it into a small inkpot that Callistus held out for her and placed the pen in Trajan's hand. Then the secretary passed her the document. She unrolled it and placed it under her husband's right hand. "This is your Will, Marcus. In it you are designating Hadrian as Emperor of Rome by adopting him as your son and heir." Plotina spoke little by little so that Trajan would surely understand. She met his rheumy gaze, but his glittering eyes pointed nowhere. The empress could not tell whether he was even able to hear her words.

"Yes," Trajan uttered. "The barbarians. We have to fight them... And the Parthians... fight them too... Why is Harpenna not here? Harpenna?!"

Puzzled, Plotina looked at the others. They shrugged, shaking their heads. Trajan was apparently delirious. Harpenna, the good angel of the Traiani household, had been dead for years...

She tried again. "Trajan! Listen to me. Please sign here." Plotina guided his hand and the reed pen in it with her own. "Here, sign here!" But the pen dropped from Trajan's hand. Scrambling, Plotina picked it up from the bed sheet and stuck it back into her husband's hand when she realized that somebody was tapping her shoulder. It was Attianus. "Pompeia," he said softly. "He is dead. Trajan is dead."

Pompeia shot a furious glance at Trajan's face and saw his open eyes. She winced - the gods had decided, calling for the Lion of Rome...

Crito stepped forward and closed Trajan's eyes. Matidia was heaving and sobbing in Callistus's arms, who was fighting the tears himself.

It took some moments to sink in. When it finally did, Pompeia tossed the scroll aside and threw herself on Trajan's chest, weeping and sobbing until Attianus pulled her away. She didn't resist him, and he walked her to Matidia's room. The ladies needed time to grieve.

Chapter 68

By noon Plotina had herself together again, but Trajan's grand-niece was still wailing. The empress reached out to her, holding her tight. "Shh, shh, Matidia," Pompeia spoke gently. "Never forget – your uncle's glory will live on. Thousands of years from now people everywhere in the world will still remember him." She caressed Matidia's mangled hair and gave her another long and heartfelt hug. Then she eased back and left the chamber.

After a quick meal Plotina headed to the imperial yacht to meet with Attianus, who was overseeing the preparations for their departure. On her way she met Crito, and Trajan's doctor had more terrible news: Phaedimus had died too...

Crito looked distraught. He said, "I still don't know whether both died from a fever or from food poisoning? But either way, Pompeia, they must have picked it up in Antioch," he added.

Plotina nodded. Phaedimus was not her concern, but his death was proof that Trajan had not just died from old age.

On the ship she found the praefect in the stateroom, drooping over sea maps. "Wait, Attianus," Plotina asked. "Trajan is dead, but we are not done here."

"What are you talking about?" he said gruffly.

"He hasn't signed the Will," the empress pointed out.

"It's too late for that now." Attianus shrugged.

"Publius, there is another way," Plotina insisted.

Attianus looked up from the scroll-littered desk, drawing together his eyebrows.

Pompeia pulled closer. "I will sign it for him."

The praefect backed away from her. "Impossible. It wouldn't count. Yes, you can sign his correspondence, but nobody would accept Trajan's Will if only you signed it. You are his widow, not a regent," Attianus explained.

"That is not what I mean. I will sign AS Trajan. Nobody will ever know..."

"Forgery? Insane! If it comes out, the Senate will come after you and nullify it."

"How would they, Attianus? We won't tell them. Matidia, Callistus, Crito, you and I will have to keep it a secret. I am sure they will play along. Publius, I am perfectly capable of imitating Trajan's signature. No one can tell the difference. I have signed in his name many times since his stroke. This will be no different."

Attianus sank into the chair behind his desk and leaned forward, clasping his hands on the pile of maps. "It is a road fraught with peril, Pompeia.

I am not worried about Matidia or Callistus not keeping quiet. They are family or quasi-family and will do whatever we tell them to, but Crito can be a stickler. He doesn't always see the big picture."

"We have to try."

Attianus heaved a long sigh. "Pompeia Plotina, you really want to go through with this? Let me think about it. For now, I will suspend our launch preparations."

Plotina's face lit up. "Thank you, Publius. For the empire's sake!"

Pompeia hurried back and found Callistus back at the inn. She pulled him aside and told him about her intentions. He growled, but didn't object. Matidia agreed without hesitating. Lastly, she spoke with Crito. He gave her dazed looks but promised to comply. They all liked the prospect of Hadrian becoming emperor.

Triumphantly, Plotina returned to Attianus. "They agreed - all of them! Publius, it's the right thing to do. Let's go for it."

Attianus held his breath. "You are not wasting any time, Pompeia. Did you make it absolutely clear to them that they must never talk about this to anyone?"

"Crystal clear."

He scrambled from his chair and paced up and down. "What about Phaedimus? His coincidental death can easily be construed as the assassination of someone who knew too much. It will cause a stir. People will look at this and ask, 'Trajan died, and who was with him? The empress and the Praefect of the Guard, both supporters of Hadrian, both involved with his education, one even his former ward - of course Hadrian is suddenly emperor. Surprise, surprise!'"

"IT DOES NOT MATTER, Publius. Let them talk. The likes of Celsus and Palma and Quietus will not get the Senate behind them. If we do this, the Senate WILL recognize Hadrian as emperor. More importantly, the Army will acknowledge Hadrian. The legions will appreciate the family connection. They have seen Trajan confer upon Hadrian the command over the eastern army. Hadrian has Trajan's name and prestige behind him. That alone counts, no matter what some generals say.

Last but not least, the soldiers are tired from the fighting. I have a feeling Hadrian will do something about that. We both know he never liked the idea of a Parthian war. He knows our limits, Publius! He will pull out of Mesopotamia sooner than later. The troops will cheer to that, and you have long recognized the futility of our efforts there yourself."

"I would have never invaded Parthia," Attianus said abruptly, stopping the flood of her words.

"Well then..."

Attianus pressed his lips together, ogling the empress.

Plotina pulled the forged Will from a hidden pouch under her *stola*, laid it on the praefect's desk and rolled it open. After a quick probing look at Attianus she picked up his pen right in front of him and painstakingly scribbled Trajan's signature on the formal document:

IMP AUG Marcus Ulpius Traianus, Princeps.

She spread drying powder on the wet ink, jiggled the scroll, rolled it up, dripped hot wax from a candle on Attianus's desk onto the paper's rim and stamped it with Trajan's imperial seal. Then she handed the sealed document to the praefect. "I take it you agree, Attianus," she intoned. "Here it is. Send it to Hadrian. Oh, wait a minute. We need to be smarter than that. If we send it now, right with the notification of his death, the act could be interpreted as rather quick. Someone could say, 'Trajan died and had a Will ready nobody knew about, how convenient!'

Instead, let us merely send the Will with a note stating that the emperor is very ill, that he has written his Will just in case and wants it to be delivered to his heir now to avoid any confusion."

Attianus shot an admiring look at her.

"Trajan would have wanted it this way," Plotina assured him. "He would have quoted Caesar's words when crossing the *Rubico*: 'Alea iacta est.' - The die is cast!"

They dispatched a courier ship from Selinus to Antioch, carrying Plotina's message and the forged Will of the Emperor Trajan.

Two days later they sent another dispatch, advising Hadrian that Trajan had passed away. A copy went forth to the Senate in Rome. Then the imperial yacht set sail to return to Antioch.

Chapter 69

Lingering on the pier of Seleucia's harbor, Hadrian stared at the vast horizon of the Mediterranean. Despite the welcome breeze it was blazing hot as always at this time of the year, but his mind was elsewhere. He was anxious to make out the sail of Trajan's yacht on the glistening water.

What had happened? Why and how did Trajan die so suddenly? And why did he make him emperor? His cousin had never promised him that. He had only mentioned once that he was entertaining the idea. Now it had happened - unless... unless foul play was involved. Plotina?

He couldn't imagine she would kill her husband, but there were other possibilities. Rumors to that regard were spreading already. His officers supported him for now, but the yacht's arrival with Trajan's corpse on board was critical.

The adoption scroll Attianus had sent appeared authentic no doubt. None of the generals had posed a challenge when he read it to them. Afterwards the legionaries had sworn the oath of allegiance to him. His immediate officers were loyal, but some of Rome's most famous military leaders would certainly disapprove. He knew them all too well: Palma and Celsus and of course his archenemy Quietus, who still commanded Palestine.

Some of them didn't like him because he was family and they were not. Some of them didn't like his attraction to Greek culture; others were hostile to his cautious approach in military matters.

They will all talk to Plotina and Attianus to investigate the details surrounding Trajan's sudden death. Much depended on these talks. The credibility of his claim to the throne for sure – or maybe not. Did he need their approval? Could he ignore them? Should he dispose of them?

He shuddered, resolved to bring these issues up with Attianus.

Hadrian's thoughts wandered to his dead cousin's last days. He asked himself over and over again: Had Trajan really adopted him on his deathbed? Even if he had, how much weight would it carry in the Senate?

Sura had told him before Hadrian's first consulship that Trajan had plans to adopt him. Inexplicably, Trajan had never come through. And he, Hadrian, had been too proud to ask.

The new emperor focused his gaze on the horizon again. Still no ship...

Then he shifted his glance to the companions near him and the port road in the back where Sabina's litter was parked. The tasseled curtains of the litter were shut to protect her from the harsh sun. They were fluttering in the squall. Her four Nubian carriers remained on stand-by. Behind the litter an escort of legionary cavalry lingered, waiting for orders.

Attianus's dispatch had advised him to expect the yacht today, but they might have to wait for hours. Attianus had also promised that Trajan's corpse would be ready for immediate inspection and cremation. As Trajan's adopted son, it would be Hadrian's duty to preside over the funeral ceremony in front of the whole assembled army.

He couldn't wait for it all to be over, but it had to be done with piety and in compliance with the religious rites of Rome's state religion.

His nearest companion, adviser Valerius Eudaemon, suddenly held out his arm and shouted, "There - a sail!"

Hadrian's gaze followed the man's arm out to the sea. He could see it too. Soon he could even make out the mast - it was the imperial yacht! The wait was over. Hadrian glanced at his other companion, General Claudius Paternus, second-in-command of the eastern army. The officer, like Hadrian dressed up in his parade cuirass and wearing his finest crimson plumed helmet, pulled up one eyebrow and said, "*Imperator*, are you ready for your Father?"

"I am," Hadrian answered with dignity. "It will be the saddest moment in my life."

Paternus shifted his head back to the sea. Neither him nor the officers behind him spoke until the yacht had tied up at the pier. Hadrian stared at the ship as if it had come straight from Hades. He clenched his teeth. His cheek bulged in and out under the pressure. Otherwise his face showed no emotion. *Dignitas! I have to uphold my dignitas, no matter the circumstances.*

The soldiers and pier workers were watching him – and Sabina, who had now opened the curtains of her litter.

Meanwhile the harbor slaves hooked up a ramp to the boat's gunwale. Then they made way for Hadrian and his entourage. Trajan's cousin headed for the ramp while Praetorian guards filed down from the ship, lined up on the ramp to escort the yacht's illustrious passengers on land.

Soon the stateroom's entrance doors swung open. First to come out was Callistus, followed by Crito, Matidia and Attianus, and finally the widowed and veiled empress. Attianus walked Pompeia down the ramp himself. Neither of them said a word as they stepped on the pier. Pompeia gave Hadrian a courteous nod. Then she stepped aside to allow the Praetorians to carry down Trajan's bier and coffin. They put the casket down before Hadrian and saluted their new master. Attianus signaled them to open the coffin. Hadrian stepped forward and drooped over the casket.

His dead cousin appeared to be slumbering, but his closed eyes were deeply recessed into their sockets. Shockingly, the cheeks looked starved. Trajan would not be presentable. Hadrian would have to call on the best Egyptian experts to improve his appearance for the cremation ceremony. Hadrian didn't want the troops to see him like that. Trajan looked indeed as if he had been very sick, but then again, Hadrian knew of many poisons that made a man look like this. It meant nothing.

He saluted one last time before his cousin and stepped back. The Praetorians lifted the emperor's coffin and made their way off the pier. Everybody else followed in their tail. Attianus remained behind, signaling Hadrian to wait with him until the procession was out of earshot. "*Ave, Imperator,*" he greeted his former ward. "A private word?"

"Sure, *Praefectus.* It's good to have you back. Tell me, what happened on this ship?"

Attianus shrugged. "Trajan fell sick after we set sail. We thought at first it was some sort of incontinence, but then he developed a fever that turned worse and worse. Crito thinks your cousin died from food poisoning, compounded by his weak heart and the stress on his body from the long campaign. He was not the only one to die; Phaedimus is dead too. Look." The praefect pointed to another, less adorned coffin that was now being carried off the ship.

Baffled, Hadrian shook his head. "And then what happened?"

"We pulled into Selinus to make it easier on Trajan, but he died the next day."

"And my adoption?"

"Unfortunately, Trajan was delirious and talked incoherently. He was paranoid somebody might have poisoned him, but there is no evidence. We tried to make him sign the Will you received, but he wasn't able to. I don't even know whether he understood what we wanted him to do. His mind was gone. Anyway, Plotina forged his signature. Nobody must ever know!"

There it was... Attianus and Plotina had acted to save the empire from trouble. Hadrian was not even surprised. Still, it was disappointing. He had hoped his cousin had indeed adopted him. Hadrian clenched his teeth.

"Dearest Hadrian," Attianus tried to soothe him. "Never mind, Trajan just didn't get around it. It would have been his wish, I am sure! For the same reasons we did it."

Hadrian swallowed hard. "Who else knows about this?" he asked.

"Callistus, Matidia and Crito. No one else. Matidia and Callistus are solid. Crito not so much, but I will take him with me to keep an eye on him." He paused. Then Attianus asked Hadrian with great apprehension on his face, "Have you announced your accession? Is the Army sworn in?"

"Of course. It was no problem. The soldiers like me. I have Trajan's prestige, and my officers are loyal to me. But what do we tell the Senate?"

"A courier ship is under way to notify the senators. They will receive the same message I sent you. I hope they will confirm your accession. That's why you should send a letter also and apologize for the hurried action you and I had to take."

"I will. There is another issue. Some of the generals will start sniffing around as you can imagine. In fact, I wouldn't be surprised if Lusius Quietus had spies out here on the pier. They may challenge us. I am thinking of Crassus Frugi and Baebius Macer, and of course Quietus, Celsus and Palma."

"I know. I will take care of Macer in Rome. Crassus, who had aspirations on the throne even under Trajan is still exiled. He will stay there – or die. The other three are more difficult to handle. You will have to replace Quietus with a governor devoted to you. I know the Moor is not your friend. Act before he does! If he has enough time to turn his men against you, you could be in trouble. Send the Moors home. Celsus and Palma can be handled in the Senate I believe.

Anyway, let's hold a War Council tomorrow. I would like to get an update on the military situation in Parthia and Armenia. I know from your dispatches that we lost much of the conquered territories and that the Jewish revolt is still ongoing. No matter what we do, we need to act decisively."

The praefect was a man of action. Hadrian was glad to have him at his side though it felt strange. He had been Attianus's ward growing up. Now he was his ex-Guardian's master... Thank Apollo, it didn't seem to affect Attianus's obedience. "Let's ride back to Antioch with Trajan's bier in our midst. People need to see who is in charge and how reverently I am handling Trajan's cremation and apotheosis. It shall be an event such as Antioch has never seen before!"

Upon their arrival in the city's forum the preparations for Trajan's state funeral were in full swing. Attianus excused himself. "I want to oversee the lodging of my men and hold conference with the other generals." Hadrian just nodded. He and Plotina retreated to his office in Antioch's *praetorium*.

Pompeia settled on his visitor's chair, clasping her hands on her lap. "Have I done the right thing, Hadrian?" she asked, her voice dripping with angst and apprehension. "It happened so fast..."

"You have, Pompeia," Hadrian assured with the highest regard. "I am grateful, very grateful. Would that I could have talked to the old man one more time though! Alas, it wasn't meant to be." His teeth gnawed on his lower lip.

"I did it for you, Publius." Tears welled in her tired eyes. She dabbed them with her handkerchief, then met his sympathetic gaze. "Don't ask me why. I just did. You deserve it. I know deep in my heart that you will serve the empire well, just like Trajan did. You are of the same incorruptible mold." She paused, looked around the chamber. "But it was certainly not easy or... shall I say... constitutional."

"Don't worry, Pompeia. Attianus and I will keep a lid on it. I am going to write a letter to the Senate today and apologize for taking the purple without their approval. I will justify it with the crisis here – and a crisis it is!" He told her the latest terrible news: Parthia mostly lost, Mesopotamia under siege, Armenia in dire straits, Jewish revolts raging in Alexandria, Cyrenaica and Palestine, barbarians invading Britannia from Caledonia and Moesia from the vast steppes of Sarmatia.

Pompeia listened, then she said. "You will manage. I see you have an awesome grasp of the situation already. I need to go now. Matidia needs me."

"Of course." Hadrian stood, strode around the desk and kissed her long hair. "Thank you, Pompeia. May the Genius of the Roman People be with you."

Chapter 70

The generals were waiting for Hadrian in the mess hall: his legionary commanders Claudius Paternus Clementianus and Rammius Martialis, his personal adviser Valerius Eudaemon, and Praefect Attianus.

When the new emperor strode into the room, the chatter died at once, and the men shot expectant glances at the new Caesar. "*Amici*," Hadrian hailed them. "I know Trajan's untimely death is fresh on your minds, but there is no time now to mourn our beloved leader. You have read the reports. The East is in turmoil. If we don't rein this in with iron determination, the empire will suffer irreparable harm. After this conference I will fill you in on the plans for Trajan's funeral."

Each officer gave Hadrian and Attianus an update from his perspective. Eudaemon summarized the conflagrations of the revolting Jewish merchants. Hadrian was aware of most of the issues, but Attianus needed to catch up. He listened carefully, asking tough questions, making notes on his wax board.

After the update, Hadrian passed his gaze from Attianus to Valerius to Martialis to Paternus. "Here is my decision," he said in the harshest command tone. "And some of you may not like it: We will evacuate the newly conquered provinces: Armenia, Mesopotamia and Parthia. The safety and territorial integrity of the empire are more important than our recent conquests. We need to concentrate on the internal revolts and the outside incursions, particularly on the Lower Danube. I will keep Arabia, however. I have not decided on Dacia's fate though I am inclined to abandon it as well. It will be a most difficult decision because many Roman settlers live there now, and the country is rich in precious metals. I will reserve final judgment for later, but discarding Dacia is on the table also."

Shocked murmurs sounded around the tables. Martialis was the first to raise his hand. "*Imperator*, I agree with most of it, but Dacia? We need to be careful. Trajan invited the settlers to live there. We cannot simply leave them now to their own designs - without military protection."

Attianus's face reflected agreement with the general, but he didn't speak.

Hadrian shot an appeasing smile at Martialis and spoke, "Have no doubt, Rammius. The decision on Dacia will be not be made lightly. For now, I am sending Quadratus Bassus to the Danube to defend our provinces there, including Dacia. He will take the very detachments we pulled away from these provinces to invade Parthia. This should give him enough manpower to drive back the invaders and quell a potential Dacian revolt.

As for the Jewish rebellions in Palestine and beyond, I want you, Claudius, to replace Lusius Quietus in Judaea. The Moor is a butcher and will do more harm than good."

Paternus acknowledged. *"Sic, Imperator."*

"You will go to Hierosolyma with my friend Valerius here and disband the Moorish cavalry. Discharge them, pay them and send them home. Valerius will travel on to Alexandria and take over as the civilian Procurator of Egypt. Keep an eye on this province for me, Valerius. However, Rammius, I want you to command our troops in Egypt as praefect. You will both report to me. In all, the three of you will be my point men to defeat the revolts and restore the peace.

In Parthia, I will recall our client King Parthamaspates and make him ruler of Osrhoene instead. That way Chosroes and his rival Vologaeses have no more common enemy and will hopefully start fighting each other again. This in turn will allow us to consolidate our position and be prepared if they decide to attack Syria. I doubt it, but we have to assume the worst." He was still not finished. "You, Attianus, will take the imperial yacht to Rome with Matidia and Plotina – and Trajan's ashes. Tell the Senate I am respectfully asking for permission to deify our late emperor and have his ashes placed in a golden urn in the vestibule of his Dacian Wars Column. Furthermore, he must not be denied in death what he deserved in life: I am asking to hold his Parthian Triumph and Games as planned and arrange for an effigy of Trajan to be carried on the general's chariot during the procession.

And Attianus, I need you to deal with the hawks in the government. Have the Senate approve my decision of consolidating the eastern border. I don't envy you. This could turn into an ugly fight with the stakeholders of conquest."

"Sic, Imperator," Attianus acknowledged like the other generals had done before him. "The formalities will be no problem, but Trajan's deification will have to wait for your own return to Rome. The policy decisions will be a big issue, but we have solid arguments. I will explain the military situation and outline why we are stretched too thin to hold the new territories. For example, our supply lines in the Arabian desert collapsed because we couldn't take Hatra."

Satisfied, Hadrian nodded. "I will stay here and command the Syrian legions until the situation is under control." He rose and left the chamber.

Outside the room he had to think of Pompeia again and how important she had been in all of this. He and Pompeia wouldn't have enough time to talk everything over because she had to go back to Rome. He would miss her.

The change of Roman military strategy in the East went over well both in the corps of officers and the rankers. Though just a week ago they had been prepared to return to the desert and complete the subjugation of the Parthian empire they were glad to stay and dig in. Parthia had been a tough nut to crack. The vast desert had made supplying the army almost impossible. There was a reason why Roman and Asian culture were so different from each other: The hot desert formed an almost impenetrable barrier for the exchange of people and goods. Alexander and the Macedonian conquest had not changed that. And the peoples of Mesopotamia – as much as they loathed their Parthian overlords – did not want Westerners in their lands. Trajan had been myopic to the cultural divide, but Hadrian was acutely aware of it and had drawn the necessary conclusions: The army was overextended and something had to give. It would be Trajan's Parthian conquest.

In Rome, shortly after Attianus's arrival, the Senate confirmed Hadrian as emperor and bestowed on him the honorific title *Pater Patriae* – Father of the Homeland. The mint issued new coins showing Trajan on one side and Hadrian on the other, celebrating Trajan's deification and Hadrian's adoption. After often tumultuous discussions, the senators also approved the evacuation of the conquered provinces in central Asia, empowering Hadrian to focus on pacifying the Middle East.

This was no easy task as the Moors in Mauretania rose up to protest the dismissal of their leader Quietus. Hadrian had to send naval infantry under the command of his faithful friend Admiral Marcius Turbo to suppress their mutiny. Turbo did so with aplomb, returned east and then finished quelling the uprisings in Cyrenaica and Egypt.

Palestine calmed down after Quietus's dismissal. Some Jews even hailed Hadrian for relieving them from the 'Butcher of Babylonian Jewry', as they called the Moor. The emperor himself stabilized the critical Syrian border to Armenia.

Half a year went by until conditions looked stable, and Hadrian and Sabina were able to set out for their long journey back to Rome. They passed through Asia Minor first and traveled up the Danube Valley to decide the fate of Dacia and conclude the war against the invading Roxolani.

EPILOGUE

Chapter 71

Several weeks later (118 AD), on the Lower Danube

"**I** still can't believe so much trouble erupted all at once in the empire. Of course, you wouldn't believe it looking at the peaceful scenery here," Hadrian mused on the imperial vessel while he watched the verdant Danube shore float by. The boat was pushing upstream, propelled by two squads of professional rowers splashing their oars into the water at a steady pace. He was on his way to meet with the governor of Upper Moesia and Dacia, Avidius Nigrinus.

Hadrian and Sabina were lounging on the elevated stern on a settee, not far from the steersman. Sabina had one elbow on the gunwale, watching the shoreline with him. The boat's captain, an experienced Danube sailor named Probus, and the Governor of Lower Moesia, Pompeius Falco, a long-term friend and ally, reclined on their sofa opposite the imperial couple.

"I feel like you, Hadrian," Falco uttered. "It is disturbing. The barbarians had apparently been waiting for Trajan to die. He must have awed them. Or maybe they were waiting for the Parthian Campaign to fail. It's irrelevant now. They did what they did, wreaking mayhem, and we had to fight back – most successfully I might add."

"Really, Pompeius?" Sabina questioned him. "What do you think the Senate will say when they hear we ordered the dismantling of the Great Danube Bridge? Trajan's pride, Apollodorus's Masterpiece! Or when they hear about us giving up Trajan's conquest to the north of the lower Danube – in addition to ceding Parthia, Armenia and Mesopotamia?"

"They won't like it, Empress, but it was the right thing to do. We couldn't take the risk, no matter the lost prestige. The bridge would have been an open invitation for the Roxolani to cross to our side time and again and pillage Lower Moesia.

As for giving up the plains of Oltenia and Muntenia and all the lands east of Dacia, by Jupiter, it would have been wonderful to keep them, but they are hard to defend. There are no natural barriers, and our resources are depleted. Don't forget, Sabina, we've been fighting wars in Britannia, Egypt, Armenia, Cyrenaica, Mauretania and Pannonia simultaneously. At least, for our settlers' sake and to keep the gold mines we kept Dacia but will now have to reinforce its northern border."

Sabina pursed her lips. "I know all that, Pompeius," she said. "But the hawks won't see it that way. They will heckle us in the Senate and jeer, 'Under Trajan, this would never happened!'

In any case, we need to position ourselves with care and be proactive about it. There is a strong faction in the Senate that does not condone our border consolidation. To them it's defeatist." She paused. "Hadrian, I have an idea. Why don't we simply retitle the transdanubian territories of Lower Moesia that we did keep as 'Lower Dacia'? If we combine this with serious re-settlement efforts, we could make the point that it's a province and therefore a logical eastern extension of Dacia, and not a part of Moesia at all!"

Falco stiffened in his sofa, but Sabina's words prompted a proud smile on Hadrian's face. *She is smart, would make a formidable politician...*

Instead of an answer he turned his head to look back at the two Praetorian escort vessels following the imperial vessel. They were identical to their own: compact, fast river galleys, twenty-five yards long and seven wide, deploying twelve rowers on either side of the hull. The blades of all three boats moved up and down at the same rhythm, their monosails unfurled.

The bulk of the Praetorian escort, however, was cantering west on the road paralleling the Danube, currently out of sight. Each night they rendezvoused with them at a river fort, town or army camp.

Hadrian returned his attention to Sabina. "My wife is right," he said. "I like the idea of making those regions of Lower Moesia into a new province and call it Lower Dacia. On paper, this makes for a new province, giving us an argument against the hawks in Rome. But Pompeius is right too. Dismantling the bridge was proper, but let me be clear on one thing: The revolts in the East erupted as a consequence of the Parthian War. I have feared that all along. The merchants, Jewish, Armenian, Egyptian, Arab, but others as well, saw their share of the East-West trade in jeopardy. If we controlled the whole Middle East AND Parthia, what would we have needed them for? What would have prevented us from establishing tolls on the ship lanes that connect Arabia and Egypt with India? Or worse, why not found a new city on strategically located Parthian territory closer to India and force all traffic through there? Alexandria would have been marginalized. Or worse yet, why not set up a Roman beachhead around our Indian settlement in Muziris and establish direct contact with all of India and even the land of silk itself, and cut out all the middlemen...

This insurrection was about trade and money. They saw their lifeline jeopardized by a Roman empire that, in their view, was spinning out of control in an orgy of conquest.

We needed to back off and do what is in Rome's long-term interest even if the imperialists in the Senate don't like it. What alternative did we have? Recruit more legions? There aren't enough Roman citizens to recruit even if we had tried, and I would never enlist provincials to the legions. The Army must never be diluted.

And for argument's sake, let's say there were enough Roman citizens to recruit, how would we have paid them? Raising more legions requires more funds that we don't have without levying more taxes, which in turn would strangle the economy. And if we had done it anyway, guess who would have screamed the most? The rich landowners who are backing the warmongers in the Senate! No matter how you look at it, the Parthian War was not winnable. I am relenting not unlike Augustus who changed his mind after losing three legions in the Germanic wilderness.

I realize I am making myself unpopular, particularly with Palma and Celsus. So I am treading lightly, and Attianus keeps me posted what they are up to. I also benefit from being Trajan's adopted son. Most senators are ardent supporters of the House of Trajan. They will go along with this, and I will treat them well."

After a long silence, Falco asked the captain, "When will we reach Viminacium?"

"In about two hours," Probus answered.

"Excellent," Falco commended him. "That means we will arrive before dawn. I can't wait to talk to Nigrinus and hear the latest news from Dacia."

"Let's hope they will be good," Hadrian called out. "After all we've been through!"

He was curious whether a courier would be waiting for them with a new dispatch from Attianus. The emperor hadn't heard anything from the praefect in over four weeks. He was getting concerned but was hiding it well because he didn't want to undermine their confidence in him. *Better to be wrong than rattling their nerves.* An emperor was a lonely man - even Sabina didn't know how forlorn he often felt.

They tied-up at the legionary fort of Viminacium, home of the Seventh Legion *Macedonica,* also a town and seat of the governor of Upper Moesia and Dacia. A detail of cordoned Praetorians was hailing them on the dock in the presence of the caparisoned Governor Nigrinus and two of his officers.

General Falco and Hadrian's guardsmen disembarked first, followed by the imperial couple.

Nigrinus raised his arm to greet them. "Hail, *Imperator.* Hail, *Augusta. Ave, Legatus,*" he shouted, hitting his gilded cuirass with his fist. Then he opened the clenched fist and stretched out his arm at the imperials until his fingers pointed exactly at the emperor and his wife. His officers snapped to attention and followed suit.

Hadrian had appointed Avidius Nigrinus the year before. The man was well connected, a former consul and legate in Greece. His uncle had been part of the Republican opposition against Nero. Both Nigrinus and his father were friends of the Greek writer Plutarch, a historian that Hadrian held in high esteem.

The emperor also lifted his arm mildly, returning the salute. "*Ave, Legatus. Ave, milites.* Avidius, what are the latest news from Dacia? What have we heard from the Jazyges? Is the province safe?"

Nigrinus cleared his throat. "Dacia is safe, Caesar. The Thirteenth *Gemina* has stumped any outbreak of insurgency. Their base is still at Apulum, but detachments are all over Dacia. We have no problems south of the Danube either. However, I am waiting for scout reports beyond the border. The Jazyges have still not made peace." Then Nigrinus turned to Falco. "I bow to you, Falco. You seem to have made more progress in Lower Moesia than I deemed possible," he said, alluding to the Peace Treaty Falco and Bassus had signed with the eastern Sarmatian people, the Roxolani. "The conditions here are different. We cannot buy ourselves out of this conflict by returning conquered lands. Moesia is core Roman territory that the Jazyges are coveting. They know my troops are still not back to their full strength."

With the vein in his temple bulging, Falco readied an angry riposte, but Hadrian cut in. "I see. You realize that all the cohorts from the Dacian and Moesian legions we sent to the East and many of the associated auxiliary units are on their way back to their units as we speak. Your legions will be back to full strength very, very soon. Within a month, wouldn't you say, Pompeius?"

"*Sic*, Majesty," Falco said with straightening shoulders.

"Excellent," Nigrinus replied unctuously. "On my end - I will let you know as soon as I know more of the enemy's moves."

Suddenly, there was commotion amongst the Praetorian horseguards. They shifted aside to let one trooper pass through their midst who was walking a beautiful black mustang to the fore.

"Borysthenes!" Hadrian cried and lunged forward to pet his favorite mustang. He fell around his neck, hugged the mustang, and brushed his spotless forehead. "What a nice surprise!"

Borysthenes whinnied, shifted his stance in excitement and snorted noisily while tossing his head up and down. The mustang was a gift of the Roxolani to underscore their commitment to the Peace Treaty with Hadrian that Nigrinus just had called a sell-out. The Roxolani were famous for their horse-breeding, and Hadrian had become very fond of the magnificent animal.

"Thank you, my friends, thank you! I thought I wouldn't see Borysthenes for another couple of weeks. I hope you didn't run him hard to get here on time. Did you?" he addressed the Praetorian horseguard.

"No, Caesar," the guardsman said unfazed. "Not at all. We treated Borysthenes with the utmost care. He is the imperial horse after all."

"All right then," Nigrinus chimed in. "Tonight you are my guests of course. Supper will be served in the Praetorium whenever you are ready. Be assured, it will be to your satisfaction. But first, get refreshed in the bath-house. My staff is waiting there for you. This way, your Excellencies, this way," Nigrinus strutted ahead, and they followed him to the legionary camp that abutted the port. Surrounded by a Praetorian detail, Hadrian and Sabina entered through the Porta Praetoria. Hadrian waved at the honorary guard of legionaries from the Seventh that waved at them behind the mighty portal, but his mind was elsewhere. *No word from Attianus? And what is going on with the Jazyges? Should he take the Seventh and cross the river? If only Turbo were here already!* Falco was an experienced general but needed to return to his own province. Nigrinus's comments, jabbing Hadrian's actions on the Lower Danube, had alarmed the emperor.

At the Praetorium they settled in the governor's quarters where they would stay during their visit in Viminacium, at least for a week, maybe longer. Nigrinus himself had moved his belongings to the chambers of his second-in-command, the *primipilus* of the Seventh.

Hadrian didn't linger in the comfortable suite – Sabina would take care of the logistics and the treasured correspondence chests – and headed straight to the bathhouse instead. He ordered the staff to admit any courier from Rome at once, no matter what the time was - even in the middle of the night. Hopefully, Mercury would be good to him tonight and send him a message.

After finishing a full bathing cycle the slaves dried Hadrian in the finest cotton towels. Refreshed, he left the building with two guardsmen and strolled around the camp, chatting with the men when he heard the clatter of a horse's hooves from the main gate. Hadrian wheeled and peered at the Porta Praetoria. A horseman galloped through the gates and was shown to the emperor at once. The trooper reined-in his horse before Hadrian, saluted, jumped off and handed the emperor a sealed dispatch – from Attianus himself!

"Thank you, soldier," Hadrian praised the Praetorian. "I was waiting for this dispatch. This is most excellent. Thank you. Go to the *primipilus* now and tell him I am sending you to take care of your horse and give you lodging for the night. Then get a good night's sleep. You will be cantering back to Rome tomorrow. I will have my answer ready in the morning."

The trooper acknowledged and walked his mount off to the Praetorium. Hadrian broke Attianus's seal on the spot, unfolded the lengthy scroll and read it while strolling back to his quarters.

> *From P. Acilius Attianus, Praefect of*
> *the Praetorian Guard at Rome*
> *To: P. Aelius Hadrianus IMP CAESAR AUG*

Dear Hadrian:

I hope this letter finds you well as you are traveling along the Danube. We heard you made peace with the Roxolani. Congratulations! At the same time, let me confirm to you that Marcius Turbo has crushed the rebellion in Egypt and Cyrenaica for good. He will send you a missive himself. However, the situation in Britannia is still critical. You may want to send Falco there as soon as you can. I am glad you decided not to give up Dacia. Turbo is now available to take over from Nigrinus. Dacia would be in good hands with him.

In Rome, your rule is not undisputed. Rumors are making the rounds that we forged Trajan's Will and the adoption document. Some say I had Trajan's secretary Phaedimus killed because he knew too much. Worse, some senators argue Trajan wanted the Senate to appoint a successor – as it did when Nerva took over. They say that Trajan had suggested in a State Council meeting once that he would give the Senate ten names from which to choose. Do you remember that? As you know, Trajan never followed through and didn't give them any names at all. Others say he had Neratius Priscus in mind as regent, assigned to organize the selection of the next Princeps.

All this is very disturbing, but I am hopeful the rumors will stop over time, and people realize that your rule is here to stay.

Another issue concerns me more. Heavyweights in the Senate such as Palma and Celsus are livid over your Augustus-inspired doctrine to keep the empire in its natural borders. They put you down as a 'Graeculus', and say you are betraying Trajan's legacy.

Undoing Trajan's conquest in the East has indeed stirred unrest in the Senate as we expected. Also returning the lower transdanubian territory to the Roxolani didn't help matters as you can imagine. Some people are VERY unhappy about this – furious, I might add. I am trying to keep the situation under control, but I am worried about Quietus's, Palma's and Celsus's plans. They are powerful and dangerous men.

I am certain Quietus is eyeing the throne for himself, and the other two believe you are not up to the task, that you are a liability for the empire. In the Senate they boasted

*the other day that Nigrinus feels the same way... I have
to therefore question his loyalty. My sources are reliable
on this even if he denies it. I understand you will be in his
province when receiving this dispatch. Be careful and see
for yourself, don't forget he has a legion at his disposal.*

*I strongly urge you to eliminate all four of these men
– in the interest of the empire. Taking the lives of senators
is never easy and certainly not pleasant, but better than
Civil War. The empire's stability is precarious enough.
We are under multiple attacks from the inside and the
outside. The Jazyges are still campaigning against us, and
the humiliated Parthians are lusting for revenge. Under
these conditions, the unity of the Army is of paramount
importance. The only way to secure it in my view is the
execution of these troublemaker generals. To me, exile is
not an option because they would be hard to watch.*

*That brings me to Crassus Frugi. This self-important
scoundrel left his exile without permission. The procurator
in charge punished and killed him. You might say, 'The
exile system seems to be working after all,' and you may
point out that you didn't follow my advice on previous
such occasions when other noblemen disputed your
legitimacy, and we neutralized them without bloodshed.*

*My dear Publius, that's correct, but the situation is
different now. The men I am talking about are heavyweights,
ex-consuls. They can marshal support in the Curia and in
the Army. Think about it. Palma was governor many times
over and fought under Trajan with distinction. Quietus is
a veteran marshal with fanatical support from his Moorish
cavalry. Both hate you for putting a priority on peace and
consolidation. They want the conquests to continue because
it's in their personal interest. The more provinces Rome has,
the more gubernatorial posts there will be. More proconsular
commands mean more financial opportunities for them.*

For what it's worth, Pompeia agrees with me.

*Dearest Caesar, I am awaiting your instructions.
Don't forget, time is of the essence.*

*Sincerely,
Your friend and servant Publius Attianus*

Hadrian put down the scroll, shaking his head. By the gods, what was Attianus thinking? The emperor did absolutely NOT want to start his reign with executions. He wanted to work with the Senate, not terrify it. *I am not Domitian or Nero!*

Trajan's relationship with the Senate had been unblemished throughout his reign. Hadrian was committed to the same path.

He showed the letter to Sabina.

"What did I tell you?" she said. "The Senate is a problem. You will have to win them over." She paused. "I believe in you, Publius. Your strategy is good for the empire, but is Attianus the right man to persuade the Senate? So much depends on him. He is not part of the Roman or even the Italian aristocracy. You should have a more credible champion in Rome, and he should not be a Praetorian Praefect. What you need is a senior statesman like Priscus, not a soldier from the equestrian order."

"I have to do it myself," Hadrian snapped. "Nobody can do it for me anyway – not Attianus, not Priscus. I have to be in Rome as soon as possible. Given what Attianus wrote in his letter, I cannot even trust Nigrinus here. I will send for Marcius Turbo to replace him, and Falco will take over Britannia.

In Quietus's case, I already substituted him as Governor of Judaea but won't have him killed or anybody else for that matter. Yes, he disgusts me, hates me, but the Moor has given much for the empire and he is the best cavalry general we have. I will not start my rule murdering him. I won't!"

Sabina arched her eyebrows. "No need to get upset, husband," she said with a soothing voice, calming him down. "But remove him and the others from positions of influence before it's too late. Attianus is right. If you tolerate them, they will interpret it as weakness and make a move against you, possibly inciting Civil War. It wouldn't be the first time. You don't want that to happen: Romans fighting Romans. It's what destroyed the Republic - it shall not destroy you."

Hadrian didn't answer. He had meant to dictate an immediate answer to Attianus's letter but now hesitated. Maybe it was better to wait until he had a chance to talk to Nigrinus. Yes, he would write his response early in the morning.

Hadrian crossed to his desk, sat down and browsed through piles of correspondence that his aides had brought from the ship. Hadrian missed Callistus. After Trajan's death his faithful secretary had retired from imperial service and was now Plotina's private secretary, living in the Traiani villa on the Aventine with her and Matidia.

Chapter 72

Falco and Nigrinus were lounging on their respective sofas when the imperial couple entered the *triclinium* for dinner. Hadrian and Sabina settled on the *lectus medius*, sharing the ranking, slightly elevated middle couch, while Falco and Nigrinus occupied the lower couches to their left and right.

"How was your journey, Majesty?" Nigrinus started the conversation.

"Uneventful, pleasant enough, I would say," Hadrian replied.

"And boring," Sabina piped up. "Nothing to do!"

"Well," Pompeius Falco said. "Our river galley was not the Domus Tiberiana or the Baths of Trajan, but I had a good time. The trip allowed me to get a lot of paper work done and send instructions back to my staff in Oescus."

"So true," Hadrian echoed him. "The amount of mail I am getting as emperor is astounding. Missives are coming from everywhere, without break, asking for instructions or guidance and even judgment in appealed criminal cases - or permission to do this and that. I will have to learn to delegate some decisions to my State Council – like legates do with your officers."

"Delegating is a wonderful thing. It keeps your mind free for the important stuff," Avidius Nigrinus agreed. "Ahh, now that our goblets are filled with the finest Falernian – here's a toast to my distinguished guests: Welcome to Viminacium! It is a pleasure hosting you."

Hadrian, Sabina and Falco held up their chalices in response and touched glasses with the friendly governor. Then pages served up the first course.

Falco was first to resume the conversation. "Avidius, what are your plans with the Jazyges? How do you plan to get them under control? Will you take the offensive or try to ambush them when they raid our side of the river?"

"For now, I have to dig in until reinforcements arrive. According to what you told me, Caesar, it won't be long," Nigrinus answered, lowering his head respectfully in Hadrian's direction. "After that and depending what my scouts find out, I may try to squash them in their own land. If they disperse, we will target their villages and burn down their houses and crops. That should make them sue for peace."

"As long as they stay north of the Danube, I don't see a need for any action," Hadrian disagreed. "I am still hoping we won't need a major presence in this area. There are bigger fish to fry."

"With all due respect, *Imperator*," Nigrinus countered. "They raided my province multiple times. Many villages close to the Danube were destroyed, the people abducted, harvests stolen. The provincials are screaming for protection - I have to heed their call!"

"Of course, Avidius," Hadrian assuaged him. "Use the additional troops and put sufficient garrisons into all threatened areas. All I am saying is that

I don't want the world to regard us as the aggressor."

"B... b... but your Majesty," Nigrinus stuttered. "The Jazyges should be punished for their acts. If we don't go after them, they won't desist."

"We will see about that," Hadrian maintained.

Nigrinus furrowed his eyebrows. He was clearly unhappy about the directive he had just received and glowered but said nothing.

Falco tried to find a middle ground. "I can see where my colleague is coming from, Caesar. I would be tempted to act the same way, but I also see a need for moderation. Avidius, the empire is under assault. We need to make tough calls, choose our battles wisely."

"Matter most? By Jupiter, my province is closer to Italia than all the trouble spots in the East or Britannia. Upper Moesia should be a priority!"

His riposte drew another frown from Hadrian.

"Excuse me, Caesar," Avidius quickly apologized. "I am so passionate about these things, I didn't intend to be disrespectful."

"No offense taken," Hadrian said, playing down his anger. *I need to probe you,* he thought. "Governor, what do you think we should be doing East? Should we go on the offensive again?"

"I am surprised you are asking me that, Majesty. Haven't we already wrapped up the unfortunate evacuation of Trajan's conquered lands?"

"We have, but you may have your own ideas on this matter, Governor."

Nigrinus shot a surprised glance at the emperor. Then he said, "I believe it's a pity we relinquished Trajan's Parthian conquest. We had reached the Persian Gulf after all. '*Tu regere imperio populos, Romane, memento.*' Isn't that our mission – to rule the world? Didn't Virgil state our Destiny in his immortal verse? Tell me, Hadrian, if I am missing something because I don't understand the world anymore. Why did we withdraw from the lower transdanubian territories but not in Dacia? It's a sign of weakness, and we will have to pay for it. That's what I think." Defiantly, he stared at the emperor.

Hadrian bobbed his head up and down, his dark eyes standing up to Nigrinus's fierce gaze. "Avidius Nigrinus, you are wrong. First of all, I don't like Virgil. Never have, never will. Read Ennius if you want to be patriotic. Second, where are all the legions we would need for such an endeavor? How would we pay them? How would we march them into central Asia? How would we keep them supplied in the Arabian desert and the endless plains of Scythia? How would you communicate with them? Look at Alexander and how quickly his generals lost their vast territories in Persia and Bactria." Hadrian paused. "Do you want to know why I ordered the evacuation of Mesopotamia?" he continued. "We couldn't supply our troops without the support of the local populations in the oases, cities and supply stations between Roman Syria and Parthia. Nobody lent us any support; everybody regarded us as invaders and competitors. They may not like their overlord, the Parthian king, either but the culture is the same, and they know his army is weaker than ours which means they can get away with more.

See, Avidius, our conquest of Greece and the hellenized world worked so well because the areas we conquered share a related culture and language and we can reach most of the new provinces by ship. If you go beyond the Euphrates, everything changes: There is the desert, but also a wholly different, yet sophisticated culture, a different alphabet, a different concept of society. We don't understand the eastern religions, customs, habits, their way of life. We understand nothing. That makes it much harder to romanize these people."

"We assimilated all of Hispania hundreds of years ago," Nigrinus challenged the emperor. "The very province you come from, and look at you now, Hadrian. You are Roman through and through. You speak and write Latin, you wear the toga, you learned our system of law, read our classics. In other words, you are no different from me than any City Roman or Italian. So much for not being able to assimilate!

We need conquest to keep the spoils of war and a steady supply of slaves flowing. Every emperor before you expanded our boundaries: Domitian added territories in southwestern Germania and northern Britannia, Vespasian and Titus defeated the Jews, Nero conquered many British tribes and made Armenia a client kingdom, Claudius started the conquest of Britannia and annexed Thrace, Tiberius conquered Cappadocia. I could go on and on.

Even your role model, Augustus, conquered extensively: the Alps and Raetia all the way to the Danube, northwestern Hispania, large parts of Asia Minor, all of Noricum, Pannonia, Illyricum, Upper and Lower Moesia - and of course Egypt, a priceless gem. And recently, your adoptive father Trajan vanquished the Dacians, Roxolani, Armenians, Arabs and even the mighty Parthians!

Conquest is our destiny. Stagnation is the first step towards decline!"

Hadrian didn't cede him any ground. "Governor, Hispania is a lot closer to Rome than Ctesiphon and easier to reach. Second, I am a descendant of Roman colonists in Hispania, not native Spanish stock. I don't compare to a native Parthian, but I may be wasting my time with you. You don't want to see the realities. What is pragmatism to me is betrayal to you. Don't you understand that all these conquests, as beneficial as they were at the time, increased Roman territory so much that we have now reached a point where the Army cannot control any more new territories?

We have grown big, too big. This ends now. I am not going to hold lands I can't send colonists to, period. Without colonists, there is no romanization. That's the difference between Dacia and Parthia. That is why I kept Dacia but pulled out of Parthia. We have reached our natural limits. Our new role is to develop, to romanize and pacify what we have – an equally honorable task."

Nigrinus scowled. Uncomfortable silence permeated the *triclinium* now. One could have heard a needle fall on the black and white mosaic floor.

Finally, the intransigent governor met Hadrian's gaze again and said, "I respectfully disagree, your Majesty. That's all. Please, excuse me now. I have duties to perform and need to review the *primipilus's* camp report."

"Certainly. You are dismissed."

Nigrinus stood and left the chamber without a final salute.

Pompeius Falco took a deep breath. "He is a tough nut - like the other hawks in the Senate and our special 'friend' Quietus."

Hadrian raised his left eyebrow. "Do you think the two will be trouble?"

"I do. The question is whether they aren't allies already."

"Attianus thinks so. He wants me to take action."

"By Jupiter! Not that I am really surprised but still... He wanted you to take out Crassus Frugi too, didn't he? But does he have any proof of a conspiracy?"

"I don't know," Hadrian said. "But I don't want to be another Nero. I will likely exile them." He paused. "Pompeius, I need you to go to Britannia. As soon as your replacement arrives, leave for Londinium. Take a fast boat and travel to Castra Regina, canter to the Rhine and board an ocean-going vessel at Colonia Ulpia for the channel crossing. I will give you an imperial travel warrant that requires every Roman commander to assist with your travel needs. Understood?"

"*Sic, Imperator.* Who will replace me?"

"Marcius Turbo, but I don't know how fast he can be here. Don't worry, I will stay on the Danube myself until the border is safe. For now, I want you to sail back downriver and stabilize the Lower Danube. You will be reinforced soon."

"And the governor?"

"I will replace Nigrinus with Marcius Turbo. I want one strong commander for all of Dacia, Upper and Lower Moesia."

"I see," Falco said. "Does he know that?"

"No. I will send his orders tomorrow."

The legate whistled. "He won't like it."

Hadrian shrugged. *What else is there to say?* He hoped Nigrinus would have the dignity worthy of a Roman senator.

After the dinner Hadrian didn't find much sleep. He tossed and turned all night. In the morning his courier left Viminacium with a dispatch for Attianus:

From: P. Aelius Hadrianus, IMP CAESAR AUG
To: P. Acilius Attianus, Praefect of the Praetorian Guard at Rome

Dear Publius:

Thank you for your letter. The information was
helpful, as always. I will make the replacements per
your recommendations. However, I will not have
Quietus, Celsus, Palma or Nigrinus executed.
By Jupiter Optimus Maximus, Attianus, I am not Nero!
Watch them but don't touch them. Let me decide their
fate on my return to Rome, but I will do the following:
Pompeius Falco is to take over Britannia, and Marcius
Turbo will replace both him and Nigrinus on the Danube.
I have no other news for you. I will inspect Pannonia
next, maybe hold some maneuvers and have the Guard
cross the Danube to intimidate the Jazyges. Five hundred
of my best horse troopers are camped here in Viminacium.
Expect my return in July and keep me
posted on any new developments.

Hadrian

Chapter 73

After sending off the courier Hadrian shared a light breakfast with Sabina and then decided to go on a boar hunt. It would be great exercise for Borysthenes, and help him clear his mind and distract him from his worries. First of all, he had to find out where to find boars in the area. The tribunes of Viminacium's garrison told him would have to at least ride an hour south from here to have a decent chance to rouse a wild hog - farther away than he preferred, but a Praetorian detail would be with him anyway.

While he was chatting with the officers outside the fort's Principia Nigrinus joined them. "A boar hunt? What an excellent idea! There is plenty of opportunity in this land. I have hunted some wonderful boars a couple of weeks ago in the southern forest, and would be happy to lead you to the area in person, Caesar."

Can I trust him? Hadrian hesitated. "Sounds great," he said at last.

Nigrinus headed straight back to his quarter to change. The governor wouldn't need his uniform for the hunt. Hadrian was already dressed in a fashionable, richly adorned tunic and wore the appropriate boots.

While camp ostlers walked Borysthenes over from his stable the emperor sent for twenty Praetorians, commanded by the young *Decurio* Gaius Verulenus. Hadrian also picked two hunt attendants from among the garrison staff. They brought a supply of javelins and trained dogs specialized in sniffing out wild boars.

Nigrinus soon returned with two of his officers. "I am ready," he said and climbed on his horse.

Hadrian nodded and gave the departure signal for the whole troop. The men cantered out of the fort through the *Porta Decumana* in pairs of two, Hadrian and Nigrinus riding at the head, followed by Gaius Verulenus and Nigrinus's two men. The attendants and their leashed dogs took the middle; the Praetorian rankers covered the rear.

It took a good hour and a half until they reached their destination, a forested area ten miles south of the river. There the hunters unleashed the dogs. They ran off in all directions, aimlessly sniffing around at first until they suddenly barked in unison, sped up and dashed off in one direction.

"The dogs have picked up scent," Hadrian shouted excited. "Attendants to me! I need one more spear right away." He tied the additional javelin to his horned saddle and galloped off, Nigrinus and his men right behind him, followed by the guardsmen. The dogs meanwhile had disappeared in the thick underbrush, but they could hear them woofing in the distance.

The hunters tried to keep up with the dogs, but the underbrush scattered the man and slowed them down. Then the barking swelled to a frenetic howl. *They have cornered a boar!* Sure enough, when he caught up with them they were circling around a grunting hog, which kept lashing out at them. The dogs were clever enough to keep their distance while they ferociously barked at the wild animal, not giving it any space to escape.

Adrenalin shot through Hadrian's veins. He ordered everybody back but the two attendants and the governor. Then he took aim at his prey and hurled the javelin. It whipped through the air but missed the boar by a couple of inches. "One more," he yelled, untying his second javelin. But by the time he was ready to take aim again, the boar and the snapping dogs had disappeared in the dense undergrowth. To follow them now he would have to dismount. Hadrian vaulted off his horse, the spare javelin in his hand, and passed Borysthes's reins to one of the attendants. He scurried after the boar, followed by the other attendant and Nigrinus. They scuttled and scrambled through the brushwood until they located pack and prey once more.

The boar had stopped, pouncing and grunting at his attackers. The frenetic dogs dodged its attacks with skill, harassing it, cornering it. *Here is my opportunity!* Hadrian did not hesitate. He took aim, but out of the blue Nigrinus jostled him aside shrieking, "For Rome!"

The governor's push knocked the javelin out of Hadrian's hands. He lost his balance and went down. Suddenly, Nigrinus held a dagger in his hand, aiming it at the helpless and unarmed Hadrian. But before the renegade governor could stab his victim, the hunting companion threw himself at Nigrinus, trying to protect the dazed emperor. The governor responded resolutely. He turned at the man and slashed his stomach. The attendant fell to the ground whimpering, covering the gash with his hands. Hadrian cried for help at the top of his lungs, and tried to reach for the downed javelin.

Nigrinus whirled and targeted Hadrian's belly when he abruptly fell forward. Two guardsmen had run him over from behind and wrestled him to the ground. Finally, they were able to pry the *pugio* from his hand and yanked him up to present him to Hadrian.

Still in shock, he rasped his order. "Tie the coward's hands!"

Nigrinus scowled, said nothing. Now his officers and the other Praetorians arrived on the scene.

"What is this?" one of the governor's men asked.

Hadrian pointed at Nigrinus. "He tried to kill me."

The men's jaws went slack. Seemingly stunned, they looked at each other.

"Caesar, what shall happen to him?" detail commander Verulenus asked Hadrian.

"Take him back to the fort. And can someone please help my brave attendant over there? He is wounded!"

The man was still on the ground, moaning. Blood had soaked his white tunic. Guardsmen stepped forward and attended to him, ripping improvised bandages from their cloaks and wrapping them around his wound to stop the bleeding.

"The injury is not deep, but we need to fetch fresh water to clean the gash," one of them said after a quick inspection.

"Do it," Hadrian ordered. "And take him to the horses." Then he looked at Nigrinus's men. They seemed not to have been in on this assassination attempt, but Hadrian had his guardsmen disarm them while he sank to the ground, shaking. The boar was gone, with the dogs still in pursuit. He could hear their muffled yapping deep in the forest, but his thoughts moved on. *Had Nigrinus had acted alone or was he part of a bigger plot? Were the hardliners involved, possibly hideous Quietus himself?* He wasn't sure. Nigrinus might just have seen an opportunity and acted on his own.

"Are you really not injured, Majesty?" Verulenus asked him with a frown, but Hadrian waved him away. He wanted to be alone. *What if there were more conspirators in Nigrinus's staff at the fort?* Hadrian decided to return to Viminacium right away. He ordered the men to mount their horses. They tied Nigrinus's hands to his back, kicked him on his horse and took him into their midst.

"*Equites Singulares*, back to the fort!"

Upon their arrival Hadrian had the governor thrown into the dungeon and interrogated him at length the same day. Nothing came of it: he claimed he had acted alone, in the spur of the moment. Hadrian also interviewed his senior officers. They seemed innocent. All the same, he ordered the Praetorians to take command of the fort, disarmed the officers of the Seventh Legion and confined them to their quarters. Then he dictated another letter to Attianus.

From: P. Aelius Hadrianus IMP CAESAR AUG
To: P. Acilius Attianus, Praefect of the Praetorian Guard at Rome

Dear Publius:

Things are moving faster than even you predicted. Nigrinus tried to kill me today during a boar hunt, but I am well. My hunt attendant held him back long enough for guardsmen to rush to the scene and foil his attempt. The courageous man is injured, but he will make it.

*Nigrinus insists he acted alone. After interrogating
his men I believe he is actually saying the truth - as
far as his local staff is concerned. However, we cannot
be certain. This may be part of a broader conspiracy.
For now, Nigrinus remains incarcerated. I have taken
away his commission and will later send him home
and exile him at his native town of Faventium.*

*Attianus, please bring in Celsus and Palma for
questioning. Find out what they know but don't inflict
pain. I give you three weeks and will wait for your report
her in Viminacium. If you need more time, send a courier.
The gods be with you. Be careful.*

Hadrian

The message would take a week to reach Rome. Assuming another week
for Attianus's report to reach Hadrian, the praefect had one week left for his
investigation.

In the meantime, Hadrian decided to distract the troops with a demonstration of power and impress the enemy at the same time. The opportunity
came two days later when scouts reported a significant number of Jayzges
near the northern banks of the Danube, twenty miles from Viminacium.

Hadrian ordered his agents north of the river to spread word that he
would lead a Roman force across the Danube, hoping this would intrigue the
Jazygian tribal leaders. How could he possibly cross this vast stream with no
bridge and no fleet nearby?

Undeterred, the emperor directed two hundred of his Praetorians to
dress up in parade uniform and form ranks on the camp's drill field on
horseback in files of two. At the same time he assembled the other three
hundred guardsmen in combat gear behind the fort's palisades, hidden out
of view.

The Praetorians gathered in their shiniest armor, wearing awe-inspiring
helmed masks made of glittering brass and silver that covered heads and
faces and were topped by a pair of yellow plumes. Enormous gilded fibulas
and brooches decorated the men's chain mail and were used to attach the
men's red cloaks to their body armor. Even the plates of their white horses
glittered. The head pieces and gilded blinders showed off spectacular embel-
lishments of mythical scenes embossed in the metal and crimson leather
strips that were connected to ring-shaped silvered harnesses.

The troopers themselves wore stamped greaves made of copper and iron. Their hexagonal shields were painted red and decorated with the intimidating scorpion blazon of the Praetorian Guard. Hadrian led the parade in person, wearing the golden imperial cuirass and a purple cloak but no helmet. The units in regular battle gear trailed behind the line-up of their parade comrades.

The moment the parade units reached the shore they wheeled about to face the water line. Hadrian let them linger there, motionless, menacing, a venomous glittering snake ready to pounce. The Jazyges were watching all this from the opposite shore. *Perfect*, Hadrian thought, and gave his signal. All at once, the lined-up horsemen splashed into the water and began to swim to the other side, on horseback, in full kit. Row after row, they went in.

To top it off the battle-ready troopers now plunged onto the scene, joining their caparisoned colleagues on either flank until the river was swirling with hundreds and hundreds of men...

The barbarians are going to ask themselves how we do that, Hadrian hoped. *Why don't the Romans drown?*

This particular maneuver was a specialty of the imperial horseguards - ever since Trajan had recruited them from the Batavians. Would it terrify the Jazyges? Soon, the rumble of disheartened men echoed from the other shore and the Jazyges fled in droves. By the time the Roman cavalry had reached the other side, they were gone.

"This will teach them a lesson," Hadrian addressed his officers, chuckling.

The parade troopers returned to camp after a short rest on the other side of the river. The other three hundred men fanned out with orders to harass the enemy and intimidate their villages. They were not supposed to engage in battle, however. The show of force was only designed to deter the barbarians with both skill and glamor.

Chapter 74

O ne week later Hadrian visited Nigrinus in his prison. "Avidius, what do you think I am going to do with you?" he asked him.

"If you were Trajan, you would let me go. But I guess you will put me on trial for High Treason," Nigrinus sneered.

"Is that what you think?" Hadrian asked while squinting at the renegade governor. "You are mistaken. I am not my Father, but I will send you home. Yes, you are a free man, Avidius Nigrinus, but you cannot leave Faventium. Is that understood?"

Wide-eyed, Nigrinus stared at the emperor, "I thank you, Caesar. Unless this is some evil ploy..."

Hadrian studied the man's face, still wondering what motivated the nobleman. *Why has he taken so much risk for his political views? Was he a hothead?*

He said, "You never liked me, Nigrinus, did you?"

"That's not it. It's nothing personal," Nigrinus insisted. "I happen to not agree with your policies. That's all. Your policies are un-Roman. You are infected by Greek views of the world. I never understood why Trajan let you rise to such power."

"Maybe he saw something in me that you don't. Maybe he saw a competent soldier where you see a *'Graeculus'*. Maybe you are underestimating both of us by only seeing Trajan's military side. There was more to the man, much more: a profound care for the empire in ALL its aspects. That's what you didn't notice: the many things he built, the human beings he protected, the institutions he nurtured.

Remember, my cousin was the first Caesar to pass a law that subsidizes orphans and the children of poor families in Italia. Now, how does this go with unfettered militarism? And his instructions to protect minorities from random prosecution, such as the Christians? And his measures to improve the lot of state-owned slaves in mines and agriculture?

The house of Trajan is not only about military might, it is also about clemency and kindness, Nigrinus! And this is why I am letting you go."

Hadrian spun round, called the guard and said, "The prisoner is free to go. Allow him access to his belongings and his horse. He will return to Italia."

Then he strode back to his quarters. Sabina was sifting through her correspondence when he walked in. She looked up, reading his face right away. "You let him go, didn't you?"

He nodded.

"Why? He will plot against you again," she warned him, frowning.

"You don't know that. Clemency might convince him otherwise." He paused. "I hope."

Sabina shook her head. "You are a fool, Publius! This is not how the world works. Remember Julius Caesar? He showed clemency to the stubborn republicans in the Senate. And how did they pay him back? With murder! Mark my word. You should at least have him sent into exile far away, under tight guard, maybe somewhere in soggy Britannia."

"I have made my decision." He glanced out the window. One of the stable boys was saddling Nigrinus's horse. The disgraced governor appeared several minutes later with a pouch on his shoulder and flung himself on the horse. He cantered off without looking back and disappeared from Hadrian's sight.

Two weeks later Attianus's answer arrived.

From: P. Acilius Attianus, Praefect of the Praetorian Guard at Rome
To: P. Aelius Hadrianus, IMP CAESAR AUG

Dear Hadrian:

With the utmost horror did I hear of the despicable attempt to take your life. I am glad you are alive and well!

I have personally interviewed Publilius Celsus and Cornelius Palma. They deny any association with Nigrinus, but I was reading unveiled hatred on their faces and dismay about your decisions. We have intercepted messages that are clear indicators of their dissatisfaction and willingness to undermine your rule. They are lobbying the Senate to reverse your policies in the East. And they are in touch with Quietus.

Hadrian, I IMPLORE YOU, PUT THEM TO DEATH. Most of the senators are on your side. I can make them pass a Senatus Consultum approving these executions. I assume Nigrinus is now on his way back to Faventium, and I know the location of the three others. I can eliminate all of them.

Caesar, I know how much you resent this, how aghast you are, but I appeal to your common sense and the higher interests of the State and the unity of the empire. If you don't act, they will take control of some army units at some point, declare one of their own emperor and march against you. It is impossible for me to know which commanders they

might persuade and how many senators and knights they
might sway. But one thing would be assured: Civil War!
We have to avoid this at any cost. If I
don't hear from you in ten days, I will act on
my own and have them put to death.
Hadrian, I know your role model is our first Emperor
Augustus. Do what he would have done. He killed when
he had to, when he needed to secure the peace and end a
century of internal wars, pitching Romans against Romans,
almost destroying our world. Quietus, Nigrinus, Palma and
Celsus are your Cassius and Brutus, your Marcus Antonius
and Cleopatra. They must die! Make your mark now – it
is your destiny. Rome will be forever grateful, and the
People will praise your wisdom for millennia to come.

> *Your friend and servant*
> *Attianus*

Hadrian flicked the scroll against the wall in disgust. No, no, no, Attianus had lost his mind! *Why me? Why do I have to bloody my hands?* Ten days, Attianus wrote. Ten days... That meant he had only three days to make up his mind as the courier would take seven days for sure to reach the Eternal City, and Attianus knew that too.

For the rest of the day he distracted himself with an easy rabbit hunt, but over supper he discussed the thorny issue with Sabina and Falco. They talked for hours, and to his horror they agreed with the praefect.

He withdrew to his chambers after that, admitting no one, wanted time to think, consult the wisdom of Rome's ancient heroes. Hadrian browsed through Rome's national epics that he always took with him on his voyages. With reluctance he opened Virgil's Aeneid, the story of Aeneas, Rome's Trojan ancestor of Romulus and Remus, who had to kill so that Rome could prosper. *Virgil has the gods tell him it's their will, but none of them is talking to me, not even Mars! And I have so many questions for them. Where is proof that the gods want it that way? What is right and what is wrong? Why do humans struggle so much? Why can't they get along? Why did Aeneas have to kill to make peace? Beyond that, why do the few often have to die to preserve the lives of the many? And why of all men do am I supposed to commit a crime to maintain peace in the empire? What is wrong with the world???*

Oh Tiberius, I understand you now - the loneliness of a ruler... How you suffered!

What can I do to make the world a better place? What makes a good emperor? How can I be remembered as a shining example?

Tears filled his eyes. One was creeping down his cheek. Stunned, he brushed it off. He had not cried since he'd been a child...

His thoughts returned to Augustus, his role model, the first Princeps, a man who had become emperor when the word for emperor had not even existed. He was the one Virgil implied when opening the Aeneid: *Arma virumque cano* – 'Arms and the Man I sing of...'

I hate you, Virgil! I always have. Why does a ruler have to shed the blood of his brothers? But that is what we had to do to pacify the world. Converting the Mediterranean by force and make it into Mare Nostrum, Our Sea, a peaceful ocean, free of warfare and pirates, open to commerce and trade. Rome enabled growth and prosperity in its vast sphere of influence.

We shaped half the known world with the sword for the benefit of all - Pax Romana, the Roman Peace.

He tormented himself for three more days, couldn't act one way or another, couldn't write back to Attianus, couldn't do anything - well aware that taking no action meant certain death for four distinguished generals and senators.

Sacrifice the few to save the many...

This is what Attianus argued. But the price! Blood on his hands, stains forever, inextinguishable. And a sour relationship with the Senate for years to come for his killing of senators and consulars, Trajan's most decorated officers. I would be doing something he never had to.

Arma virumque cano...

In the end, Hadrian decided by not deciding. Attianus convened an extraordinary session of the Senate and put his and the emperor's political enemies to death - Nigrinus in Faventium, Quietus on the Via Latina on his way to Rome, Celsus in Tarracina, Palma in Baiae.

Hadrian cried bitterly when he heard of their executions.

Arma virumque cano Troiae qui primus ab oris - "Arms and the man I sing of. Troy's shores he once left forever".

Virgil, *Aeneid*

Glossary

Aedile: Senior Roman magistrate.

Aeneas: Mythical Roman figure. Son of Venus, father of Julus, forefather of Romulus and Remus, the legendary founders of Rome. According to legend he came to Rome from Troy, escaping its destruction around 1200 BC. The epic poet Virgil describes his adventures and struggle to reach Central Italy in the national epic 'Aeneid'. The Julian family including Julius Caesar and Octavian Augustus, Caesar's great-nephew, traced their ancestry back to him. Virgil makes Aeneas the moral equivalent to the first Emperor Augustus, who restored the peace by winning and ending Rome's endless civil wars in the first century BC.

Aesculapius: Roman god of health. This deity was imported in 291 BC from Epidaurus, Greece, as the result of a plague in Rome and following the advice of the sacred Sibylline Books. Supposedly, a barge landed at the Tiber River near Rome, transporting a huge sacred snake. The snake was released and swam to the Tiber Island. This place was then chosen as the site for the future Temple of Aesculapius. The same year the plague stopped, abruptly vindicating the Sibylline Books. To this day the stick of Aesculapius and the sacred snake entwined around it are the symbol for medicine in the western world.

Agri Decumates: An area in southwestern Germany conquered by the Emperor Domitian, today largely comprising the modern state of Baden-Wuerttemberg, Germany.

Ahuramazda: God of the Parthian people, a quasi-monotheistic deity.

Ala: Auxiliary cavalry unit in the Roman army, 500 – 1000 men strong, equivalent to a legionary cohort. It consisted of 10 - 20 *turmae* (squadrons).

Alans: Nomadic people that lived between Black Sea and Caspian Sea, north of modern Armenia.

Alpes Graiae: Today the southern Swiss Alps between Rhone and the Italian border, east of Lake Geneva.

Amici: Lat. friends.

Amici Comitesque: Lat. friends and advisors.

Amphitheatrum Flavium: The Flavian Amphitheater was the biggest gladiatorial arena in Rome, today referred to as the Colosseum, a term coined in the Middle Ages. It is a huge elliptical-shaped arena hosting 50,000 spectators, and Rome's landmark building. Like all other arenas and theaters with the notable exception of the Circus Maximus, people were seated by gender and social class. Construction began under Vespasian and was inaugurated ten years later by his son Titus in 80 AD. The Colosseum is truly colossal, the biggest and most impressive ancient Roman building still standing. Amphitheaters of this type were built all around the Empire, but none of them approached the size of Rome's Colosseum.

Antioch: Today Antakya in Turkey. Capital of the Roman province of Syria since 67 BC and seat of the Governor with the official title 'Legatus Augusti Pro Praetore' (Imperial Legate of Praetorian Rank). One of the biggest cities in the Roman Empire, named after the Greek General and King Antiochos.

Aquae: Today Calan, Romania.

Aquae Mattiae: Today Wiesbaden, Germany.

Aquileia: Today Grado, Italy, north of Venice.

Aquincum: Today Budapest, capital of Hungary.

Arabia Felix: Lat. fortunate Arabia. That's what the Romans called a new province on the Sinai and eastern Palestine, annexed in 105 AD by General Palma under orders from Emperor Trajan. The term describes the former Kingdom of the Nabataeans with the capital of Petra, which was immensely prosperous due to the incense and myrrh trade passing through it.

Argentorate: Today Strasbourg, France.

Armenia: The large Kingdom east of Asia Minor in the Caucasus that Romans and Parthians many times fought over. Since the reign of Nero a treaty stated that its king had to be approved by Rome. Culturally however, it was much closer to Parthia. Trajan made it a Roman province in 115 AD. It became a Roman client kingdom under Hadrian.

Arrius Antoninus: Grandfather of the future Emperor Antoninus Pius (ruled 138 – 161 AD).

Artaxata: Capital of ancient Armenia, today Artasat, Armenia.

Asia Minor: Modern Turkey. Roman territory containing many different provinces, among them Asia, Cilicia, Galatia, Bithynia and Cappadocia.

Atropatene: Parthian client kingdom southeast of Armenia.

Augusta Praetoria: Today Aosta, Italy.

Augusta Raurica: The oldest Roman colony on the Rhine, near Basel, Switzerland, and located between the modern villages of Augst and Kaiseraugst.

Augusta: Lat. Empress.

Augustus: First Roman Emperor (born in 62 BC, ruled 30 BC – 14 AD). Augustus (meaning the 'Elevated One') was an honorary title given to him by the Senate. His original name was Octavianus (Octavian).

Aureus: Roman gold coin (pl. aurei).

Ave: Lat. hello (pl. Avete).

Bactria: Today Afghanistan. Visited and conquered by Alexander the Great as the first western commander to reach this remote province of the Persian Empire in the fourth century BC.

Baetica: Roman province in southern Spain (today called Andalusia).

Baetis: The Guadalquivir River.

Baiae: Upscale coastal resort between Rome and Naples.

Balceus: Expensive shoe worn by the rich on solemn occasions (pl. balcei).

Banat: Southwestern part of Dacia. Trajan occupied it after the First Dacian War and incorporated it into the Roman province Moesia Superior.

Batavians: Germanic tribe on the Lower Rhine. Famous for their horse skills, Trajan recruited them into his Personal Guard as Governor of Lower Germania and later into the Praetorian Guard.

Belgica: Today Belgium. One of the four Roman provinces in Gaul (France).

Bithynia: Roman province in northwestern Asia Minor, today part of Turkey.

Bonna: Today Bonn, Germany.

Borysthenes: The Dnieper River in southern Russia, also the name of Hadrian's favorite horse.

Brundisium: The Italian port city of Brindisi on the southeastern coast of Italy.

Brutus, Marcus Junius: One of Caesar's infamous murderers, a member of Rome's famous families. He died in 42 BC fighting Mark Anthony and Octavian on the battlefield of Philippi in Greece.

Buridava: Today Ocnele Maria, Romania.

Caca: Latin obscenity.

Caesar, Julius: Roman politician, writer and general (100 BC – 44 BC). Hugely influential for his dramatic state reforms. He conquered all of Gaul (France) between 58 and 50 BC, murdered in 44 BC by conservative senators that envied his accomplishments and their loss of power. There are indications that Mark Anthony was in on the plot.

Caelian Hill: One of the Seven Hills of Rome, east of the Palatine.

Calidarium: Hot poolroom and sauna in a Roman bath.

Caledonia: Scotland.

Caligae: Lat. army sandals.

Campus Martius: Large area between Forum Romanum and the Tiber north of the Forum. It was not originally within the city limits, but rather an open field used for military exercises and to hold public elections. At the time of Trajan, buildings such as theaters, stadiums, offices, baths, temples and cemeteries occupied the Campus Martius.

Capitoline Hill: One of the Seven Hills of Rome, location of its imposing Jupiter temple and Rome's core fortifications surrounding the temple precinct. It inspired the American founding fathers to name the seat of Congress in Washington after it.

Capitoline Trinity: The gods Jupiter, Juno and Minerva. Christianity transformed it into the Father, the Son and the Holy Spirit.

Cappadocia: Roman province in eastern Asia Minor. Established in 18 AD by the Emperor Tiberius (located in eastern Turkey).

Capreae: Capri, beautiful island at the southern end of the Golf of Naples.

Cardo Maximus: Main street in any Roman town stretching from north to south.

Carnuntum: Petronell near Vienna, Austria. In Roman days the location of a legionary base.

Carrhae: Today Harran, Syria. Location of a battle between the Triumvir Crassus and the Parthians in 55 BC. Crassus lost and was taken prisoner. Known for his greed, the Parthian King poured molten gold down his throat to kill him most painfully.

Castellum Mattiae: Today Kastel, Germany.

Castor and Pollux: Roman gods of salvation, also the patron gods of the Roman Cavalry.

Castra: Lat. fort, fortress.

Catilina: Ambitious Roman politician who attempted a coup d'etat in 63 BC, the year of Cicero's consulship.

Catull: Famous Roman writer of love poems, lived 84 – 54 BC. His hometown was Verona.

Centum Cellae: Today Civitavecchia, Rome's modern harbor. Built by Trajan when the port in Ostia could no longer handle Rome's ever increasing cargo and passenger volume, even after the emperor had added an extra basin at Ostia which is visible to this very day.

Centuriate Assemblies: Legislative assemblies of the Roman people in the days of the Republic. The wealthier citizens were automatically allocated a majority of the votes. The Centuriate Assemblies were the most important assemblies, electing Rome's top magistrates, consuls and praetors, and decided over war and peace. Since the days of Augustus they had ceased to be relevant. To keep up with tradition, the Centuriate Assemblies were however not officially abolished. Nerva's Agriculture Law became the last bill in the history of this venerable institution which it was allowed to voted on. He wanted to show his commitment to the rule of law after Domitian's tyranny.

Centurio: Military rank in the Roman Army, comparable to captain.

Century: Military unit of 80 soldiers, divided in ten contubernia.

Charax: Parthian port town in the Persian Gulf, south of modern Basra, Iraq.

Chatti: Significant Germanic tribe in what is today the state of Hessen, Germany.

Chauci and Frisii: Northern Germanic tribes east and north of the Lower Rhine.

Cilicia: Roman province in what is today southeastern Turkey.

Circus Maximus: Largest of all the arenas in Rome. Rectangular and almost 2000 feet in length, it covered the valley between Palatine and Aventine. Accommodating up to 250,000 (!) spectators, the arena was huge and used for horse races, processions and triumph marches. The Circus Maximus was the only stadium where spectators were not seated by gender. Ovid tells us it was therefore a great place to pick up women.

Clausurae: Lat. enclosures. Barricades to obstruct and manage the travel of invaders or nomadic peoples across valleys and other natural corridors of communications and movement.

Clibanarius: Lat. heavily armored cavalryman of Parthian origin. He and his horse were dressed in scale or chain mail armor from tip to toe. The armor pieces were interlocked and made from bronze or iron. The main weapon was a long lance and the long sword. A clibanarius also had maces for close combat. Clibanarii units charged in formation and intended to crush their usually lighter armed enemies on impact.

Clients and patrons: An ancient system of give and take and a cornerstone of Roman society.

Colonia Claudia (in full: **Ara Agrippinensium**): Capital of Lower Germania Province, today Cologne, Germany.

Colonia Ulpia Traiana: Today Xanten, Germany.

Comes: Lat. companion. In the military, term for a ranking officer on special imperial assignment. In the late empire, the term was used for commanders of whole armies. From that the English word 'Count'.

Comitia Centuriata (lat.): See Centuriate Assemblies.

Commagene: Small Roman province in Asia Minor (modern Turkey), north of Syria and bordering both Armenia and Parthia. It was established by Vespasian.

Concordia Excercituum: Lat. 'Unity of the Armies': An Imperial motto that was propagated when civil unrest or war had broken out and needed to be quelled.

Congiarium: Accession bonus for the urban *plebs* (people) in Rome.

Consul: Top Roman magistrate. It was the second most important office in the empire. A consul started his office at the beginning of the year (in January) and left office on December 31st. Following this example and to this very day an American President is always inaugurated in January. Many elements in the American constitution are also modeled after the Roman Republic, which men like Washington, Jefferson, Madison, Hamilton and Franklin had carefully studied before breaking away from Britain.

Consul Ordinarius: Lat. regular consul. The signifier *Ordinarius* was added at times to indicate this was the regular consul, ordinarily elected by the Senate, as opposed to a suffect consul who could be added later in the year because either a *Consul Ordinarius* had died or the emperor decided to appoint another consul mid-year. In the Republic the year was named after the two *Consules Ordinarii*. The rank of *Consul Ordinarius* was more prestigious than *Consul Suffectus*. He also outranked him.

Contubernium: Roman military unit consisting of eight soldiers under the command of a *duplicarius* or *optio*. In the infantry, ten *contubernia* made up a century, commanded by a centurion. In the cavalry, four *contubernia* made up a *turma*.

Corduba: Modern Cordoba, upstream from Italica on the Guadalquivir.

Cornicen: Lat. hornblower. Roman soldier who used big tubas to communicate orders in battle or to announce a general (*legatus*).

Ctesiphon: Capital of Parthia, one of the greatest cities in the ancient world, abandoned under Arab control in the 8th Century AD. It was located about twenty miles southeast of Baghdad.

Crassus, Marcus Licinius: Roman senator and general, famous for quelling the slave revolt under Spartacus in 70 BC. He was Rome's richest man, a modern Rockefeller, and in 60 BC allied himself with Caesar and Pompey, forging a triumvirate.

Crito, Titus Statilius: Trajan's physician.

Cubiculum: Lat. bedroom.

Curia: Name of the building that housed the Senate, also used as a synonym for Senate. The Curia still standing in the Forum Romanum dates from the time of Constantine.

Cursus Honorum: From Lat. honos = honor or public office, and cursus = path. It was the traditional career path for Roman magistrates. These officials were originally appointed by election only, later by the emperor and his staff. Age limits applied for each office, and it was desirable to hold an office at the earliest allowed age.

Cursus Publicus: The state-operated mail service. It delivered mail between officials and officers. Its messengers used state-owned horses and other means of transportation. A system of inns provided lodging on their journeys throughout the empire. At these hostels the couriers could enjoy meals and change horses to complete their journey with almost no interruption. The ancient world did not have a concept for a truly public mail service.

People commonly handed letters and other mail to their friends or family members when they travelled to the right destination. The well-heeled often used slaves as messengers if they had no access to the *Cursus Publicus*.

Cyrenaica/Cyrene: Today the area of northeastern Libya.

Dacia: Modern Romania. Ancient Dacia comprised Transsylvania, the Banat and Walachia.

Daci (Dacians): People of Dacia. The *Daci* were of Thracian descent and more sophisticated than their Germanic neighbors. They had a central government and fortified cities. Culturally, they were influenced by the Hellenistic cities of the Black Sea coast and their Roman, Germanic, Scythian and Celtic neighbors. Parts of northern Dacia were even populated by people of Celtic, Germanic and Iranian (Roxolani) origin. The country was rich in precious metals, particularly gold and silver.

Decurio: Rank in the Roman military, equivalent to sergeant.

Dignitas: Lat. honor, dignity.

Dinar: Roman silver coin (Lat. *denarius*, pl. *denarii*). To give an indication of its value, under Augustus the Praetorian Guard's annual military pay was 275 dinars per soldier.

Domina: Lat. female form of *Dominus* (master), the mistress of the house and wife of the head of the household (*pater familias*).

Domitianus, Titus Flavius: The Emperor Domitian (ruled 81 – 96 AD)

Dominus: Lat. master.

Domus Traiana: The villa of the Traiani family in Rome, situated on the Aventine Hill.

Donativum: Imperial accession bonus for the Army, usually paid out in cash by a new emperor, sometimes over a period of time to avoid excessive immediate spending by the soldiers. Trajan paid only half the customary amount because the soldiers had just received a *donativum* at Nerva's accession to the throne.

Drobeta: Today Turnu-Severin, Romania.

Drusus: Roman general and son-in-law of Augustus. He campaigned in central Germany and even reached the Elbe in 9 BC.

Duplicarius: Lat. A rank in the Roman auxiliary cavalry, equivalent to lieutenant (literally someone who is getting double pay).

Dura-Europus: Roman fortress on the Euphrates River, today an unsettled ruin town in modern Syria.

Duumvir: One of the two top magistrates in any Roman or Italian town, comparable to a mayor. Similar to the consular system of the Roman Republic, a Roman city was governed by two elected magistrates who shared power, called the duumviri (lat. 'The Two Men'). Despite the imperial system of government at the head of state, local government remained a democratic affair, and much money was spent to win an election. The graffiti in Pompeii prove that these elections were highly competitive, remindful of our own present time.

Egeta: Modern Brza Palanka, Serbia.

Elegeia: Modern Erzurum, Turkey.

Epona: Horse goddess worshipped in western Europe including Italy and Rome, originally of Celtic origin.

Equites Singulares Augusti: Name of the Imperial Guard under Trajan. They were handpicked cavalrists, in Trajan's and Hadrian's days usually recruited from Germanic tribes like the Batavians. Comparable in their reputation with American marines, they were able to swim across a river on horseback in full armor.

Esquiline: One of the Seven Hills of Rome.

Euphrates: Key river in Mesopotamia. It formed the borderline between the Roman empire to the west and the smaller Parthian empire to the east (today Iraq and Iran). Further north, it was the demarcation line between the Romans and the mountain kingdom of Armenia, often contested between Rome and Parthia.

Falx: Dacian infantry weapon. A thin and long sickle-like but straightened sword with a sharp tip. A fierce blow with this weapon could slash a helmet, killing the soldier instantly.

Famous Families: The nobility in Rome that contributed most to the senators and consuls of the Republic, e.g. the Julii (Caesar), Claudii (Tiberius, Claudius), Antonii (Mark Anthony), Cornelii (Scipio, Sulla), Licinii (Crassus, Sura), and others.

Fates (pl.): Roman deities of destiny.

Fenugreek: Lat. *Faenum Graecum*, Greek hay that flowers in the mid-summer time.

Fiscus: Lat. treasury.

Flamen Dialis: The Priest of *Jupiter Optimus Maximus*, Rome's highest god, the 'Best and Greatest Jupiter', equivalent to the Greek Zeus.

Forum Romanum: The heart of Rome, a large rectangular valley between Capitol and Palatine, littered with sumptuous temples, basilicas, state offices, shops and markets. It was the political center of the city during the time of the Republic and housed key institutions even in the empire, such as the Senate, State Treasury, Public Archives and the College of the Vestal Virgins.

Frigidarium: Swimming pool room in a Roman bath.

Gades: Today Cadiz, Spain.

Gallia: France.

Gemonian Stairs: Lat. *Scalae Gemoniae*. A marble staircase in the Forum Romanum that allowed you to walk from the Senate building up to the Temple of Juno Moneta on the eastern part of the Capitoline, the castle mount (*arx*). It was sometimes used gruesomely to toss the dead bodies of enemies of the State. Tiberius, for example, did so with the traitor Sejanus and his family seventy years before the Dacian Wars.

Gladiator: Sword fighter in the arena, usually a slave or criminal or prisoner of war who was forced to fight to the death. Some gladiators became well paid public heroes and were sponsored by rich aristocrats.

Gladius: Lat. sword. Term for the short Roman infantry sword, two feet long, double-edged and very sharp.

Graeculus: Lat. Little Greek. A term Romans used to label one of their own as a lover of Greek culture, customs and arts. The diminutive makes it derogatory.

Grammaticus: Teacher of literature and critical text analysis.

Groma: Surveying tool to line up building, streets and roads in a straight line.

Guntia: Today Guenzburg, Germany.

Hades: In Greek mythology the grim and dark underworld of the Dead.

Hadrianus, Publius Aelius (Hadrian). Roman Emperor 117 – 138 AD, successor of Trajan.

Harpastum: Roman ball game, similar to modern rugby and popular in the military.

Hatra: Strategic Parthian fortress and town in Mesopotamia.

Hibernia: Ireland, which was never occupied by the Romans.

Hispalis: Today Seville, Spain.

Homo novus: Lat. 'New Man'. An expression for a newcomer to Rome's patrician class, who was not born into one of the Famous Families, usually a Roman citizen from Italy or the provinces, like Trajan's father.

Horti Sallustiani: Opulent gardens built by the Republican politician Sallust. They became imperial property after Tiberius, but were at times partly open to the public.

Ides of September: 13. – 15. September.

Illyria: Today Dalmatia. The Romans conquered it in the reign of the Emperor Augustus. Illyria includes parts of Bosnia, Serbia and Croatia.

Imperium maius: The legal power of the top magistrate in the empire, subordinate to no one. It signified supreme executive authority over the City of Rome and the empire as a whole.

Imperium Romanum: Lat. Roman empire.

Impluvium: Lat. low square basin to hold rainwater, located in the middle of the atrium of a Roman villa. Rainwater was channeled to fall from the roofs into this shallow pool. Down below the water was collected in a cistern. Other than collecting rainwater the *impluvium* served to embellish the atrium.

Italica: Trajan's hometown. Today a ruin town under reconstruction near Seville, Spain.

Juno: Roman goddess, wife of Jupiter and mother of Mars. She was the goddess of the home, marriage and frugality.

Jupiter Optimus Maximus: Often abbreviated as IOM, he is the figure at the top of the Roman hierarchy of gods, equivalent to Zeus in the Hellenistic world. *Optimus Maximus* means 'Best and Greatest'. It expresses the huge importance of this god as the patron god for all Romans. His temple stood on the Capitoline Hill and was the largest temple in the city.

Lararium: Altar for the family gods called the *Lares*.

Lares: Lat. family gods, usually displayed in the form of small bronze figurines. Soldiers often brought them along on campaigns like charms to hold them in their hands in a quiet moment while reciting sacred verses spoken to invoke the favor of the deities.

Latifundia: Vast country estates usually owned by a senator, used for agricultural production and operated by large numbers of slaves. Some latifundia were state-owned.

Latium: Name for the region around Rome. Rome was one of several Latin tribes.

Latona: Latin name for the Greek goddess Leto, mother of Apollo and Artemis.

Lederata: Today Palanka, Serbia (sixty miles east of Belgrade).

Legate: Commander of a legion, comparable to a general.

Legatus Augusti: Lat. 'Sent by the emperor', anglicized 'Legate'. Term for a provincial governor directly reporting to the emperor and usually in command of one or more legions. There were different ranks among the emperor's legates: *pro praetore* (of praetorian rank) or *pro consule* (of consular rank). A proconsular legate ranked the highest. He was sent to govern as consul outside the homeland (Italy). Only senators could climb to that rank.

Legio (pronounced lay-ghee-o): Modern Leon, Spain. Legionary fortress and city in the Roman province Hispania Tarraconensis, base of the only legion stationed in Spain in Trajan's time.

Legion: Precursor of a modern division, the main unit in the Roman military, between 4,000 and 6,000 men, mostly infantry. The standing army of the Roman empire consisted of 20 – 28 legions plus the same number of auxiliary troops, about 300,000 men total.

Lex Agraria: Lat. Agriculture Bill.

Librarius: Lat. military accountant in charge of managing logistics and supplies, also administrated the distribution of a soldier's estate.

Lictor proximus: Senior attendant of the emperor on campaign.

Limes (pronounced lee-mass): Lat. border or limit. The term describes Roman border fortifications crossing through Germania. The *limes* separated Rome's Germanic provinces (Upper and Lower Germania) from the free Germanic tribes north and east. Construction for these continuous walls began under Domitian and was completed by Trajan. Hadrian rebuilt parts of it in stone, replacing the older wood palisades.

Livia: Wife of the Emperor Augustus (lived 57 BC – 29 AD).

Ludi Romani: Roman equivalent to the Olympic Games of Greece. Originally a one-day event on September 13 honoring the Roman patron god *Jupiter Optimus Maximus* (Zeus), they were established by Tarquinius Priscus, fifth King of Rome in the sixth century BC. By the time of Domitian, the Games covered the period between September 4 and September 19. They included a variety of horse and chariot races, sacrificial events, plays, as well as track-and-field and gymnastics competitions. Rome's population was obsessed with the horse races. They were even more popular than the gladiatorial fights in the Amphitheatrum Flavium (Colosseum).

Lugdunese Gaul: One of the provinces in Gaul (France) with the capital of Lugdunum (Lyon).

Lugdunum: Today Lyon, France.

Magi: The 'wise men' of Parthia, a state council complementing the Arsacid nobles council, which only included the Royal Parthian Family and its relatives and sister clans. The idea was to put men in places of influence not based on birth but merit in order to balance the often random Royal Family. The system didn't work, however. On the contrary, it contributed to the many squabbles characteristic of Parthian rule.

Marcomanni: Numerous Germanic tribe that at the time of Trajan lived in what today are northern Bavaria and the western Czech Republic. It is the ancient Roman term for the people of southern Bavaria who settled south of the Danube after the fall of the Roman Empire.

Mare Germanicus: Lat. North Sea.

Mare Nostrum: Lat. Our Sea, a term the Romans coined to describe the Mediterranean after eliminating Carthage after the Second Punic War. Initially an expression to indicate a claim, it became reality under Augustus when the Mediterranean was completely under Roman control and would remain so for another 400 years.

Marius, Gaius: Roman politician and general (156 BC – 86 BC). Seven times consul, he reformed the Roman army and defeated the invasions of the Germanic Cimbri and Teutones tribes. He also engaged in a doomed Civil War against the conservatives in the Senate under Sulla to enact land reforms for his veterans.

Mars: Roman God of War.

Mars Ultor: Lat. Mars the Avenger, a title given to the god of war Mars by the Emperor Augustus after he had successfully avenged the assassination of his great-uncle Julius Caesar at the battle of Philippi in 42 BC.

Matisco: Today Macon, France.

Mauretania: Roman province in northwestern Africa, today Morocco and western Algeria.

Medicus: Lat. doctor.

Melitene: Today Malatya, Turkey.

Mentula: Latin obscenity.

Mercury: In Roman mythology the son of Maia and Jupiter, the messenger of the gods, equivalent to the Greek Hermes. He was portrayed with a winged hat and shoes - attribute to his speed when running errands for the gods.

Milites: Lat. soldiers.

Minerva: Roman goddess of the crafts and trade guilds (Athena in Greece). She was especially worshipped by Domitian.

Misenum: Navy base south of Rome, base of the western mediterranean fleet of the Roman Navy.

Mithraeum: Sanctuary of the bull-slaying God Mithras who was popular in the Roman Army. A *mithraeum* was a place for the worshippers of Mithras to assemble and propitiate. It often had two levels to allow the acolytes to be bathed in the blood of a bull being slaughtered above them. The religion hailed from Persia and was monotheistic like Christianity.

Moguntiacum: Capital of Upper Germania Province, today Mainz, Germany.

Mola Salsa: A cake of ground barley and salt, used in religious rituals and meals.

Mons Caelius: One of Rome's Seven Hills.

Morava: River in Moesia Superior Province (today eastern Serbia).

Mos Maiorum: Lat. customs of our ancestors. The term describes the traditional ancient Roman customs and laws. It is a collective term for Roman piety and the respect for their ancestors and way of life.

Muses: Greek deities of the Arts.

Muziris: Roman settlement in India on the Periyar River on the southwest coast of India near what is today the town of Pattanam. Most recent archaeological finds confirmed its existence. Scholars had suspected its location for the longest time from reading a first century shipping handbook called the Periplus of the Erythraean Sea.

Naissus: Today Nis, Serbia.

Nauta: Lat. sailor.

Neapolis: Today Naples, Italy.

Nefas: Lat. unholy. Days were called *Fas* when priests determined them favorable, and *Nefas* when not. No business was allowed on *nefas* days. The calendar before Caesar's reform had 58 such days, a significant number. They were marked as N in the calendar.

Nemausus: Today Nimes, France.

Neptune: Roman god of the sea (equivalent to Poseidon).

Nero, Lucius Domitius Ahenobarbus: The Emperor Nero (ruled 54 – 68 AD). His imperial name was: Nero Claudius Drusus Germanicus Caesar.

Nerva, Marcus Cocceius: The Emperor Nerva (96 – 98 AD).

Nicephorum: Today Bagga, Syria.

Nicomedia: Today Izmit, Turkey. In Trajan's time, it was the provincial capital of Bithynia in Asia Minor.

Nicopolis (ad Istrum): Today unsettled, just west of Draganovo, Bulgaria.

Noricum: Roman province north of the Alps, includes southeastern Bavaria and most of Austria.

Nubia: Kingdom south of Egypt, today the area of northern Sudan.

Octodurum: Modern Martigny, France.

Oescus: Near what is today Nicopol, Bulgaria.

Olt: River in today's eastern Romania east of Dacia.

Oltenia and Muntenia: The southeastern plains of Romania.

Oppian Hill: Small hill in Rome, west of the Esquiline.

Ornatrix: Female slave specialized in beauty treatments.

Osrhoene: Roman client kingdom northeast of Syria, today located in northeastern Syria and parts of southeastern Turkey.

Ostia: Rome's original port at the mouth of the Tiber.

Oxyporium: Roman salad dressing made with cumin, ginger, green rue, dates, pepper and honey.

Paedagogus: Teacher for Greek and Latin.

Palaestra: Lawn surrounded by porticoed walls to form a courtyard in a public Roman bath for exercising, wrestling and playing ball games.

Palatine: One of the Seven Hills of Rome, location of the imperial palace. Our word palace derives from it.

Palatini: Lat. members of the palace staff.

Palmyra: Today an unsettled ruin town in modern Syria.

Paludamentum: Lat. red army cloak.

Pannonia: A key province south of the Danube in Central Europe, today overlapping eastern Austria, western Hungary and parts of Serbia.

Pannonia Superior: Western (Upper) Pannonia.

Pannonia Inferior: Eastern (Lower) Pannonia.

Pater familias: Lat. head of the Roman family. The *pater familias* held absolute power. In the early days of the Republic he could even decide over life or death of any family member.

Pater Patriae: Lat. Father of the Fatherland. Honorific title for Roman statesmen instrumental in defending the State against enemies from within or without. The title was first bestowed upon Cicero in the year of his consulate (63 BC) for squashing the conspiracy of Catilina. Julius Caesar received the title also.

Patres Conscripti: Lat. fathers (=senators) and added members of the Senate. The official formula used to address the whole Senate in session.

Pax Deorum: Lat. peace with the gods, enacted through the correct observance of public and private rituals.

Pax Romana: Lat. Roman Peace. Expression describing the absence of war and turmoil on the territory of the vast Roman empire and used by Roman historians to justify their expansion beyond Rome and Italy. Trajan's reign marked the beginning of a particularly stable period in the empire that lasted until about 160 AD.

Penates: Roman deities, together with the *lares* considered as the protectors of the household. The name literally means 'gods of the store cupboard' because figurines of these deities were placed in the atrium cupboard. The *penates* were also the spirits of the pantry, insuring the integrity of stored food. To keep the *penates* satisfied a household always kept a small symbolic offering of fresh fruit for them on the table.

Peristyle: Large garden surrounded by a colonnaded portico.

Pillars of Hercules: Ancient term for the Straits of Gibraltar where the Mediterranean meets the Atlantic Ocean.

Pilum: A widely used javelin in the Roman military. It was six feet tall, its tip was made of iron and buckled on impact to entwine itself with the enemy's shield or armor. A hit forced the punctured soldier to drop his shield nor could he throw the *pilum* back at the legionaries. A *pilum* could be thrown over a distance of up to 50 feet. Sometimes tiny holes were drilled into the iron tip to make the missile whistle while airborne and intimidate the enemy.

Placentia: Today the Italian city of Piacenza, south of Milan.

Plebs: Lat. the common people.

Pontifex Maximus: Supreme Roman Priest, an office for life that could not be delegated. The words mean 'Greatest Bridge Builder' because the officeholder was supposed to gap the bridge between humans and gods. The *Pontifex Maximus* was in charge of making sure the Roman people lived and acted according to the wishes and expectations of the gods. In the context of Rome's state religion and its hierarchies, the *Pontifex Maximus* directed all other priests. He also supervised the famous Vestal Virgins so they would not violate their vows of virginity and keep attending to the sacred hearth of the city for the well-being of the State. In the later secularized empire, the office was largely ceremonial. Julius Caesar was a famous *Pontifex Maximus* and used the office to reform the Republican calendar, replacing it with the one still in use today. At the end of the empire in the West the pope took over this office. His official Latin title is in fact *Pontifex Maximus*.

Pontus Euxinus: Lat. Black Sea.

Populus Romanus: Lat. People of Rome.

Porolissium: Modern Moigrad, Romania.

Porta Decumana: Southern gate of a Roman fort (at the opposite end of the Porta Praetoria).

Porta Praetoria: Main (northern) gate of a Roman fort.

Portico of the Dei Consentes: A small portico shaped in a thirty-degree angle at the southern end of the Tabularium (State Archive). It housed statues of Rome's twelve counselor gods, the *Dei Consentes*, supreme gods in the Roman pantheon and worshipped since the days of the Republic.

Poseidon: Greek god of the Sea. The Romans called him Neptune.

Praefect: Title for the commander of the Praetorian Guard, also title for the chiefs of certain imperial agencies and the governor of Egypt.

Praetor: Roman magistrate, second only to consul.

Praetorian Guard: The emperor's personal guard, also in charge of defending the city of Rome. Their barracks were in the northeastern part of the city. It was established by Augustus and comprised six to eight cohorts.

Praetorium: Central building in a Roman camp or fort. It housed the commander of the legion, the legate.

Primipilus: Lat. First Spear. Senior centurion of a legion and the legate's military deputy. The *primipilus* was a career officer and the operative manager of the legion. He reported directly to a legate, who typically was a senator, often a consul, proconsul or propraetor. The *primipilus* was also in charge of the legionary camp. Every soldier in the legion reported to him, with the only exception of military tribunes who formed the legate's immediate staff. The position is comparable to a brigadier general.

Primus inter pares: Lat. first among equals.

Princeps Senatus: Leader of the Senate, its most senior member and always a former consul (consular).

Princeps: Lat. First Man. Another word for emperor. Introduced by Augustus who refused to be called emperor. Trajan went back to that tradition and called himself *Princeps* also. The Senate honored that by naming him '*Optimus Princeps*', the Best First Man.

Principium: Largest building in a Roman fort or camp. It housed the offices, treasury and standards of a legion, also the figurines, images and altars of the different deities a legion was dedicated to.

Proconsul: Governor of consular rank.

Propraetor: Roman magistrate holding office outside of Rome, sometimes governor of praetorian rank.

Pterygae (pronounced teriguy): The studded stripes of a Roman soldier hanging from his belt for protection.

Pugio (pronounced poo-ghee-o): Roman dagger, about one foot long, used for self-defense and carried by military messengers, officers and at times of civil unrest by civilians underneath their toga. It played the role of modern hand weapons. The *pugio* was versatile, practical and deadly.

Pulcher: Lat. beautiful.

Puteoli: Modern Pozzuoli, coastal resort town near Naples, Italy.

Quadi: Germanic people in northeastern Austria and the Czech Republic.

Quaestor: Roman magistrate. The lowest rank in the magistrarian hierarchy who could hold a seat in the Senate. At the time of Trajan, quaestors had different roles: Twelve of them worked as financial administrators in senatorial provinces, four assisted the consuls in Rome, two held administrative functions in the Senate house and two worked in the imperial bureaucracy.

Quirinal: One of the Seven Hills of Rome, today seat of the Italian President.

Quirites: Lat. citizens.

Raetia: Province in southern Germania between the Alps and the Danube, today the southern heartland of Bavaria (Oberbayern county).

Ranisstorium: Location unclear, possibly modern Piatri Craivii, Romania.

Roma Aeterna Est: Lat. Rome Is Eternal.

Roxolani: Nomad warrior people east of Dacia in what are today Moldavia and the southern Ukraine.

Saguntum: Today Sagunto, town on the east coast of Spain.

Salve: Lat. hello (plural: Salvete).

Samnites: A warrior people in central and southern Italy. Rome defeated them in three difficult wars in the third century BC.

Samosata: Today Samsat, Turkey.

Sarmizegethusa: Today Dealul Gradistei, Romania (north of the Transylvanian Alps).

Satala: Modern Kelkit, Turkey.

Satrap: Title of a Parthian or Persian feudal king ruling his fiefdom on behalf of the high king in Ctesiphon. Many were members of the Arsacid Royal Family.

Saturn: Roman god of seeds and crops.

Saturnalia: The Roman winter solstice festivities honoring the god Saturn. Celebrated on December 21, it was later transformed by the Catholic Church into Christmas.

Satyr: Greek woodland spirit, thought of as half human, half goat. The Romans identified him with their fauns. He was a pastoral deity with horns and goats' hooves. Satyrs were deemed lustful and often portrayed with oversize genitals chasing females.

Scorpion: A torsion artillery engine capable of projecting arrows, bolts or javelins up to a distance of 420 yards. It could be mounted on a cart and served as the army's first choice of field artillery. Each century had one such catapult. The scorpion belongs to the family of ballista artillery.

Scythia: Roman term for the land north and northeast of the Black and Caspian Sea, today mostly Russia and the Ukraine.

Sejanus: Praetorian Praefect under the Emperor Tiberius. He tried to assassinate Tiberius, but the plot was exposed and he was executed.

Seleucia (pronounced Selu-kee-ah): Major Parthian city on the Tigris, founded by Alexander's General Seleucos, today in the greater Baghdad area.

Senatus Consultum: Majority vote of the Senate, abbreviated with SC on Roman coinage.

Senatus PopulusQue Romanus (SPQR): Lat. Senate and People of Rome, to this very day the symbol for the city of Rome.

Senatus Consultum Ultimum: Irrevocable majority vote of the Senate to decide on matters of the highest importance.

Servian Walls: Republic-era walls that used to surround Rome. By the time of Trajan they had not been in use for over three hundred years. They were likely built after Gauls had defeated the Romans in 387 BC and pillaged the city. The Servian Walls were based on previous, but less complete fortifications that are ascribed to the legendary King Servius Tullus, hence the name.

Sic: Lat. yes.

Sinae (pronounced Sini): Lat. the Chinese.

Singidunum: Today Belgrade, capital of Serbia.

Sirens: Mythical women with bird bodies in Homer's Odyssey that attracted sailors to their island with mesmerizing songs to kill them and suck the blood out of their bodies. The term made it into most western languages and is now also figuratively used, e.g. in the expression 'alarm sirens'.

Spatha: Roman cavalry sword, one foot longer than the shorter infantry sword, the *gladius*. It gave the user a wider range when wielding it on horseback. Like the *gladius*, it was double-edged and very sharp.

Stipendium: A legionary's salary.

Stobi: Strategically located Roman town in Macedonia Province at the confluence of the rivers Crna and Vardar (in northern Greece).

Styx: Boundary river to the underworld of the Dead (Hades).

Suffect Consul: Surrogate Consul, an office originally created to replace a Consul that had died or stepped down during his term and designed to bridge the gap until the next elections. In the empire it often turned into an additional consulship used by the emperor to reward his loyal supporters in the Senate.

Suiones: Roman term for the Germanic tribes in what is today Sweden.

Sulla, Lucius Cornelius: Roman aristocrat, politician and general (138 BC – 78 BC). Defeated King Mithridates of Pontus who had overrun the Roman provinces of Pergamum and Greece in Asia Minor. Sulla won a terrible Civil War against the reformer Marius to defend the interests of the Senate. He was cruel, but effective.

Tarraco: Capital of Hispania Tarraconensis, today Tarragona, Spain.

Tepidarium: Moderately heated intermediate poolroom in a Roman bath.

Terra Sigillata: Expensive bowls or planters made of burnt clay, usually red.

Testudo: Lat. tortoise. A military siege formation in which centuries of soldiers held up their shields and interlocked them over their heads for protection, forming a human 'battle tank'. We know from Trajan's Column in Rome that the emperor used it often in the Dacian Wars when taking enemy strongholds.

Thrace: A country annexed by Rome under the Emperor Claudius. Today covering parts of northeastern Greece, Bulgaria and the European side of Turkey.

Tiberius, Claudius: The Emperor Tiberius (ruled 14 – 37 AD), also called Tiberius Julius Caesar.

Vespasianus, Titus Flavius (Vespasian): The Emperor Vespasian (ruled 69 – 79 AD).

Vespasianus, Titus Flavius (Titus): The Emperor Titus (ruled 79 – 81 AD).

Traianus, Marcus Ulpius (Traianus): Father of the Emperor Trajan, Roman senator and general.

Traianus, Marcus Ulpius (Trajan): The Emperor Trajan (ruled 98 – 117 AD), protagonist of this novel, referred to as Trajan in most western languages. His Latin name was identical to his father's - a frequent Roman tradition.

Tribune: Military officer, comparable to colonel.

Tribunicia potestas: In the Republic the constitutional right of a People's Tribune to initiate and veto legislation from either the Senate or the People's Assemblies. The People's tribunate was a powerful office. The Assemblies elected their tribunes directly. The office was designed to counterbalance the influence of the Senate. In the empire it became an imperial privilege. All its powers were conferred upon the emperor once he was confirmed by the Senate.

Triclinium: Lat. dining room.

Trireme: A type of war galley with three rows of oars on either side.

Triumvir Monetalis: One of the three administrators of the imperial mint at Rome.

Tropaeum Traiani: Lat. Trajan's Trophy. Today this Roman settlement is called Adamclisi, situated in modern Romania. It is the location of a huge war monument, drum shaped and faced in marble, that Trajan had erected to honor the fallen Roman soldiers of the Dacian Wars and at the same time to deter nomadic tribes from entering the empire.

Tullianum: The State Prison in Rome located close to the Capitoline Hill and the Senate. It was used to temporarily house and then execute high-ranking enemies of the State. The execution was not a public act, but performed inside the Tullianum. Rome did not have any prisons holding people as punishment.

Tunica laticlavia: A Roman tunic with a broad purple seam signifying a military tribune (*tribunus militum* or *tribunus laticlavius*).

'Tu regere imperio populos, Romane': A quote from Virgil's Aeneid – 'Rome, you shall reign over the peoples.'

Turma: Lat. squadron of cavalry, usually 40 riders, commanded by a decurion.

Upper and Lower Moesia: Two Roman Danube provinces, today Serbia and Bulgaria, respectively.

Ubians: Germanic tribe originally populating the southeastern shores of the Lower Rhine near Colonia Claudia (Cologne). After being defeated, the Romans moved them to the western shore of the river.

Vambrace: Armor used to protect the forearm.

Varus, Quinctilius: Governor of Lower and Upper Germania under Augustus. He was ambushed, and his three legions completely annihilated in 9 AD by an alliance of Germanic tribes under the Cheruscan Arminius. The disaster made Augustus cancel his plans to establish a permanent Germanic province between Rhine and Elbe.

Velabrum: The small valley between the Capitol and Palatine Hill in Rome.

Verres, Gaius: Infamous governor of Sicily (73 – 71 BC) who pillaged the whole province without shame. Indicted by Cicero, he had to pay compensation and was forced into exile.

Vetera: Roman fort near the modern German town of Xanten on the Lower Rhine.

Vexillation: Lat. detachment, usually several centuries, squadrons or cohorts that were grouped together and temporarily assigned to a different legion, expeditionary corps or region.

Via Sacra and Via Nova: The main streets in the Forum Romanum. The Via Sacra (lat. Holy Street) terminates at the Colosseum. The Via Nova (lat. New Street) is an offshoot connecting the Forum Romanum to the Palatine.

Vigintiviri: Lat. 'Twenty Men', a collective term for officials serving in different Roman supervisory boards. They were in charge of the mint, street maintenance, and worked in the courts. Membership in the Vigintiviri College was compulsory for young patricians and plebeians alike if they aspired to become a member of the Senate. The emperor and his staff appointed the prospective candidates.

Viminacium: Legionary camp and city on the Danube in the province of Moesia, today Kostolac, Serbia. It was Trajan's headquarters during the Dacian Wars.

Vindonissa: Today Windisch, Switzerland.

Vir Vere Romanus: Lat. a true Roman.

Virgil: Publius Vergilius Maro, 70 – 19 BC, famous national poet of the Romans. A gifted writer of epics and poetry. Financially supported by Maecenas and Augustus, he helped lay the ideological and moral foundation for imperial rule.

Zalmoxis: Supreme god of the Dacians, a sky god who was also worshipped as the god of the Dead.

Zeugma: Today an unsettled ruin town in modern Syria.

Maps

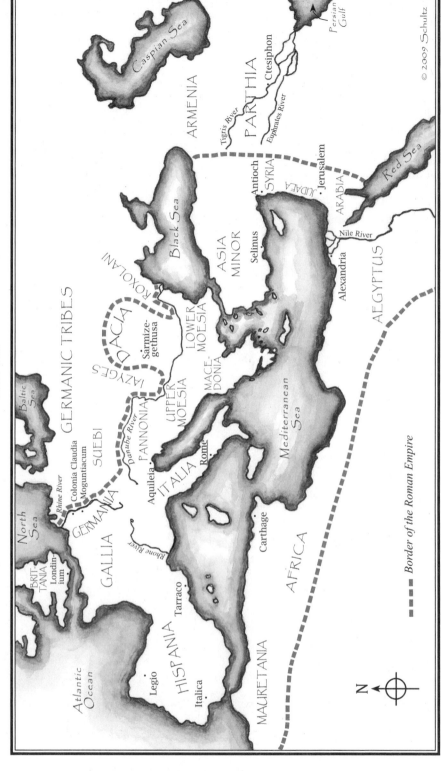

The Roman Empire
120 AD

ARMENIA

PARTHIA

Tigris River

Euphrates River

Ctesiphon

Persian Gulf

Caspian Sea

© 2009 Schultz

Red Sea

Black Sea

Antioch

SYRIA

JUDAEA

Jerusalem

ARABIA

ASIA MINOR

Selinus

Nile River

Alexandria

AEGYPTUS

ROXOLANI

DACIA

IAZYGES

Sarmizegethusa

LOWER MOESIA

UPPER MOESIA

MACEDONIA

GERMANIC TRIBES

SUEBI

Danube River

PANNONIA

Aquileia

ITALIA

Rome

Mediterranean Sea

Baltic Sea

Rhine River

Colonia Claudia
Moguntiacum

GERMANIA

GALLIA

Rhone River

Carthage

AFRICA

North Sea

BRIT-
TANIA

Londin-
ium

Tarraco

HISPANIA

Legio

Italica

Atlantic Ocean

MAURETANIA

N

■ ■ ■ *Border of the Roman Empire*

Palestine
66 AD

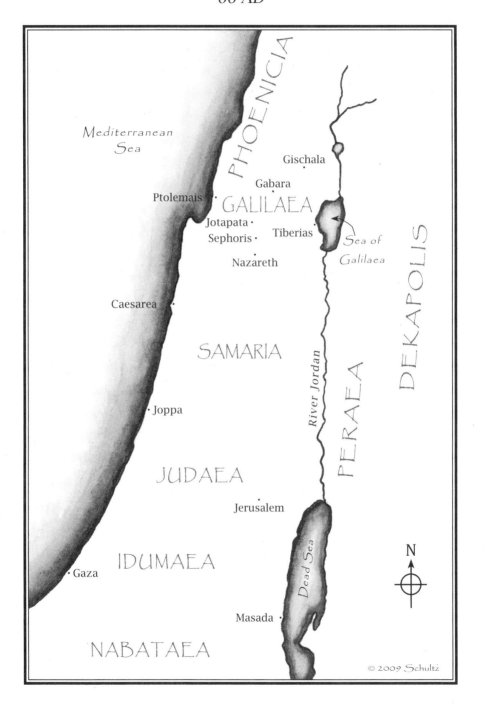

Rome
120 AD

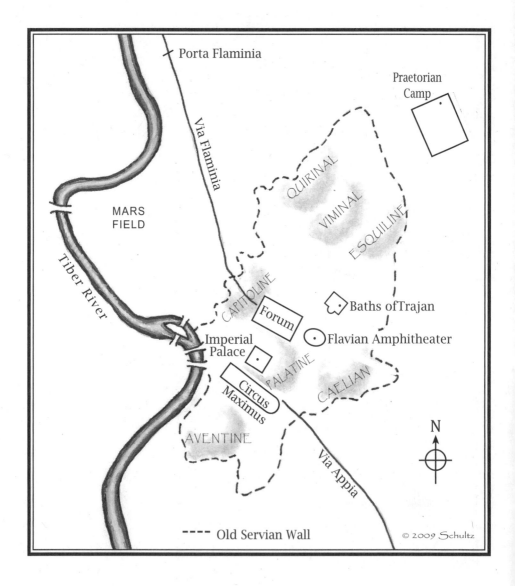

Porta Flaminia

Praetorian
Camp

Via Flaminia

QUIRINAL

VIMINAL

ESQUILINE

MARS
FIELD

Tiber River

CAPITOLINE

Forum

Baths of Trajan

Flavian Amphitheater

Imperial
Palace

PALATINE

CAELIAN

Circus
Maximus

AVENTINE

Via Appia

N

- - - - Old Servian Wall

© 2009 Schultz

The Rhine Frontier
120 AD

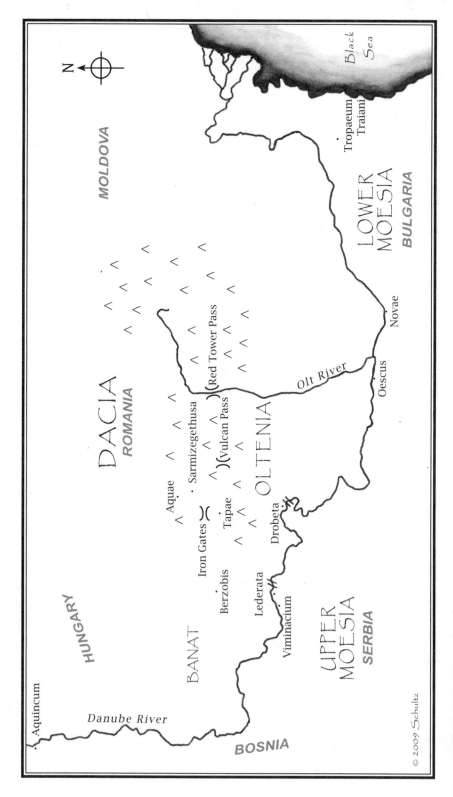

Dacia
98AD

© 2009 Schultz

The East
115 AD

A note to the reader:

This story is based on the life of the Emperor Trajan. It is fictional but adheres to the known facts with few exceptions. However, the historical record is littered with gaps, and some events are murky or controversial. My story fills in those gaps *sine ira et studio* - as Tacitus would say - with an interpretation based on plausibility and in the interest of the story.

Most characters in this book are historical, but not all of them are: most importantly Callistus, Claudia Aemilia and Telerion.

On Trajan becoming Nerva's successor:

Nerva's decision-making process to pick Trajan as his successor was in reality more complicated and took more time and effort than a novel can cover without boring the reader. Nerva and his Council had to consult not only the generals and governors of the empire, but also the key factions and aristocratic networks in the Senate because senators were often governors. The whole process likely took all of 97 AD and was accelerated by the Praetorian mutiny in the fall of that year.

Trajan was ultimately chosen not only for his military skills (there were other equally qualified officers like Pompeius Longinus and Lappius Maximus), but because he was at the intersection point of the empire's leading families through social, political and familial ties covering many different geographies: Rome and Hispania Baetica through birth, Gallia Narbonnensis through marriage and Asia Minor through Plotina's narbonnensian connections. He was therefore acceptable to different key constituencies and power brokers. Of all the candidates he was the only one with the right age (42) to be a balanced and yet energetic ruler.

On Trajan being governor of Pannonia at the time of his adoption:

This is conjecture based on Julian Bennett's Trajan biography. The conventional view has him as governor of Upper Germania at the time of his adoption, as outlined by John Grainger in his monography on Nerva and Birley's book on Hadrian. To me, Bennett's argumentation seems more plausible. Unless we find conclusive proof in the archaeological record, there is no certainty on the matter.

On names:

For authenticity's sake I have chosen to use the Latin names for ancient towns and cities, with few exceptions like Rome itself (*Roma*), Antioch (*Antiochia*), Carthage (*Carthago*) and some others. Mountains, rivers and certain geographic areas remain with their modern names. After all, they largely look the same today whereas towns and cities have morphed beyond recognition. For example, today's Cologne looks completely different from Roman *Colonia Claudia*. Referring to it as Cologne would give a completely wrong impression. However, the Rhine is still the Rhine even if its exact geographic position has somewhat changed. Likewise, Spain still looks much the same even if it was called *Hispania* in Roman times.

Carnifex:
The assassin Carnifex's real name was **Saturnius**. I made this change because the reader might easily confuse him with the similarly named rebel Governor **Saturninus**. Carnifex means butcher.

Lucius Licinius Sura:
Sura's position at the end of 97 AD is unclear. Some scholars have him as governor of Lower Germania BEFORE Trajan arrives in Colonia Claudia. I do not follow this assumption and have him as *consul suffectus*, partnering with Tacitus in November of 97. In my conjecture, Trajan then appointed Sura governor of Lower Germania so he could help him, Trajan, establish himself with the Rhine legions. Sura was a loyal friend he could trust in this delicate transition period.

Claudius Maximus:
This Roman soldier who hunted down Decebalus is a historical figure. His tomb was found in Macedonia. On it, the man claims his deeds including the successful pursuit and capture of Decebalus, King of Dacia.

Timeline

Year	Events
54	Death of Claudius, Nero emperor at the age of sixteen
56	Trajan born
66-72	Jewish War
67	Trajan's father, Marcus Ulpius Traianus, commanding the famous Tenth Legion in Judaea
68	Nero commits suicide
68-69	Civil War
69	Vespasian emperor
72	Fall of Masada
73-76	Traianus governor of Syria province
75	Trajan enters the army as laticlavian tribune under his father's command in Syria
77	Trajan transfers to Germania province
78	Trajan marries Pompeia Plotina
79	Death of Vespasian, Titus emperor, eruption of Mt. Vesuvius
81	Trajan quaestor, death of Titus, Domitian emperor
87	Trajan takes command of the Seventh Legion *Gemina* in Spain
89	Revolt of Governor Saturninus, Trajan takes the Seventh to Germania, punitive campaign against the Chatti
91	Trajan ordinary consul for the first time
92-93	Trajan in command on the Rhine
95-96	Trajan in command in Pannonia province
96	Domitian assassinated, Nerva emperor
97	Trajan defeats the Suebi, Nerva adopts him in absentia as Nerva Caesar, Trajan now co-emperor, departs for Germania to reorganize the frontier
98	Death of Nerva, Trajan emperor, then residing on the Rhine in Colonia Claudia, executes Nerva's insurgent Praetorian Praefect, Suburanus appointed Praefect, Tacitus consul, writes *De Germania*, Trajan inspects the Danube frontier
99	Trajan enters Rome

100	Trajan consul together with Frontinus, Pliny the younger delivers the *Panegyricus*, Hadrian marries Trajan's niece Sabina
101-102	First Dacian War, Decebalus defeated, Trajan accepts Dacian surrender
103	Trajan consul for the fifth time, together with Laberius Maximus, establishes accord with the Senate and is hailed as *Optimus Princeps* (Best Emperor)
105-106	Second Dacian War, destruction of Sarmizegethusa and death of Decebalus, annexation of Dacia, huge spoils of war, Tacitus publishes the *Historiae*
107	Trajan's Dacian triumph in Rome, Hadrian appointed praetor
109	Trajan's Baths and aqueduct dedicated
111	Pliny governor in Bithynia, corresponds with Trajan about the Christians, Antoninus Pius marries Faustina
113	Trajan's Column dedicated, death of sister Marciana, completion of Trajan's Forum, Basilica Ulpia and the Markets, death of Pliny, Trajan goes east and begins his Parthian campaign
114	Trajan deposes the usurper Parthamasiris and conquers Armenia
115	Trajan conquers Mesopotamia, Jewish agitations begin
116	Trajan enters the Parthian capital Ctesiphon and captures Babylon, was voted *Parthicus* and granted a triumph by the Senate, Jewish uprisings all over the East, Parthian counter-attack and Roman withdrawal, Tacitus publishes the Annales
117	Trajan suffers a stroke and sets sail for Rome, dies at Selinus in Cilicia, Hadrian submits adoption papers and declares himself emperor in Antioch, Trajan cremated at Seleucia, his ashes are returned to Rome and placed in the chamber at the base of his Column

Acknowledgments

Many thanks go to the people that helped me with this book: my wife Jayne Schultz who spent endless hours proofreading the manuscript, fishing out inconsistencies, designing the page layout, dust jacket and drawing the maps; my friend Rich Deleissegues, who helped me put the final touches on the text; Anne Schott, who provided early feedback on the basic concept of this novel and Peggy Warner for her editing support.

My gratitude extends to the ancient writers: Dio Cassius, Eutropius, Pliny the younger, Dio Chrysostom, John Xiphilinus and Aurelius Victor, but also to the many modern scholars and biographers who analyzed the material and compiled it into our history books, particularly John Grainger (*Nerva and the Roman succession crisis of AD 96~99*), Julian Bennett (*Trajan-Optimus Princeps*) and Anthony Birley (*Hadrian-The restless emperor*). Julian Bennett's Trajan biography is the ultimate authority on the great emperor. His Indiana University Press book was my enduring companion, supplying me with the known details of Trajan's life.

I also owe the unknown artists and sculptors of Trajan's Column in Rome without whom the world would have no detailed record of the Dacian Wars. In fact, two scenes in my book are lifted from the venerable column, standing tall to this day and resisting the ultimate grinder, time: Decebalus's capture and the decapitation of Dacian combatants by Roman auxiliaries.

And I would like to thank my Latin teacher, Werner Mueller, who brought the Roman world to life in his class, inculcating me forever with a passion for antiquity.

I have done my own research for this novel, including years of study and extensive travelling to the applicable archaeological sites throughout the Mediterranean. Any errors are my own and I ask forgiveness up front.

La Mesa, California, on the Ides of January in the year 2762 AUC
(*Ab Urbe Condita* – Since Rome Was Founded)

C.R.H. Wildfeuer

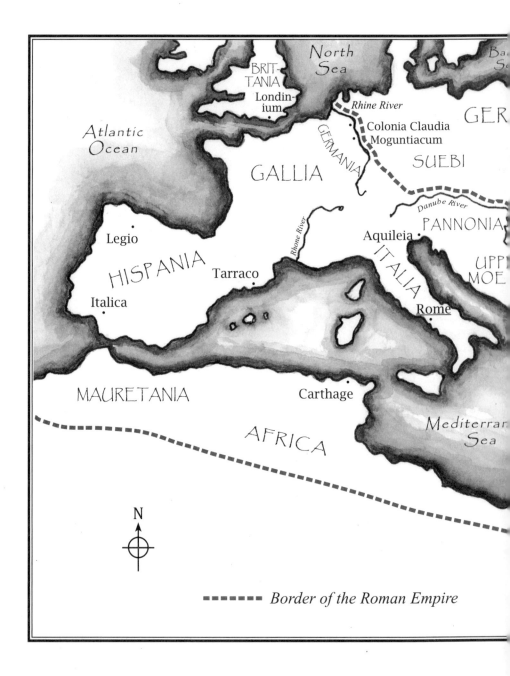

North Sea

BRIT-
TANIA

Londin-
ium

Atlantic
Ocean

GALLIA

GERMANIA

Rhine River

Colonia Claudia
Moguntiacum

GER

SUEBI

Danube River

PANNONIA

Legio

HISPANIA

Tarraco

Rhone River

Aquileia

ITALIA

Rome

UPP
MOE

Italica

Ba
S

MAURETANIA

Carthage

AFRICA

Mediterra
Sea

N

------- Border of the Roman Empire